MW01131155

NAGA QUEEN

SHE WAS AWARDED A MEDAL FOR HER WWII EXPLOITS

by

Pauline Hayton

Naga Queen

For information address:

Pauline Hayton
3446 13th Ave SW
Naples, FL 34117 USA

Cover by Lance Buckley. Email: lance@lancebuckley.com

Books by Pauline Hayton

A Corporal's War
Myanmar: In my Father's Footsteps
Naga Queen
Grandma Rambo
If You Love Me, Kill Me
Still Pedaling
Extreme Delight
The Unfriendly Bee (Children's book)

Royalties from the sales of my books go to support the education of more than 100 children at remote Mount Kisha English School, Magulong Village, Manipur, India.

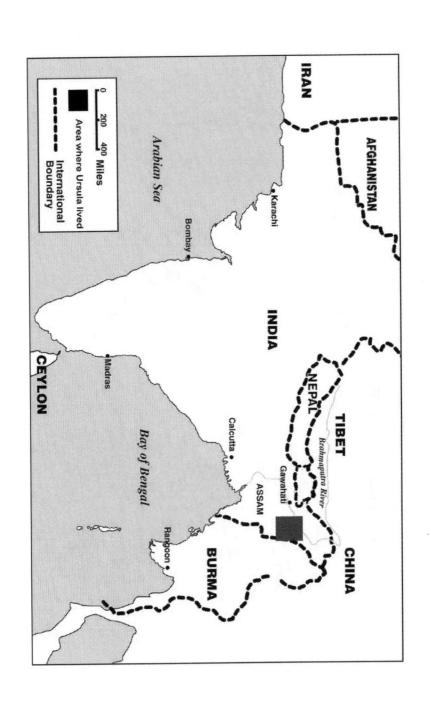

"Manipur Road Station next stop, miss-sahib," the Indian conductor announced in his singsong accent.

Ursula inserted her bookmark and closed *The Count of Monte Cristo*. Her stomach fluttered. She had sat by herself for hours while the train rattled along in dim light, the track hemmed in by dark jungle, all made murkier by grimy windows. The train clattered into a clearing. The long, dreary journey was ending, and in celebration, a burst of sunlight flooded the compartment, cheering her.

She stretched her long legs and gazed through the window with interest, eager to leave the train and hoping Lexie would be there to meet her.

Ursula rummaged in her handbag, found her diary and on a fresh page scribbled, October 28th, 1938, 7:30 a.m. Hurrah! After all the commotion and confusion of the four-day journey from Calcutta, I'm finally to escape the confines of this blasted train!

In the gold powder-compact's mirror, she touched up her lipstick, and studied her tawny hair, which she'd had cropped for the trip. The short style made her look younger than her twenty-three years she thought, almost schoolgirlish. She wasn't sure she liked it but was grateful for the ease it gave her in managing her hair. She snapped the compact shut. It had been two years since she'd seen her friend Alexa, and she wanted to look good.

The train screeched to a jerking halt in a hissing gasp of steam. Ursula stood up, and staggered, feeling wobbly, a ghost of the train's motion still in her body. She brushed her blue linen skirt in a vain attempt to remove the creases then moved along the corridor to an open door. Shading her grey eyes from the sun's glare, she looked around for Lexie and caught sight of a conspicuous halo of red hair. Ursula watched Alexa's excited, freckled face, as she bobbed along the platform, peering into carriages, deftly dodging porters and the few travellers descending from the train. She and Lexie seemed to be the only Europeans at the station.

"Lexie!" Ursula called, waving her white handkerchief. "Lexie!"

Lexie broke into a run and Ursula jumped from the train to hug her tightly.

"It's so good to see you."

"At last," Lexie said. "I've missed you."

"Thank goodness you're here. I've been in India only four days, and I feel as if I've been wrung out and hung up to dry."

Ursula had thought she knew what she was coming to, but the reality was so different—the masses of people, jostling bodies, the pungent smells.

"It's all been so strange and nerve-wracking," she continued. "I didn't realize it would be such a long, difficult journey from Calcutta, and it didn't help that I don't speak one word of the language. But, Lexie, it's all been so . . ."

"What?"

". . . fascinating!"

Lexie laughed at her friend's spirit. "You'll be all right now. I'll take care of you, and we'll soon have you speaking some Hindustani."

Lexie bustled about, organizing the porters loading Ursula's luggage into her little Austin car then took Ursula to the tin-roofed travellers' bungalow.

"This is where I stayed last night," she said. While Ursula looked on with interest, her friend reeled off some Hindustani to the caretaker. Two minutes later, he brought a pitcher of water for Ursula to refresh herself followed by a welcome cup of tea.

Ursula poured more tea. "I'm looking forward to making up for lost time. It's been far too long. Have you made any friends in Imphal?"

"Not close friends, more social acquaintances. They're very proper. We ladies lead a leisurely life out here. But oh, Ursula, we're going to have a marvellous time." Lexie settled her cup on its saucer. "We've a long drive ahead of us. Won't arrive in Imphal till evening. Are you up for it?"

Ursula laughed. "Wouldn't miss it for the world, if it means spending the next few months with you."

They set off along a straight road, a gash in the thick jungle covering the foothills. The car trundled along the bumpy tarmac pressed on both sides by tall spindly trees reaching for daylight. Rising from the congested undergrowth, vines and choking creepers ran riot, clinging to trunks and wrapping round branches. A steep escarpment of blue-black hills covered in rainforest towered on the horizon.

"I've been so looking forward to this," Ursula said, "but when I arrived in Calcutta, well, nothing prepares you for the smells, and the crippled children begging—and the hordes! It's so different from my travels on the Continent with Grandmama. I used to think I was worldly but . . ." Lost for words Ursula shook her head.

Lexie glanced at her passenger. "It *is* a shock to the system, isn't it? Thank goodness Richard took some leave and met me in Calcutta, otherwise I'm sure I'd have been overcome by it all."

"Ah, Richard. How is that brother of yours?"

"He's doing as well as can be expected, working in the Indian Civil Service. In fact, we have him to thank for this whole adventure. It was his idea to invite you."

"Do you remember the last time we were in a car together?"

"When we were on holiday in Scotland, the Oban rally," cried Lexie in glee.

They smiled at memories of Ursula veering round tight corners in her MG, spraying mud on the luckless spectators. They had needed woollen jumpers on that windswept day.

"A little different from riding in my Austin, wasn't it?"

"A wee bit. Have you adjusted to your new life as your brother's hostess?"

Lexie pursed her lips in thought before replying. "I enjoy being with Richard. He encourages my independent nature. Only about a dozen Europeans live in Imphal, mostly administrators, and most of them are older. Some of them seem to have been in India forever. In fact," said Lexie, laughing, "they're positively fossilized. Did your parents put up much opposition to your coming?"

"Surprisingly, no. When your letter arrived, the prospect really ruffled poor Grandmama. 'You can't possibly go gallivanting off to India unchaperoned,' she said. But I insisted she write to Mummy about it. Mummy was obviously keen for me to come because she replied that I was to be given 'all help and encouragement to book passage on the next available ship to India.'"

"Gosh, I wouldn't have expected that. Any idea why she was so in favour of it?"

"No. It was amazing! In no time at all, I was on my way, and after several weeks at sea, I was being ferried up the Hooghley River to Calcutta. That part was much easier than I expected."

Eight miles later, Lexie stopped at a sentry post to show their papers. As the car accelerated, she told Ursula, "We've just entered the Naga Hills."

The landscape changed. First, the road took them into a high, narrow gorge then climbed a steep incline beside a turbulent stream. The road twisted and turned, squeezing along the bases of rugged cliffs, passing large boulders, stands of giant fern, tall slender bamboo, and trees that blotted out the sky.

"Lexie," Ursula said, a tinge of reverence in her voice, "the scenery's heavenly!"

Lexie grinned. "I did it all for you. A bit different from the English countryside, isn't it?"

Ursula could not stop looking about her. "It's so wild and awesome."

The car bowled along, climbing and curling round tight bends. Turning a sharp corner, they startled a small group of hillmen who darted to safety at the side of the road and stared in surprise at the two women in the Austin.

Ursula returned the stare, twisting round in her seat to watch as long as she could. Unlike the slim Assamese of the valley, these men were stocky, with slashing cheekbones and Mongoloid features. Hard muscles rippled under coppery skin, and they were, somehow, beautiful she thought. They were naked except for small black kilts round their hips and plaid blankets covering broad shoulders. Strands of brightly coloured beads adorned their necks.

A fleeting recognition startled Ursula, a memory piercing the deepest recesses of her mind—and then it was gone.

"Lexie! Who are those people?" she asked, in a voice filled with awe.

"Those? Why, they're Nagas, of course."

"Of course," Ursula murmured. She felt vaguely unsettled and rummaged through her mind for some touchstone. Why had these men stirred her so?

They stopped for lunch in Kohima, a mountain village 4,800 feet above sea level where the Deputy Commissioner had his headquarters. The village perched on a saddle between two mountain ranges, overlooked from the south by Japvo, a 9,000-foot mountain. The hot sun beat down on the handful of red-roofed bungalows spread out along spurs.

Ursula and Lexie left the restaurant they had found in the one-street bazaar, which catered to the needs of the few government workers and the small garrison of Assam Rifles.

"Take a good look, Ursula, this land is going to be your home for the next five months."

"Do we have time for some snaps?" Ursula reached into the car for her new, precision-made, technically advanced Leica camera in its leather fitted case. It had been an extravagant purchase, but she was glad of it now to record this enchanting place.

Lexie smiled at her friend's excitement. "When you've finished here, we'll drive to a better viewpoint."

Stopping outside the town, they found a clear view of the hills. Ursula climbed from the car, pressed the Leica to her face and sighted through the viewfinder. To the east lay wave after wave of mountain ranges, blue fading to violet and gray in the hazy distance. The only way to reach them was along trails winding tortuously round spurs and chiselled precipices, up jungle-clad hills and down deep, steep slopes. Native villages with dingy smoke-stained thatched roofs sat on top of every ridge in sight. The ridge slopes had sharp inclines and thick woods except for the hillsides in the town. These were cleared for cultivation and covered in terraced paddy fields, which, at this time of year, were filled with parched stubble.

She paused, lowered her camera, heart beating fast as she gazed upon the panorama before her. *I belong here!* The thought startled Ursula. Her pulse throbbed; a surge of joy had her grinning

"Ready, Ursula?" Lexie called. "Still another ninety miles to go."

In the twilight, the Austin came to a stop in front of a brick bungalow. Familiar flowers, snapdragons, lilies, and pansies, crammed the small, neat garden's borders. The two women, stiff from their long journey, eased themselves from the vehicle and stretched legs and backs. Richard hurried down the veranda steps followed by two servants who took the luggage indoors. Richard and his sister could have been twins save for his neatly trimmed moustache and the hue of his hair, more auburn than Lexie's titian-red.

"Good, you're back safe and sound," he said. "You resisted catching up on old times with some rally driving." Richard turned his attention to Ursula. "Hello, Ursula."

He accepted a kiss on the cheek from his sister and shook Ursula's proffered hand. "Welcome to Imphal. Long journey from the station. You must be all in. I hope you're hungry. Cook has food ready when you are."

Lexie showed Ursula to her room. The four-poster bed, chest of drawers and the writing desk were a rich mahogany, the walls whitewashed. A flower-patterned Indian rug of subtle browns, greens and yellows covered the dark floorboards.
"The bed's pulled away from the wall so insects can't hide there. And use your mosquito net at night; it wouldn't do for you to fall sick while you're here. I'll be back in a jiffy once I've washed my face and powdered my nose."

"This is lovely, Lexie!"

"Of course it is." Lexie grinned, enjoying Ursula's delight. She patted the marble-topped stand. "There's water in the jug, soap and towel. I won't be long."

Ursula sighed happily, contemplating five whole months of adventure. She poured water from the rose-decorated jug into the matching basin and washed her hands and face. What sort of insects lurk behind a bed, she wondered gazing round her room for clues while she dried her hands. She had just finished combing her hair when Lexie reappeared.

"Ready?"

"Yes, and I'm ravenous."

The simple meal of chicken curry, rice and fresh fruit salad was ambrosial.

"Lexie told me you wanted to go to Oxford to study archaeology," Richard said over port. "Why didn't you? Change of heart?"

Ursula expression did not reveal the sudden stab of pain she felt at this question. The loss of her dream had left a wound, still raw. She decided to spare Richard the tale.

"No change of heart, change in circumstances. The Depression, you see. I was pulled out of boarding school and sent to live with Grandmama."

"Couldn't you live with your parents?" asked Richard.

"With Daddy a commander in the Royal Navy, he and Mummy live wherever he's posted. When I wasn't at boarding school I usually stayed with my grandparents. I grew up listening to uncles and great uncles who had all been in the services, telling the most marvellous stories, and I was bitterly resentful I wasn't a boy. I so wanted to have my own adventures, but I was told women didn't involve themselves in that sort of thing."

They adjourned to the veranda to relax over drinks.

"Surely you realize how difficult it is for unconventional women," Lexie said to her brother. "We're brought up to support our husbands in whatever they want to do, not what we'd like to do.

"That's not fair, Lexie!" he cried. "Some unconventional women I could mention have the most wonderful brothers! Why do you think I asked you to come and join me in India?"

"Lexie's lucky," Ursula said. "You're a rare brother. Do you remember, Lexie, how we made a solemn vow?"

"Oh yes, on top of Mount Blevan. We promised to support one another in living life on our own terms."

"And so we are!"

"What stands out in my mind," Richard said, "is the pair of you competing in the car rallies."

"In my beautiful MG! Lipstick red and a fine match for Lexie's hair."

Lexie set her glass down, her face alive with excitement. "Oh, we had such fun! Roaring round in the mud, giving the men a run for their money."

"It's a pity we had to wait until I was twenty-one," Ursula said. "But buying that car was a good way to spend the first year's income from my trust fund, wasn't it?"

Richard raised his glass. "Oh, I approve."

"Ursula didn't let on she'd bought it. I was waiting on the quay at the Isle of Skye to meet her, when she just drove off the ferry in this flashy red sports car and announced we were going to take part in the Oban rally."

Under the spell of the port, the evening's beauty and friendship rejoined, the three relished their stories all over again.

Richard chuckled. "Kindred spirits, that's what you are, kindred spirits. Dare-devils." He poured more wine. "I hope you'll find enough excitement while you're here, Ursula. Imphal may be the capital of Manipur, but it isn't really a town, more a group of villages."

"Surrounded by mountains and cut off from the outside world," Lexie added. "We're quite isolated, seventy miles from the Burma frontier in the east, accessible only by a mule track, and the nearest British station at Silchar is one hundred and thirty miles west by track over the mountains. The only people who come to Imphal are those with business here. So, we have to do the best we can to amuse ourselves."

"Mind, you won't be bored," Richard said. "We have golf at the Club, tennis at the Residency, and polo, of course. To the south is Logtak Lake, where we go duck shooting. The hunting really is excellent in this area. Are you any good with a shotgun, Ursula?"

"I've managed to bag a pheasant or two, but I haven't handled a gun for some time. My father taught me to use one when I was thirteen. Richard, I do want to thank you again for putting me up."

"Completely selfish of me! Lexie finds life here rather dreary despite our pastimes, and I was sure she'd go running back to England, leaving me all alone here. Your job is to keep her fully occupied."

Lexie gulped her port and protested, "Richard! You know the pastimes are fine. It's just that most of the people are so dull and stuffy."

"I can't argue with you on that point, Lexie. But look at the pair of you. Your eyelids are heavy, and you seem on the verge of sleep. Why don't you retire for the night? And now that Ursula's here," he said, his blue eyes twinkling, "you can start the day refreshed ready to get up to mischief tomorrow."

*   *   *

Ursula lay in bed, her hands linked behind her head, staring into the darkness. Richard's remarks about her lost career had stirred a sadness and an anger that were deep in equal measure. Her thoughts turned to the day of her twenty-first birthday, the memory so vivid as to cause her face to colour. Grandmama had expected her to be jubilant on informing her that she now had a trust fund, which would provide a comfortable annual income. Instead, when Grandmama left the room, Ursula had leaned against the frame of the French doors and watched the rain slide down the glass. Her eyes flashed with anger and unshed tears. Her fingers rubbed along the string of pearls round her neck as she pondered an injustice so profound, it would scar her forever.

She was seventeen and had arrived from boarding school to spend half-term at Grandmama's house in Kensington. That first afternoon, Grandmama called her into the drawing room. Grandmother Bower, her father's mother, sat in one of the large wing chairs. The white lace antimacassar covering the chair back accentuated the blue rinsed, finger-waved hair. Grandfather Bower stood in front of the mantelpiece, as stiff as the hearth irons, while Grandmama Graham, looking frail and worried, sat on the edge of a chair, her hands clasping and unclasping.

"Ah, Ursula," Grandmother Bower said, her expression business-like. "Come, sit down. We need to talk to you." She motioned Ursula to the wing chair opposite.

Grandmama pressed the bell push to summon Janet, the maid, to bring afternoon tea. Grandmother Bower continued, her voice gentle but firm, broaching no argument. "I'm afraid the family has suffered an embarrassing financial setback, Ursula. Because of our losses in the stock market, we no longer have the money to keep you at Roedean. I've written to your parents about the situation, and they agree, albeit reluctantly, that there's no other way. You are to leave school at Easter and stay here in Kensington with your grandmama, who has been suffering with her health. We feel it would be beneficial if you were here to look after her."

Ursula stared aghast at the strait-laced, formidable woman before her, too afraid of her grandmother to utter one word of protest. Grandfather Bower spoke up, his nasal voice droned on sealing her fate.

"There's your younger brother to consider. The money we have must be devoted to his university education." His voice became brisk. "As for you, well, we regard the cost of your Oxford education as a luxury and a folly. Girls really don't need a career, do they? They always end up getting married."

In one devastating swoop, Ursula was robbed of her opportunity to go to Oxford to study her passion—archaeology.

Then, on her twenty-first birthday, Grandfather Bower had sent a letter informing Ursula she would start receiving a small annual income from a trust they had provided for her.

Ursula had crushed the letter in disbelief.

All along, there had been money set-aside for her and having reached the magical age of adulthood, it was money she could have *now* but not when she had needed it most.

Ursula's eyes became moist as she remembered how she had wrapped her arms round herself and almost cried at the unbearable disappointment. She did not understand why they hadn't given her the money earlier for her education. She had been clever in school, had dreams of creating something of value on her own account. She had read with hunger and total

11

involvement the monographs and histories of prominent archaeologists, their excavations, their findings, and she had thrilled at the reports of Sir Leonard Woolley's excavations at Ur of Chaldees. And she knew for certain she didn't want to live her life through any husband she might have. There would be no satisfaction with that.

Ursula blinked back the threatening tears then smiled in the darkness as she remembered how the exquisite idea of buying a bright red MG sports car had popped into her head. She'd picked up a cushion from the sofa and twirled round the room with it in her arms. Then she had stopped in surprise as a further joyful idea formed. She would take part in the Scottish car rallies instead of sitting on the sidelines full of longing to compete. Still hugging the cushion, she had stood in front of the French door, looking through the rain at the buds and new blooms in the soaked garden. She was no longer a girl but an adult woman. She would henceforth live life to the fullest, make up for her stolen dreams and her four years of misery at being stuck in Kensington with Grandmama.

Now here she was in India with her best friend Lexie. Ursula stretched and turned over. They were going to have the time of their lives.

In the morning, Ursula awakened to a symphony of new sounds and whether she was hearing screeching monkeys, squawking birds or cheeping frogs, she had no clue. "You'll sort out what's what soon enough," Lexie told her and added that Richard had left for work already. "I'll take you for a drive round the area, if you feel up to it."

"Of course, I feel up to it. I want to see everything and take lots of photographs."

They had only driven a few yards when Ursula wanted to stop and admire the beauty of the bougainvillea festooning the neat bungalows and splashing the walls with vibrant magenta and pink. On the outskirts of town, she photographed Lexie standing under a spreading Banyan tree, measuring, Ursula was told, four hundred feet across and separating the road, which passed on either side. They passed groves of wild bananas and feathery bamboo surrounding the villages. Paddy fields covered the Imphal Plain, and Ursula could see row upon row of terraced paddies on the hillsides. In the distance, in every direction, towered the blue-tinged mountains of Manipur, and at every opportunity, Ursula whipped out her camera to record it all.

"When will I meet the other residents?" asked Ursula.

"We'll go to the Club tonight. It won't be very entertaining, but you'll meet the crowd. After that, I'm sure we'll be invited to play cards or call for afternoon tea and gossip. They'll be wanting to see a new face."

"Do you think you'll stay long in India?"

"It's socially limited here, but I do like its exoticness," Lexie said. "And lucky you, this is the best time of year to be here. In May, the monsoon arrives, and it all changes.

"So I heard from other passengers on the ship."

"But you can't imagine! We have tremendous thunderstorms. Rain pours like waterfalls, and the paths turn to muck. Streams flood and become raging torrents, and the rice fields turn into lakes. With all the rain and greyness, it's utterly dismal."

"So that's why people visit between October and April."

A pair of bright green birds flew low across the path in front of them. Craa-aak-aak one squawked, a call Ursula recognized from the morning.

"Parrots!" she cried. "I've never seen such a variety of bird-life. I've lost count—wagtails, orioles, hawks, kites, and lots of others I don't recognize."

"We've more exotic wildlife than birds. Look." Lexie pointed to a stand of scrub-oak. "See?"

Ursula had to look hard at a shade-freckled branch of the oak before she saw the well-camouflaged animals. "Monkeys!"

"And before you go home," Lexie said, "you'll see wild elephant, deer, snakes. I'll have to teach you which ones are poisonous, and even if you don't see any leopards or tigers prowling about, I'm sure we can find you some pug marks."

"Pug marks? Just the thing to take home as souvenirs. Do they fit in one's luggage?"

Lexie threw back her head and laughed, and Ursula felt a surge of relief to have someone her own age to share some fun.

*　　*　　*

Ursula settled into the leisurely lifestyle of the European community. She played golf and tennis. Sitting under shade trees, she chatted on manicured lawns, and twice a week the ladies of the community watched the men's polo matches. They went duck shooting in the swamplands at Logtak Lake and shopped at the Canteen and the Imphal bazaar.

Two weeks after Ursula's arrival, she and Lexie were relaxing on the veranda one evening, sipping gin and tonics when Lexie asked, "Are you enjoying yourself?"

"Why, yes. Yes, of course. It's all very pleasant. Much better than being stuck in Kensington."

"But...?"

"No buts. Everything's fine. I'm enjoying my visit and spending time with you."

"Come now, Ursula Graham Bower, be honest. Do you think you'll survive several more months of this?"

As Ursula struggled for the correct, polite response, her fleeting expression of dismay confirmed Lexie's suspicions.

"You'll soon be bored once the novelty wears off, won't you? Well, never mind. Because I know you so well, and being the cunning person that I am, I've arranged for you to meet Colonel Taylor, the Civil Surgeon."

Lexie's smile was inscrutable.

"Lexie, really! I don't need a dance partner, thank you, and I don't need to see a doctor to cure incipient boredom."

"Yes, you do! Yes, you do!" Lexie was bouncing in her chair with excitement. "I've been busy, and I've a wonderful surprise. Colonel Taylor and his wife are going on a tour to Ukhrul, and they've offered to take us with them."

"Lexie!" Ursula clunked down her glass, splashing the contents over her dress. "Oh, that's wonderful!" she said, brushing the gin from her clothes. "When do we go?"

"In two days, so we'll have to get organized."

Just then, Richard arrived home, having spent the evening at the Club. "Well, Lexie," he said, climbing the veranda steps, "you've certainly set the cat among the pigeons."

"Did I? What happened?"

"You know how Colonel Taylor likes to take a rise out of people at times? Well, he informed the men, with a twinkle in his eye, that he was going to take you both on his next tour and then sat back to watch the reaction."

Richard imitated in turns the blustering, pompous, responses. "'I've never heard of anything so preposterous!' Can you guess who that was? No? Never mind. Then there was 'How could you allow your sister to make such a crackpot decision?' The Commissioner's response was the mildest. All he said was 'Don't you think they're being rather foolish?'"

Ursula and Lexie giggled.

"Our plans seem to have ruffled a few feathers," said Ursula.

Richard chuckled. "I'd say plucked rather than ruffled. The old hens! Serves them right too."

The next two days were a flurry of activity as Ursula and Lexie sought out supplies and clothing for the trip, which they squeezed into *jappas*, the tall, covered, carrying baskets plaited of cane and bamboo used for hill transport.

On the appointed morning, the colonel's car arrived at the bungalow door. Colonel Taylor was a sturdy man with a square and florid face, his hair slicked back and fixed with pomade. His wife would have been considered plain but for her amiable personality and large violet eyes. Ursula and Lexie scurried about, collecting odds and ends they had overlooked, before rushing out to the car. In her excitement, Lexie slipped on the veranda steps and cried out as she fell. She winced in pain as she tried to sit up.

"Oh blast!" she said, between clenched teeth. "I've twisted my ankle."

Colonel Taylor lifted her onto the lowest step and knelt to examine her.

"Sorry, Alexa, my girl, I'm afraid you won't be going on this trip."

He picked her up and carried her indoors. Ursula shouldered both *jappas* and followed them. Inside, the colonel lowered Lexie onto the long rattan couch and told the houseboy to bring cold water and bandages. While he wrapped her ankle in damp, deftly intertwined bandages, Lexie looked forlornly at Ursula. Suddenly, she realized Ursula had brought both *jappas* into the bungalow.

"No, Ursula! No! You must go on this tour. I will not allow you to stay here with me and miss the fun. I will not!"

"How can I possibly go off and leave you like this? It's not right."

"Of course, it's right! We arranged this especially for your benefit, didn't we, Colonel? Besides, we don't want the men in this town thinking we got cold feet and backed out at the last minute."

16

Mrs. Taylor spoke. "She's right, Ursula. There's no reason for you not to come if Alexa insists that she doesn't need you for the next two weeks."

Ursula looked at Lexie, then the colonel and Mrs. Taylor, and back to Lexie.

"I *would* like to go, Lexie. Are you sure you'll be all right?"

"Of course I will. Now be off with you. I've held you up far too long."

The Riley Falcon, its sliding roof open to the rushing air, bounced along the Yamgangpokpi road, heading east with Colonel Taylor at the wheel. Beside him sat Vasuki, the compounder, the title given to a native trained to be a medical assistant. Ursula sat in the rear with Mrs. Taylor. The road was rutted and the ride jarring. When Ursula was not looking out of the window at all the new sights, Colonel Taylor regaled her with his experiences as a Civil Surgeon. At times, she felt she was a child again, listening to some of her great uncles telling their tales. By nightfall, they reached the foothills, where they ran out of road on the outskirts of a Naga village.

"We're leaving the car here," Colonel Taylor said. "From now on we'll be on foot." He and Vasuki started pulling *jappas* and bags from the car.

"What do you think of the accommodation?" asked Mrs. Taylor, nodding towards the mud-walled rest-house with its shaggy, thatched roof.

"Well, it's not exactly the Ritz, but it'll do," said Ursula, laughing.

Colonel Taylor went into the village and arranged for six porters to join them in the morning. They arrived in the pre-dawn light, hoisted *jappas* on their backs, and then the group set off walking in file. As the sun rose, the party entered the outer foothills. With the brightening sky, Ursula saw where erosion had carved red gullies in the arid, treeless slopes. The track ploughed on through dense dry grass. Ursula trudged behind one of the porters, whose tread was light and spry, despite the burden balanced over his brow. She couldn't time the walk but guessed from the sun and from the ache in her calves that they'd been at it for at least three hours. The trail climbed out of the

18

heat, leading the perspiring group to wooded areas, cooler climes, and refreshing breezes. As they moved into the inner slopes, the surroundings changed, becoming greener and more luxuriant. At times, they walked through woods where crisp, dry leaves crunched under foot, and bright blue sky sparkled above bare tree branches. Other times, the path plummeted into steaming tropical forests full of large, shiny, leathery leaves, fern fronds, and choking vines.

Travelling along the track, a ledge on the hillside, they spotted a group of Nagas waiting for them and the medicines they brought.

"Here we are, our first batch of patients," announced the colonel.

The porters travelled on to the next rest-house, apart from the porter carrying the medicine *jappa*; he slipped the strap from his forehead and set his load on the ground. Ursula studied the Nagas: men, women and children, semi-naked people smelling of sweat, and wood-smoke. They were short in stature and wore bright, bead necklaces. Big silver rings stretched their ears. Some were standing; others squatted behind eggs and fruit placed on the ground, brought as offerings for medical treatments. Seeking safety behind parents, chubby, dark-eyed children stared with fascination at the strangers. One man, wrapped in a red blanket with black trimming and imposing despite his lack of height, came forward to greet Colonel Taylor. The two spoke in a language new to Ursula.

"Who's that man in red?" Ursula asked Mrs. Taylor.

"That's the village headman. He wears a red blanket because red is the colour of authority. These are Tangkhul Nagas. You can tell by their haircuts."

Ursula had noticed the sides of the men's heads were shaved, and the top was shaped like a crest, standing up like a cropped horse's mane?"

"So there are different tribes of Nagas."

Mrs. Taylor nodded.

Ursula watched as Vasuki spread a cloth on the ground and laid out the ointments, salves and medicines. The headman beckoned a man with a large sore on his leg to come forward.

19

Colonel Taylor used a scalpel to cut away the dead flesh then administered powdered M and B 760. Ursula was amazed at the hill-man's silent stoicism in the face of such pain.

Mrs. Taylor looked at Ursula with admiration. "Most civilians can't bear to watch my husband at work and yet you're riveted."

"I can't look away."

Mrs. Taylor smiled. "You're also a delicate shade of green."

"I'm definitely queasy. What are you using on the sore, Colonel Taylor?"

"It's a sulphur drug," the colonel explained. "It cleans the ulcer and starts the healing." He nodded towards the compounder where a number of Nagas had lined up. "Vasuki is using a 90% alcohol solution on his patients. They've got scabies. It's common among the Tangkhuls."

The dispensary lasted an hour, after which the Nagas presented the colonel with their gifts and departed. Vasuki began packing the medicines.

Ursula watched the colonel sterilize his hands with a rinse of Dettol antiseptic. "What other sorts of illnesses do you treat?" Ursula asked.

"Minor things, usually. Malaria, bronchitis, worms. Then we have septic wounds and, as you saw, ulcers to deal with. These can be horrendous. And of course, we perform minor operations such as lancing abscesses and extracting teeth. We're kept busy on these tours," the colonel said, drying his hands on a small towel. "There's a small hospital for Indian patients in Haflong, but that's over a hundred and twenty miles away. Imagine trying to carry a patient there over this terrain."

"It would take days, weeks," Ursula said.

"Right, and besides, the Nagas won't go there. That's why we make these tours. I provide the only medical attention these people are likely to receive."

Vasuki finished packing, and they moved on.

"You're holding up well to the walking, Ursula. Ready for the next march?" the colonel asked.

Ursula grinned. "I'm managing, but I'll be rubbing my calf muscles tonight."

"From what Alexa told us about your walking holidays in Scotland, we knew you would be fine," Mrs. Taylor said.

The group travelled on, coming across two more groups of Nagas requiring treatment. Late in the afternoon, they arrived at an earthen-floored, mud-walled, decaying bungalow nestled in a compound hedged by cacti. Ursula looked round the sparse accommodation, which had open rafters holding up a thatched roof where legions of sparrows were nesting. That could make the evening meal interesting she thought.

By some miracle, no bird droppings landed in their food or mugs of tea. Over the meal of chicken stew, rice, and oranges made from the Naga's offerings, Ursula, bubbling with curiosity, asked about the hillmen.

"The Nagas belong to a headhunting culture," Colonel Taylor told her as he cut into an orange. He noticed Ursula jump with shock. "As recently as three years ago, in the Somra tract area, they were taking heads. Mr. Mills, who was then Deputy Commissioner, took the Assam Rifles on an expedition into the hills to rescue slaves taken by the Nagas to be used as sacrifices."

"Slaves! Sacrifices! I don't believe you! The people we saw today were so pleasant, happy and laughing—and so *nice* to us," Ursula said.

Colonel Taylor swallowed his orange segment.

"Hard to grasp. Of course, the Nagas you saw today live nearer to civilization and have been administered by the British authorities for some years. We put a stop to the fighting between rival villages, so the opportunity to take heads was removed."

"Don't let their headhunting past upset you, Ursula. We've always found the Nagas to be extremely courteous and helpful to us," Mrs. Taylor reassured her.

"Oh, I'm not upset, just amazed. What do they do with the heads? Have you seen them? Will I? I'm finding it all so fascinating."

Early in the morning, before the sun's heat boiled away the mist swirling in the hollows, they began the usual four hours daily walk. The track dropped into a deep valley and led them onto a gruelling climb as it zigzagged up the opposite side to the next crest. Following the path along the crest, Ursula paused to gaze upon the sea of ridges stretching to the horizon and on Naga villages scattered on hilltops above staircase rice terraces, which plunged two thousand feet to meet the paddy fields of the valleys.

"I can't explain how I feel about this scenery," she told her companions. "It's absolutely mesmerizing. Do you mind if I take some photographs?"

Colonel Taylor patted Ursula's shoulder. "Make the most of it, Ursula. This may be a once in a lifetime trip."

The colonel's words jarred Ursula, and for a split second, she almost fell into the pit of resignation she had lived in since moving in with her grandmother. Then she rallied, straightened her shoulders and, set her jaw. You're wrong, Colonel, she thought. Dead wrong. My life has changed, and here in the hills, I've changed. I'm not going back to my old life, ever.

Perhaps what had struck her about that first glimpse of Naga men was their aura of difference. They were different from the men of England, just as their land was different from the muddy tweeds and murky skies, the brick houses, tarmac roads, slate roofs and cold rooms, and the class system that, taken altogether, defined her own country and confined her.

They moved on, following the trail through a ravine and over a wooden bridge at a boulder-strewn stream, where they found another group of Nagas to treat. Ursula played peek-a-boo with the children and managed to gain their mothers' trust enough to take some photographs. The ratchet sound of Ursula cocking the Leica and the "sha-cuck" of the shutter delighted the children, and they chortled with each picture snapped.

After ten days of hiking and holding dispensaries, the group ate dinner in their final night's basic accommodation.

"Now tell the truth, did you enjoy the tour as much as I think you did, Ursula?" asked the colonel.

"Colonel Taylor, how could you ask such a thing? It was hot, sticky, dirty, uncomfortable—and I loved every minute of it. The Nagas were fascinating; the scenery was breathtaking . . . I'd go back in an instant."

The colonel and his wife smiled at Ursula's enthusiasm.

The next morning they hiked back to the car. Before turning the ignition key, the colonel twisted in his seat to regard Ursula. "You did well, Ursula, my girl. You never groused or pouted or protested, and you kept up your spirits and ours. I'm looking forward to seeing a few disappointed faces when I tell them about it at the Club."

Ursula fell silent. She had, in fact, felt totally at home during her ten days in the Naga Hills, as if she had rediscovered a world to which she had once belonged and from which, by some accident, she had been estranged. She felt unsettled returning to Imphal, her own race and her own community as if she was no longer connected to that life.

Ursula had barely handed her *jappa* to the servant and entered the bungalow before Lexie was pouring tea and offering sandwiches. She launched into her questions. "How was it? Anything like you expected? Did you enjoy yourself? Would you do it all over again?"

Ursula finally managed to get a word in edgeways, "I don't know. It was a bit much."

For a moment, Lexie was crestfallen, then she saw the twinkle in Ursula's eyes. Leaning forward, she threatened, "Ursula Graham Bower . . ."

"Oh, Lexie, yes, I would do it again in the blink of an eye."

"Marvellous!" whooped Lexie, relaxing back into her chair. "I thought you would, so I've made arrangements."

"What! What arrangements?"

"Don't worry. You'll have a week to rest, then we're going with Mr. Jeffery, the State Engineer, to Tamenglong and the Barak River on his tour of bridge inspection."

Ursula jumped up from her chair and hugged her friend. "Lexie! You're adorable, an angel and brilliant!"

"She wasted no time after you left with Colonel Taylor," Richard said, entering the room. He was followed by a lean, wiry man with black hair and a large, strong nose. "She hobbled around on that gammy leg of hers determined to stir up some action, didn't she, Jeffery?"

"She certainly did. If you two ladies are game, so am I."

Ursula found his deep melodic voice pleasing.

"Ursula, meet Mr. Jeffery. Mr. Jeffery, meet Ursula Bower," Lexie said.

Jeffery shook Ursula's hand. "Hello, Ursula. I hear you've just spent ten days in Manipur's eastern subdivision."

"Yes and I had a wonderful time."

"Hmm." Jeffery cocked his head and scrutinized Ursula with narrowed eyes. "We'll be touring in Manipur's western subdivision. Things will be even more primitive than on Colonel Taylor's tour. We'll be overnighting in jungle camps and travelling mainly on native paths rather than tracks. I assume you have the appropriate gear," he said, pointing to his olive green shirt with its flapped and buttoned patch breast pockets and his voluminous biscuit-coloured shorts and sturdy boots.

"Yes, we have our jungle uniforms," Lexie said.

"Will we meet with Nagas?" Ursula asked.

"Definitely," Jeffery said and explained that at Tamenglong they'd have contact with three tribes, the Kabui, Zemi, and Lyeng, who form a group known as the Kacha Nagas."

"The word is out about our trip with Mr. Jeffery," Lexie said. "We're going to be in for some strong criticism over the next few days, I'm afraid."

Lexie was right. The next evening, they went to the Club with its high ceilings, dark, rough beams and unadorned, whitewashed, plaster walls. The long bamboo sofa with its chintz-covered cushions was reserved for the senior ladies of the community, who sat making small talk about the frustrations their Indian servants caused them. In the small dining room, white-coated Indian attendants waited to serve dinner. The lounge was dotted with groupings of sturdy, handsomely carved, rosewood chairs and rattan tables and sturdy, handsomely carved middle-aged men. "As rigid and inflexible as the furniture," Lexie quipped.

As the three friends walked into the lounge, voices fell silent. The palm-leaf fans hummed overhead as Richard settled them at their table and ordered drinks.

"Sorry I have to leave you here by yourselves for a while. I'll be in the smoking room, talking with the Commissioner." Richard looked around. "It looks like a hostile crowd."

Ursula could see some of the ladies of the community eyeing them and whispering toxic comments to one another behind raised hands. She caught several hostile stares trained at her.

"We'll be fine. Don't worry, Richard," Ursula said. "Just a few ladies thrilled to have something to gossip about."

Mrs. Birchall, stiff in her whalebone corsets, was the first to approach them. Her jowls quivered as she asked in a voice of patently insincere concern, "Are you sure you know what you are doing, my dears?" Her tone intimated her certainty that they did not.

"It's so kind of you to be worried about us, Mrs. Birchall. But we'll be perfectly safe with Mr. Jeffery," Lexie answered.

Mrs. Huntley, sitting with friends at a nearby table, lifted her nose and sniffed with an air of righteous indignation and stage whispered, "What about their reputations?"

Lexie snickered and winked at Ursula who struggled to suppress her laughter, rolling her eyes to the ceiling instead.

A captain in the Assam Rifles brought them drinks and stayed long enough to tell the two women, "Have you any idea what you're proposing to do? This is a two hundred-mile march you're going on, not a jaunt. You'll *never* stand the marching."

As he departed, Ursula watched his retreating back. "All this so-called concern is so comforting, isn't it? Well, you said yourself they're practically fossilized. I see now what you mean. I'm not daunted, are you?"

Lexie grinned as if in a conspiracy. "Hardly," she said, lifting her glass to make a toast. "We will support one another in living life on our own terms."

Ursula joined Lexie in renewing the oath. Their glasses clinked.

Richard reported later that he and Jeffery had faced their own inquisition in the smoking lounge. One of the regulars had growled at him, "No responsible brother should allow such a thing. What if they became sick? They'd have to be carried in."

"I told him I thought he was underestimating the capabilities of the fairer sex. Then the magistrate had remonstrated Jeffery. 'You ought to know better.'"

Richard told the women that Jeffery had coolly stood up and addressed the room. Without rancour, he had said firmly, "Gentlemen, your attitudes smack of the nineteenth century not the twentieth. Times have changed. The young ladies have plenty of pluck, perhaps more than some of you here. Now, if you'll excuse me . . ."

"And with that," Richard said, "he swallowed the last of his whisky and left."

Rain sheeted down. On the quagmire road, the car slid and slithered in foot-deep mud, crabbing its way to the starting point in the bazaar. Ursula and Lexie remained enthusiastic as they met with damp porters trying to shelter themselves and the baggage between the cigarette stalls under the dripping peepul tree. Most of the porters had accompanied Jeffery on previous tours, and they greeted him warmly. They hoisted the loads onto their backs and filed up the slope enveloped in shrouds of mist and drenching drizzle.

"We're off now. No second thoughts!" Ursula said.

Clothes were soon soaked. Dusk dimmed the skies.

"I hope this weather isn't an omen," Lexie said.

"A bit different from the Ukhrul side, isn't it?" Jeffery said, cheerfully. "That's the dry side of Manipur. This western side's wetter, as you're finding out. We're several days' march from the Barak River. Don't get too disheartened; the rain will stop eventually."

After two days' soggy marching and two nights spent in hastily erected jungle camps trying to dry socks and clothing by the fires, Ursula's spirits were sagging when, as promised, the rain stopped. The clouds lifted to reveal the razor-back ranges covered in dark, dense rain forest. On the fourth day, after toiling up three thousand feet of murderous slopes, they reached Tamenglong. Naga interpreters came to meet them just below the summit, bringing rice-beer to refresh the party before they clambered up the last quarter mile to the top of the ridge.

The two women studied the milky white, opaque rice beer in their mugs.

Jeffery noticed their hesitation. "First *zu?*"

Ursula and Lexie nodded.

Jeffery saluted them with his mug then gulped down the liquid. "Cheers. Drink up. It tastes fine."

Before an audience of watching porters and Nagas, Ursula sipped her rice-beer.

"Well, how is it?" Lexie asked.

"I would say it's an acquired taste, but I'm thankful for anything to quench my thirst right now. How about you? What's your verdict?"

Lexie sipped the *zu* then drank a mouthful. "It's quite pleasant!" she said, surprised.

At the top of the ridge, the group looked down on the small hill station.

"There you are, girls, Tamenglong," Jeffery said. We'll be stopping here for a day. That bungalow on the highest crest is the Subdivisional Officer's bungalow. Below it, on the other crest, is the rest-house. Most of the other homes you see are for the clerks and interpreters. We'll be invited to dine with the SDO tonight. He's always glad to have company."

They gazed down at the small town. Red tin roofs, peeping like poppies from the surrounding greenery, were strewn along a low spur, which thrust out over the Barak valley.

Jeffery pointed ahead. "There's the Naga village perched right on the end of the spur, see it? Keep your camera handy, Ursula. You'll see plenty of Nagas here."

Ursula was already removing the Leica from its case unable to resist the green, undulating hills that were Tamenglong's backdrop and the metallic streak of the Barak River, glistening in the sunshine. A sparkling sliver revealed a distant waterfall.

That evening, the delighted SDO, Jim Harvey, a slim man with an unruly blonde quiff and boyish charm, welcomed the two young women and Jeffery as dinner guests. He couldn't hide his amazement at the boldness of their adventure.

"I'm sure that set a few tongues wagging, Jeffery."

"It certainly did. You would have thought the idea of condemning forward-looking women would have died a death by now. After all, we've had people such as Florence Nightingale, Madame Curie . . . "

"And the *extraordinary* Amelia Earhart," added the SDO. "First person ever to fly solo across the Pacific. Imagine that!"

"Lucy Walker, the first woman to climb the Matterhorn," Ursula added.

"And *we* only want to see where Mr. Jeffery goes on his tours," Lexie said.

The following day, while Jeffery organized porters and equipment for the next leg of the tour, Lexie and Ursula explored an ancient stone fort on the outskirts of the town. They sat in the shade of the walls enjoying the cooling breeze. Lexie spoke first. "I'm having a wonderful time. And, knock on wood, my ankle is giving me no trouble, despite all the dire warnings we received about the walking."

"I love it here, Lexie," Ursula said, her voice wistful. "I'm totally at home in the hills. I feel complete, as if I never want to return to civilization."

"We're poles apart from our old friends, aren't we? Most are married or chafing at the bit to find some suitable chap." Alexa lifted her face to the sun. "This is wonderful, a fantasy that's become reality. We have sixteen days left. We'll make the most of them."

Sixteen days seemed too few for Ursula. She was a lover newly infatuated, but the mysteries and charms of her loved one, this land, would never wear out for her. She thought of her life in England, the expectations and restraints imposed by grandparents who had robbed her of her Oxford education and Grandmama, a sweetie really, but not the best companion for a young girl. She took a deep breath. Enough of bleak thoughts. Today she was triumphant. She had slipped her leash and was running free with the one person who knew her best.

The morning saw them on the march again down through the Kabui village where shy villagers watched their progress from doorways and porches. Jeffery smiled, called greetings and waved to the villagers as he walked along the street. Ursula and Lexie followed his example, waving and smiling to the Nagas. On the far side of the village, the path curled over the edge of the spur plummeting from view. The group filed along the twisting turning trail as it plunged through fields, woods and grassy slopes, leading the party down into the forest. They descended through a long tunnel of bamboo. Lichen-speckled milestones marked the distance travelled. Legs began to ache; their boots chafed their feet. The cooling breeze died away as they descended into the clammy, muted world of the steamy valley.

Flies buzzed round their ears. Mosquitoes zoomed in to attack. Ursula slapped at the pests biting her forearm and calf.

"We'll stop to rest awhile and eat, but not for too long; the mosquitoes will see to that," Jeffery said, slapping his neck.

They ate sardine sandwiches, gulped down some tea and moved on.

Delicate bamboo gave way to giant varieties with wide five-inch stems reaching sixty feet into the air. Soaked in perspiration, they moved through the dank, decaying undergrowth until finally they reached level ground.

Jeffery nodded towards roaring sounds hidden by thinning jungle and river-grass. "There's the river. Do you hear it?"

The blaze of sunlight after so long in the darkness of the forest made them squint. They walked across dry water channels, sandbanks and through reed beds.

"There's a welcome sight," Ursula said, as she spotted the camp, a cluster of bamboo huts underneath the high suspension bridge.

"Ready to rest your legs, girls? I am."

"Yes, me too," Lexie said.

"I must admit, I've had enough marching for today," said Ursula.

"Settle in," Jeffery said. "I'll be checking out the bridge, after I've had a drink of tea."

While Jeffery clambered about the bridge, testing, tapping, inspecting, the boys lit fires, and soon the odour of chilli stew filled the air.

That evening, around the campfire, Ursula observed Jeffery with the natives. He was tolerant and patient with the hillmen, relaxed and friendly in their company, and he treated them as equals. As he squatted to chat with them or moved about, his body movement shadowed theirs in a subtle mimicry. It was obvious he respected their world and his acceptance appeared to have earned the Nagas' trust.

"I've been watching you with the Nagas," Ursula said when he joined her and Lexie by the fireside. "You're comfortable with them, not at all like the Europeans at Imphal."

"Oh? And how are they in Imphal?"

"Well, they make fun of the natives. They're condescending. They're…"

"Whoa," he stopped Ursula, who was indignantly building her case against their bigotry. "The Europeans at Imphal are like any small group anywhere that feels isolated and threatened. They're wedged into a world with a different culture and standards, and they're filled with fear. That's understandable, don't you think?"

"And it's mainly the people who aren't administrators who feel that way, isn't it?" Lexie said.

"Um. On the whole, the administrators appreciate the cultures they're taking care of. Remember, most Europeans are only here for a few years, and then they return home. They pull their customs and their own moral standards around them and close ranks in order to feel safe."

"You don't need to feel safe then?" Ursula asked.

"I don't feel threatened by the human differences," Jeffery said. "I feel stimulated. I learn something new about human nature on every trip. The Nagas are shy but courteous. They're helpful but not ingratiating." He laughed self-consciously. "I guess I'm a very lucky man. I love my work."

The fire crackled and sparked in the darkness. More brown bodies crowded round, Nagas who had come to visit out of curiosity. The murmur of voices and laughter felt as warm as the fire. Mists flowed into the valley. The moon shone argent behind the hazy screen.

Suddenly, a slashing whoosh tore through the peace.

Ursula heard a thud close to Lexie and Lexie's scream. Ursula and Jeffery leapt up. A machete was angled from the ground, inches from Lexie's thigh. "Good God!" Ursula shouted, pulling Lexie to her feet. "Are you all right?"

Shocked and shaking, Lexie asked, "What happened?"

Ursula looked to Jeffery, ready to take her cue from him on whether or not their lives were in danger. She was surprised when he laughed.

A Naga yanked the machete from the earth and held up a small, now headless, writhing snake.

"It's a krait," Jeffery told her. "They're deadly. One bite and you'd have been dead in seconds. This young man saved your life."

The Naga threw the snake away. Lexie grabbed his hand, vigorously pumping it up and down. "Thank you. Thank you. Thank you," she kept repeating. Jeffery took her hands and stilled them in his. "Come on, Alexa, you'll shake his hand off if you're not careful." The young Naga seemed surprised and pleased at her gratitude, and when the interpreter translated Jeffery's words, everyone laughed in relief.

On the sandbank next morning, over twenty Nagas swarmed about, cutting down bamboo and tying the stems together into long triangular rafts built with low platforms to keep the riders dry as the waves washed over the bases, which rode low in the water.

Jeffery, grinned at Ursula and Lexie's anxious expressions. "Hang on tight. They can tilt and dump you in the river, but I've never known a raft to capsize."

"How reassuring," Ursula said, dryly, stepping aboard, "we may get dumped in the water, but the raft won't capsize."

The boatmen, one forward and one aft, pushed the rafts from shore until knee deep in water before hauling themselves aboard. With the boatmen poling and paddling, the flotilla coursed south along the Barak River. Sometimes, the boatmen jumped into the water to guide the rafts over shallows and fords. Other times, the travellers carried the rafts and equipment past surging rapids and cascading waterfalls. Then there were the long pools where the gliding rafts rippled the glass-smooth, jade waters. The river carried the party deep into a green world of wild jungle. Lexie and Ursula whispered in the muted atmosphere. Chattering monkeys disturbed the silence. Snapping twigs and rustling leaves marked the retreat of disturbed wild boar. Otters slipped into the water when the rafts approached.

The party camped in small clearings hacked from the forest.

In the mornings, twice Jeffery pointed out the pug marks of curious tigers that had visited during the night. Once shown, Ursula could clearly pick out the evidence on the paths and sandbanks. For days, they journeyed in this beautiful paradise, marvelling at the dark green, shiny plants, colourful squawking birds and iridescent butterflies as large as tea-plates. When not overawed by this unspoiled beauty, Ursula remembered to take some photographs, and as she did, the surety of her plan took over. She would come back.

But how?

Who would come with her? Would she be safe, accepted by the Nagas? What if she became ill? She stopped herself. It was all too silly. It wasn't going to happen.

The stream widened. A suspension bridge came into view.

"This bridge carries the Silchar track. Our river journey ends here," Jeffery said, as the rafts moved to shore by the bridge.

Ursula's heart sank. "I feel like I've come to the end of a dream."

"Don't worry. It's not over yet. We'll be camping here tonight." Jeffery stepped onto the sandbank. "Looks like we've got visitors," he said, moving away to greet a crowd of Kabui Nagas who had travelled seven miles from their village for a final meal with their friend. The rice-beer flowed; the food cooked; the fire glowed. Ursula struggled to control her despondency in order to enjoy this last get together with the Nagas.

The next morning, Ursula stood and stared at the dead fire's ashes. A wave of despair hit her.

"Penny for them," Lexie said, coming up behind Ursula.

"Just saying goodbye—the trip, the experience, the wonder, you know."

"Yes, I know. It's been wonderful, hasn't it?"

The porters picked up their loads, and the entourage filed off. Ursula kept her eyes focused straight ahead, refusing to allow herself to look back at the deserted camp, afraid she would embarrass herself by crying.

At Silchar, they took the train to Haflong. After the beautiful surroundings of the Barak, Ursula felt claustrophobic in the grimy train. The Nagas she saw hanging round the stations, selling oranges, were mere shadows of the glorious people in the hills. She fretted and slept all the way to Haflong, from where they journeyed to Imphal, just in time for Christmas.

Ursula joined in the festivities as best she could, but anyone could tell she was preoccupied. While they strolled back from the bazaar together one afternoon, Lexie asked, "What's going on? Your mind is elsewhere most of the time. What is it?"

Ursula hoped and believed her friend would fully understand. "The trip with Mr. Jeffery changed me, Lexie. I've been thinking about it, and I've made up my mind. I'm going back."

"Back? Into the hills? Who will go with you? It wouldn't be fair of me to leave Richard again. How are you going to manage it?"

"I've been working things out. I feel quite crazy, but I have to go back. I have my allowance. I can afford one servant and a few porters, and perhaps I could borrow some equipment."

Over breakfast next morning, Richard talked to Ursula. "Lexie tells me you intend to go off into the hills by yourself. I can't say I don't have some misgivings about it. No European woman has ever done such a thing. Are you sure about this?"

"Absolutely, so don't try to dissuade me."

"No, I won't do that, but it's not as simple as taking a trip to the Isle of Skye. I've been giving it some thought. You'll need permission from Jimpson, the Political Agent, and if your money will stretch to it, it may be worth your while talking to Colonel Taylor about taking some medicines for the Nagas."

Ursula, filled with admiration for this wonderful brother of Lexie's, raved, "I knew you would think of something! You're a whizz!"

"Thank you, Ursula." Richard made a bow and flashed her a huge grin before continuing. "And while you're waiting for Jimpson's decision, Colonel Taylor could give you a crash course in first aid and Manipuri—and I'm sure he'd put a word in for you."

"Richard! That's a wonderful idea!" Ursula jumped up and kissed him on the cheek. "Thank you so much for not discouraging me."

"Would it have done any good? Besides, Lexie's all for it, aren't you, Lexie? Anyway, I have it on good authority that the Deputy Commissioner at Kohima has a great interest in the Nagas. If he hears that you want to study them and take photographs to record their culture, he may vouch for you."

"With him and Colonel Taylor and possibly Jeffery speaking for Ursula, surely she'll have a good chance at getting permission," Lexie said.

"Who knows?" Richard said. He turned to Ursula. "You're a first. A woman going off into the hills by herself, it's never been done before."

"Then I need all the help I can get. Keep your fingers crossed."

*   *   *

In the days that followed, Ursula refused to allow herself any thoughts that permission to go into the hills might be denied. Instead, she studied first aid and treatment of the most common ailments she'd come across. She learned some Manipuri, bought medicines, drew up lists of items and equipment she would need, and then pared them down. There would be few porters on this trip to carry the loads. She arranged to borrow camping equipment: a camp bed, chair, table and bath, some cutlery, cooking pots and a plastic picnic-set. She set aside some linen shorts and cotton shirts bought for a song in the bazaar and, for the chilly nights, a sweater and a golf jacket. To keep her feet comfortable on the long marches, Ursula chose Pathan-style sandals and thick army socks. She packed a battered copy of *The Tropical Dispensary Handbook* Colonel Taylor had given her, then checked her camera and made sure she had plenty of yellow boxes of Kodak film and a carrying bag for the rolls of negatives. And when all this was done, she waited.

Ursula and Lexie continued to join the ladies at the Club, where they were greeted by whispers that Ursula was "not sound," and "a mere slip of a girl with crackpot ideas." Proclamations such as "Whatever would the world come to if the ladies thought they could just go off into the jungle whenever they felt like it!" were wearing, and overhearing a pronouncement that it would take a miracle for the Political Agent to give her leave to go brought Ursula close to tears.

She was beginning to agree with that opinion when the letter arrived. She tore it open and skimmed the contents. "Lexie, it's on! I can go!" Then her voice became shrill in panic, and she grabbed Lexie as a drowning man might grab a life belt. "I don't know if I can do it! I've hardly any money, a single, solitary servant, and there are kraits and tigers, and do I even know enough to treat the Nagas?"

"See here, Ursula Graham Bower, you can do it, and you will do it," Lexie declared. "Colonel Taylor is lending you a reliable man to be your servant, and he's found you a good compounder. Ouch! Ursula, you can let go of me now."

"Right." Ursula relaxed her grip on her friend. "Yes, you're right."

"Once you're trekking through the hills, you'll be fine. I know you will."

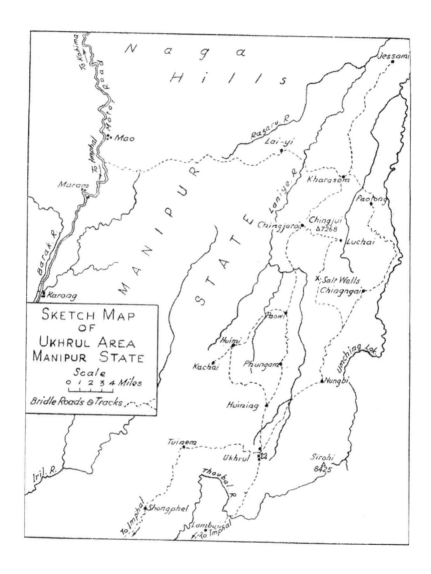

N a g a

H i l l s

Jessami

To Kohima

Mao

Razaru R.

Lai-yi

Motor Road

To Imphal

M A N I P U R

Kharasom

Loniye R.

Faolong

Maram

Chingjui
△7268

Chingjaroi

Luchai

Barak R.

S T A T E

X Salt Wells

Chiungngai

Karong

Yaowi

Umching Lok

SKETCH MAP
OF
UKHRUL AREA
MANIPUR STATE

Huimi

Kachai

Phungam

Scale
0 1 2 3 4 Miles

Nungbi

Bridle Roads & Tracks

Huining

Tuinem

Ukhrul

Sirohi
8425

Iril R.

Thoubal R.

To Imphal

Shongphel

Lambui

To Imphal

Ursula shivered as she climbed into the truck, telling herself it was because of the cold January morning. Her servants loaded the paraphernalia into the back then piled in on top of it. Acting with a confidence she didn't feel, Ursula waved goodbye to Richard and Lexie and set off for the foothills. The further she travelled, the smaller and more alone she felt.

Silently, she chivvied herself. You've done this twice before, and you can jolly well do it again. Nothing to it really, piece of cake. She looked out the window, unconvinced.

On this expedition, she had decided to go to Ukhrul, Nungbi and the Tangkhul Naga country. Her companions were Abung and Jafar. Abung, about forty, small even for a Kabui Naga, had an unruly mass of black hair. Ursula, at five feet nine inches, towered head and shoulders above him. Colonel Taylor had praised Abung's loyalty and his ability to speak some English, but warned that his cooking left a lot to be desired. Jafar, the compounder, had prematurely white hair cut in the English manner; he was a patient Manipuri, a kind gentle minister of medicines.

The truck sped across the dry Imphal Plain, whipping up clouds of dust as it headed for Yamgangpokpi. From there, the journey would be on foot. Ursula hired six porters, and off they marched. Arriving at the first village, the porters downed *jappas* and demanded more pay. Abung, acting as go between, came to Ursula with the news.

"Tell them the miss-sahib's not having any of it," she told him. "If they don't like it, they can leave."

Abung carried Ursula's words to the porters. They shrugged, picked up their loads and without further ado went on, taking it all in their stride.

Three days after leaving Imphal, they arrived at Ukhrul. The town stretched along a ridge, 6,000 feet above sea level. To the north stood the Naga Village. The group spent a day in Ukhrul to refit and re-organize its equipment. Late morning, Ursula called on Jeff Duncan, the Subdivisional Officer. He was lean and ruddy with burnished sun-bleached hair. He shook her hand.

"Good morning, Miss Bower. I received word you were coming. How can I help?"

"Please, call me Ursula. I need your advice on where to go and what to see about Naga culture that would be interesting, or rather, most interesting."

"You could start with the Naga village here. It's quite large, three hundred houses. You'll be able to see the style in which they're built. Then there's Khulen and Khunao, two Nungbi villages near a bed of clay, which gave rise to the pottery industry there."

He brought out a map, spread it on his desk and pointed out a circular route for her to follow. Finding paper and pencil, he drew a map and handed it to her.

"Here, this will make it easier."

"Thanks Jeff. May I call you Jeff?"

Duncan nodded.

"I'll go and take a look at the village now," Ursula said.

With Abung by her side and the camera round her neck, she visited the Naga village.

"This is a big village, miss-sahib. Many villages are much smaller," Abung told her.

Ursula studied the houses. Behind soot-stained porches, the fronts of the houses were covered in wooden boards with the whole covered by straggly thatch. A few houses had enormous crossed bargeboards thrusting out from the thatch like the antlers of a giant stag.

"Why do some homes have wooden shingle roofs and house horns on the gables?"

"Those houses belong to the richer Nagas, miss-sahib. The horns show that the owners have given several Feasts of Merit."

"What's a Feast of Merit?"

"It costs much money to give a Feast of Merit. A man who is rich enough, and wants the village to look up to him by having the house horns, pays for sacrifices, usually mithan and buffalo, and the village has a big feast. He also pays for dancers to come from nearby villages. Nobody goes to the fields on feast days."

Ursula walked along the street, which descended in a series of stone-faced platforms. Tall genna-posts, wooden posts stripped of bark and set up to commemorate feast days, huddled together, casting long shadows in the afternoon sun.

Ursula took out her camera and, in order to assure the Nagas that the Leica was harmless, took pictures only of the surroundings: an oriole in a tree, a distant view, and flowers peeping from the side of a house. Eventually, the courteous but shy Nagas, not wanting to offend the European woman, allowed her to take their pictures. Some were pleased at her interest. Young mothers sat on porches, holding chubby infants as they smiled quizzically into the Leica. Proud young men posed for the lens, or perhaps just for Ursula.

Next day, the party set out for Nungbi Khunao. They marched through sparse pinewoods, the rusty-brown pine needles soft under foot. In the clearings, Ursula paused to look at the views of the hills against cornflower-blue skies and cotton wool clouds. She could barely contain her joy as she soaked in the beautiful surroundings.

Late in the afternoon, they arrived on the outskirts of the village, where they were met by a headman and escorted to grass and matting huts prepared for their stay. The villagers presented her with two goats, ten bunches of bananas, two-dozen oranges, a basket of lemons, some eggs and three bottles of rice-beer.

Ursula was feeling composed and very much in control until her first casualty approached.

A man limped in from the village with a burned foot. Ursula took a deep breath and tried not to look at Jafar, her compounder, for support. Even if she did not know what she was doing, she must strike an air of confidence for the Nagas to look up to. She knelt to study the raw, oozing wound. She disinfected the wound, smoothed on a salve and bandaged it up. Out of the corner of her eye, she saw Jafar nodding his encouragement. She stood up straight, feeling ten feet tall. Towards dusk, patients came thick and fast—a dog-bite, sores, broken rib, cuts, wounds, coughs—and a baby with boils. The whole side of his head, having gone septic, was one mass of black scabs and pus.

Ursula felt a flutter of fear in the pit of her stomach on seeing the child. "Word must have spread," she said to Jafar, putting her shoulders back and rolling her neck. She picked up the antiseptic and a swab.

"The headman told me they have been without medical treatment for two years."

They took turns working on the screaming baby, battling scabs with swabs soaked in antiseptic. The more matter they cleaned away, the more appeared, and when the scabs came off, more pus oozed from his head. At last, they finished. With his head bandaged, his crying ceased. They would see him next day. The clinic continued for two hours until Ursula, exhausted, fell onto her bed. Biting winds whistled through every crack and crevice; the bitter cold disturbed her sleep. She was almost awake when she heard Abung's discreet cough outside. When she didn't grumble, "Go away," it was the signal that it was safe for Abung to enter with her early morning cup of tea.

"It will be half-past six," he announced in fuzzy Manipuri.

"I'm sure it is," Ursula muttered half-asleep.

Ten minutes later, a village woman brought a huge brass jug of fire-heated water for Ursula so she could wash.

After breakfast, Ursula walked with Abung to the village, eager to take pictures of the potters at work. Plumes of brown smoke rose above the rooftops from the kilns. Villagers watched two potters already at work in the street. A third potter appeared. Ursula looked on as he stripped off his red cloth and wrapped it about his hips to work bare-skinned from the waist up. "To keep it clean," Abung informed her. She began taking pictures of the potter pounding stones into dust then mixing the dust with powdered clay and water to make a pliable mixture. He used no wheel. Half the mixture he fashioned into a flat round base; the other half he formed into a cylinder by shaping the clay round a section of bamboo. With the cylinder added to the base,

43

he refined his work, patting, shaping, and stretching until satisfied. Then he added two rolled pieces of clay for handles, smoothed it and cut the pot free at its base. Ursula clicked away, taking final pictures of the potter posing with his pots before they were placed in the kiln.

*   *   *

As Ursula and her servants were sitting by the campfire that night, a man appeared from the darkness. He was thin, almost gaunt, and grubby.

"Abung, ask him what he wants," Ursula said.

"He is called Luikai," Abung told her. "He is a Tangkhul drowning in debt from his wife's funeral. He wants to work for you to earn some money."

Ursula looked at the shivering man in his ragged cloth. "Oh, I see," she said dismayed, thinking of her strained budget, but, damn, she wanted to help the poor man.

Jafar spoke up for him. "It would be a very kind deed if the miss-sahib agreed to help a struggling man. The gods will look upon you with favour, miss-sahib, and we can find plenty for him to do."

Luikai fidgeted, anxiously waiting for her decision, all the while scratching himself with some vigour.

"Very well, I'll take him on, but for goodness sake see what he's scratching at."

Abung interpreted. Luikai perked up. Jafar beckoned Luikai to sit next to him and examined his skin in the firelight.

"He's got the itch, miss-sahib."

"Smother him in ointment first thing in the morning. I don't want any of us catching scabies."

*   *   *

From Nungbi, the group filed down the trail before turning north to the hills that had captured Ursula's heart during her tour with the Civil Surgeon. She overflowed with happiness, loving everything; the primitive camps, the marching, the misty

44

mornings, treating and meeting the Nagas and learning about her glorious surroundings. Nothing, absolutely nothing, could be better than this.

They had developed a routine. At dawn's first light, Abung, wearing his servant's attire of white jacket and trousers, brought her a cup of tea and water to wash. Next, the staff packed the equipment, the porters loaded up, and off they filed along the trail. Ursula and the compounder stayed behind to hold a final dispensary. Usually, they were away by eight, but they could not predict when they would arrive at the next camp; that depended on how often they had to stop to dispense medicines and treatment at the villages along the way. These sessions helped the Nagas to be more trusting and confident with Ursula, enabling her to use her camera to capture the child peeping from behind his mother, the distinctive Tangkhul hairstyle, and wizened faces with sagacious, knowing eyes. On reaching camp, they managed to eat and rest for a while before the nightly dispensary, which lasted as long as daylight.

Large numbers of patients, usually brought by the headman, crowded round, pushing close and in their eagerness to receive attention, jostling Ursula and the compounder as they tried to work. In the villages, the scenes were the same, only without a table to put out the medicines, they improvised with a bench or even used the floor. Conditions were hardly sanitary with bare feet kicking up dust and flies getting into the ointments.

Through Abung and Jafar, she asked the hillmen why they did not use the hospitals at Imphal, Ukhrul and Tamenglong. Abung translated that it was too unfamiliar and inconsistent with their traditional ways.

"What do they do for medical help?" Ursula asked.

"They do without," Abung told her.

"The few drugs and treatments we are providing relieve much suffering," Jafar said.

Yes, they do, thought Ursula filled with the strange happiness that is a heady mixture of pride and compassion. She finally approved of her decision to make this trip, and the fact that she was helping the hillmen outweighed any silly objections

45

to her sex or her commonsense. Being right is gratifying, she thought, and she had been dead right.

The group moved on to the east, then north, from camp to camp, with Ursula industriously adding to her collection of photographs. Travelling through fields and woodland, they climbed a large hill to reach Chingjaroi.

Jeff Duncan had told her it was an unusual community, a mixture of Tangkhuls and Angamis, who had come from surrounding tribes to settle in what had been an abandoned village after Kuki raids had killed or driven out the original occupants. Through intermarriage, the Tangkhuls and Angamis had merged to form a unique culture.

On Ursula's first day in the village, strong blustery winds blew in. Dust and leaves were flying everywhere. Bitterly cold air whistled round the houses and howled through the treetops. She returned to her draughty basha to tell her servants, "We'll be staying here for a while. It's an interesting place, and hopefully these gales will blow over in a day or two."

"It is March," Abung said with resignation. "The winds will blow for a long time."

"Then we'll stay as long as we can," Ursula said.

Climbing up and down the steep steps of the village streets, accompanied by Jafar and Luikai carrying the medicine *jappa*, Ursula roamed around the three settlements that made up the village. They held dispensaries outdoors in the wind and dust, but once they were over, Ursula took photographs and scribbled notes at every chance to record the fascinating customs she discovered.

Luikai, the stray they had taken on, was proving his worth. With Ursula and Abung prodding him to wash, his new hygiene, coupled with the successful treatment of his scabies, had turned Luikai into a presentable young man. Indeed, the village girls often followed him around, flirting and chatting with him. He learned to perform a variety of useful chores: scrubbing, washing, and chopping wood, delighting Abung with his willingness to work hard.

When the day arrived to leave the village and head south, the village elders accompanied Ursula as far as the ford. Their farewells were affectionate and tearful. Through Abung they told her the village felt honoured that Ursula, a lone British woman, had shown interest in their lives, had felt safe living among them, and had given them much medical help. Ursula's heart filled with a fondness that surprised her.

"Abung, tell them I'm the one who's honoured by being allowed into their lives."

After crossing the river, Ursula's group faced a steep climb. She turned to watch the Naga elders in their red blankets moving up the far slope until they disappeared from view among trees stripped bare by the wintry winds. Within half-an-hour of starting the climb, Ursula felt feverish, aching in every cell and fibre of her body.

Influenza.

With no drugs left to ease her pains, she could only hope for a quick return to health.

For Ursula, it was a march made in hell. Tortuous steps replaced the usual pleasure of climbing and walking. She felt like Alice in wonderland, the trail appearing to extend before her eyes, stretching, alive, moving the night's resting-place further and further away. She eventually staggered into camp, feeling on fire with pointed rocks in her skull, and rested until Jafar opened the dispensary. Then gritting her teeth, she struggled to her feet.

A young Naga in his twenties stepped forward. Thickened skin covered his face; nodules on his nose and cheeks had broken down into discharging sores.

"Jafar, what is it?"

"Leprosy."

They were talking to the young man when the crowd made way for a woman limping towards the table, accompanied by a boy about eight years old. She wore makeshift soles tied to her feet with string. On examining her, Ursula and Jafar discovered the soles of her feet were covered in sores, leprosy sores. Her eight-year-old seemed to be all right.

This is all a hallucination thought Ursula. The world cannot have turned so vile so quickly. Her own body was wracked with fever, her temples beat hotly and her eyes burned with migraine.

The boy turned to smile at his mother. Ursula bit her lip to stop herself from gasping in dismay when she caught sight of the leprosy lesions on his back.

They tried to persuade the woman to go to the leper asylum at Kangpokpi, but she refused. Feeling helpless and frustrated because they had nothing in the dispensary for the treatment of leprosy, she could only send the lepers away.

Her pride and self-satisfaction waned, and now, in her impotence, she thought that perhaps the ladies of the Club had been right. She was too weak for the wilderness, too sick to cure, too helpless to help.

Next day, Ursula struggled on to Ukhrul. Even though she still suffered from the flu, they did not halt there. Short of money and low on supplies, they travelled on to Tuinem where they stayed for a day, and Ursula rallied enough to capture on film the Tangkhul weaving industry. Flattered by her interest and grateful for her medical help, the village decided to commemorate the occasion with a gift. As she sat outside the headman's house sipping rice-beer, he presented her with a beautiful white cloth to cheers from the villagers.

Ursula draped the cloth over her shoulders. Abung spoke with the villagers and when they laughed, she looked at him for an explanation.

"I say you make good Tangkhul."

The thought stunned Ursula. Then after a pause she said cheerfully, "Yes, I would, a tall one."

Abung told the Nagas, who burst into more excited talking. Ursula wished she understood. That night the village sang and danced for her. It was a sad farewell next morning.

Disconsolate, unwilling to think about her trip ending, Ursula hiked the last leg down to the plain where a truck waited to take them to Imphal. As they drove from the hills, Ursula's influenza-induced aches and pains began to ease at last, replaced by another kind of suffering, the agony of an aching heart.

As the truck pulled up outside the bungalow, Lexie hurried outside to greet Ursula. The friends embraced then, holding Ursula at arms' length, Lexie scrutinized her. "You look like death."

"I've had the flu."

"Come inside and put your feet up. You can tell me all about it over a cup of tea."

Revived with rum cake and several cups of strong tea, Ursula felt the colour return to her cheeks.

She regaled Lexie with the events of her tour with gusto then added, "For the first time in my life I've known responsibility, loneliness, worry, and exhaustion. I've been revolted by wounds and filth and hampered by lack of the language. You may think I'm insane, but I'm going back if it kills me."

Lexie laughed. "I tried to bet Richard five rupees that that's what you'd do, but he refused. He thought you'd go back too."

They spoke of the Isle of Skye, where the two of them had enjoyed many walking holidays. In the Scottish hills, Ursula was restored and made whole. The suffocating burden of looking after her grandmother and the haunting spectre of thwarted dreams evaporated in the breeze among the heights and heather.

"Ursula, do you remember how you cured yourself of vertigo?"

"How could I forget?"

"You risked your fool neck by climbing up the steepest slopes and balancing on the outcrops until you were cured."

"It was a sound method."

"Well, now you're at it again. Only with bigger hills to climb. You have more gumption than I'll ever have. I couldn't do what you've just done. I almost envy you."

"No need, Lexie. It's a purely selfish joy I feel when I'm helping the Nagas. It feels wonderful to be actually doing something useful with my life, and I want more of it before I go home."

"I wish I could come with you, but Richard would draw the line at letting me go without an official in the group. I'll just have to soak up your tales when you get back."

For the week Ursula was in Imphal, busily making arrangements for another tour before her return to England, Lexie stayed by her side, partly to take vicarious pleasure from Ursula's preparations and partly to act as a shield, protecting Ursula from the chilly attitude of the British community. Richard pointed out that Ursula was so resolute and involved in her preparations she was oblivious to the snubs.

"They haven't seen what I've seen," Ursula said. "Why should I listen to them?"

Abung and Luikai would accompany Ursula again. She went to see the Civil Surgeon Colonel Radnor, the blustery old walrus who had replaced Colonel Taylor.

"I'm no admirer of your jaunts into the hills, Miss Bower," Colonel Radnor said, "but I recognize the value of medical assistance reaching the isolated Naga tribes, and for that reason only, I will assist you. I have one compounder to spare."

"Colonel Radnor, I'd be grateful for anyone I could get as long as I can return with medical help for the Nagas."

Radnor harrumphed and petted his moustache. "The compounder I have in mind has been troublesome, having twice been transferred for dishonesty. It will be a last chance for him to reform. You'll have to keep a tight rein on the medicines. Keep them with you, and issue them yourself. The man is not to be trusted."

Within a week, Ursula was ready to leave Imphal. Her new compounder, Suizhakhup, with his sulky expression, had an arrogance, an air of disdain, and Ursula knew he would rather be anywhere else but on this tour with her.

It had been pouring with rain for days. The truck laboured along the muddy the road. With the vehicle either stuck in the mire or slewing left or right, the journey was nerve-wracking and slow.

"We're going to have to turn back," Ursula told the Sikh driver. "We're never going to make it."

"Do not worry, miss-sahib. I will get you to Yamgangpokpi in one piece," he promised time and time again. He was as cheerful and optimistic as Suizhakhup was dour.

The truck finally slid to a sideways stop at the travellers' bungalow on the edge of Yamgangpokpi village. Ursula breathed a sigh of relief.

"I'm not sure how you managed to get us here in one piece, but I'm very pleased you did," she told the driver with a nervous laugh.

That evening, Abung slipped and hurt himself as he was carrying cooking pots to the kitchen and tore a nasty gash in his calf. Ursula despatched Suizhakhup to clean and dress the wound. With everything unloaded, she entered the rest-house. She had just sat down when she heard angry voices coming from the servants' quarters. With a sigh, she stood up and walked over to see what was happening. She saw Suizhakhup outside his room, his Kuki features more sullen than usual, arguing furiously with the caretaker.

"What is it? What's going on?" Ursula demanded.

Suizhakhup pointed inside. "I am not sleeping there. It is filthy. I will leave if you expect me to sleep in such filth."

His room was splattered with blood, stank of raw, festering meat, and the grisly remnants of a carcass were flung here and there.

"Why is the room like this?" she demanded of the caretaker.

"He," Suizhakhup said, pointing with distain at the caretaker, "slaughtered a cow in there."

"Get your things. You can't stay in this muck. You'll have to sleep in my house tonight." The last thing Ursula wanted was to share her quarters with Suizhakhup.

Suizhakhup's sulkiness intensified. He darkened like a stormy sky, and if looks could kill, the caretaker would have died on the spot. "I do not wish to stay in the miss-sahib's quarters."

"Anything is better than this bloody room, and if you won't sleep there and you won't stay in my bungalow, then sleep in the rain and be food for the tigers for all I care."

Ursula turned on her heel and headed for her bungalow. Suizhakhup picked up his *jappa* and followed.

The next day, they marched seventeen miles along the steep track to Lambui. A mile from the village, Luikai jogged up to Ursula and Abung, fell into step with them and announced, "I am leaving. I'm going home to cultivate my fields."

Ursula was livid. "Why have you chosen to tell me this here? You could have told me in Imphal. It's so damned inconvenient for you to decide to quit now! Where the hell will I find a replacement?"

Luikai looked down, dumb in the face of Ursula's wrath. He didn't need Abung's translation to understand her annoyance.

She turned away seething with anger and stomped along the track. Luikai trotted meekly after her. Ursula was still fuming at dusk when they reached Lambui. She didn't trust herself not to give him another tongue-lashing and stayed on the veranda while he made the beds and prepared the rest-house as a peace offering. She watched as he worked. His frightened face and his constant anxious patting of the sheets eventually seemed comic: he reminded her of Charlie Chaplin being overly contrite. Ursula grinned, shook her head and went in to look. Abung followed her. Ursula told him, "Luikai seems scared."

In a fatherly way, Abung jollied Luikai, who clutched a sheet to his chest and in a terrified voice promised not to go until the miss-sahib gave him leave.

In the morning, Abung brought her tea.

"Abung, I've been thinking. Did the compounder try to make Luikai leave?"

"I do not know, miss-sahib, but I do not like the man. He reeks of dissatisfaction."

Ursula silently agreed.

They marched on to Ukhrul, and after arranging her route with Jeff Duncan, set off for Luikai's village Nungbi Khunao. On the outskirts of Ukhrul, they met a party from Luikai's village, who gaped and gaped at Luikai. The last time they had seen him, he was shabby and penniless, the object of a village lawsuit, and now, here he was, wearing a Tuinem cloth, carrying the miss-sahib's lunch, looking cleaner and fitter than they had ever seen him before. Having been instrumental in Luikai's metamorphosis, Ursula delighted in seeing him affluent enough to offer his cigarettes to the headman and the group.

Abung translated the conversation for Ursula.

"You look well, Luikai," from the aloof headman, looking as if he were not sure how to react to this new Luikai who had been the village object of scorn and distain.

"Yes, I've been to Imphal, and I've got two new cloths. I'm a house servant. I get cigarettes every day, and I'm learning Hindustani from the cook. How's Auntie?"

"Your aunt is very well."

"That is good. I'll see you at Nungbi tonight. So long."

Ursula noticed the headman's frosty demeanour

"Why was the headman so cold towards you," Ursula asked Luikai.

Abung translated that Luikai had been the village scapegoat and commanded no respect, and, until he worked for Ursula, he had been poor. "He still owes money to the moneylender, but now Luikai is faring well, and the headman is jealous of his prosperity."

The two groups moved on. Further along the path, Ursula's group met another party from Nungbi Khulen. At first they only stared at Ursula. Then she heard a gasp and what she assumed was the Tangkhul equivalent of "My God, it's Luikai!"

Luikai was so taken by surprise Abung had to pull him out of her way. Near the village, they met one of his cousins in a group of girls going to the fields. Looking at him with admiration, Ursula heard her as she whispered, "It's Luikai."

Luikai's chest swelled. His walk took on a confident swagger.

Wanting to ease Luikai's money worries and help him be more accepted by the village, Ursula decided to give him an advance on his wages. That evening, she went with Luikai to the moneylender, who had lost the debt document.

Of course, he has, thought Ursula. They drew up another one in both Manipuri and English then signed it, witnessed it and dated it until Ursula was satisfied they had an airtight contract agreeing that Luikai had paid off his debt. She handed fifteen rupees, three weeks wages, to Luikai. Tears of gratitude slipped down his face. The moneylender rang the money professionally.

"This is a bad rupee," he said.

Ursula took the rupee from his fingers. "Here, I'll change it." She handed him another. "I take it the matter is now concluded?"

Abung translated. All agreed. Luikai was now free from debt.

*   *   *

At Nungbi, the cold winds were still blowing, and the huts were just as cold and draughty as Ursula remembered them. They stayed for two days then, on the day they were due to leave, the weather changed. The wind dropped, and Ursula awakened to warm sunlight shining through chinks in the matting walls, dappling the earth floor. She lay in bed looking at the patterns until Abung brought her tea, poured water into the washbasin and left to prepare breakfast.

Ursula slipped out of her pyjamas and washed, pleased not to be shivering with cold. She was reaching for her underwear when the door crashed open and a man entered. He stood unrecognised in a shaft of blinding light. Ursula shrieked, dropped onto her camp bed and covered herself as best she could with the towel. She then saw the intruder was Suizhakhup.

"I'm not dressed yet. Go away!"

He ignored her and sauntered to the medicine *jappa* standing in the far corner. He placed his cigarette in his mouth, while he removed the lid. Crouching down, cigarette dangling from his lips, he studiously unpacked the medicines. Ursula sat dumbfounded. The door flew open. A surge of pushing, jostling patients spilled into the room.

Ursula could not believe that Suizhakhup had not heard her. "What is it? Is it urgent? I want to dress. Come back later."

The Tangkhuls froze, shocked to see the miss-sahib sitting on the bed with only a small towel for cover. Ill at ease and not sure what to do, they looked down at the floor and shuffled their feet until one patient moved outside, and the rest followed in silence.

The compounder squatted over the medicines, his back towards Ursula. She sensed his malicious pleasure as he selected bottles, held them up, and studied them one at a time before putting them down.

"I want medicine," he said, defiantly tossing the words over his shoulder.

Then Ursula understood. He had deliberately set out to humiliate her and had brought the Tangkhuls into her room to humiliate her that much more.

Trembling with rage, she rushed across the room. "Get out! Leave right now! Go on! Get out! Get out!"

He rose to his feet with feline grace and strolled from the room. His attitude was sheer malevolence.

Ursula slammed the door. She leaned against it shaking. Tears glistened in her eyelashes. She hurried to dress; her trembling fingers fumbled as she struggled into her clothes. Outside, silence in the camp. Ursula's chest heaved, struggling to catch ragged, shallow breaths. She needed to breathe. She sat on the bed and breathed deeply until she composed herself then stepped outside into the sunlight.

In the space in front of the bungalow, she saw a pile of baggage, packed, ready for leaving. Beside it squatted the compounder. The moment Ursula's shadow reached him he began to complain.

"You were very rude to me. I was only looking for medicine. I cannot work when I receive such rudeness. I have no choice but to return to Imphal."

With that, he turned his face away but not quick enough to hide a triumphant smirk.

Ursula took stock of the treacherous man in front of her. What kind of man contrives such a devious scheme? Here he is, she thought, ready to desert them, having orchestrated the perfect excuse to gain his freedom, having ruined her trip to the north, having put an end to her photographs and the medical help she promised the villagers there. He knows it would be impossible to find another compounder, and he planned his defection with as much mortification for her as he could muster. He thinks he's gained the upper hand. Well, Suizhakhup, you can think again. Come hell or high water, you're making the trip, and the hillmen are going to get their medicine.

"Suizhakhup," Ursula said in honeyed tones, "I'm so sorry I was rude to you in my room. You must have been hurt and upset by my outburst. It was uncalled for. Please accept my profuse apologies."

Suizhakhup's mouth fell open, his cigarette stuck to his lower lip or it would have fallen. He had not expected Ursula's eloquent apology. He was in the trap. Ursula could almost hear the clang of the cage door slam shut. She managed to keep an earnest expression of regret on her face and not gloat at his quandary. Exultation could come later. He tried to re-establish his advantage, but it was a lost cause. Ursula continued her conciliatory words with sweet skill then waited, thinking if he leaves me after this, it will be out and out desertion, and he'll lose his hospital job.

The compounder rose to his feet. He had been outplayed and knew it. "I will stay," he said, almost choking on the words.

The servants and porters, watching from the sidelines, heaved a sigh of relief and moved away to finish packing. Half an hour later, they were on the road to Chingngai. Ursula felt drained, but the sulky compounder with his glowering looks was still with her.

So was another new man, a tall, lean Tangkhul called Chinaorang. Now that Luikai was squeaky clean and trained as a house-servant, Ursula needed Chinaorang to carry the medicine *jappa*. He turned out to be an exceptional porter. On leaving the last village behind, he strode away at a fantastic pace despite his sixty-pound load, reaching camp well ahead of everyone. Like Luikai, Chinaorang was working to earn money owed because of the love of a woman. He was a poor man who had fallen in love with the daughter of a wealthy family. Her parents would not allow them to marry and quickly married her off to a rich youth from another village. Unhappy in the marriage, the young lady sent word to Chinaorang who went to her rescue, stealing her away from her husband. It ended in court with Chinaorang convicted of wife stealing and being fined one hundred rupees, a small fortune to a man of Chinaorang's means.

The party headed north. Only one ridge away, to the east, was the Burma border. The people here had barely been touched by the outside world, and when Ursula tried to take photographs, they took flight like skittish colts. Ursula wanted most to take pictures of a Tangkhul girl from the Somra Tract, who wore such large, heavy crystal discs in her ears they had to be held by a string across the head or they would have torn the lobes, but the girl refused to pose.

The day they were to move on, Abung brought disquieting news along with Ursula's morning cup of tea. "Miss-sahib, Luikai and the porters have word that the Tangkhuls of Somra village, just across the border, have killed two Manipuri traders and taken their heads."

"Are they sure of this?"

"It is just a rumour, miss-sahib, but it would be wise to be careful."

"It certainly would. Thank you for the information, Abung."

Ursula pondered what to do. Should she continue on her route or move away from the Somra Tract? Her understanding was that the Nagas took heads only in battle, but here were some peaceful traders who had supposedly lost theirs. If the rumour were true, would they attack a white woman and her staff? She thought it unlikely and decided to continue as planned to the Kuki village of Paotong.

Stopping for lunch beside a bridge, Luikai struggled to open the container of rice-beer he had unwisely corked. The cork shot out, hit the bridge roof, and ricocheted off on to the path. The strain of headhunting reports had perhaps made her giddy, but Ursula laughed until her sides ached at his shocked face. To keep the miss-sahib laughing, Luikai gave an impromptu comic performance, his imitation of a singing European.

Gasping for breath between shrieks of glee, Ursula said, "Sounds like a dyspeptic steam whistle. Who is it, Luikai? Me? Mr. Duncan?"

Luikai diplomatically refused to say, only wagged his head no, no, no behind a raised finger.

They set off to tackle the steep climb to Paotong. Ursula teased Luikai, who was panting, while she wasn't. "But miss-sahib," he protested, "when you take one step, I have to take three."

Ursula laughed. It was true. The Nagas were small people, while her long legs strode the miles away. Even carrying her own *jappa* did not slow her down.

"Miss-sahib, why do you come to give medicines?" asked Luikai, as they marched along.

"Because there's no one else to come, and many Nagas are ill with no one to help."

He responded with an outburst of Tangkhul. Ursula smiled. Being far from proficient in the language, she was unsure whether Luikai thought her crazy, a saint, or both.

Among the patients at the Paotong dispensary was an old woman who came for liniment. She took a shine to Ursula and tried to give her a chaw of tobacco and a string of noxious dried fish.

Ursula's stomach churned from the stench.

"Abung, tell her she's too kind, and it's not really necessary to offer me a gift."

Grinning toothlessly, the woman persisted. Abung was wise enough to the ways of the sahibs to see Ursula's revulsion at the gifts and her anxiety that she might give offence by refusing. His eyes twinkled in mirth.

"She insists, miss-sahib. You are going to have to take them."

"I know full well what you're up to, Abung," Ursula said.

Trying to look delighted, she took the proffered offerings and quickly handed them to Luikai, who bore them majestically away. Her predicament even brought a smile to the compounder's lips. As the old woman walked away, Ursula sent Abung an accusing look. His shoulders started shaking, and before long, he dissolved into hearty laughter.

"You looked so funny, miss-sahib."

Ursula laughed too. "I'm sure I did."

Five days after leaving Ukhrul, they arrived at Kharasom, the most northerly Tangkhul village. The porters were to go back from here. By the light of the hurricane lamp, Ursula, half-dead with fatigue, toiled over letters to go with the porters. It was late when she heard a tap at the door. In came Abung bearing a gift.

"Abung, what's this?"

"I thought the miss-sahib looked depressed. I made some bread to cheer you up."

She was touched by his thoughtfulness, gave him a warm smile and took the misshapen loaf. She broke off a small piece and ate it. It looked like sponge cake but tasted faintly bitter and tough. Nevertheless, she told him, "Thank you, Abung. This is delicious."

Delighted with the compliment, he slipped out the door.

Of such gestures, small and large, are friendships forged. Of such friendships are families made, even without a blood relation. Ursula felt, for the first time, an important part of a large, difficult, but loving family—the Naga.

Ursula planned to rest for several days at Kharasom. During the morning, the camp bustled with activity with much soaking and scrubbing of clothes and lines of washing billowing in the breeze. Spicy smells of bubbling curry came from the pot on the fire. Ursula paid the porters, who had gathered for their pay, and they finally left for the village. She had barely sat down to sew a tear in her blouse, when a giggling apparition ran past. Going to investigate, she found Luikai in Abung's jacket, trousers and scarf, the attire of a house-servant.

"You look like heaven knows what," she said.

Luikai paraded in front of her thrilled with his outfit, even though the sleeves and trousers were inches above his wrists and ankles.

Just then, Chingjaroi headmen strode into camp, bringing a hen. They were directed to the compounder. Ursula could see there was a problem from their serious faces.

Suizhakhup came to her. "A woman in their village is very sick after giving birth. They need us to go at once."

"We'd better pack and get a move on." She called Chinaorang. "We'll need porters. Run to the village and find some."

She next enlisted Abung and Luikai, who hurriedly served food then ran about packing damp washing and clearing everything away. After an hour of productive chaos, the group filed out of camp. Half running, half walking in the stifling heat, they reached the camp at Chingjaroi as dusk was falling, only to be told the woman lived in the Christian village two miles further on. Ursula left her party to settle in, and with Suizhakhup and Chinaorang carrying the medicine *jappa*, she hurried down the trail after the headmen. Ursula's hair stuck to her damp forehead, and her blouse was darkened by sweat when, at last, they arrived at the village.

They were led to a tall house silhouetted against the dimming twilight sky. The headman spoke at the closed door. It creaked open. Ursula was hit by a gust of fetid warm air. Taking the *jappa* from Chinaorang, she and the compounder followed the headman inside. A woman led them to the middle of the oblong room where a fire burned. Beside it sat a man, cradling a whimpering baby wrapped in rags. The woman shut the door then went to the hearth to stir a pot of rice.

Ursula struggled to breathe in the sweltering house. The room reeked of food, smoke, stale clothes and sweaty bodies, but beyond these smells was another—the sickly stench of infection. She looked round the murky soot-stained interior littered with clothes, hoes, baskets and the assorted jumble of a Naga household.

"Where's the patient?" she asked Suizhakhup.

He asked the man with the baby who pointed to the far wall. The sick woman was lying on a bed of rags in deep shadows. Ursula winced at the sight. The woman's face, her body, even her fingers were grotesque, so swollen and purple that she seemed at first to be a kind of monster, barely recognizable as human. The headman spoke to her. At his words, she slid off the bed and dragged herself to the fire for Ursula and the compounder to see her better.

The light cast by the flames revealed her predicament. The woman's vagina was a mass of festering pus-filled wounds.

"She had a difficult labour," Suizhakhup said, after conferring with the headman. "The village midwives had to deliver the child by hand."

Ursula looked down at the swollen, poison-filled body, the ugly results of their handiwork. Her blood ran cold at the thought of the midwives' gnarled, filthy hands and twisted nails caked with years of dirt, poking in the birth canal to pry the baby free.

Ursula and the compounder set to work. For an hour, they knelt beside the fire, working in the light cast by the flames.

Engrossed in watching the treatment, members of the household forgot to tend the fire. When the flames died down, Ursula grabbed the electric torch. She and Suizhakhup took turns holding it, while the other swabbed, cleaned and disinfected the injuries with antiseptic.

The heat, the work, the fumes of throat-catching disinfectant mingling with the fetid odours of the house and the ripe stench of infection, hit Ursula like a punch to the solar plexus. Bile flooded her mouth. Her gorge rose. She broke out in a clammy sweat. Feeling she was about to pass out, Ursula bolted for the door. The cold night air was tonic. On the porch, she filled her lungs until she felt stronger.

Funny, she thought, how she had never put the star formations to memory, but they were there above her, burning against the clear night sky just as they might be in England. The pinpoints of light spelled out a kind of code: eternity, shelter, charity. Below the house were pine-covered ridges. The headmen and Chinaorang were squatting by the wall.

"Will she be all right?" asked one of the headmen. "She is my cousin."

Chinaorang interpreted.

"Yes, she'll be all right," Ursula said, sure she was lying. Straightening her shoulders, she went back inside to the young woman she thought would soon die.

The compounder was waiting for her. Whatever else she thought of him, Ursula would be the first to admit that he was a worthy man in a crisis, and nothing seemed to put him off. She had been told the best compounders shrink from no illness, disease or wound.

Two pairs of hands were needed to apply the dressing. He took the syringe, lying sterilized in its little pan, and gave the sick woman an injection of quinine.

Nothing for it now but to wait.

Ursula helped the exhausted patient to her bed. Her thick, black hair, wet with sweat and coarse as a horse's tail, brushed against Ursula's supporting arms. As the patient lay down, she turned her head, murmuring words of thanks.

The compounder packed the *jappa*. He and Ursula moved to the door. Then Ursula turned back. The husband, still holding the baby, watched them, his face pinched with misery. Ursula wanted to say something, reassure him. She sought for the right words. Unable to find them, she resorted to the brisk language of the medical profession.

"That's all for now. We'll come in the morning. Just a day or two, and she'll be better."

The cool sweet smelling air of the street was a welcome relief from the malodorous air inside.

The compounder marched off into the darkness of the Christian village to spend the night with his friend, the pastor.

Chinaorang sat back against the *jappa*, pulled the strap over his head and then had his friend haul him to his feet. Chinaorang jounced and shifted the *jappa* to adjust his load. From a nearby house, a headman brought ten pine-torches, giving off the stinging scent of burning resin with their smoky blaze. After handing them out to the men standing around, the party set off in single file along the steep path to the camp, with the headman leading the way. The flickering torches created a tunnel of light, casting distorted shadows in the coal-black night as the group walked between the thick tree trunks of the pine forest. Meteoric sparkles fell to earth briefly igniting the pine needles, until tramping feet coming from the rear stamped them out.

Ursula tramped along amid the fluttering torches. She felt safe in this small band, the bright flames making a protective cocoon against the terrors of darkness. With a shock, she recognized how primeval an experience she was having and that primitive man must have felt like this after discovering the power of fire.

An hour's walking brought them to Ursula's camp and for Ursula, a return to the commonplace. A worried Abung greeted her, wringing his hands until assured all was well. She had only been in camp an hour when a messenger arrived with a note from the compounder requesting medicines for infant diarrhoea.

Suizhakhup didn't return until noon next day. His eyes were drooping, his features haggard, and he was exceptionally sulky and prickly.

"How's the patient doing?" asked Ursula.

"The woman is improving. I gave her another injection. I think she might pull through. I did not sleep because people pulled me from my bed all night long to attend to babies." He yawned. "The Christian village is full of infant diarrhoea. One of them died, and now I'm going to sleep."

With that, the compounder went off to well-earned and deserved sleep, leaving Ursula to hold the dispensaries alone.

That evening, Ursula talked with Suizhakhup. "If you're sure the woman is out of danger, we can go on with the tour as planned."

"We have treated many people here. We are almost out of drugs, miss-sahib. It would be best if I went back to Imphal for more."

Ursula mulled over Suizhakhup's suggestion. It was the most sensible course of action with more than half the tour in front of them, but even after his recent commendable performance, she didn't trust this schemer to return.

Against her better judgement, she agreed. "You're right. We will need more drugs," and, doubting that she would see him again, she said, "You can set off in the morning." She made a list of items she needed—cinchona, bandages, Septanilam tablets, sulphur ointment, zinc, diarrhoea mixture and phenacetin. Next morning, the compounder left camp heading south, while Ursula returned to Kharasom.

Abung stared, startled. "Tomorrow we're leaving for Jessami," Ursula had told him when he came to collect her teacup. He turned to leave then turned back again.

"Do you think that is wise, miss-sahib?"

"Wise? Of course it's wise. Why do you say that?"

"Better we go to another village, miss-sahib."

"What's wrong with going to Jessami?"

"I . . . They . . . Nothing, miss-sahib, nothing."

With a frown creasing his brow, he hurried away. Ten minutes later, Ursula stepped outside to go into the village to hold a dispensary. Luikai approached.

"Miss-sahib, not good to go to Jessami."

"What is wrong with going to Jessami, Luikai?"

"It is not a good place, miss-sahib."

"Well, unless someone can give me a good reason not to go, we're going there tomorrow."

Luikai's expression became serious, and he turned away. Puzzled, Ursula looked at his stooped back then shrugged and set off for the village. Chinaorang followed with the medicine *jappa*. He, too, tried to persuade her not to go; he could not or would not explain why. Ursula set her jaw and entered Kharasom. Running after them, Luikai followed through the village gate.

A woman suffering with a large, smelly, jungle sore arrived at the dispensary. It was so bad Chinaorang put his cloth to his face. Luikai turned green. Ursula took out the vapex smelling salts, took a big sniff as a precaution against fainting, and rolled her shoulders back ready to start work.

"Miss-sahib, I do for you," Luikai gallantly offered.

Ursula shook her head, passed the vapex to Luikai and then took hold of the knife.

Luikai fled.

"I will do it myself," the woman offered, holding out her hand for the knife.

Understanding her gesture, Ursula patted the woman's arm. "No, it's all right. I will do it."

The woman clutched Ursula's sleeve, and Ursula clasped the patient tightly with a free hand. A friend repeatedly patted the woman's back, offering comfort during the operation to cut away the dead flesh. Despite the pain, the stoic patient uttered not one sound and afterwards, hobbled away well pleased with her treatment.

During the dispensary, Abung arrived from camp with Ursula's collection of photographs.

"Show them to the village," she said, "while I finish up here."

Abung showed them in batches first to the young men, and soon to the entire village, which ended up congregating on the veranda of the *morung*, the men's house. Some were of Abung, two were of the village elders and some were of Luikai and Chinaorang, taken after they had borrowed Ursula's scissors for a haircut.

Ursula was particularly pleased with those snaps, feeling she had captured the very essence of the hillmen. The two Tangkhul men were glorious, with long tails of hair flowing from their Mohican-style manes. Chinaorang looked regal in her white cloth from Tuinem. That afternoon, villagers came in droves to her camp, dressed in their best, eager to have their photographs taken too.

Ursula sought out the village headman to discuss using villagers as porters for the journey to Jessami. She did not need Chinaorang to interpret the headman's obvious uneasiness and the apprehension in his voice. And still no one would explain the lack of enthusiasm for going to Jessami.

"If no one will give me grounds for not going to Jessami, then we are going first thing in the morning," pronounced Ursula to her staff and the headman.

Not wanting to offend the miss-sahib, the headman organized porters, who duly arrived at Ursula's compound early the next day. Her staff and the porters moved at her bidding and according to her orders, but more slowly than usual, she noticed. What was wrong?

The dusty road to Jessami meandered through sparse jungle, scrub and thickets. At a Kuki village, Ursula spent over an hour treating the myriad of minor ailments common to the hillmen before moving on along the wooded ridge. They left the trees behind during the afternoon when the path made a sudden drop down through fields until it widened into a broad, well-worn path that led to the gates of Jessami village.

Arriving late in the afternoon, they were met by the headman, alerted to her visit by the earlier arrival of her porters. He led the way to their camp. Ursula was pleased to discover it was in good shape, and the villagers had provided eggs, vegetables, chickens, and rice-beer for Ursula's party. Despite the courteous welcome, her entourage was still behaving strangely. The Tangkhul porters recoiled in horror from the rice-beer as if it were poisoned. They stared petrified at the headman as if he were Rakshasa, the demonic troublemaker who delights in feasting on human flesh as the grand finale to his evil deeds. They cowered together in camp, peering wild-eyed over their shoulders each time a villager passed by, and instead of going into the village that evening to relax and drink rice-beer round a fire with the villagers, they chose to stay in camp near Ursula. But for the pang of concern for the mental health of the porters and her servants, Ursula found it all so comical it almost made her grin.

After the next morning's busy dispensary, Ursula relaxed in her hut reading Evelyn Waugh's *A Handful of Dust*. Her head jerked up as the door flew open. Abung, Luikai, Chinaorang and all the porters spilled inside. Babbling, agitated, wide-eyed men packed into the tiny room; men so spooked and traumatized they were gibbering incoherently; men who kept turning their heads to look behind them as if expecting the devil himself to appear.

"Boy! Boys! Whatever is the matter?" Ursula demanded.

The men started yelling and pointing behind them.

"Shush, now! Be quiet!" Ursula raised and lowered her arm to signal silence. The outcry subsided. "Abung, what is it?"

"*Jadu!*"

"*Jadu?* What's that?"

Abung stuttered in terror, "Buh-by the gate. Suh-something has been puh-put by the gate. To harm us."

"Black magic?" Ursula said, astonished.

She pushed past the men and strode to the village gate. The men surged onto the veranda to watch, but ventured no further. Abung, as Ursula's lieutenant, reluctantly shuffled after her, but even he stopped ten feet from the gate. He pointed to a small bamboo basket at the foot of the tall hedge, which surrounded the camp. Ursula turned back to Abung. "This is the problem?"

He nodded, his expression wary.

"It looks harmless enough, Abung."

Ursula walked over to take a closer look. Inside lay a white egg, and on top of that, tied to it with string, was a piece of lint smeared with ointment. The ointment had to have come from that morning's dispensary. She straightened up and looked back for Abung. She found herself alone, Abung having retreated to the safety of her veranda. On the other side of the gate, at a safe distance, a group of Jessami men gathered, silently watching Ursula.

She walked back to Abung. "Could this be some sort of sickness ceremony?"

He shook his head and stubbornly set his chin. "*Jadu!* It is *Jadu!*"

Ursula wondered how she could deal with it without her staff and porters getting the wind up. She returned to the gate. Acting with a confidence she did not feel, she picked up the basket by its handles, and holding it out in front of her, carried it back to the hut. The men shrank back, parting like the Red Sea before the hexed object.

Ursula stood there not knowing what to do next. Then, from the corner of her eye, she spotted the headman at the cookhouse searching for her staff. He seemed bewildered, wondering why no one was about.

Ursula called him over. He padded across the yard amazed to find all the men squeezed onto Ursula's veranda.

Ursula showed him the basket. "What's this?"

The headman's jaw sagged and trembled; his skin paled. He stepped backwards raising his palms as if to fend off the basket. Shock left him speechless.

"*Jadu*," Abung pronounced, settling the matter.

The porters crowded round the headman, shouting and yelling. The more daring of the Jessami men came over to poke their noses over the porters' shoulders or stick their heads through any gap they could find. They whispered and stared at the contents of the basket. Ursula was still holding it out to the horrified headman, who could not tear his eyes away from the hideous object. Losing patience, she forced the basket into the headman's hand, removing the scrap of lint as she did so. Whatever imagined power that scrap of lint possessed, she meant to burn it later with much pomp and ceremony. Surely, that would neutralize any black magic threat it held and cheer up her crew.

The stunned headman held the basket. The crowd fell silent. As if jolted by an electric shock, the headman thrust the basket into the hands of a small boy standing next to him, who carefully carried it off to the village at arms' length. Ursula, her tone sad rather than angry, expressed through Abung her dismay that the village had acted so despicably against her. Head held high and shoulders back, she retired to her hut with as much dignity as she could muster.

Once inside, she peered through the largest crack she could find in the wall to see what would happen next. A minute later, she saw the headman turn away looking downcast followed by the jabbering men. Tears of shame flowed down the headman's cheeks before he reached the cookhouse. They had tried so hard to make Ursula's group welcome, to make her visit pleasant, and it had all been ruined by some secret witch.

To express her displeasure, Ursula spent the day sequestered in her hut. She picked up her book, putting it down ten minutes later unable to concentrate. She paced the room then started pulling clothes from her *jappa*. They were fraying; blouses paper-thin; shorts positively ragged; sandals worn out. She picked a shirt in reasonable condition and put it to one side. She would keep that for her return to Imphal. As things stood, she'd soon have to wear her pyjama jacket as a shirt in order to stay decent.

Occasionally, Ursula peeped through the cracks in the walls to check on the Tangkhul porters. They huddled in a corner of the compound holding a palaver, glancing round wide-eyed with fear as if expecting to be dragged off by some demon at any minute.

She realized that Jessami was considered a nest of wizards and that was the reason her staff had not wanted to come, and now the porters were so jittery she expected them to do a moonlight flit that night.

Abung was jumpy the whole day, but along with Ursula's lunch, he brought information. "The headmen have called a meeting in the village, miss-sahib."

Later in the day, he told Ursula, "They have not found the man who did the *jadu*. They are going to have a public cursing tonight."

That night headmen called the villagers together. Young men of the village had laid a banana tree trunk in the centre of the meeting place then searched homes to ensure everyone attended. The headman moved through the crowd, taking a census, of sorts, and announced that no one was missing. Then it began. In a strong voice, he called upon the people to cut and curse and slay the tree trunk.

"This tree-trunk is acting as proxy for the culprit who brought shame on our village. Everyone must curse the evildoer, and because everyone is involved, he will curse himself and so will die."

The screaming crowd surged forward, calling down evil upon the guilty one. In a frenzy of destruction, the Nagas hacked and slashed, sweating in the torchlight, which played like liquid over the muscles of their gleaming bodies. Razor-sharp machete blades flashed orange, black and yellow, reflecting torch flames. With grunts and yells, the villagers swung their large knives to cleave and chop the tree trunk. Wood splinters and shards flew everywhere. The odour of freshly chopped wood mingled with

70

the pungent smell of sweat, and the pulverized tree trunk disintegrated into fragments and sawdust.

It was over.

Next morning, Abung, almost his old self again, brought Ursula's tea and washing water.

"Are the porters still with us?" Ursula asked.

"Yes, miss-sahib. Everyone is here."

"That's a relief. Thank you, Abung."

Thirty minutes later, Abung returned accompanied by the headmen holding out an olive branch: gifts of fowl, eggs, beer, rice, and pumpkins. Through Abung, they made it clear that the *jadu* was the work of one person; it was not an insult from the people of Jessami.

Seeing that the headmen with their solemn, shamed expressions were filled with anguish over the witchcraft and truly wished to make amends, Ursula graciously accepted the gifts.

"I am reassured by your actions, and I'll be happy to remain at Jessami for a few more days."

The matter was never mentioned again.

"I'd better get on with a dispensary, hadn't I?" Ursula said to Abung. "Tell Chinaorang to fetch the *jappa*."

When they walked into the village, the Tangkhul porters tagged along, sticking like barnacles to Ursula, feeling safer keeping her in sight. It took a day or two before the porters were confident enough to wander into Jessami without her to enjoy some rice-beer.

Ursula and her men spent the next five evenings in the village, watching the young men display their prowess. The villagers and her staff competed in spear-throwing competitions, stone-putting and long jumping. She provided cash and cigarettes for prizes. Youths and girls dressed in their finery. Horn and brass rings adorned arms and legs; beaded necklaces bounced on their chests, and feathered headdresses bobbed and swayed as they danced for Ursula to the accompaniment of drummers, singers and cymbals. Large bamboo torches lit the site. Chickens, roast pig, rice and vegetables provided the feast, and rice-beer flowed.

Suizhakhup returned after a surprisingly swift journey, finding Ursula still at Jessami.

He came back! Now that was a turn up for the books, she thought. At first, Ursula considered she had judged him wrong, but then amended her opinion. In all likelihood, the Civil Surgeon at Imphal had driven the compounder back with threats.

To give the villagers the benefit of the new supplies, they stayed for two more days before setting out on the return trip to Kharasom. The long strenuous march along ridges, up steep and wooded slopes in the heat brought them to the village. Arriving tired and hungry, they found the village gate shut.

"Open the gate, the miss-sahib is here," called Abung.

The request was ignored, as were further pleas to open the gate.

Eventually, Abung demanded they bring the headman to the gate. It took twenty minutes for the summoned headman to arrive.

"Miss-sahib," Abung translated, "smallpox has broken out at Lai-yi, and every village for miles has closed its gates. Lai-yi has been sending messengers for days to see if we were back, but Kharasom drove them away and would not let them stay. They left a letter begging us to come and save them." Abung handed Ursula the letter the headman had given him.

Frowning in consternation, she took the scribbled note then beckoned to Suizhakhup. They walked through the half-unpacked camp to her hut.

"I'm vaccinated for smallpox. Are you?" she asked.

"Yes, miss-sahib."

"What about the others? Better see who's safe."

The compounder made the rounds of the camp and reported back to Ursula.

"Only you and I are safe to go into the danger zone, no one else, miss-sahib."

"Even if we went to Lai-yi alone, we have no lymph or lancets. The best thing we can do for Lai-yi is send for help."

"The quickest way to Imphal is through the infected area, miss-sahib," Suizhakhup informed her.

"Well, we can't send a runner that way. He'll have to go round through Ukhrul. How far do you think it is to Imphal? Ursula took out her map. "Eighty miles?"

"Yes, miss-sahib."

"Ask Abung to bring Chinaorang, while I write a note to go with him."

Within an hour, Chinaorang was racing down the path. He was relieved at Ukhrul, where the Duncans found a fresh runner to take the letter on to Imphal. By the evening of the second day, the letter was in the Civil Surgeon's hands.

Colonel Radnor wasted no time. Before the sun rose the following morning, a medical team was on its way to Lai-yi, arriving at the stricken village only four days after Ursula had written the letter, but not soon enough to prevent the deaths of thirty people.

Ursula spoke with Abung and the compounder. "The whole area could shut down if it looks like the epidemic is spreading. I've decided to move south. I'm concerned that if we wait too long, we won't be able to find porters."

"That is good, miss-sahib. The villages west of Paowi will need medical treatment, and we will be within easy reach if they need our help at Lai-yi," Suizhakhup said.

"Tomorrow we go to Chingjaroi, miss-sahib?" Abung asked.

"Yes, we do."

*　　*　　*

The next afternoon, the pockmarked headman met Ursula's party as it approached Chingjaroi village. She pleased him with a gift of a packet of Players cigarettes.

"You must take care," he told her. "There is a black panther on the prowl. It has killed three of our cattle since you were last here. We sit up at night to try and kill it, but it has been too cunning for us."

"Then we will take care. How is the woman we treated?" she asked.

The headman beamed. "The woman is better."

Ursula and Suizhakhup exchanged smiles.

"We'll call to see her in the morning, Suizhakhup."

Ursula decided to cool off with a swim in one of the deep pools in the river and then do some watercolour painting. Luikai and Chinaorang went with her. While Chinaorang fished in the shallows using only his fingers, she bathed and dived from the rocks. Luikai surprised her by coming into the water and swimming a dog paddle. Most Nagas did not swim.

Ursula sat on a rock and allowed the sun to dry her while she thought of what life held for her in England, her family's expectation that she would eventually conform, do the business, find a man to cherish, marry and have his children. She felt as alienated from those goings on as a schoolboy. It was not for her. It could never be. She was thrilled to be busy with this adventure and these natural people.

Having washed his loincloth with soap, Luikai sat around in his cloth like a petticoat. Men strolling home from the fields stopped for a dip in the river. One stark-naked man moved too close to where Ursula was dressing. Luikai, on guard, squatting on the rocks above her pool, yelled to warn him away from the area.

Dressed and refreshed, Ursula brought out her case of Windsor-Newton watercolours: a varnished wooden box with small lozenge-shaped tablets of colours inside, along with a slot for two sable-tip brushes and a small plastic cup for water. Curious Nagas gathered round.

"Go on, dip in," she said.

The Nagas hesitated. Laughing, Ursula dabbed yellow ochre on Luikai's nose. With much hilarity, a rush of fingers dipped into the colours. They decorated their bodies, dabs of vermilion, streaks of cobalt blue. Some borrowed Ursula's brush to daub paint on the paper. A lively free-for-all developed, each man trying to out do the others by spreading the most colours on himself. The Nagas' spontaneity delighted Ursula. Europeans would have been too concerned with appearing foolish to play like children.

That evening, she relaxed in the compounder's hut drinking rice-beer and listening to her staff sing, thinking what a blissful day it had been. Outside, smallpox was on the rampage but that seemed a long way away.

*   *   *

After breakfast, they entered the village. Chinaorang, having returned from Ukhrul, carried the medicine *jappa*. They managed to find the house, which in daylight was no longer scary but merely the shabby abode of a poor family. Ursula knocked on the door. A young woman with a glowing complexion opened it. She was holding the baby and looking at the group, bewildered by their appearance on her doorstep.

They asked for the convalescent and attempted to enter the house.

The woman protested, blocking the doorway to prevent entry. Ursula and the compounder insisted. Pandemonium broke out with everyone talking at once and everyone talking a different language. Hearing the ruckus, the headman hurried over and plunged in. Eventually, he made himself heard. "This is the one! This is the one!"

Stunned silence. Ursula and the compounder, startled by the change in the woman in just ten days, gawped at her until she blushed.

"I can't believe it!" Ursula said. "The last time we saw her she was a mass of festering wounds and her body was bloated with poison. Look at her! She's healthy and wholesome as if she's never ailed a day in her life."

The headman translated. The woman suckled her baby and laughed shyly, flustered and self-conscious from their continuing incredulous stares.

As they left the house to hold a dispensary, Suizhakhup said, half in wonder, "I think God was with our medicine the night we came here."

Ursula patted his shoulder. "I think you're right."

Leaving Chingjaroi and travelling westward, the party clambered up Naga paths and then down. The inclement spring weather grew steadily worse. Luikai squelched along in the pouring rain behind Ursula, holding his cloth over his head. By the time they reached Huimi, everyone was dripping.

That night, Chinaorang reported sick with fever and an infected cut on his leg.

"We'd better turn back," Ursula told Suizhakhup. "That's a nasty gash on Chinaorang's leg. We can take a short cut over the hills to reach the Ukhrul-Chingjaroi road and make for the camp at Phungam tomorrow."

In pouring rain next morning, they climbed through the misty forests to the top of the ridge. Chinaorang was limping. The men were gloomy and coughing. Luikai woefully predicted pneumonia for everyone. After the climb, came the descent. Like the others, Ursula shivered and slithered on the downward trail, longing to reach the comfort of camp. Low-lying clouds enveloped the hillside; a gusty wind sprayed their faces with fine rain. Through eyelashes dripping raindrops, a relieved Ursula caught sight of the camp's thatched roofs, but on walking into the compound, her heart sank. The villagers had not been expecting them, and the camp was in a state of disrepair. Abung organized the collecting of firewood, all of it soaking wet, so that the fires smoked incessantly. Rain dripped through leaking roofs onto the earth floors. In Ursula's hut, she and Luikai moved the camp bed from place to place, but not a dry spot could be found. The villagers brought mats, which they spread over the roofs in an attempt to stem the leaks. Less than an hour later, a wild storm blew them off. It was the last straw. Weary and disgusted everyone gave up the struggle against the elements and went to bed.

During the next two days' journey, the weather began to clear. The men's spirits lifted along with the steam rising from the ground after each rainfall. With no road from Huining to Tuinem, the group travelled along paths leading to fields. At first, the going was easy, but as the paths forked and became less distinct, Chinaorang broke a green frond at each fork to guide the stragglers. When the path disappeared completely, they scrambled down the length and breadth of the steep hillside by the banks of water channels and wet rice-terraces until they reached the valley floor.

On arriving at the river, Ursula was disconcerted to find there was no bridge. Travellers had to cross the swirling brown water using a row of stepping-stones three feet apart. She took a deep breath and jumped. Landing on the first stone, she stuck there, wobbling precariously. On the riverbank behind her, she could hear Abung shouting directions. She glanced back. Luikai was shaking his head at her foolhardiness. The jabbering porters were spread out and waving their arms.

Ursula turned her attention back to the river. A group of Tangkhuls, working in the fields on the far side, heard the commotion. One man, seeing her difficulty, dropped his hoe and ran over to help. He raced down the steep bank, charged full-tilt into the river and waded across to Ursula. The brown water surged against his sinewy thighs. The man, muddy from his work and without a stitch of clothing, as was the custom when working in the fields, grasped Ursula's hand. His strong arm steadied her, guiding her from stone to stone to the far bank. Ursula clung to him, too concerned with reaching the bank safely to be embarrassed by his nakedness. Behind her, she could hear Abung's raucous laughter ringing out at the impropriety of her predicament. Safely across, she thanked the Tangkhul then watched the men cross the river. It was her turn to laugh when Abung almost lost his footing half way over. Pity he kept his balance, she thought with a smile. Revenge would have been sweet.

After a short rest, they set off for Tuinem. The higher mid-April temperatures left Ursula tired, hot, and sticky by the time they reached the village in the early evening. She had to hold the dispensary alone, as there was no sign of Suizhakhup, who turned up hours later after completely losing his way.

The finishing touch came on the next and final night of the tour at the Shongphal rest-house. Instead of the quiet evening Ursula wanted to mentally prepare for the return to civilization, the drunken watchman picked a fight with the porters. She was livid at having to go and break it up. She was livid until, walking back to her hut, her sadness about reaching the end of these incredible transformative months engulfed her. She might have cried but her emotions did an about turn, replacing sorrow with relief at giving up the responsibilities of the tours and a longing to see Lexie and Richard again.

It was late afternoon, and the heat of the day was waning. Ursula relaxed with Richard and Lexie on the veranda, watching the changing swathes of colour in the darkening sky. The houseboy slipped an ornate silver tray, holding three glasses of gin and tonic, onto the cane table. Richard took his glass and raised it to Ursula.

"I propose a toast. To Ursula, Queen of the Naga Hills, intrepid explorer and adventurer."

"I hardly feel like a queen," she said.

In her bedroom mirror, Ursula had seen the dark circles under her eyes and the skin stretched tight from exhaustion despite a healthy suntan.

Richard continued. "A woman of outstanding beauty, who has more guts than any man I know. Thanks to you, Ursula, we'll be the talk of Imphal for many weeks to come."

"Thank you, Richard," Ursula said, bowing her head to him with an impish grin, "but if you'd seen me when I returned three hours ago, you might have had a different opinion. It's amazing what a long soak in a bath tub and clean, freshly ironed clothes can do for one."

"Her travelling clothes were reduced to rags," Lexie said. "We threw them away."

Ursula looked apologetic. "I've a confession to make. I rescued my sandals. I decided to take them back to England as a memento of all the miles I've walked."

Lexie laughed. "Of all the souvenirs you could take home, you're taking those dreadful sandals! They're about to disintegrate!"

"I do have some other items I'm taking home. I'll show you after dinner. I have a mouth organ, a trap, and a shuttle used in weaving, all made from bamboo, and I also have a cane-work shield. Oh, and I have lots of photographs."

"It's a long journey from the home country to India for so few souvenirs," Richard said. "Do you think you'll adjust to life in London again after all this adventure?"

"I'm taking home much more than those and you well know it, Richard. I'm the luckiest woman in the world. I've always known that I'd have to return home. I made a point of capturing the hills and the Nagas in my mind and my senses to take home with me in my heart. Whenever I need to, I'll pull those memories out and savour them. Not many people experience in their whole lifetime the joy or the learning I've had since landing in Calcutta. I can't thank you enough for inviting me to stay."

"Look what I'd have missed if you hadn't come," Lexie said. "Without you, I wouldn't have gone on tour with Mr. Jeffery. Anytime you want to come back, you'll be welcomed with open arms."

"Thank you, Lexie, but I doubt I'll be able to come to India again. I've just read one of my letters that arrived while I was away. It seems Mother hoped I'd find a young man while in India. Her very words were, 'It's often said you only buy a one way ticket for a young lady going to India with all the lonely, suitable young men in the Indian Civil Service.' Mother's going to be dreadfully disappointed that after paying my passage I'm not at least engaged. I'm sure they won't do it again. I rather think they'll wash their hands of me, at least as far as marriage goes."

*   *   *

Ten days later, Ursula was in a truck rattling along the road to the railway. As she passed each landmark: Maram village perched on a hill, the pass at Mao, and the neat bungalows of Kohima, the lump in her throat tumbled to her heart where it settled like a heavy weight. The road plunged downwards to Manipur station. The train carried her away to the docks at Calcutta and the ship waiting to convey her to England.

It was a bright, breezy day as the tugs manoeuvred the liner into Tilbury dock. Ursula hung over the rail trying to catch sight of her younger brother Graham, who had been sent to meet her. Seeing him, she waved. The gangplank went down. Ursula disembarked among the throng of passengers and hurried to Graham. He smiled warmly and held her at arms length to look at her.

"You're looking great. Life in India agreed with you."

"Yes, it did. I didn't want to come home. But it is good to see you. I've brought all kinds of interesting titbits to show people."

After a generous tip to the porter for loading Ursula's luggage into the car, they made their way to Tower Bridge to cross the River Thames for the A3 road, heading southwest to their parents' house in Weybridge.

"I wanted to pick you up in my spiffing, new sports car, but Mother insisted I drive her car. She didn't think we'd fit all your luggage in the Alvis. Does eighty-five miles an hour top speed, but it doesn't have much room for luggage." As Graham strained his neck to look at Ursula's left hand, the car swerved towards the opposite lane.

"What are you doing? Watch the road!"

"I was looking for an engagement ring."

Ursula laughed. "I know that was Mother's plan, but my own didn't include looking for a husband. I only wanted to escape my life with Grandmama." She paused to swallow down the lump that appeared in her throat, turning her head to look through the window at the passing houses before continuing. "India was wonderful, the best experience of my whole life. Now that I'm back, I feel as if I've left a part of me behind."

"Go on then, tell me about it."

"I will, later. Bring me up to date with your news. How was Cambridge?"

"Just finished my finals."

"Oh, good. You'll have the summer free. We can spend some time together."

"Well, actually, Ursula, we can't. I was hoping you would have cheering news of a betrothal for Mother and Father to take the sting out of my own news."

"Your news? You haven't got a girl into trouble, have you?"

Graham chuckled, but the smile disappeared to be replaced by a soberness Ursula had rarely seen in her brother. "No, nothing as simple as that. I intend to break the news tonight, tomorrow at the latest. There'll be hell to pay."

"May I ask what this big announcement is about?"

"You'll find out tonight, at dinner, but I think you'll be proud of me."

*   *   *

Grandparents Bower and Grandmama were invited to dinner that evening. Except for Graham, the family, infuriatingly, found Ursula's interest in "the natives" puzzling.

Commander Bower carved the joint of roast beef. "I'd have thought there would have been enough to interest you in Imphal, what with the polo, tennis and shooting, without risking life and limb in the wilds."

"Weren't there any dashing young officers to interest you?" Mrs. Bower asked, helping herself to some cabbage before passing the tureen.

"Not really. There was only a handful of Europeans in Imphal, and they were quite stuffy. I became interested in photographing the Nagas instead."

"Why you involved yourself with those people is beyond me," Grandfather Bower said, "but then, you've always been a queer one. Archaeology, wasn't it?"

"Yes, Grandfather, I was interested in archaeology."

"A profession held in high regard," Graham said, supporting his sister.

"For gentlemen," Commander Bower said. " Still, it may have been more suitable than photographing naked Nagas."

Ursula sent Graham a look across the room urging him to speak. Responding to his sister's silent plea, Graham stood up and tapped his wineglass with his dessert fork.

"I have an announcement to make." He squared his shoulders as if bracing himself for their disapproval. "You know I always wanted to join the Navy, but you ignored that and put pressure on me to find a civilian occupation. Well, it's not going to happen. I took the bit between the teeth and enlisted. I'm sorry there's going to be a big ruckus about it just as Ursula's returning home, but any fool can see we'll soon be at war. How the blazes could I not enlist?"

"Graham, you're an insufferable fool!" his father exploded.

"Graham, bravo!" Ursula said. "I didn't know you had it in you. What service?"

"I joined the Marines yesterday. I'm leaving tomorrow for officer training school."

The commander was furious. "Whatever were you thinking? Did we or did we not decide you should follow a career in the diplomatic corps?"

"After all our sacrifices for your education, how could you ignore our wishes?" Grandmother Bower said.

Ursula spoke up. "But Graham has always wanted to enter one of the services, haven't you, Graham? It was you who ignored his wishes," she said, turning to her parents.

"You've done well in your naval career, Father," Graham said. "I'm sure I'll do well too."

With war imminent, Mrs. Bower feared for her son's safety but was only able to express her concern with anger. "How could we have had such wayward children?"

Ursula felt suffocated on hearing her mother's words. "If you'll excuse me, I'll retire."

Heated voices continued in the drawing room as she crossed the parquet hall and ran up the carved wooden staircase.

Later, when the house became quiet, Ursula tiptoed to Graham's room. She tapped on the door and slipped inside. Graham was sitting on the window seat, smoking his pipe and looking out at the moonlit garden.

"Hello, Sis, thanks for the support."

She joined him on the seat. "Are you all right?"

"Of course, the tirade didn't last anywhere near as long as I thought it would," he said, cheerfully.

"I'm pleased you stood up to them. I came to see if you were harbouring any doubts."

"None. I only wish they'd given you the chance to go to Oxford. You'd have made a great archaeologist."

Ursula touched her brother's wrist. "Listen, Graham. I was extremely upset at the time, especially when I was made to live with Grandmama, but if I'd gone to Oxford, I wouldn't have had my wonderful experiences in India. Until I went there, I always felt I was up against a brick wall. I was never allowed to do what I wanted, and then, in Assam, I had six of the most wonderful months one could ever imagine."

"Your face was glowing as you talked about the hillmen. I've never seen you looking so radiant."

"I can't explain how marvellous it was. I fell in love with the Nagas and the Naga Hills. I've never felt like that before—alive, useful, as if I really belonged. I feel like there's no other place for me in the whole wide world. And I wish you the same in the Marines. Now I'm back, I feel out of place."

In the silence that followed, Graham seemed to be following his own train of thoughts.

Eventually, Ursula said, "One of us must escape living for others' expectations and do what one wants. I just don't know what I'll do with my life now. Mother wants me to join the St. John's Ambulance Brigade. She thinks I'll be needed when the war starts."

"That's not much of a substitute for what you left in India. Do you think they would listen if I tried to persuade them to send you out there again?"

Ursula Laughed light-heartedly. "I doubt it. You've already rocked the boat quite enough. I don't think you'll have any influence in this household for a long time."

Piles of black and white photographs buried the study's large oak desk. Ursula was sorting through them, trying to select her best pictures, when her mother peeped round the door.

"Hello, darling, I was just wondering why the study door was open. What do you have there?" she asked. Mrs. Bower entered the room followed by her friend Mrs. Southcott.

"They're snapshots of my trips in the Naga Hills."

Mrs. Southcott strode across the Persian rug. "Snapshots, you say?" She picked up photograph after photograph. "These are excellent, Ursula. You have a considerable talent for photography. Most professional! Tell me about them." She made herself comfortable in the fireside chair.

Ursula's mother, dazed by Mrs. Southcott's interest, lowered herself into the nearest armchair.

Using various photographs to illustrate her tales, Ursula recounted some of the details of her adventures with the Nagas. Her mother sat as if watching a game of tennis. Listening intently, she looked at Ursula, then Mrs. Southcott whenever she murmured, "How interesting."

As Ursula finished, Mrs. Southcott looked to Mrs. Bower. "We must ask your daughter to give this talk to the women at the WRVS." She turned to Ursula. "Would you like to do that, Ursula?"

"Why, yes, but I've never done any public speaking before," Ursula said, flushed with excitement and pleasure at Mrs. Southcott's interest.

"All you have to do is tell the ladies your stories as you've told them to me. They'll be fascinated. Will July 7th be convenient? We already have a speaker arranged for that afternoon, but I know she wouldn't mind stepping down."

"Well, if you think they'll . . . that is, I'd be happy to do it."

*   *   *

Ursula's interest in her subject, her enthusiasm, her recounting of details so dear to memory, made her lectures engrossing. She held her audiences spellbound, showing her slides and imitating Suizhakhup, Luikai or Abung and telling stories of the krait and machete, the diseases and rains, the heat and terrain and the extraordinary generosity of spirit of the hillmen. Her talks were such a hit, Mrs. Southcott arranged for Ursula to speak before several organizations and academic bodies. She was also introduced to learned anthropologists at the Pitt Rivers Museum at Oxford University, and the Royal Central Asian Society, London. Encouraged by their interest and appreciation, Ursula wrote to Professor Hutton at Cambridge University, who invited her to meet him.

She found him in his dark oak-panelled office, strewn with piles of books and papers around the desk and floor in organized clutter. Professor Hutton cleared a place for Ursula to sit and squinted over his half-spectacles perched on the end of his nose.

She told him first about the black magic at Jessami and how she had dealt with it. He bobbed his head listening, signalling that this was all familiar to him.

"What would you have done in that situation, Professor?"

"Well, of course, it's best to avoid such situations if at all possible. But there are those tribes with a reputation for black magic, using it to scare and blackmail other villagers into doing what they want. One has to use a firm hand. From what you tell me, you did well, Miss Bower."

"Thank you, but how would you have dealt with it?"

"As it happens, I have a useful formula for just such an occasion, which I used when I was Deputy Commissioner at Kohima. If you want to curse an unidentified culprit who has used black magic against you, you must take an egg and stand outside so that the heavens above and the earth below can see what you are doing. Then you tell the assembled villagers that you are going to deal with the perpetrator. You hold up the egg and then recite something impressive. I used Greek. *The Iliad* did the trick. The hill tribes will be awed by your actions and believe you have strong magic. I used this technique to settle tough disputes, and I developed a reputation for being exceedingly efficient with it."

"I don't know enough Greek, but I do know a lot of Victor Hugo by heart. I'm sure if I ever go back, none of the Nagas would understand French."

Professor Hutton removed his glasses and wiped their lenses with his handkerchief. "Miss Bower," he said, "The Nagas are remote and have not been studied much. There's a field of research to be done with them. We have written observations on many parts of their culture, but we would also like to have them recorded on film. There may even be a small amount of funding available for that purpose. Will you give the idea some consideration?"

*   *   *

With the promise of financial help for another tour of the hills, she poured her energy into working on a programme for her winter expedition. Even the monumental expenditure for film, equipment, and fares could not dampen her excitement. She booked her passage.

Her mother feared Ursula was becoming obsessed with the Nagas and worried she was facing a severe disappointment, as the likelihood of war loomed closer. By August, sailings were being cancelled. Ursula's booking changed twice. Then on September 3rd, Britain declared war on Germany. The day before she was due to sail, Ursula, a volunteer with the St. John's Ambulance Brigade, was called to ambulance stations. Ursula had no sooner put down the telephone after taking the call than it rang again. "Graham! Is everything all right?"

"Of course it is. I'm just calling to congratulate my favourite sister on her escape and to wish you bon voyage."

"Oh, Graham!" Ursula's voice was anguished. "I'm not leaving. I've been called to ambulance stations. I have to cancel

my berth and go to Grandmama's. I don't feel I can leave
England now."

"Well that's a hell of a sacrifice you're making to do your
patriotic duty. Can't I persuade you to change your mind?"

"I can't bring myself to leave England under these
circumstances. I wouldn't be able to live with myself. Perhaps
when the war's over . . ."

Ursula moved into her old room in Grandmama's house,
and settled down to wait for Germany to attack, and tried to
resign herself to never see Assam and the Naga Hills again.

* * *

Knitting sweaters. Ursula and the other women ambulance
drivers sat in the garage knitting sweaters. She was burning with
frustration and indignation. She had given up her dreams again,
this time for king and country and her country had her knitting
sweaters. In the past two months since volunteering, there had
been nothing else for them to do.

To Imogen, a fellow volunteer, she said, "Aren't you getting
a bit fed up with this sitting around?"

"Yes, I am. We sit here day in and day out not being very
useful, in an organization that's not very well run. There're
commandeered furniture vans and other emergency ambulances
standing idle in the garage, and *nothing's* happening."

"No wonder they're calling this the Phoney War," another
woman said, nimbly clicking her knitting needles. "I feel like I'm
all dressed up with nowhere to go."

All dressed up with nowhere to go. The phrase struck a
chord in Ursula. She gathered her needles and yarn and stood
up. "Time for me to say goodbye, ladies."

"Where are you off to?"

"I'm leaving the London Ambulance Brigade," Ursula
announced. "I'm going to do something more useful."

That evening, Ursula told her grandmother, "I left the
ambulance service."

89

"Why on earth did you do that? I'm surprised by your cavalier attitude, Ursula." Grandmama paused, "Was there any difficulty when you told them you were leaving?"

"No. I told them I'd come back when they sent for me, handed in my gas mask and tin hat, and off I went. Nobody objected."

"What will you do now for the war effort?"

"I'm not sure, but I need to do more than sit around knitting."

Next morning, Ursula had barely finished her toast when her mother rang.

"Grandmama told us you left the ambulance service. Your father and I have spent most of the night discussing what to do with you."

"Mother, I . . ."

"Let me finish, Ursula," Mrs. Bower said. "We don't really understand why your photographs have created so much interest in academic circles, but you must be of some use, and we are gratified. Also, Graham has been urging us for weeks to send you back to India. So," Mrs. Bower paused to take a deep breath before saying, "we think you should see if you can book passage."

Ursula gasped then laughed with relief at her mother's suggestion.

"I've already made enquiries, Mother, but with the country at war, I feel I'd be abandoning ship."

"That may well be, but with both Graham and your father in the services, it will be a comfort to know that at least one Bower will be somewhere safe and far away when the war turns nasty."

On the last day of November, Ursula received a call telling her to report at once to Liverpool. It was a cold, cloudy day when she left war torn Europe on *The City of Benares* to join a convoy headed for the safety of the Far East.

Ursula stepped down from the train onto Manipur Road platform. She looked around at the forested hills and took a deep breath. Old life left behind: new life beckoning. She lifted her face to the sun as if receiving a blessing then placed her hat with its broad brim on her head and gave it a satisfied tap into place.

Lexie hurried over. Ursula put her hands on her friend's shoulders and grinned. "I'm ecstatic. It's wonderful to be back. I almost can't believe it." Richard came up beside his sister. "Hello, Richard," Ursula said, giving him a kiss on the cheek. "I'm so happy!"

After checking that Ursula's baggage and equipment were safely in the care of the porters, they strolled to the travellers' bungalow. Ursula's steps were light and frisky.

"Slow down, Miss Bower, you're cavorting like a spring lamb," said Richard laughing.

Halfway up the hill, the watchman approached and handed Ursula a letter from Mr. Jimpson, the Political Agent. Gaily, she tore open the envelope. It contained a pass for the road. She scanned the letter and stopped in her tracks, her smile disappearing as she read the last line: *I regret that at this time it will not be possible for you to tour the hills.*

Ursula gasped as if punched. "Oh. Lexie . . . !" She held out the letter, averting her face to hide her trembling chin and eyes brimming with tears. She struggled for control and turned her head toward the distant hills. She felt like a child being torn from her mother.

"Oh gosh, Ursula! What a cruel blow!"

Lexie handed the letter to Richard. His expression grew dark. "Come. Let's move on to the rest-house. We'll figure something out over a cup of tea."

For once, Richard was out of ideas. There was nothing to be done. Ursula gazed ahead with unfocused eyes during the long drive to Imphal. Early next morning, dressed and ready when only the servants were stirring, she was sipping her second cup of tea when Lexie and Richard arrived at the breakfast table. They glanced at each other with relieved smiles. The old Ursula was back.

"Good morning, darling. You look much, much better," Lexie greeted her.

"I feel better. I've decided to speak to the Political Agent to see if we can sort this out."

"Good," Richard said. "And if he won't change his mind?"

Ursula raised her eyebrows. "If he won't, I intend to strangle him, beat him with a cudgel and shoot him with your shotgun."

*　　*　　*

In Mr. Jimpson's office, Ursula laid out her plans, her arguments, her reasoning about why there was no just cause to deny her access to the Naga Hills. He remained adamant. She began pleading. "But Mr. Jimpson, I've travelled all the way from England to do this research. I have a responsibility to some important anthropological societies. I've spent a lot of money buying equipment and supplies. I really must do this. I have medicines for the Nagas."

Her voice faded as she realized she was having little effect. Afraid that if she did not stop, she would lose all self-respect and start grovelling, Ursula fell silent.

"Miss Bower, I don't wish to seem unkind, but there *is* a war on, and we must protect the area and the residents in whichever way the British government sees fit. I'm truly sorry for your disappointment, but I cannot make any exceptions." Mr. Jimpson rose from his chair and came round the desk. "If I can be of help in any other way . . ."

"No, no. Thank you for your time," Ursula heard herself say.

She stumbled down the Residency's steps into the dusk, biting hard on her lower lip to stop noisy sobs from escaping. Tears streamed. Round and round cantonments she walked, not daring to return to Richard and Lexie in such a state. She passed bungalows filled with light and people talking and laughing. Something inside had died, and she could not cope with her grief. Too tired to walk any further, too tired to think anymore, and too tired to do anything but sleep, Ursula returned to Richard's house and retreated to her bedroom. She fell fully clothed onto her bed, and in the night's shadows, she watched the hypnotic blurred circle of the overhead fan until she fell into a fitful sleep.

"What do you intend to do?" Lexie asked two days later as Ursula returned to the bungalow after a morning making arrangements.

"Well, I'm not leaving. That would signify failure, so I've arranged to rent the small forest bungalow."

"Richard and I are concerned about you. You seem despondent."

"I'm feeling utterly miserable, but I'll keep busy, and I'll soon be all right. Tell Richard not to worry about me. *You* may worry all you want, of course."

Lexie laughed. Ursula had not completely had the stuffing knocked out of her.

During the next two weeks, Ursula struggled with a depression that threatened to swallow her up. She distracted herself from her misery by furnishing her new home, collecting a staff, and improving her Manipuri language skills. By grasping tightly to the normal daily routine, she managed to prevent the dark feelings of hopelessness and worthlessness from overwhelming her. She isolated herself from other residents at the hill station, not daring to risk an unkind word or thoughtless act which might send her so far down into the darkness she would not be able to find her way out. And then, in the middle of it all, Luikai returned.

Shocked by the melancholy engulfing the miss-sahib, he determined to cheer her up. He was clownish and silly in an effort to make her smile; he tempted her with tasty dishes, but she ate little. She hid herself in the bungalow and saw no one but the servants. Concerned, Luikai approached one of his friends, a pockmarked Tangkhul, who sold dogs in the Naga market and asked him to come to the house.

Luikai appeared at her door with the dog-seller.

"Miss-sahib, you buy a dog from this man?" Luikai managed to say.

Ursula told him, "No," and closed the door.

Luikai told his friend, "Hurry back and bring a pretty puppy to the miss-sahib." An hour later, the man returned. Luikai called the miss-sahib to the door. The pedlar was tugging a piece of string. At the other end, playfully resisting, was a black and white ball of fluff. Despite a slight softening, Ursula remained resolute, until the puppy took a tumble onto his nose.

"Oh, poor thing," she said and picked up the fleecy bundle.

The trader took his opportunity. "Only one rupee, miss-sahib. Very good dog for only one rupee."

She looked at Luikai's encouraging expression.

"All right," she said, resigned. "We'll take the dog. One rupee, you say?"

Luikai watched the pup lick Ursula's face. As she stifled a giggle, she saw Luikai's relief and was filled by a surge of affection for her loyal servant.

"Your money is not wasted, miss-sahib. If you decide you do not like him, I can always cook him."

"Luikai!" Ursula cried in mock horror at his jest, protectively snuggling the young dog to her chest.

They named the pup Khamba. He was black with a white face and chest like a Border Collie but destined to grow much bigger to the size of a Chow. The discovery that he was infested with worms had Ursula writing to her mother, asking her to send worming powders ASAP. Her spirits lifted watching Khamba tumble and tussle with Luikai. She laughed when the pup tried to chew bones almost as big as himself or tackled a large beetle he found in the grass. It's no easy thing to ignore a dog's devotion to you, she thought, and he was company for her, which she didn't mind. He didn't want to talk. He didn't judge her or mind when her thoughts drifted to some inner painful place. He nestled in her lap, while she read a book. And now and then, she would catch him gazing at her with his preposterous, comic, grave small face, and she would feel almost happy.

As her emotions healed, Ursula's optimism and determination returned. She travelled to Shillong to see Mr. Mills, the Governor's Secretary and Director of Ethnography in Assam. Philip. Mills was tall and lean with a long, thin face. There was something kind and wise in his manner and his smile. He greeted Ursula with a firm handshake. From behind small metal-rimmed spectacles, his intelligent eyes appraised the determined face of the young woman before him.

"Mr. Mills, I've travelled all the way from England with funding from the Royal Central Asian Society in London in order to film Naga culture. I desperately want to go into the hills, but I've been refused permission because of the war."

"Yes, I know. No civilians are being allowed into the Naga Hills. I met Colonel Taylor some months ago. He told me about your travels among the Nagas. I can't arrange for you to travel in the Naga Hills, but I do have some other avenues you may wish to explore, Miss Bower."

"You do?"

Mr. Mills rifled through a drawer in his desk and brought out a manila folder.

"I've a list of hill tribes here. We'd like to know more about them, and I'm sure they would be of great interest."

He turned the sheet of paper for Ursula to see from her side of the desk and running his finger down the list read out the names. Occasionally, he paused, tapping his finger on a name, to point out why he thought that tribe would be of interest and where it was located, but Ursula wasn't listening. A name on the list, North Cachar, a district fifty miles west of Imphal, had caught her eye.

Animated, Ursula said, "I've read about the Zemi Nagas in North Cachar. They're similar to the Kabui I'd hoped to study."

"As well as the Zemi, there are other tribes and archaeological remains that are well worth seeing. It's a large district with much of interest."

"Then North Cachar it is," Ursula said with jubilant determination.

"Come to dinner tonight, Miss. Bower. I'd like to discuss your tour further."

After dinner with Mr. Mills and his down-to-earth wife, they settled on the veranda.

Over a glass of brandy, Philip Mills talked to Ursula. "Let me tell you why I need your help. I won't go into detail about what happened in North Cachar before it came under British rule in the nineteenth century, but the Kacha Nagas arrived in the Barail area first. Later, there came surges of Kuki immigrants, who settled wherever they could on the over-populated land. There have only been two major disturbances since British rule. One was the Kuki uprising of 1918, and the other was the Naga troubles of 1931. The effects of both are still being felt today."

"How?" Ursula asked.

"Well, the Zemi Nagas have been strongly disaffected towards the government, and I'd like to know why. That's where you can help."

"You want me to find out why they've turned against the government?"

"Yes. We know it was shortage of land for growing food that caused the Kuki uprisings."

"North Cachar's a large area, isn't it? I'd have thought there was room for everyone," Ursula said.

"You *have* been studying! Large, yes, but unfortunately, it is mainly steep slopes, unsuitable for agriculture. Competition for land between the Kukis and the Nagas was strong. Normally, the situation would have been settled by warfare, but under British rule, the conflict could not be solved that way.

"In 1918, the Kukis rebelled against the British government, and while the hills were in turmoil, the Kukis took the opportunity to settle their grievances against the Nagas before we managed, with the Nagas helping the troops, to re-establish order. It was a bad do. We know of at least five Zemi who took Kuki heads during the uprising.

"Ten years later, the Kacha Nagas—the Zemi, the Kabui and other tribes, grew restless. They still had many bitter grudges against the Kukis and planned to massacre them. The government barely managed to prevent the Nagas from carrying it out. When the government intervened, the Nagas saw it as being on the side of the enemy and fought against the troops. In 1931, it was the Kukis' turn to be loyal to the government and assist in quelling the Naga uprising. Since then, the Naga tribes, apart from the Zemi, have settled down."

"What caused the Kacha Nagas to stage an uprising?"

"I don't know the whole story, but apparently, an old prophecy told that one day a Naga king would come, drive out the British, and rule over all Naga tribes. In 1929, a seer from Kambiron called Jadonang declared himself the Naga saviour and started a new religion. The government was aware of his activities, but he wasn't breaking the law, so they took no action against him.

"Soon afterwards, four Manipuri traders disappeared on a trip to Silchar. Although searches and inquiries were made, no trace of them was found until a year later when a drunken Kambiron buck boasted of killing them. When the Political Agent and Subdivisional Officer arrived at Kambiron to investigate, they searched the village and recovered cloths, pots, and other objects, which had belonged to the Manipuris. They started digging on the outskirts of the village and found the Manipuris' remains and evidence of human sacrifice. It was enough to hang Jadonang for murder and to jail for several years the bucks who had carried out the deed."

"They were involved with human sacrifice? Colonel Taylor told me some things about this, but it's hard to fathom. I've not read anything about the Nagas engaging in such religious practices."

"Jadonang had created a new religion that blended elements of Christianity, Hinduism, and the Nagas' Animist religion with a few creations of his own. The government wrecked his temples and shot his sacred python, which the Nagas worshipped as a deity. That should have been the end of it, but Jadonang had a disciple, a sixteen-year old girl, Gaidiliu. Thinking she was too young to go to jail, the Political Agent made the mistake of sending her home, not realizing that during the previous two years the girl and Jadonang had been worshipped as gods. They'd also grown rich by demanding allegiance and tribute from the inhabitants of their Naga Kingdom. Those who were reluctant were forced to comply under threat of exile."

"They must have had a tremendous hold over the people. How did they manage it?"

"Jadonang and Gaidiliu promised their followers a life of feasting and plenty that attracted all the ruffians and robbers in the area to their side. The two so-called gods used these thugs to enforce their power.

"When the Political Agent sent her home, Gaidiliu bolted north to her gang and her faithful followers. Within days, the whole Kacha Naga country erupted, and the government began hunting her down. Troops were sent to all three districts of Kacha Naga country—Manipur, the Naga Hills, and North Cachar. Outposts were set at strategic points, searches were instituted, patrols went out, and local movement between villages was severely restricted. But Gaidiliu, guided by her North Cachar agent, Masang of Kepelo, remained at large. Most of the Zemi were on her side. Those who spoke against her were killed. The villages that supported her used beacons to signal the movements of patrols. Also, the country was a warren of game-trails, paths, caves, forests, and secret hideouts. To make matters worse, she was often present only in spirit, and patrols, sent out on the best information, only found Nagas dancing solemnly before an empty throne. To crown it all, she was concealed for three months within sight of the outpost at Hangrum. The village went out to worship her in secret, and when she left, she told Hangrum that they could attack the outpost without getting hurt because she had cast a spell on the *sepoys'* rifles; their bullets would be as water and could not harm them.

"The villagers, armed with nothing more than bamboo spears, charged the outpost in broad daylight, running down a slope on which the *sepoys* commanded a field of fire. The *sepoys* fired the first volley over their heads. Encouraged that no one had fallen, the howling villagers charged on. The next volley was sent into them at thirty yards range. It's a mystery why only eleven villagers were killed out of the hundred or so who charged down the hill."

Ursula swirled the brandy in her glass and shivered. "Do you think she really believed in her powers?"

"I don't know about that. It was in her interests to keep the uprising going. Wherever Gaidiliu went, there were agents to support her religious movement. Whether it was by selling 'Gaidiliu water' as a cure-all, even though the water only came from the village pond, or by performing her healing ceremonies for the sick faithful for a large fee, they collected tribute on her behalf and took commission. Above all, they took great care that she stayed at large. When the ordinary villager grew tired of it, and it was he who was being harried and fined by the pursuing government, her thugs took care of him too. After a few dissenters had been found dead, it was harder than ever for officers to gather information. But it had to come to an end one day, and it did.

"She travelled to the fringes of the Angami country, where a Kuki caretaker of Lakema rest-house heard of her whereabouts and passed the information on to me. At that time I was Deputy Commissioner at Kohima. We knew she had spies in Kohima bazaar, so one day, with much fanfare, we sent off a false expedition in the wrong direction, while the real one left unnoticed at dusk on a thirty-mile night march. The expedition found her sentries drunk after celebrating their safety, thinking the expedition had gone on a wild goose chase. The *sepoys* swarmed over the palisade and surrounded her house. She began to shriek spells and called on her bodyguard to resist, but the men, possibly remembering Hangrum, laid down their spears and surrendered. She was screaming and scratching, kicking and biting when the *sepoys* brought her out. The only casualty was a corporal when she gave his thumb a good bite."

"And that was the end of it?"

Mr. Mills poured more brandy and swept a fall of lank hair off his long brow before answering. "Not quite. It was funny really. When they brought her to me at the rest-house a few hours later, she told me it was hard work being a goddess; people wanted to worship her night and day, and she never had time for a bath. Could she have one please? So she had her bath, in the rest-house, surrounded by sentries."

Ursula was enthralled. "What happened to her?"

"She was sent off to Manipur for trial and sentenced to fourteen years for abetment to murder. Her agents escaped the raid. Thirteen of them went to take revenge on the Lakema caretaker. They didn't find him at home as he'd gone to Kohima to collect his pay, but they did find his wife and children. They strangled them all and set fire to his house. We captured two of the ringleaders, Masang and Ghumeo. Ghumeo is still in jail. Masang was released after serving six months."

"When did all this happen?"

"Eight years ago, and since then the Nagas have been disaffected. This is where you can help me. There must be a reason. As things stand, it's quite obvious they're not going to confide in a government official and certainly not a man."

Mrs. Mills, who had been quietly listening all this time, lifted her head to watch Ursula's face as she spoke. "But you see, Ursula, there's a sporting chance that a young lady on her own, one with sympathetic feelings towards the Nagas, might get to the bottom of it."

Ursula's face lit up. "That's a challenge I can't resist."

"You understand, it could be risky," Mr. Mills said.

"I've never had any trouble with the Nagas so far; I don't expect any now."

"Good. I'll talk to the Subdivisional Officer at Haflong. He'll help you get started."

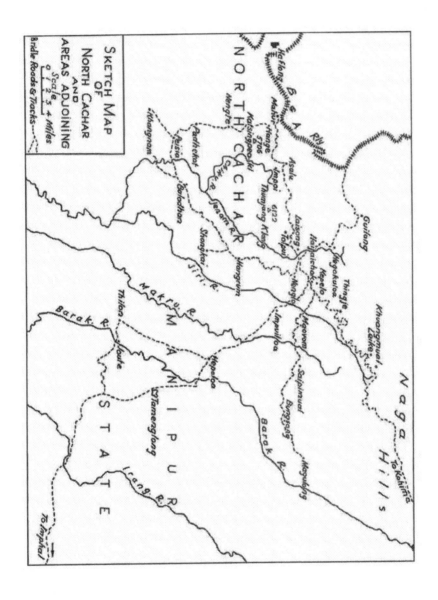

A month later, after a farewell dinner with Lexie and Richard and promises to write often, Ursula was in a truck heading for Manipur Road station at Dimapur. In the back with the equipment was her Tangkhul Naga staff, Luikai and Chinaorang, doing their best to control Khamba, who was jumping, squirming, and barking excitedly at this change in his routine.

Jack Dawson, the Subdivisional Officer, a slim, easy-going man with mousy hair and the bluest eyes Ursula had ever seen, met them off the train at Haflong rail halt. She noticed he seemed pleasantly surprised and taken with her, but quickly stowed his feelings. They strolled up to the hill station at the top of the ridge, around which the railway ran in a large loop.

"We'll get you out to the Barail as soon as we can," he told her, "probably in a day or two. In the meantime, you can stay in the travellers' bungalow and explore the town. It's still the administrative centre of the subdivision, but it's a quiet backwater now."

"It looks so pretty, almost like a park," Ursula said, looking at the slopes dotted with pines and oaks, surrounding a serpentine lake.

"It used to be a resort for the Cachar planters, but the new road to Shillong was its downfall. See those bungalows, they're just rotting away."

"How sad, and it's so enchanting," Ursula said. They walked along the cobbled footpaths lined with blossoming trees. Haflong stood where the rolling grass-covered hills of the Western Plateau met the towering Barail Range.

While her staff readied the bungalow, Ursula discussed her needs with Jack.

"I'll need a permanent base, somewhere I can stay for a year and central enough for me to go out on my tours."

"Laisong might fit the bill. It's about twelve miles from the railway. I'll send a runner to the village to see if they'd be willing to look after you. You'll also need an interpreter," the SDO said.

"I'll have to think about that."

"I need to make arrangements for my mail and medical supplies, too."

Jack directed her to the post office, after which she collected Khamba and strolled through the small bazaar. She saw her first Zemi and her heart sank; they were dirty, bedraggled and listless, hanging round the bazaar. Most seemed to be in a daze from opium addiction.

Rain delayed the start of Ursula's tour. She wrote letters home and to Lexie and strolled through the town to gaze down on a rainbow in the valley below. Then, finding a dank copy of E. M. Forster's *A Passage to India* in the bungalow, she settled down to read until the rain stopped.

Curious writer, she thought. He seemed to approach his women characters with an animosity almost as strong as Grandfather Bower or the ladies of the Club, but in a distinctly different mode and manner. She rather liked parts of the book anyhow and read it all.

One morning, a tall Zemi, wearing his headman's scarlet blanket and a red hibiscus tucked into a hole in a distended earlobe, strolled round the corner of the bungalow to where Ursula was reading on the veranda. He carried a bottle of rice-beer in one hand and a fowl in the other, gifts for the English woman he had heard was going to live with the Zemi.

His name was Gumtuing. Although the Naga could speak a little Hindustani, communication was made easier with the help of the struggling, temporary interpreter Jack had found for Ursula. Gumtuing came each of the next two days, delighting Ursula with his stories about the Zemi, which helped her gain some understanding of Naga village life.

One story was about Dinekamba from Impoi, a seventeen-year-old, who fell in love with an orphaned girl living with her uncle and aunt in Laisong. She returned his affection, and although Zemi tradition supports lovers, maintaining that they should have their way without interference, her uncle obstructed the suitor at every turn. Dinekamba was poor and therefore undesirable, particularly when the girl had many, more eligible suitors in Laisong.

When the uncle forbade his niece from seeing Dinekamba again, they decided to elope. One morning, the girl told her aunt that she was going into the forest to collect firewood. She took her axe and basket, in which she had hidden her trousseau, and met Dinekamba. Later that day, they were seen travelling together on the road to Impoi, and that night, they settled as man and wife in the back room of Dinekamba's brother's house.

At any other time of year their union would have been recognized, but it happened in the middle of the harvest. There is a strict taboo on anything that might interfere with the harvesting of village crops. The next day, a delegation of headmen and relatives arrived at Impoi to insist that she return until the harvest was over. The meeting lasted all day. Priests, headmen, and relatives argued the merits and implications of the situation until they were hoarse. When her uncle promised she could marry Dinekamba in the spring, the girl agreed to return to Laisong.

As soon as he reached home, the uncle swore that she would never marry Dinekamba. No one took much notice, assuming he was reacting to his loss of face. After all, the promise had been made by the village elders.

The following spring, when the marriage season began, the headmen of Impoi arrived in Laisong in response to Dinekamba's anxious requests. They went to the uncle's house and formerly requested the girl, who was by now six months pregnant. Hurling insults, the uncle refused to hand her over and denied any such promise had been made. The girl began to cry. Dinekamba threw his cloth over his head and began to wail. The headmen from Impoi sent for one of their headmen, Namkia, who worked as a government interpreter. He took leave of absence and, with his expert knowledge of tribal law, came to sort out the matter.

A week later, Namkia walked into Laisong followed by Impoi's village elders. In a fierce skirmish, Namkia found the uncle's weakness. The hard up uncle had found a wealthy suitor for the girl. Namkia ruthlessly launched a barrage of accusations and condemnations of the family's money-grubbing ways. He scorned them for breaching the Zemi tradition of indulging lovers and condemned the uncle for breaking the promises he had made. In a triumph of rhetoric, Namkia prophesised disgrace and disaster for the family. During Namkia's onslaught, the uncle did not manage to inject one word to promote or defend his cause. Outsmarted but not yet defeated, he agreed to acknowledge the marriage if Dinekamba could pay the marriage price.

Namkia went in for the kill, and a duel ensued over the marriage-price. Back and forth they haggled. The uncle wanted sixty rupees in cash and sixty rupees worth of goods. Namkia beat the uncle and his family down to twenty rupees, a necklace, one pig and a cooking-pot. The vanquished uncle and his family members were left in the dust, stunned and crumpled. The girl was Dinekamba's at Dinekamba's own price. To soothe the uncle's feelings, Namkia left them with a pot of beer and then went home to Impoi to share the news.

Everyone in Impoi was happy, and when the couple returned, the celebrations began. However, a year later the girl was returned to her uncle in disgrace. She turned out to be a thief, constantly taking things from every house in Impoi. Dinekamba had paid for the items she stole, worked off the debts and begged for her at the village council, all to no avail. When the whole village demanded her banishment, Dinekamba's brother sent her away for the sake of the family name, leaving a heartbroken Dinekamba to weep alone in the back room.

Ursula clapped her hands. "Gumtuing, you're a master storyteller. I enjoyed it very much."

The interpreter explained Ursula's words. Gumtuing swelled with pride, pleased he had made the miss-sahib happy with his story.

The following day, another Naga, Masang of Kepelo, appeared also wearing a red blanket, the mark of a headman.

Masang was short and barrel-chested, his black hair cut in a pageboy bob. Ursula remembered his name from Philip Mills' history. Masang had been an acolyte of the goddess Gaidiliu. Like a spy in enemy territory, his watchful, dark eyes missed nothing. Masang told Ursula the government had made him a wet-rice demonstrator to teach the people how to build walls and water channels for rice terraces.

"Why did the government employ you to do that?" asked Ursula. He had been part of the Naga uprising, after all.

"Before Mr. Mills came, nobody had enough land to support themselves," Masang said. "There was much fighting among the tribes because the Zemi needed a lot of land to lay fallow in their food growing cycles, and when the Kukis wanted land to cultivate, they used Zemi fallow land. The Zemi protested, but the British government did not understand the Zemi system and gave Zemi land to the Kukis. The Zemi felt the government had betrayed them by taking away their land. Then Mr. Mills came. He knew what to do. He set up a system of wet-rice farming for the Kukis and Zemi, and he needed an Angami like me to show them how to grow the rice," Masang said, puffing up his chest in pride.

"And maybe," he grinned knowingly, "he wanted to keep me from being involved in any further troubles."

Did the plan work, Ursula wondered. She'd wager that Masang was as wily as a fox.

At the beginning of March, in the company of the SDO, Jack Dawson, Ursula left Haflong with her staff. With the group were Masang and Gumtuing, who had decided to go along too. They caught a train to Mahur where the Haflong-Kohima bridle path brushed alongside the railway, and the imposing, dark, forested Barail loomed over the rail halt. A short distance past the bazaar, on the far side of the tracks and across a stream, stood a tiny rest-house where they spent the night.

Next morning, they marched along an easy road at the base of the Barail, and after dispensary visits to two villages, they reached their first stop at Asalu. The camp was in a pleasant, grassy area dotted with trees. A wood lay between the camp and the village consisting of thirty houses with thatched, steep-pitched roofs. They all faced onto a higgledy-piggledy street of bare earth with large flat gravestones here and there. There were two *morungs*, which Ursula knew were "bachelors' halls", that were three times bigger than a family house. The *morungs*' large front rooms served as clubs and dormitories for men and youths. On the village outskirts stood granaries on stilts. A handful of plum and pomegranate trees grew along the edge of the wood.

Ursula and Jack strolled through the woodland. It reminded Ursula of a beech wood in Hampshire. The headmen came to greet them. Over bamboo cups of rice-beer, Jack informed the headmen that Ursula would be living in the area for one year to learn about Naga culture.

"The miss-sahib will also care for people at her clinic wherever she travels. I want her to be well-received by the villagers and treated hospitably."

As they sat with the headmen, a man entering the village caught Jack's attention.

"Thank you for your warm hospitality," Jack said, rising from his low stool to take leave of the headmen. "We must talk to that man coming into the village. Is he one of your villagers?"

"No, sahib. That is Namkia from Impoi."

"I recognize that man over there," Jack told Ursula, as they walked along the street. "He's an ex-government servant. He resigned from his job as interpreter a few months ago. He's the man you need for your tour. Let's go and talk to him."

They approached a muscular man in his thirties. He was tall for a Zemi but still shorter than Ursula.

"Good afternoon," Jack said. "You're Namkia, until recently a government interpreter. Is that right?"

Ursula regarded the man with interest and wondered if this was the Namkia of the elopement story Gumtuing had told her. If he took the job with her, he would be a critical part of her everyday life. He seemed intelligent enough. He was rugged and handsome with strong cheekbones.

Namkia looked impassively at Ursula and the SDO. "Yes, sahib."

Jack nodded towards Ursula. "The miss-sahib is an important lady. She will be touring the villages in the area for one year. She needs a good interpreter, and you're the man I want for the job. You are also to be the miss-sahib's bodyguard. You must keep her safe at all times. The government would not look well upon you if anything happened to the miss-sahib. There'll be no problem with that, will there, Namkia?"

Ursula saw Namkia's lips tighten with annoyance instead of smiling with pleasure at being given the opportunity to work for her, yet he bowed to the authority of the Subdivisional Officer.

"No, sahib."

"Splendid, splendid," Jack said, pleased to have settled that problem. "Come back to our camp, and I'll give you a red blanket."

Namkia remained quiet while they walked through the woods. As he accepted the red cloth, symbol of his position and authority, his expression was indifferent, even when Khamba barked at him and tried to chew his toe. Then he left, returning to his village a mile away to collect his things and say goodbye to his wife and family.

"Namkia looks capable, but he's obviously not keen to work for me," Ursula said.

Jack gave a rueful grin. "I did have to twist his arm a little, didn't I? Namkia isn't your typical government employee. From what I remember, he has a mind of his own and a strong sense of what's right and wrong, and when he saw things happening which clashed with his moral code, he spoke up whatever the cost. It didn't go down well with harried overworked district officers who want unquestioning compliance from employees. Namkia resigned because he realized he was not cut out for government work. He had to apply many times before his resignation was accepted. Although he often infuriated officers, he was loyal and honest, an accurate interpreter, an expert in tribal law, and a notable man among the Barail Zemi. You'll be in good hands with him looking after you."

In the morning, Ursula and Jack climbed the hill to Impoi, where Namkia joined the tour. They were travelling to Laisong, Ursula's base for the next twelve months. The road was nothing more than a rocky shelf running along the escarpment, curling ever higher through tall mountain forest to where thinning trees gave way to scrub and old fields. At 4,000 feet, they reached the pass, from where Ursula, looking east, could see ridge after tree-covered ridge sweeping south as if formed by a giant garden rake until they blended with the sky and the clouds and the haze of the horizon.

The group travelled downwards to the grassy foothills then scrambled upwards like mountain goats for four hundred yards before Jack spotted the *morungs'* roofs standing out above the surrounding thicket.

"Laisong," he said.

Ursula's heart, already pounding, throbbed now with anticipation. Here was her new home.

The path widened and led into a wood to emerge later into the rocky village street through an alleyway messy with chaff, dung, and refuse washed there by rainstorms from higher ground. The village stood on a spur, which sloped from the main range. Walking along the steep street, they passed an old man sitting in front of his house mending a basket. Without pausing from his work, he looked up and gave a friendly smile.

"This seems to be a fair sized village," Ursula said.

"About eighty houses," Jack answered.

They came to a wide space in the street where two enormous water troughs stood like dugout canoes.

"That bamboo pipeline feeds the troughs from a spring in the hills behind the village," he told Ursula. "This stone here . . ." He broke off on spotting one of the headmen approaching. "Tell the miss-sahib about the jumping stone, Namkia, while I go ahead to greet the headman."

Dutifully and without modulation, Namkia told the tale. "This stone is a sacred stone used in Naga festivities where the men from the *morungs* show off their jumping abilities. Heads taken in war are buried beside it."

Not exactly rude thought Ursula, but he doesn't enjoy being my interpreter. She hoped she could win him over. It was going to be tedious if she couldn't, and he was almost cold enough to make her miss the arrogant Suizhakhup.

While Ursula looked around her, Namkia joined Jack and the headman.

A *morung* stood at each end of the space. From the highest end, Ursula looked east past craggy cliffs and an immense chasm to a valley flanked by barren hills. Beyond the lower *morung*, the street dropped steeply, the houses ended, and the path forked. One branch fell away through a stonewalled gateway and disappeared down the cliff; the other climbed up round the small hill on the end of the spur.

"Ursula," Jack said, returning with Namkia and the headman, "we've been invited to partake of some rice-beer while your staff prepares the camp."

As they squatted on low stools in the dark interior of the headman's house, other headmen joined them.

"How is the village ruled?" Ursula asked Namkia.

He asked the headmen and interpreted, "Laisong is like most Naga villages. It has a village council of four headmen and four village priests who rule the community. The headmen are chosen by a hereditary leader who is a landowner."

Namkia told Ursula and the SDO that the village had planned a great celebration to honour the miss-sahib. "Five villages have been invited. In two days, there will be a feast and dancing so the miss-sahib and the Zemi can meet. The miss-sahib will be expected to buy a mithan for the feast. It is the custom."

"That's wonderful, Namkia. Tell the headman I am very happy to be given the chance to meet everyone." Ursula turned to Jack. "What's a mithan?"

"It's a kind of domesticated buffalo used for special occasions and sacrifices. Looks like the bison you see in the Altamira cave paintings."

The sun was low in the sky when Ursula and Jack climbed to the thatched camp. It looked Lilliputian perched on an aerie surrounded by vast expanses of plunging shadowy abysses and colossal dramatic ridges topped with dark forest. To the south and east, the spur's sides fell sheer in grassy cliffs; to the north was a wooded ravine. Eight hundred feet below, the Jenam River flashed like a vein of precious metal among the rocks then

111

flowed into an open green basin to meander through bamboo and reed-beds before disappearing into the labyrinth of spurs.

All in all, this is a fine place to call home, Ursula decided, comparing this vista to the view of Grandmama's garden and the back of the brick house from the next street along.

"Will you be all right here?" Jack Dawson asked.

"Quite all right," she said.

Two days later, headmen and their dance teams began arriving in Laisong from the surrounding area. Namkia helped Ursula in negotiations to buy a bull mithan. The headman's chest swelled with pride as he told her, "Never in the history of the Zemi has there been such a gathering as this. We invited five villages and nine have arrived."

Within days, the camp and village were overrun with interpreters wearing red-fronted waistcoats. The steep village street bustled with the comings and goings of scarlet-clad headmen. Men and boys wandered among the huts or sat in front of the *morungs* engrossed in decking themselves out in their finery, while all the men and youths of Laisong were engaged in capturing the mithan.

Ursula and Jack strolled to the camp. "You'll see a good show when the festivities begin," he said. "I've been told there're one hundred dancers here. Dancing is taken seriously. It's a tribal art. Each village has its special dances and its dance celebrities. Troupes of young men and girls go round the area performing their dances for a fee, usually paid for by a rich villager who wants to be a bigwig in his village."

"I'll have my camera at the ready when the dancing starts. I don't want to miss a thing."

Mid-morning, Masang, devoid of his usual grin, entered the camp gasping and sweating, his hair tousled and full of burrs.

"Come! We need you to help catch the mithan," he called to the men then charged out of the camp followed by Ursula's staff.

From the camp, Ursula and Jack could see the mithan, a dark speck in the valley a mile away, intent on resisting capture by the men fanned out around him. They watched until the beast was caught. An hour later, the triumphant captors were leading it through the village to be tethered to the sacrificial post below the lower *morung*. Ursula's dog, Khamba, seemed to think he was part of the festival. He was everywhere underfoot, and his excited bark could be heard all over the village.

Ursula and Jack entered the village for Ursula to film the ceremonial killing. As well as the mithan, a buffalo was tethered to the post. The butcher approached the beasts. He gently scratched the mithan's forehead, distracting the animal's attention from the spear poised behind its shoulder. Suddenly, the man drove the spear into the mithan's heart. With a terrible moan, the beast dropped to its knees, blood spurting in looping strings from its nose and mouth. Even before the mithan crashed to the floor, the butcher drove a spear into the buffalo's heart. The buffalo brayed, coughed out a massive gasp and crumpled. Ursula flinched behind her eyepiece but kept shooting the cine-camera.

"Are you all right?" asked Jack.

"Perfectly. I once saw a horse shot dead when she had broken her leg in the hunt."

In Naga fashion, the carcasses were hacked into pieces. Eager hands carried the meat away, and before long, a hot chilli stew, enough to feed five hundred people, was bubbling in the cooking pots. Khamba circled the stew pots stealthily, as if waiting for a chance to help himself to the meat.

The feast began. Bolstered by the flow of rice-beer, the murmur of conversation became a deafening roar. By nightfall, the village was bouncing. Then in the darkness, a lone drum began to beat, then another, and another, as the leaders gathered their teams together.

Ursula and Jack joined the villagers congregated round a large area at the top of the spur, which had been levelled for the performers. Among the spectators were the singers with cymbals and drums. Excited children squatted on the ground in front of the crowd. Young men brought twelve-foot high, bamboo torches from the *morungs* and placed them round the field. The flames flared in the wind like big, roiling pennants.

Lights bobbed in the dark street as the teams flowed in, their torches blazing orange trails against the indigo sky. A hundred or more dancers, youths and girls, slipped through the crowd and formed into lines along opposite edges of the field. The men on one side started a slow but lilting song, each line being repeated by the men opposite. Drums and cymbals joined in, and the dancers began to sway, picking up the rhythm. Moving slowly at first, they dipped and curled, moving round and round, winding, twirling, meeting and parting till the whole spur pulsated with a writhing serpent of dancing figures. Elaborate hornbill-feather headdresses glimmered in the torchlight. The young men's backs glistened and the girls' bare shoulders gleamed crimson under the flickering flames.

Beside Ursula in the dark, Jack Dawson tossed back his beer. She felt his gaze on her. The drums thundered

The pace quickened. Singers and drummers undulated to the tune. With prancing, controlled steps, the leaders moved off the ground, followed by the long lines of dancers. Faster and faster they moved; leaping feet reached higher; billowing hornbill feathers, rising and falling, moved in and out of the flames' red glare. Throbbing drums and pounding feet shook the ground. Ursula's feet tingled from the vibrating earth. Dance followed dance; burned out torches were renewed; the full moon floated across the sky, and still the dancing continued in a haze of abandonment until tinges of dawn's first golden light touched the spur.

This was the Zemi welcome to Ursula.

The next day, Ursula and Jack parted company. The sensual intensity of the dancing and carousal from the night before left Ursula feeling as if they had shared something almost intimate in the dark. She was relieved he had to leave. She had no desire to deal with lonely, lovesick swains and wanted to focus only on her work, no distractions. She did have a giggle seeing his bloodshot eyes and didn't envy him the long march ahead in his hung-over condition. The SDO returned to Haflong, while Ursula went in search of the best places for fieldwork. Masang and Gumtuing decided to stay at Laisong for a few days before travelling to Guilong.

Ursula turned south to Hangrum, mindful of Mr. Mills' need to understand why the Nagas had turned away from the government. At Nenglo, she held a dispensary, wormed forty children, and stayed overnight. Chinaorang struggled to prevent Khamba from chasing the villagers' goats. Arriving in Hangrum next day, the village's dramatic setting took Ursula's breath away. The smoke-stained houses, a medley of many shades of brown (walnut, almond, chocolate, and mushroom) stood on a knife-edged ridge looking out onto range after blue-green range of the Manipur Hills. On the other side, razorback spurs swept down to the Jenam River.

Ursula's group entered the village. Not one woman or child could be seen. Khamba prowled, investigating. The men of the village sat like scowling statues and would not answer their calls of greeting.

The silence was ominous, hostile. She looked at Namkia for reassurance but found little; in fact, he looked more stern and watchful than usual. Chinaorang scooped up Khamba and held the dog tightly. Luikai stayed so close to Ursula he almost stepped on her heels. The sullen Hangrum men sat in rows on the house platforms. Suspicious stares followed Ursula's party as it walked the quarter-mile long street, Ursula expecting any minute to be hit by a thrown stone.

Safely through the village, Ursula asked Namkia, "What was that all about?"

"They think you are a government spy. They do not like the government. It is only nine years since the *sepoys* fired on the men, burned the village, and punished the people."

They arrived at the run down rest-house.

"Namkia, when we've got this place organized, I want you to tell me about Hangrum. Mr. Dawson tells me it's the most powerful village in the area. If I can win them over, I'd like to do some studies here."

After dinner, Namkia sat with Ursula round the fire. He retold the story of the goddess Gaidiliu and how Hangrum had sheltered her, how, when she left to travel north, she urged the villagers to attack the military police outpost, promising that the *sepoys'* bullets would be turned to water by her magic.

"A hundred men charged down the hill in broad daylight armed only with sharpened bamboo because their spears had been confiscated by the soldiers. Eleven villagers were killed. The survivors fled, and the whole village took to the jungle with very little food. They hid for three days, listening to gunfire as the *sepoys* killed all their livestock and burned the village."

"No wonder they dislike the government," said Ursula.

"There is more. They became cold and hungry in the forest and lit a fire to cook some food. The *sepoys* saw it and came and rounded them up. The soldiers left the women and children in the village to starve because all the grain stocks had been burned and the animals killed. They took the men, who had been without food for three days, and marched them forty miles to the railway at Haflong and gave them nothing to eat.

"By the time they reached Asalu, the Hangrum prisoners were dropping from exhaustion and hunger. While the *sepoys* rested and ate, the headman of Asalu ran round every house to collect some rice and every cooking pot he could find to feed Hangrum's men."

"Why did the soldiers treat the Nagas so badly?"

Namkia drew himself up and looked directly into Ursula's eyes. "Those who do not know us think the hill tribes are dog-eating savages to be treated with contempt."

"How wrong they are, Namkia. I hope to show that with my study of the Nagas."

Namkia's shoulder's relaxed a little on hearing Ursula's words, but his face remained impassive as he continued. "The SDO at Haflong was the son of a wealthy Indian judge. He had his own airplane and wanted an airfield for it. He set the prisoners to work. It was not legal for him to do this, have prisoners build his private airfield, but he did not care. He gave the men little food and no pay. They were under guard like convicts, yet they had not had a trial."

Ursula was incredulous. "They were being used as forced labour? Surely someone must have done something about it."

Namkia told her that rumours must have got back to Shillong, because the authorities started to ask questions. The SDO, probably to cover up what he had been doing, sent the Hangrum men back to their village with no food and no money. But the village had been wrecked. There were no grain stocks or livestock left. The prisoners had picked up the 'flu in Haflong, and as they made their way home to Hangrum, they just fell into the undergrowth and died of the 'flu, pneumonia, and starvation.

"Those poor men!" cried Ursula, "Those poor men!"

Namkia looked sideways at Ursula. He seemed surprised by her strong feelings for his people. He continued, "The Asalu and others told me that for weeks afterwards, they kept finding the bodies and skeletons of men who did not make it to Hangrum. That is why Hangrum does not like the government."

Ursula nodded her head. "I see." She stared thoughtfully into the flames. Here was the start of her report to Mr. Mills, who surely must have suspected something like this was at the bottom of it all. She would write it all up as soon as she returned to Laisong.

Feeling nothing could be gained by staying in Hangrum, Ursula turned north to Guilong where she hoped for a warmer welcome.

During the four-day march, she asked Namkia, "How do you think we'll be received at Guilong?"

"I don't know, miss-sahib. There was also shooting there during the troubles, but not as bad as at Hangrum."

Doesn't sound promising, thought Ursula, glumly. This might not be the best area for her research.

Before they reached Guilong's village gate, villagers came to greet them, forcing cups of rice-beer into their hands.

"Looks good, Namkia," Ursula said.

His expression was non-committal.

As she started down the village street, adoring crowds mobbed her. A sea of faces and pressing bodies surrounded her. Hands pulled her by the wrist, tugged at her clothes, and pried open her hands to make her accept their gifts. She couldn't move.

"Namkia!" she finally called in desperation.

He forced his way through the crowd to Ursula's side, pushing villagers away.

"For goodness sakes," she shouted over the din, "let's find the camp and settle in."

Namkia ploughed through the crowd with Ursula hanging on to his blanket until they reached her hut. Masang and Gumtuing appeared. She was delighted to see them. Masang always cheered her with his infectious grin. Although he acted the clown, Ursula was well aware it was an act, which hid the deeper man. Here in Guilong, he seemed puffed up with pride and particularly pleased with himself. She noticed Namkia was scowling and his greeting to the two men curt, and she wondered at his animosity.

While in Guilong, she could give the matter no consideration.

The villagers gave her no peace or privacy. No matter whether she was eating, sleeping, resting, and even during her evening bath, villagers piled into Ursula's hut. There was no polite request to speak to her. The invaders just plopped down and began uttering inane phrases over and over like a mantra. Namkia, sitting on the floor near Ursula, his expression one of distaste and boredom, translated each phrase: "Oh my mother,

Oh Queen, Oh Goddess. You are our mother, you are a goddess, there is none greater, there is none better than you."

At first, Ursula was completely confounded and even a little amused. Then the adoration became tedious. If her interest waned and strayed back to her book, or to Khamba, or if she tried to talk to Namkia, the villager's hand would tug impatiently at her clothes, demanding she pay attention to his recitations.

"Mother, Mother, you are our mother. Oh my mother, I am very happy. Oh my mother, bless me, say good words for me. Oh my mother, you are our mother, you are a goddess; there is none greater than you."

She tried barring the door to her hut, but sooner or later, an arm forced its way through the woven bamboo, hurling the bar to the ground to reveal at the open door an aggrieved villager angry at being shut out. Nothing Ursula did or said made any difference. In the end, she gave up and resigned herself to the outpourings being foisted upon her.

"What's the matter with these people?" she asked Namkia. "One village treats me with distrust and suspicion, and another drowns me in adulation."

"I don't know anything. Ask Masang."

"Masang? What would he know about it?"

"He is the one to ask."

With that, Namkia left to go into the village to drink rice-beer in one of the *morungs*, leaving Ursula even more puzzled and unable to concentrate on her book. When Masang showed up the next day, Ursula asked him why the people of Guilong were so overwhelming in their welcome.

He flashed a wide grin. "They are pleased to see the miss-sahib."

"Yes, I can see that, but why are they so pleased?"

He smiled disarmingly. "It is a great honour that you come to the village."

Ursula gave up. She was getting nowhere. Namkia, who had been translating as if it left a bad taste in his mouth, abruptly left the hut, putting an end to any further conversation with Masang.

On Ursula's last evening, the village had an impromptu dance in her honour, a farcical affair completely disorganized and lacking synchronization. The drummers pounded out a rhythm at odds with the choir's singing. Instead of the swaying, curling unity she had seen in the dancing at Laisong, the dancers of Guilong strayed and clashed until not one but two dances were in progress. It was with great relief she left next morning for Laisong.

Jack Dawson was in the village when Ursula returned. Khamba romped up to him, and Jack bent and roughed the dog's fur then straightened up to greet Ursula. "How was the tour?"

"Remarkable! Fascinating people," Ursula told him, laughing. "I'm beginning to think at least half of them are as mad as hatters." She went on to describe her experiences.

"So, you're going ahead with your fieldwork?"

"Definitely! The Nagas I've come across are extremely interesting. I'll have plenty of material to take back to England at the end of the year."

"Then Laisong will be the best place for your centre. I'll make arrangements for the village to build a permanent camp for you."

Construction began on Ursula's new camp, and the commotion of building overtook the usual peace of "the aerie", Ursula's nickname for the high spur. With Luikai and Chinaorang on leave, she searched the village for some servants to go on another tour with her. She chose Ramgakpa, a sturdy youth from Gobin to be the kitchen-hand, and Degalang, a gangly youth from Impoi, as dog-boy to care for the half-grown Khamba. They joined Ali, the cook, a highly strung, lanky, Moslem Manipuri brought from Haflong.

Her ten-day tour included another visit to Hangrum where her reception was as cool as the first. Ursula returned to Laisong through the valley below the aerie. Looking up, she could see the new camp perched like a sentinel on the high spur. The golden, newly thatched roofs, visible above the low scrub-jungle, sparkled in the morning sunlight. It was exhilarating to see her quarters looking so noble, but the climb to reach them was a trial.

The sun beat down, and on the steep climb up the valley sides, heat radiated from the baked earth. Trickling perspiration stung their eyes and soaked their clothes. Faces sizzled in the sun's glare.

As Ursula dragged herself up the last rock steps, she paused to heave a sigh and feel the cooling mountain breeze start to dry her steaming body. This tramp, required every time she left Laisong, was more strenuous than any walk she'd made on the Isle of Skye. She smiled and leaned into the uphill path to her new home.

Ursula's bungalow, made of bamboo matting on a timber frame with a roof of thick, grass thatch, was cool and airy. It had five rooms and two verandas. The men's quarters and the cookhouse stood fifteen feet behind the bungalow tucked into the base of a craggy precipice of the Barail Range. An elderly man greeted Ursula with a cup of water.

"His name is Hazekiemba," Namkia translated. "He wants to be your caretaker and look after the camp when you go on tour."

Ursula took the offered cup, gulped down some water and studied the old man. "He's got the job," she told Namkia. "Anyone who has the initiative to know I need a cool drink right now deserves it."

Luikai, back from leave and newly married, walked across the compound to Ursula. "This is a good camp, miss-sahib. Do you like it?"

"It's a fine place, Luikai. We'll be happy here. Will you bring the *jappas* in?" she said and entered her bungalow.

While the *jappas* were unpacked, she looked around at the tall posts and the solid roof-beam eighteen feet overhead. Like a child at Christmas, she inspected all the rooms, looked out her bedroom window at the view of the valley and gasped with delight

This would be home for the next twelve months. She could have jumped up and down with joy.

She ate her first meal sitting by the hearth, savouring the experience of being in her own home instead of a travellers' house. Then, worn out by the gruelling morning's march, Ursula went to sleep for the afternoon in her shuttered bedroom. She slipped beneath the covers into a realm of contentment and took a moment to exult before exhaustion overtook her.

She woke with a start. It was dark. She looked at her watch and saw it was half past one. She had been asleep less than an hour. Ursula lay on her bed, her senses straining, trying to understand the tension she was feeling. She heard a door banging. The bungalow began to creak. The wind was getting up. Ursula ran to the window. Menacing black clouds, driven by powerful winds, swirled over the valley.

The heavy veranda door, slung from an overhead beam, flapped like a loose sail in a gale. Khamba started barking. Ursula tried to pull the door shut. It lashed about, lifting wildly when the wind grabbed it from her hands.

"Damn the ruddy thing!"

She wrestled with the door then heard a tap, a rattle, more taps, and then hail struck, pelting the bungalow with golf-ball sized hailstones. The whole bungalow leaned over groaning, the sound lost under the roaring onslaught. Small hailstones, twigs, and scraps of leaves blew through the back eaves and up over the inner partitions to shower down over everything. Panic-stricken, Khamba dashed around in a frenzy. Ursula fought to fasten the second door, but Khamba bolted past her and ran outside. She lunged after him and caught him as he balked under the stinging blows of hailstones. She dragged him inside and, using all her strength, managed to force the door shut.

Striking hailstones sounded like a thousand bombs' terrifying overlapping explosions.

Her heart was hammering. Through the open window, she could see hailstones racing horizontally like shot across the spur before being flung into space by gusts of wind.

She cast anxious eyes around the listing bungalow and slipped a leash on Khamba.

"We'll be killed if we try to leave in this!" she shouted to her cowering dog. "Come on, Khamba, we'll stand by the front wall! We'll have more chance there if the house collapses."

A tense twenty minutes later, the roar faded, the wind decreased, and the house seemed to right itself, creaking upright like an old woman standing tall. Ursula waited for the last of the stones to fall then, filled with apprehension, ran over to the cookhouse to see how her staff had fared.

Ali stepped outside as Ursula arrived. He was hysterical, babbling noisily, his arms flapping, and his feet doing an agitated jig. He yelled in Manipuri.

"I need a new cookhouse. It's all flooded. I must have a new one, at once."

"Ali, it's all right. Calm down."

Ursula pushed past him into the cookhouse, leaning like the Tower of Pisa. The only damage she could see was melting ice flowing across the floor. Luikai and Ramgakpa were sitting on a bamboo bench looking strained but calm.

"Are you all right?" she asked.

Luikai nodded. Ursula patted Ramgakpa's shoulder then stepped outside and looked round. A carpet of hailstones several feet deep covered the area at the back of the house where they had landed after bouncing off the cliff. A small grass hut from the old camp had been ripped to shreds. Looking back the way the storm had come, Ursula gasped.

There had been little damage in the lee of the Barail, but the exposed north side of the spur was a desolate wasteland. Hailstones had reduced the scrub jungle to a stark landscape of bare twigs. In a mile-long stretch, every leaf had been torn from the trees. Tree bark was left scarred and splintered. Banana trees looked as if they had been machine-gunned. Masang and Hazekiemba, her new caretaker, came running up from the village. "Ish!" "Whoosh!" they kept exclaiming in astonishment. Namkia strolled up and casually asked if she was all right.

"We're all right. What about the village?"

"The hailstones killed all the animals caught out in the open. Even some of the young men sheltering under benches in the *morungs* were hurt, but no one has been killed," Namkia told her.

"We'll need a gang of men here to clear the hailstones away, Ursula said. "Better fetch the medicine *jappa*, Namkia. Let's see what we can do for the injured in the village."

* * *

Two days after the hailstorm, Ursula decided to make a start on her ethnographical work. During the six months she had spent trying to obtain permission to tour the Naga Hills, her films and photographic equipment had been sitting in Haflong. It was time to go and collect them.

Ursula and her staff had not even reached the top of the pass on the way to Asalu, when fever whacked Ursula with the force of a wind-driven hailstone. She reeled and staggered. She had never been ill like this before. Every bone in her body felt squeezed by scalding pincers. Sweat bathed her feverish face. Nauseous and in agony, she struggled on with the march.

Degalang and Ramgakpa flashed anxious glances at Namkia each time Ursula stubbornly refused help. "I can manage," she insisted, even though she obviously could not. Ali muttered to himself about her foolishness. Eventually, Namkia took a firm hold of her arm to support her as her legs buckled.

At the camp in Asalu, Luikai and Namkia attempted to carry Ursula into the hut.

"Put me down this minute. I won't be carried." Ursula pushed them away. "I can go indoors by myself."

She leaned against the wall for support as racking chills shook her. Her teeth chattered, and she pressed her hands to her ears to stop the explosion of pain in her skull. Her men stood numbly, not sure what to do. Ursula could not stop a moan and at this, Ali, agitated more than ever, let out a screech and raised his arms to the heavens.

"Allah, see this woman! See this woman! She is quite mad. Mad!"

He stormed into the hut, arms flailing. Ursula could hear him stamping about, ranting and raging to Allah to save him from stubborn miss-sahibs. Despite her pain, Ursula chuckled grimly at his tantrum, feeling almost as hysterical as the cook. Her eyes glistened with angry tears.

"I've surrounded myself with toothless tigers. Out of the way!"

She staggered inside and collapsed on the bed.

The cook was jumping up and down, shouting at Namkia, "Do something! Do something! Take care of the miss-sahib!"

Namkia was without pity. "I'm going to drink beer with the men of my village." He moved to the bed and tossed a blanket over Ursula.

Shaking and shivering in the grip of chills, Ursula whispered to Namkia, "I f..feel really b..bad. S..stay within c..calling distance."

But Namkia was already leaving. "Oh, take some medicine and get better," he called over his shoulder.

The cook began shrieking. "Namkia should take care of the miss-sahib, and he's gone off to get drunk!"

Luikai ushered Ali towards the kitchen away from Ursula. Ali shouted at the boys and manhandled them into the kitchen. He was upset because Namkia drunk was a man filled with rage, a rage he tended to vent on the hapless cook. Namkia would return from the village and start screaming insults and abuse, and instead of keeping quiet, Ali would be foolish enough to retaliate.

Ursula's body shook uncontrollably. Through the haze of her delirium, she could hear the commotion in the kitchen as the cook continued his high -pitched yelling to the accompaniment of clattering pans.

Anger burned her up as much as the malaria. In lucid moments, she raged about what she would say to Namkia.

Just wait till you return you heartless brute. You leave me in this state to get drunk. I'd better last till morning because I want to give it to you with both barrels, Namkia.

When morning came, Ursula's fever still had not broken, but she was alert enough to hear Namkia slip into the hut. She pushed herself from the pillows by her elbows to look into Namkia's defiant face. She could feel her eyes glowing feverishly in her flushed face and the poison that burned through her first like fire then ice. The world made half-sense and the echo of Ali's screaming seemed incessant, everywhere.

"You!" she yelled at Namkia. "May God forgive you because I won't, you worthless piece of flesh. You'd rather get drunk than tend to your duties, would you? Go! Go drown yourself in beer. May you rot in hell, Namkia! In hell!"

Ursula fell back mumbling incoherently. Namkia's eyes widened with fear at this curse put upon him. He looked around and spotted Ali staring at him from the doorway. Namkia, annoyed that the cook had seen his fear, ordered, "Bring me water and a cloth!"

The cook's eyes narrowed. He wagged his finger at Namkia. "Not good. Not good to leave the miss-sahib."

"Go! Bring me some water. Now!"

"Don't come back here in a bad temper, shouting at me and telling me what to do. When the miss-sahib is well, you will be dismissed. Yes, ha-ha—dismissed!" Ali retorted before stomping away.

Subdued by Ursula's curse against him, Namkia nursed his employer through her chills and ramblings, feeding her quinine and washing her face with cool water throughout the day.

Whenever she came out of her stricken, hellish half-sleep, Namkia was there.

At last the fever broke. Ursula woke early next morning, her clothes and bedding saturated. She looked round and saw Namkia sleeping on the floor beside her bed. She stretched down her arm and touched his shoulder. "Namkia, I'd like a cup of tea."

With one fluid movement, he was on his feet. He looked down, his eyes not meeting hers.

"It's all right, Namkia. I'm glad you're here."

Two weeks later, after recovering from her fever and having collected her films from Haflong, Ursula began settling in Laisong. She was busy sorting out journals, files, notes, negatives and film canisters when an interpreter arrived from Haflong bringing bad news. He handed Ursula a letter from Jack Dawson, SDO, which read: *Sorry to disrupt your work, Ursula, but for your own safety, you must return to Haflong at once. There's a report of trouble among the Zemi, only a day's march away, and another rising is possible.*

Exasperated, Ursula cried, "Oh, for goodness sake! Anyone would think this tour was jinxed!"

She called Namkia and gave him the news.

With a face like a tombstone, he leant on the back of a chair and repeated what he had told her many times before. "I am only a jungle man, and I can't do work properly for the sahibs. I want to chuck up the job and go home. And I'm so upset I shall never take service with any sahib again."

There was no other Naga interpreter available. Ursula levelled her gaze at him. He stonily returned her stare.

As the news spread, headmen and her Naga friends descended on the bungalow to protest her departure. In his misery, Gumtuing wept quietly out of a window, thinking she would not see. Luikai was in tears because Ursula was unhappy, and Namkia gloomed all the deeper.

Next day, after hours of protests and inquiries from surrounding villages, where people could not understand why she had to leave, Ursula tried again to persuade Namkia to go with her.

"I do not want to go to Chenam. I am only a jungle man. I am upset. I'm going home."

Ursula stopped listening and silently parroted Namkia. And I don't love anybody. I'm going back to my village to sulk, so there!

Namkia raved on, repeating that he was not right to serve the sahibs. Finally, it was all too much for Ursula. Feeling emotionally and physically fragile from the fever and the bad news, she burst into tears. "Oh, get out! I don't want to see you again."

Namkia stomped out.

Luikai came to see her. "Mother, I will go with you to Chenam and so will Chinaorang," he told her.

Ursula tried to smile. "Thank you. I'm glad someone wants to help me."

By bedtime, Namkia, who had the duty of sleeping in the miss-sahib's house as a guard, had not returned. Ursula waited . . . and waited . . . and finally gave up and locked the door. She was climbing into bed when there was a shaking at one of the doors.

"Who is it?" she called and switched on the torch.

A small apologetic voice answered, "Me, miss-sahib."

She unbarred the door and in slipped Namkia, looking abashed and carrying an armful of bedding and a hurricane lamp.

Bringing her tea in the morning, Luikai told her they had all given Namkia a tongue-lashing for making trouble and putting their jobs at risk. He had only been gone five minutes when Ursula heard the sounds of an almighty row at the cookhouse. She threw on some clothes to investigate and found Ali weeping with his baggage packed. Close to tears, she threw her hands in the air and shook her head unable to speak.

Namkia intervened. "Today we are all upset. Tomorrow and the next day it will all be forgotten. We, the miss-sahib's servants, will all go with her. All of us."

Namkia sent a look of reparation to Ursula, and for soothing the cook, she forgave him everything. She hadn't fully recovered from the malaria which seemed to return, or some milder but still pernicious version of it. Nevertheless, once again, she dragged herself along the trail, arriving at Haflong exhausted, numb with despair and her plans in tatters.

She received another blow when Namkia told her, "Luikai is not well. He needs to see a doctor."

"Tell him to come and see me, and I'll have a look at him."

"He needs to see a doctor," Namkia insisted.

Ursula looked at Namkia's unyielding expression.

Ursula sighed. "Very well, Namkia. Go with him to the doctor."

Namkia returned alone.

"Where's Luikai? What's wrong with him?"

"Luikai has to stay in the hospital. He has V.D."

Namkia handed Ursula a note from the doctor, warning that Luikai had both gonorrhoea and syphilis and that the syphilis was in the contagious stages. She would need to watch that his contacts did not develop syphilitic chancres. And by the way, as the hospital could not meet the cost of the expensive treatments he required, who would be paying?

"Do you know where he got it?"

"He lay with a Manipuri tart, while he was on leave. Then he got married."

"Good grief! He must have been hiding it for weeks. His wife may be infected. Send someone to Nungbi to take his wife to the hospital. What about Chinaorang? Take him down as well, just to be on the safe side. No wait, I'll take him. I need to tell the hospital I'll pay for whatever needs to be done."

The doctors decided to keep Chinaorang in isolation in case he too was infected.

Ursula vented her frustration to Jack Dawson. "It's already the beginning of June, and I've barely started my research. I feel I'll explode if I don't make a start soon."

129

"You may find something of interest on the plateau," he told her. "It's away from the trouble, and there're some urn-fields and plenty of Naga villages."

So, leaving the two men in the doctors' care, Ursula travelled to the western plateau to explore the villages there.

It was the wet season. In the deluge-soaked jungle, leeches were active. By day's end, Khamba dripped with blood, and blood stained Ursula's blouse. It was Namkia's job to remove the leeches from Ursula's body, but some she had to deal with herself as the creatures attached themselves to places she could not possibly allow Namkia to go. With shade trees scarce on the rolling hills of the plateau, when it wasn't raining, the sun's glare and the ferocious heat exhausted Ursula as she toured the Naga villages, taking notes and scrambling among the ruins. Unlike the villages of the Barail where Zemi culture survived intact, the villages of the plateau were small and poor, their income mainly derived from selling produce and wares in Haflong bazaar.

There were Christian communities, converted by American Baptist missionaries, and Pagan communities, but in every village, the vitality and exquisiteness of Zemi culture had withered to a mere trace of its former glory. It was all so disappointing. Ursula knew for certain that this was not where her main work must take place, but for the sake of comparing this Naga lifestyle to that of the Barail, she would continue her notes.

Namkia, too, was uncomfortable in this decaying culture. He was so unsettled by the move from the hills to the plains that each evening, with much pouting and shouting, he gave notice.

And each evening, Ursula ignored him.

The urn-fields, consisting of stone monoliths ranging from eighteen inches to six feet in height, provided the one bright spot of the tour. There were a number of small urn-fields, but the main one was outside Bolosan where several hundred urns stood tall above the tangle of jungle grass. Ursula clambered among the monuments. Each pear-shaped urn, cut from a single

131

block of stone, stood on its narrower end. Mills had mentioned these, but his description hadn't done them justice, not by a long chalk.

"Lift me up," she told Namkia and Ramgakpa, hopping about with excitement. "There should be a hole in the top. I want to see."

They knelt down on one knee and bent the other leg so Ursula could stand on their horizontal thighs to peer into the top of the stones.

"Look, Namkia! Look!" she called. Cylindrical holes had been cut into every one of the broader tops. "Mr. Mills found charred human bones in some of these holes. He surmised they must be connected to funeral purposes. Do you know anything about the stones?"

Ramgakpa and Namkia took turns helping the other see the holes. A look of understanding passed between them. The sun had got to the miss-sahib. They were, after all, only holes.

Namkia shrugged. "No, miss-sahib, they are very old and were here before my ancestors."

"They're a mystery, Namkia. No one knows who made them," Ursula said, full of enthusiasm.

"Huh!" Namkia said.

Delighted with the well-preserved urn-fields, she made copious notes of her findings. The rest of the tour was dull and exhausting, but preferable to staying in Haflong. The travellers' camps were in deplorable condition, and it was hard-going walking in the stifling heat. One day, coming across the only shade tree for miles around, Ursula called a halt in the middle of the long, hot march. Sweat glistened on their faces and wet skin shone in the stillness of the inferno. The group sat with their backs against the tree trunk. Ursula mopped her face and neck with her handkerchief and fanned herself with her straw hat. Ramgakpa fetched water from a nearby stream for Ali to make tea and to refresh a panting Khamba, who flopped down at her feet to sleep.

Unexpectedly, Namkia began to talk in a soft and conversational tone, not his usual reluctant curtness. Ursula held her breath, afraid of breaking the spell.

"My ancestors founded the village of Gareolowa and were the headmen there. It became the third largest village in the Asalu area." He spoke with pride. "My village and all the Asalu Nagas struggled to survive after the government gave our lands to the Kukis. I went to the SDO and asked permission to settle Impoi, where I'd discovered a small area of rested land."

"What did he say?"

"He refused, but I kept asking." Namkia grinned and looked at Ursula. "Every time I went to the office I was 'that blasted Naga again.'"

Together, Ursula and Namkia chuckled at the SDO's exasperation with Namkia's persistence. "Eventually, he gave permission. We have been three years at Impoi. It is better there. It is higher than Asalu, and we are all healthier."

"If you settled the village, you must be Impoi's headman."

Namkia shook his head. "I am the second headman. I refused to be headman because it is not according to custom. I am not of a founding family. I do not 'belong' to Impoi."

"So how did you become second headman?"

"My brother-in-law, who is 'of' Impoi, gave me some house-sites in the village so that I could have a voice on the village council."

Namkia continued to tell Ursula about his village, his wife, and his two children. She soon realized that senior headman or not, Namkia was the real the leader.

Well, well, Namkia, I'm so pleased you opened up, she thought. She knew already that she could depend on him, despite his grumbling and threats to quit. She hoped now that they could become good friends. Her happy mood lasted all day even when, as usual, Namkia gave notice again that evening.

After one month's fieldwork on the plain, with nothing more of interest for Ursula to explore, she returned to Haflong at the end of July and went to see Jack Dawson.

"Has the trouble died down?" she asked.

"There was no uprising, Ursula, just a storm in a teacup. A woman set herself up as a prophet in a village in the Naga Hills, a day's march beyond the North Cachar border. Seems to have been a bit of a lunatic really. Made her prophecies while lying in the water trough."

"That conjures up a peculiar picture."

"Yes. Not a very convincing pulpit, is it? But the Zemi believed in her. Caused quite a stir. The Deputy Commissioner from Kohima arrested her, and once she'd been removed and the headmen dealt with, things died down."

"Marvellous! Now I'll be able to return to Laisong."

"Well, I don't think that's a good idea just yet. Laisong is too far away in the event of trouble. I'd rather you made Asalu your base for now."

Ursula argued her case for returning to Laisong, but Jack would not budge. With Chinaorang and Luikai joining her now that they had been pronounced fit, and with Khamba in tow, she moved to Asalu.

They spent the first few days repairing the bashas, making them weatherproof and comfortable for a lengthy stay, and she learned how mischievous Namkia could be.

Namkia knocked on Ursula's door.

"Yes, Namkia. What is it?"

"It's about the tigers. Every summer they leave the heat of the low ground and move into the hills. We usually get one around here. They kill the cattle until someone shoots them or the cold weather makes them leave."

"Are there tigers in the area now?"

"I have not seen the signs. I am telling you this because I do not want you to be afraid. I have told Chinaorang and Luikai there might be tigers in the area. I am going to play a trick on them."

Whoever would have thought it? Namkia's a prankster, at least against Tangkhul Nagas.

Ursula managed to keep a straight face. "Thank you for warning me. Don't scare the boys too much, will you?"

Early the next morning, Chinaorang went to the water hole to fill his buckets unaware that Namkia had been there before him, faking tiger tracks. As Chinaorang bent over to fill a bucket, he saw a pug mark and another. They were all around him. A terrified screech escaped his lips before he ran to the safety of the camp. The agitated cook started banging his pots and pans, disturbed at the thought of a tiger roaming nearby. The noise and his raised voice brought Ursula to the kitchen. Namkia explained the problem.

"Then you should go and investigate the situation," Ursula told him, aware of the hoax, "to make sure we're safe."

Namkia strutted bravely away, managing to keep a straight face in the midst of so much panic. Thirty minutes later, he returned to report that the tiger seemed to have been passing through and not to worry. But less than a week later, he reported

135

to Ursula that there really was a large tiger in the area. Pug marks indicated that it regularly used the path to Asalu, and its route brought the animal to within thirty yards of camp.

Ali was becoming more and more uneasy with each passing night. When Namkia returned from Asalu, convivial after an evening drinking rice-beer, Ali jabbered that the tiger had been in camp.

"I heard its paws padding between the bashas and smelt its breath through the walls."

"You're crazy, always seeing things that aren't there."

Despite his scepticism, Namkia picked up his spear and crossed the compound to Ursula's hut.

"Miss-sahib, will you hold up the lamp and keep watch, while I take the other lamp to look round?"

"Namkia be careful," Ursula said, promising herself to buy a shotgun at the first opportunity.

Namkia searched for tracks. Finding none in the camp, he went out along the road. Still he found no signs of the tiger. He strode back to Ursula with the air of a man impatient with such nonsense.

"There is no tiger," he declared and headed for the men's quarters.

Ursula was not surprised when she heard him lashing into Ali. The cook retaliated, and a full-blown argument ensued. Ursula left them to it and went to bed.

Next day, Ursula asked Namkia, "What were you and Ali arguing about?"

"I told him he was a foolish old woman, hearing and smelling tigers that weren't there. He told me I would never have dared to go in search of the tiger if I wasn't drunk." He puffed himself up with indignation. "I was not drunk last night, miss-sahib."

Ursula could tell he was deeply wounded by the insult. "I know you weren't, Namkia."

"I'll wait then get my revenge," he said.

A week later, Namkia decided the time was right. He went to Ursula. "The men know the village woodcutters have been frightened by a tiger roaring in the forest. It's time to have my revenge on Ali for his insult. Will you help?"

"Oh, what the hell! Yes, I will."

Namkia grinned and divulged his plans.

That evening, Namkia retired early to the spare hut, pretending to be ill with fever. He waited until Ali and the others went to bed and, when all was quiet, crept into the tall grass near the cookhouse where he thrust through the grass, flailing his arms and lashing out with his feet. He roared and roared with all his might then beat a hasty retreat to his quarters.

On cue, Ursula covered Namkia's getaway by shouting out of her window. "What's that? Is there a tiger about? Are you all right?"

There was no response.

"Boys, I'm really getting worried. Are you all right over there?"

A moment's silence was followed by a wretched wail as the voices of Ali, Chinaorang, Luikai and Ramgakpa blended into a woeful chorus of "Something! Tiger!"

Ursula stepped onto the veranda with Khamba by her side. Some minutes later, the men came across. Ali was shaking with fear. Holding the kitchen lamp high, he had summoned all his courage to lead the group to Ursula. Ramgakpa was glancing fearfully all around, while Chinaorang and Luikai, armed with pieces of firewood, brought up the rear. As soon as they reached the veranda, their tongues loosened. Over and over they told Ursula about the tiger. With each telling, the tiger's actions were exaggerated beyond recognition.

Ali stopped in mid-sentence, looked at Ursula then scolded her.

"You should not be out here on the veranda when there is a tiger about. Tigers have plucked sahibs from their offices and pounced on miss-sahibs in their baths. I know this."

To distract Ali from his grisly tales, Ursula asked, "Where's Namkia? Has anyone seen Namkia?"

The staff called for him, eventually eliciting a muffled reply. Namkia appeared, bundled in his blanket. The men started a garbled tale about the antics of the tiger.

"It was so close its roars shook the walls," Ali was saying when Namkia grabbed Ali's arm and pointed into the darkness.

"Look!"

Ursula started. With one jump, Ramgakpa landed inside Ursula's hut. Chinaorang and Luikai tightened their grip on the firewood determined to defend Ursula with their lives. The cook stared wide-eyed into the ominous darkness. Ten seconds later, he was jumping up and down in excitement. "Yes, I see it. I see its eyes. It's going downhill!"

Stunned, Ursula stared over Ali's shoulder at the dark curve of the hill and saw nothing.

It was all too much for Namkia. He spun round and would have clung to Ursula, weeping with laughter, but the veranda post got in the way. He held onto the post, choking noises coming from under his blanket where he buried his head until he managed to control himself. He lifted his head, met Ursula's eyes and shook his head in disbelief at the impressionable cook.

Ursula decided to calm things down. She scanned the area with her torch. "The tiger seems to have gone. Go to your quarters and try to get some sleep."

"Who will stay with you?" asked Chinaorang.

"I have Khamba. He will warn me if the tiger comes."

Reluctantly, Chinaorang joined the others in the staff quarters.

Inside her hut, Ursula marvelled at Namkia's complex personality. He was intelligent, but had a boy's sense of humour. He had an innate wisdom, was rigid in his attitude to right and wrong, and became irrational if unjustly treated. He fumed like a two year old, pouted, and many times deserted her to get drunk. Yet despite his shortcomings, he would be a stalwart friend in time of trouble. He could teach her the Zemi language and laws."

She really liked this man. She trusted and needed him, and although he was always threatening to leave her, somehow she knew he would stay.

In the staff quarters, the men were too excited to sleep. They repeated the story, adding numerous embellishments, while Namkia sat admiring and praising their fortitude. Over the following days, the tiger story developed into a legend. Then Ursula overheard Namkia tell the men the truth.

"There was no tiger. It was me. Ask the miss-sahib; she knows."

Ali was incensed. "The miss-sahib would never have been involved in such a plot. Never!"

*   *   *

The real tiger remained in the vicinity, causing mayhem. Every night and early morning, it strolled along the road close to Ursula's camp, much to the consternation of the cook, and every evening, the villagers herded their few cattle into the thicket for protection.

One evening, Ursula was keeping Namkia late, while she made notes on tribal law. A ghastly bellow from the village brought the scratching of Ursula's pen to an abrupt end. She stared at Namkia, startled. Then they heard shouts, the crack, crack, crack of shotguns and frenzied barking from the village dogs.

"One of the cattle has fallen prey to the tiger," Namkia told her.

Khamba growled deeply then barked sharply.

"Quiet, Khamba!" Ursula said. "I'll buy a shotgun as soon as possible, Namkia. I'll feel much happier then."

Later, she and Namkia learned that Ramgakpa had been in the village that night doing some courting. When the tiger struck, he and three other young men were sitting on the porch of the girls' dormitory, waiting their turn to go inside to canoodle with their girlfriends. Seconds later, panicked cattle and the mithan herd were stampeding along the village street. As one, the boys leapt for the safety of the dormitory and became wedged in the doorway. Their frightened cries of "Tiger!" and grunts as they struggled to push through woke the girls who began to scream. The young man already inside, enjoying time with his girl, began to swear. Ramgakpa, freeing himself from the jam, fell headlong through the doorway and landed on the earth floor. Yelling loudly, the three other youths tumbled inside one after another,

139

landing in a heap on top of Ramgakpa. The air exploded from his lungs with a loud gasp. Lying stunned, struggling to breathe, he heard the inner door fly open. The old woman in charge burst into the dormitory, screeching, cursing, and waving a burning piece of wood from the fire, ready to attack as violently as any tiger. The five youths scrambled to their feet, threw their cloths over their heads and hurtled out the door before they could be recognized. They tore along the street not stopping till they reached the safety of the lower *morung*, fearful of repercussions from their calamitous courting and terrified of the prowling tiger.

Next day, as Ursula approached the kitchen to talk to Ali, she heard loud guffaws from the men, and as they came into view, she saw Ramgakpa looking sheepish. She had understood the Naga word for tiger and looked quizzically at Namkia for an explanation of the hilarity. Walking with Ursula to her basha, he related Ramgakpa's escapades to Ursula. Her concern turned to laughter.

"It's like something from the Keystone Cops," she said, shaking her head.

*   *   *

Shortly after this excitement, Namkia brought his brother-in-law, Haichangnang, to be the mail-runner. Ursula took to the simple, child-like man immediately. Only a week later, his small daughter died of diarrhoea, an event marked by the death-cry from the village.

Ursula was reading in her hut when she heard grunts as if a heavily laden porter were approaching. As she rose from her seat to see who it could be, Haichangnang appeared in the doorway, his face contorted with grief, his cheeks and chest bathed in tears. The grunts had been his sobs as he ran up the path. Haichangnang fell at Ursula's feet, wrapped his arms round her knees, and began to wail and cry out in Zemi.

"Haichangnang, come on now. Get up!"

Ursula lifted the little man to his feet then stepped outside to call Namkia and pulled him inside. "Haichangnang is distraught. Find out what's wrong."

Before Namkia could utter a word, Haichangnang, now standing calmly, his expression solemn, asked in a rational tone of voice for poison from the miss-sahib's medicine. He needed to die now. He could not bear thinking of his little daughter going along the dark road of the dead all by herself.

Namkia and Ursula talked and soothed and persuaded until they convinced Haichangnang to remain alive for the sake of his remaining baby.

The simplicity of their reasoning worked. Haichangnang decided to live.

At the end of August, Jack Dawson paid Ursula a visit.

"I've good news," he told her. "The authorities believe the area is likely to remain free of any further unrest. You can return to your camp at Laisong whenever you wish."

Ursula's face lit up. "At last! I can't wait to get on with my work."

Luikai and Chinaorang went to Ursula's hut, having heard the news.

"Miss-sahib, we've decided not to go to Laisong but to return to our villages and families."

"Oh, boys, you've been with me the longest of all my staff. I'll be so sorry to see you go."

She had helped Chinaorang and Luikai be cared for when a deadly disease placed their lives in danger, and Luikai had lifted her spirits when she would have sunk into despair. They were family.

The morning they left, she gave them cigarettes and a week's extra pay as a bonus and stood in her doorway, sadly watching them walk down the path and out of her life.

Arriving at Laisong, Ursula was gratified to find that Hazekiemba, the caretaker, had taken good care of the camp while she was away. He rushed over to greet her and excitedly led her to the water supply, which had been installed under orders from the SDO. Masang and Gumtuing, who had travelled with Ursula's party, followed her round as she examined the camp. They came to the garden and looked at the stony soil. Namkia joined them followed by the caretaker.

"It is a sad garden with no vegetables," Masang said. "It needs seeds and manure."

Looking at the barren patch, Ursula could not have agreed more.

"Sambrangba's uncle, the headman, pushed him into the gardening job," Hazekiemba told her. "He is not very keen."

She made the garden a high priority in order to stretch her already over-extended budget. For a week, they carefully tended some small green plants. Ursula and Sambrangba were watering the plants, pleased with how healthy and strong they appeared, when Hazekiemba came to look. Puzzled, he shook his head and asked, "Why is the miss-sahib growing weeds?"

Sambrangba threw down his rake in a temper and began arguing with the caretaker. Ursula stepped between them. "Boys, stop this!" She called for Namkia. "What did Hazekiemba say?" she asked as soon as he appeared.

Namkia spoke with the men then stared at the plants. He pointed at the garden. "Hazekiemba says you are growing weeds."

"They're weeds? Sambrangba, you're my gardener. Didn't you know they were weeds?" He picked up the rake to give himself time to think of a reply. Ursula, exasperated by the waste of effort in growing weeds, did not give him a chance to speak. "Set to at once and dig the garden, and add plenty of manure. We must get some seeds planted."

She was relieved to see the peas and beans thriving by mid-September.

*   *   *

With Ursula committed to staying at Laisong, Namkia informed her, "Laisong is the stingiest and most unhelpful village in the area. Everybody knows it. It's had weak headmen for years. The village is really run by three bullies from the lower *morung*. You would have been better off at another village."

"It's a bit late telling me now that I'm settled in. Why didn't you tell me before?"

But Namkia didn't hear her; arriving visitors had caught his attention. Ursula turned to see three men strutting through the compound towards her.

Namkia moved forward to meet them. The men told Ursula, through Namkia, that they had some great business schemes in mind, which they were sure would be of interest to the miss-sahib. They would be greatly honoured if she became their business partner. All she had to do was provide the capital, and they would see to everything else.

"Namkia, tell them I'm flattered that they should consider me for a business partner, but I'm not interested."

And Namkia did.

She didn't need her growing knowledge of the Zemi language to tell he was being rude and abusive in sending them on their way, and by the expressions on their faces, she was sure the three would hold a grudge against her, and, dear god, probably plot some revenge.

Ursula settled into life at Laisong and enjoyed Jack Dawson's occasional visits despite his barely hidden interest in her. In her letters home she described her matriarchal existence, painting an amusing picture of herself and her staff. Being taller than all of them, she felt like Snow White with her seven dwarfs: Hazekiemba, her elderly caretaker, Namkia, Degalang, Ramgakpa, promoted to house servant now that Luikai had gone, Sambrangba, who, she hoped, would soon develop green fingers, Haichangnang, the mail-runner, and Ali, the cook.

With the arrival of autumn, the early rice was harvested. Villages celebrated harvest festivals with the feast called Pokpatngi, which included the traditional mithan chase. Ursula had already missed Asulu's and Impoi's festivities, so when Hegokuloa invited her to their feast, she went at once, just in case Jack pulled her out of the area again.

After climbing through fields of ripening rice surrounded by low-lying cloud and soaking drizzle, Ursula and her staff arrived at the camp at Hegokuloa.

The mithan hunt was to be held first thing in the morning. At dusk, the young men gathered to pad the horns of the two buffaloes, which were cheaper than mithan. One was a young animal with horns of no consequence, the other a large, temperamental bull with magnificent horns. The men threw him down with a struggle then wound layer upon layer of heavy creeper around his horns before wrapping each with bark. During the padding of the horns, Namkia explained what would happen, speaking slowly in Zemi and only resorting to English when Ursula could not understand.

"The chase is a test of courage. The men chase the bull. As soon as someone has tight hold of the tail, he yells at the top of his voice. The men from his *morung* race to the spot; the first to arrive catches the horns, while the rest beat off the rival *morung* and help bring the bull to a standstill. Then they work together to throw it. No throw, no win. They pad the horns for protection so no one is killed. In Asalu, the men often chase unpadded bulls. Look at this," he sneered, "they have piled on so much padding the bull struggles to lift his head."

Next morning, in the gray-tinged darkness before dawn, Namkia woke Ursula. She threw on her clothes, gulped down her cup of tea, grabbed cine-camera and film and hurried with her staff to where the runners were gathering round the bull. Her staff joined the other men in stripping off cloaks and necklaces until they were wearing only their small kilts. Except for Haichangnang, who had a poisoned hand, and the cook, who was no athlete, all of Ursula's staff was competing. The Hegokuloa runners were fortified by ceremonies and rice-beer.

Ursula looked at her team with concern. As far as she knew, they had not received any such benefits before leaving the camp.

Without warning, the street emptied. Children were shut indoors. Every house-front was battened down except where one or two bolder women peered round doorjambs. Haichangnang and Ursula stepped back into the shelter of the nearest porch. She checked and readied her cine camera. The village priest took a stout stick. With one stroke of his machete, his assistant cut the bull's tether, and as he did so, the old priest whacked the bull hard on the rump.

The beast threw up his weighted head in astonishment. Finding himself free, the bull sprang into action. Down the street he cantered, his snorting breath coming in bursts. A pack of jostling, shoving men ran headlong after him. They swarmed between the *morungs*. Bare, brown backs, shaggy, black heads and blue kilts filled Ursula's lens. She captured the levelling of a woodpile and the destruction of the water-pipeline as the men fell, were trampled, and then scrambled up to run again. The bull swerved to the right, crashed through a garden, cleared a stile, and vanished into the jungle with the men in hot pursuit.

The deserted street, now a desolate waste ground, was littered from one end to the other with debris from the demolished woodpile. Water spilled from the still-shaking pipe.

The headman invited Ursula and Haichangnang to his hut for a drink. They perched on three-legged stools in his fire-lit room and drank rice-beer from pint-capacity banana-leaf cups. Suddenly, they heard shouting in the distance indicating the bull had been thrown. They leapt from the stools, shoved their drinks into the hostess's hands (to be poured back into the family beer-vat for economy's sake) and dashed outside.

Down the street they ran towards the noise, surrounded by several small boys with the same idea. They raced through saplings and thickets then down a twisting path, fearing they would be too late. The group plunged into the woods, heading for the shouting and came upon a gully. Undaunted, they hurtled down it and scrambled up the far side only to come face to face, not with a captive buffalo in the hands of the young men, but an unrestrained, rampaging bull. All the young men had taken refuge in the trees and were ho-ho-ing to drive him away. Catching sight of Haichangnang's red blanket, the bull bellowed, lowered his head, pawed the ground then charged—all in the space of seconds. Ursula's eyes widened. She yelped. The huge head was aimed at her. She saw, above, a Naga frantically beckoning and with Haichangnang flew up the slope, fear making them as nimble and quick as monkeys. Haichangnang bundled her into a natural cage of saplings where the Naga had taken refuge and dived in after her, the bull so close behind he felt its hot breath on his back. The three stood in the thicket, chests heaving, staring at the bull stomping and snorting only a few feet away.

The buffalo trampled the undergrowth, clearing a space where he rushed up and down, head up, saliva stringing from his mouth, scenting his adversaries but unable to find them. When Ursula realized they were safe in the thicket, she tore her eyes away from the bull and looked around for her team. There was no sign of them in the trees, which were crammed with Hegokuloa runners. One agitated man clung to a thin sapling directly above Ursula's head, shouting and waving at the bull. In his excitement, he flung himself about, causing the branch to tip down so low his foot landed on Ursula's head. With every shriek, Ursula ducked. Head and foot bobbed like a pair of birds in some strange courtship ritual, until the bull whirled away and charged into the undergrowth. Men dropped from the trees before his tail disappeared from view. Into the jungle they ran. And for the second time that morning, Ursula and Haichangnang found themselves alone. They waited several minutes until sure it was safe to venture from their hiding place then, with fear like a spur in their rumps, sprinted back to the village as fast as they could.

When they arrived perspiring at the headman's house, the first person they saw was Namkia sitting gingerly on a stack of folded cloths. He was covered in thick dust, burrs, stripes of sweat and bloody scratches. Between long gulps of rice-beer, Namkia told how the team had fared.

"When the bull ran through the garden and jumped the stile and ran down the narrow path, I found myself in the lead. I raced after him. I almost touched his tail. Then the path and the bull twisted to the right. I overshot the turn straight into a small ravine. I lost my footing, landed on my backside and skidded twenty feet down a rocky bank."

"Ouch," Ursula said with sympathy. "Is that why you're sitting so delicately? Your backside?"

Namkia nodded, wincing in pain as he adjusted his seat. He continued with the tale. "When I crashed into the stream at the bottom of the ravine, I found I'd caught up with the hunt, which had come round by the normal route." Namkia gave a rueful smile. "I leapt into the chase again, and soon I was in the lead with Ramgakpa. First, Ramgakpa grabbed the tail, then I grabbed the tail, but the bull shook us off. Everything was confused. There were men everywhere trying to snatch the bull's tail, and then Ramgakpa grabbed the tail again. I fought my way to the horns and hung on. The bull set off with the pair of us flapping about and holding on, as you would say, for grim death. The bull tried to wipe me off on a tree."

Namkia showed Ursula his skinned arm.

"The bull suddenly stopped. It was going to turn on Ramgakpa, but I grabbed a loose end of the padding and wrapped it round a sapling . . . made it fast. And there we were, clear winners with the bull caught and Ramgakpa on the tail.

"Then the Hegokuloa men arrived. They saw we had the bull but started shouting that they wouldn't allow a visiting team to win on the home ground. We were arguing . . . almost came to blows, when the bull broke loose. Everyone scattered. When we stopped running, we decided we weren't going to compete with such an unsporting team. As we left, the bull chased them up into the trees."

"That must have been when Haichangnang and I arrived on the scene," Ursula said, proceeding to tell Namkia about her own exciting time.

Mid-morning, a man arrived at the headman's house to say they needed his gun to shoot the bull. The padding had worked loose, and now the bull had bare horns and was too dangerous to be tackled.

Namkia felt vindicated. "Heaven has been revenged for Hegokuloa's lack of sporting spirit," he proclaimed.

Most of the disgruntled runners had returned to the village to start the chase of the second bull still tied up on the flat space in front of the upper *morung*. Ursula and Haichangnang positioned themselves with the camera on the porch of the lower *morung* almost opposite. Namkia and the rest of Ursula's staff refused to participate, sulkily drinking rice-beer during this chase, which ended in a fierce fight between the two *morungs*.

When the ruckus finally died down, Namkia came to help Ursula climb down from a woodpile, where she had taken refuge to continue filming the fight until her film ran out.

"Are all harvest festivals as lively as this, Namkia?" Ursula asked as they walked back to their camp.

"Yes, but usually the host villagers are better sports."

"And the fighting, is that usual too?"

Namkia laughed. "What's a festival without a good fight?"

"I was nervous. It was pretty violent."

"There has been worse. It was over before the women came out."

"Women get involved too?"

Namkia laughed even harder at Ursula's incredulity. "You'll see in good time."

Arriving at her basha, Ursula collapsed exhausted onto her bed and slept before she could give the matter more thought. That evening, she held a dispensary to patch up the day's casualties. The headman urged her to stay for some serious drinking, but Ursula and her team had had enough. Besides, it was going to be several days before Namkia would be able to sit down. They said goodbye and marched back to Laisong to recuperate.

As the vegetable garden flourished under Ursula's watchful eye, Namkia redoubled his efforts at teaching her Zemi and told her all about Naga law and customs.

One evening, Namkia explained women's place in Naga society. "Married women take no part in public life."

"Not at all?"

"No, girls only make brief appearances on public occasions when they carry beer to the men as they work."

"But Namkia, I've seen girls dancing at the feasts."

"Well, of course. They're the main attraction of every dance, and a dance is a public occasion. They don't become as skilled performers as the men because they marry early and give up the art; but even though they can't dance so well, pretty girls are always worth looking at."

"Hmmm," Ursula responded, smiling at the twinkle in his eyes. "If they don't go out into society much, how do they meet the men they will marry?"

"Girls start sleeping in their *morungs* when they are eight years old, same as the boys. It's not decent after that age for children to sleep in the same house as their parents. The girls still work at home during the day, and then they go to the *morung* at night. Boys and girls will always find ways to meet. Boys see the girls while they are working at home, or in the fields, and then the boys sneak into the *morung* at night to see their sweethearts; and that's how the girls choose their husbands."

"What about a married woman's place in society?"

"Women can never appear in court; they must be represented by a male relative. Also, they can't enter the main hall of a *morung*."

"Is that taboo?" asked Ursula, wondering how such rules would affect her research.

"Not taboo . . . immodest. It *is* taboo for a man to eat game killed by a woman. It is unclean, unnatural. Hunting is a man's job."

"So, the men are dominant in Zemi society."

"No, that is not so. In the village, women have the most influence, even though they've almost no legal rights. You see, men do the heavier work such as house building, basketry and clearing the jungle. Men's work takes a long time and shows little profit. It's the women's work that's valuable. They cook, brew beer, pound rice, carry wood and water, sow, weed and reap; they spin, dye, weave and sew; they keep house and raise a family. They have a strong influence."

"Are you saying that behind the scenes they are the real rulers of the community?"

Namkia pondered Ursula's question. With some reluctance, he admitted it was so. "Many times I've heard men dismiss their wives' opinions and plan to do this, go there, do that and then come back in the morning to say, 'My wife won't let me?'"

Ursula laughed at Namkia's imitation of boastful men turned to mice and then asked, "Namkia, how will Zemi law regarding women restrict the work I want to do here?"

Namkia looked at Ursula thoughtfully. "I will talk to the headmen of Laisong about this."

*   *   *

Within a week, Namkia had arranged to speak for Ursula before the village council. Her case would be heard during the afternoon before all eight village officials—the two senior and two junior headmen, the two elderly village priests and their two assistants. As was the custom, the case would be heard in public.

Ursula sat on the sidelines as Namkia made his proposal to the council. "The miss-sahib," he told them, "has honoured us by coming to live with us and wanting to understand Zemi culture. However, this is difficult because she is a woman and an outsider. If the council would consider adopting her into the community as a Zemi, she would be very grateful."

As soon as he finished, the less savoury elements of Laisong, particularly the three young men who had approached Ursula with their business deals, shouted in opposition. Other people began shouting their support of Ursula's petition, and all the while, Ursula looked on amazed at this vehement public argument, wondering what was being said.

During all the yelling, the old men listened quietly, conferring with one another. When the outcry died down, the senior headman lifted his hand to signal their decision. "Will the miss-sahib agree to be bound by Zemi law and not stand on her rank as a European and expect to be outside the law and customs?"

Namkia translated for Ursula.

"Zemi laws and customs are fair and just. I will abide by them," she told him.

"In order to see the village ceremonies, the miss-sahib must be of the village. She must belong to the upper girls' *morung* with full members' rights," the headman said.

Namkia again translated. Ursula agreed.

"How will the miss-sahib pay her membership dues?"

Namkia suggested she be allowed to pay with tea.

The headman nodded. "Agreed."

"Also," Namkia held himself tall and looked round the assembled villagers, "people have been whispering about my staying with the miss-sahib and my relationship to her."

Ursula's head jerked up. Namkia had spoken slowly enough for her to grasp the meaning of his words.

"While she is being adopted as a Zemi, I wish to become her brother so that her reputation and mine and that of my family are protected."

"Do you agree to this?" the headman asked Ursula.

"Yes."

The elderly village priest stood up and motioned towards Ursula, but spoke to Namkia. "I take the miss-sahib as my daughter. I proclaim you to be brother and sister under Zemi law, and now the council is dismissed.

Namkia walked up to Ursula. "My sister, it is time to bring out the rice-beer and celebrate. You are now a Zemi, and you have a new brother."

Funny! She had already been through more with Namkia in their months together than she ever had with Graham, her actual brother. Equally funny, she thought, was Namkia's protective and touching sense of propriety.

During the party that followed, people brought small gifts to Ursula: a fowl, pumpkins, a basket, eggs, tokens of their pride that she had asked to become a Zemi. A week later, she was informed that as a resident of Laisong in house number seventy-eight her taxes were due.

The supernatural was a normal part of Naga life. Sometimes, Ursula's staff saw mysterious lights on the surrounding hills, insisting they were "spirit-fires", and sometimes, there were alarms at night, with half the men claiming they heard cries and eerie whistling. To Ursula, a born sceptic, the "spirit-fires" always looked like burning brushwood, and although she heard the cries, she could not identify the animal making them.

One day, woebegone and seeming smaller than ever, Haichangnang approached Ursula. "Mother, I am not happy in my quarters. The door is being shaken at night, and I hear pattering noises as if a pig or dog is running."

Ursula was unsympathetic. "Maybe you should drink less *zu*, Haichangnang, and then you won't be troubled by such things."

But Haichangnang continued to be disturbed, so much so that he moved in with Hazekiemba.

Soon afterwards, during dinner, Ursula was in the living room, sitting at the camp table eating pumpkin soup. She was reading by the light of a hurricane lamp, her book propped against the sauce-bottle. With her spoon halfway to her lips, she heard a faint noise behind her. She spun round, to look at her shuttered windows normally held shut by a bar across the frame on the inside. She could see the bar, which fit so tightly it took a sharp tug to dislodge it, sliding out on its own as if someone or something invisible were pulling it. Ursula gasped. The bar fell with a clatter to the floor. Ursula rushed to the door and called, "Namkia! Hazekiemba! Come quickly!" The men searched around the bungalow and the camp but found nothing.

A few nights later, after an uneventful evening, Ursula and Namkia turned in. Ursula snuggled down in her camp cot;

Namkia curled up on the floor against the far wall to be able to respond quickly to protect her from any danger or intruders, be they human or beast.

Hearing a scuffling noise coming from the storeroom, Ursula sat up.

"Namkia, I can hear rats . . . in the storeroom. Go and check it out."

Namkia pulled his blanket round him. "It is not rats. It's only the spook. I am not going."

"Namkia, I want you to check for rats in the storeroom."

"No."

"Why not? Are you afraid?" The truth being that Ursula herself felt some trepidation—otherwise she would have gone.

Namkia yawned. "No, I am not afraid."

"Then go and see."

"The spook doesn't steal eggs or chew tea-packets. Why leave a warm bed on a cold night to look for something that's invisible."

"You can't know for sure until you have a look."

"Yes, I can. It's the spook."

Ursula could still hear the scratching sound. She looked at Khamba sleeping soundly at the bottom of her bed. Surely, he'd be rattled and barking if there were unearthly goings-on around here. Of course, he would.

"Very well, I'll go myself."

She braced herself to face the icy air, threw back the covers and, shivering in her pyjamas, got out of bed. Namkia sighed. Muttering it was a waste of time, he wrapped himself in his blanket and trailed after Ursula. They padded to the storeroom behind the white beam of the electric torch with Khamba dutifully but drowsily loping behind.

The storeroom was small, ten feet square, with bamboo shelves on three walls and bamboo matting covering the floor. She searched along the shelves and behind the *jappas*, and although she could still hear the noise close by, there was no sign of rats in the store.

"See, there are no rats. It's the spook," Namkia said over his shoulder as he made his way back to his sleeping place.

Cold and puzzled, Ursula gave up and hurried back to her warm bed. An hour later, the noise was so loud and persistent it woke her; Khamba who was usually roused by the smallest sigh or scratch of a match-head, slept on.

Ursula flung back the covers. "This time I'm going to find it. There has to be something solid to account for this row." She put on her coat and returned to the storeroom, followed by the still-reluctant Namkia. Khamba did not budge. Ursula looked in and under everything. She ran the torch along the rafters. After half an hour's intense hunting found nothing, she gave up and went to bed with the scratching still audible.

Ursula and Namkia experienced one more visitation. It was the night the cook and staff went to a village party. Namkia stayed behind on his usual bodyguard duty. He and Ursula sat talking by the fire. Around eleven o' clock, they heard the murmur of voices in the cookhouse, only fifteen feet away from the bungalow. Thinking the men had returned, Namkia stood up. "I want to talk to Ali," he said and left by the back door.

Ursula continued sitting by the hearth, listening for the sound of normal conversation, but heard nothing.

Namkia returned.

"Everyone's very quiet out there. Do they think I'm asleep?" asked Ursula.

"My sister, no one is there. The quarters are locked up tight just as the men left them when they went to the village."

Ursula and Namkia looked at one another in silence then turned in without a word.

Ursula discovered the Nagas believed the spur to be haunted. Before Ursula's arrival, it had been used as a burial-ground for suicides and other ill-fated deaths. Many villagers claimed to have seen inexplicable lights moving there in the small hours. Namkia explained, "They think they must have disturbed a burial when they built the camp, or the arrival of humans living on the spur has unsettled the supernatural powers here." Ursula held her tongue. She could not argue against such theories anymore.

The disturbances continued for several more months, diminishing in frequency until they stopped altogether. Rat noises continued as they had before, during and after the disturbances. As Namkia pointed out, the noises of the spook and the rats were manifestly different.

Lassu arrived at Laisong, brought by the same Tangkhul dog-peddler who had sold Khamba to Ursula. Lassu was a young bitch with the same black and white markings as Khamba, only she had four white paws. She had one blue eye and one brown and licked Ursula's face and wagged her tail in a paroxysm of greeting and good cheer. Ursula bought her thinking she would be good company for Khamba and a fine mate. Then too, the idea of their roly-poly puppies tumbling around the place was appealing.

Another addition to the compound was Monsieur Coty, the kitchen cat. He was affectionate, with a honey-beige coat, and a remarkable talent for catching rats. He became Ali's close companion and, Namkia claimed, a trickster cat that delighted in trying to trip him as he brought Ursula's meals.

One morning, Ali came to Ursula, telling her that the night before the cat had pelted through the cookhouse drain in such a frenzy he left fur on the top edge. He leapt screeching onto Ali's bed then dived beneath the covers where, quivering in fright, he snuggled close to the cook.

With much hand wringing, Ali told Ursula about the incident. "I knew at once the cat had met a leopard," he ended.

"Ali, there's never been a sighting of a leopard or even a pug mark around the camp. Are you sure?"

"Yes, I know it. There is a leopard."

"All right, Ali. I'll ask the boys to look around," Ursula said, wondering if this was another figment of the hysterical cook's imagination and wishing Namkia was not away on leave.

Two nights later, Ramgakpa was serving Ursula dinner, when four piercing shrieks, followed by a commotion in the men's quarters, shattered the peace. Ramgakpa dumped the dishes on the table. Ursula dropped her spoon. Both rushed to the windows and leaned out calling, "What's happening? Are you all right?" It took some time before they could make themselves heard over the noise then two or three voices answered together, "Something! Something!"

"Something? Ramgakpa, what do they mean, something?"

"One of the men must have come across a big cat because Nagas believe that if you mention a great cat in his hearing, he comes to take you."

"Oh, my goodness!"

Ursula and Ramgakpa continued to lean out of the windows. "Is anyone hurt? Do you need help?" Then they saw the staff coming over in a bunch as if joined at the hip, carrying all the lamps, spears and machetes they could lay their hands on. Old Hazekiemba huddled in the centre of the group, spluttering and gasping as if he had seen a ghost.

On reaching the bungalow, the agitated men began yelling their account of the evening's events. Ursula eventually managed to make sense of the garbled tale. Hazekiemba had gone into the jungle to relieve himself. Even though it was almost dark, he was not concerned when he heard gentle rustling in the bushes heading his way, assuming it was a village pig still on the loose. When the bushes parted, and full-grown leopard stepped out a mere fifteen feet away, he was horrified. "He looked at me," Hazekiemba said. "I could tell he was annoyed. He must have been expecting to find a goat. For a few moments, we both stayed still, then I ran screaming to the camp expecting him to leap on my back, but he didn't follow or attack. He must have slipped back into the jungle."

Ursula warned them all to take extra care and to secure their quarters and silently cursed herself for not yet having a gun.

The very next evening, it was Ali's turn. He was taking a break, sitting on the bench outside the cookhouse at dusk. Looking beyond the garden, he saw a village dog crawling on its belly towards the hen-house intent on stealing a hen. The cook picked up a stone and running hurled it at the creeping shape. The shape stood up and walking away revealed itself to be a leopard. Ali gasped, clutched his chest in terror, ran screaming to the cookhouse, slammed the door shut and refused to come out until morning.

Each day, these stories were told to Ursula with increasing urgency of tone.

Two nights passed. Namkia was still on leave and Ramgakpa, on bodyguard duty, sat by the fire with Ursula. All was quiet in camp. With the men in the village, Ursula and Ramgakpa were alone. From outside the bungalow, they heard the crunch of gravel accompanied by the low, coughing grumble of a leopard. Ursula and Ramgakpa looked at one another in consternation. They stiffened, eyes wide with fear as the leopard twice padded round the house close to the walls, then it was heard no more.

When Namkia returned from leave, obviously hung over after a night's drinking, all rushed to tell him of their experiences with the leopard.

Ursula told him, "I'm concerned, Namkia . . . the way it walked round and round the house . . . I thought it might be injured and thinking of breaking in."

"There is no leopard. We would have seen signs. No, my sister, it is all imagination," he said, not wanting to be troubled while still in his happy haze.

"Well, I daresay you'll change your tune when you come face to face with it," snapped Ursula.

"It will not happen," he answered, with a smug grin.

What did happen was the leopard attacked and mauled Lassu. Sitting in her bungalow, Ursula and Namkia heard the dog's yapping then pained yelping followed by Khamba's growling and frantic barking. Namkia picked up his spear and a lamp. "Stay here!" he ordered and ran outside with the lamp in one hand and a spear in the other. He called to the men as he passed their quarters, "Come! Ramgakpa, Degalang! Arm yourselves! Come!" Following the sounds of barking, they found Khamba standing protectively over Lassu. She lay motionless. Blood poured from claw marks to her back and sides. Thankfully, the leopard had not ripped out her guts by tearing at her underbelly. Degalang began to cry. Ramgakpa picked her up and raced to the bungalow. Khamba ran beside him. The men followed. Namkia brought up the rear, peering all around him, his spear ready for action. Ali, accompanied by Degalang for protection, rushed to the cookhouse for hot water.

Ursula met Ramgakpa at the doorway. "Oh my poor Lassu! Is she alive?"

"Yes, Mother, she is still breathing."

Ursula cleared the camp table. "Put her there, Ramgakpa. Namkia, fetch the medicine *jappa.*"

Ramgakpa gently placed the dog on the table. Ali arrived with hot water.

"Come close, boys. Hold the lamps high. Give me plenty of light," Ursula told Ali, Ramgakpa and Degalang.

With Namkia helping, Ursula set to work washing the blood away, cutting off Lassu's thick coat, swabbing the wounds clean with disinfectant, and stitching the worst ones. Khamba kept sticking his nose over the tabletop to sniff at Lassu and nudge her paws. An hour later, Ursula tied her last stitch. Lassu was barely alive. Ursula straightened and stretched her aching back. Pushing the hair out of her eyes with the back of her hand, she said sadly, "We'll just have to see how she goes from here."

"I'll take her to my room, Mother," said Degalang, looking sorrowful. "She is my responsibility. I will stay up all night to watch over her."

"Take good care of her. I'll check on her in the morning."

The men trailed back to their quarters, Ramgakpa and Degalang carefully carrying the wounded dog.

As Lassu recovered from her ordeal, it would be Ursula's turn to meet the leopard.

*   *   *

Making her way down the slope from the house to the latrine before retiring, Ursula reached a turn in the path and stopped in her tracks. Was that something moving up ahead? She glanced at the crescent moon, wishing it were brighter then stared again at the path in front of her. Shrubs and tufts of grass dotted the slope beside it, but Ursula was sure she could see an extra shadow on the path, a crouching shadow, only ten yards away. Ursula cursed her hurricane lamp for not casting enough light to reveal the object barring her way. She hesitated and scrutinized the shadow. With a start, she realized the shadow was looking at her with large green eyes.

If that's the leopard and it attacks, she thought, I've had it. All I can do is throw the lamp and scream. But what if the eyes belong to a village goat, won't I look a fool if I run yelling? I'd never live it down.

She took a step forward holding the lamp as high as she could. The two glowing eyes vanished as the gray smudge wheeled round and slunk along the path with feline stealth to the edge of the bushes. It stopped and rose to its full height. The leopard turned to glare at Ursula then slipped away between the shrubs.

Ursula froze. "Namkia! Namkia!" she called, her voice shrill.

She could hear him talking with a friend some distance away on the village path. "Hold on," he called back casually.

Some minutes later, he strolled towards Ursula, standing as a statue. Seeing her waiting, her attention sharply focused on the edge of the scrub, he realized something was wrong and broke into a run.

"My sister, what is the matter?"

"I saw green eyes."

Namkia stiffened.

"One eye or two?"

"Two."

"If it was one eye," he said firmly, "it was a demon. If it was two, then it was a leopard. And either way, you're safer in the house."

Namkia grabbed Ursula's shoulder, spun her round, and rushed her along the path before him to her bungalow. He had barely pushed her through the doorway when the leopard came round the corner of the house.

Ursula glimpsed the animal, and in the same instant saw Namkia's spear launch into the air. It shot across the veranda, sliced hard into the animal and stuck. The big cat leapt in shock, snarling and twisting, then fell with a choked screech and coughed up blood. It attempted to lift its head and front paw. Its green eyes, bright and strong for a second, glared at Namkia until life faded, eyelids closed, and the head sank onto the veranda. The big cat twitched and a last shudder ran across its flanks and haunches. The staves of its rib cage stopped heaving. Namkia knelt by the big cat. "It's all right, my sister. The leopard is dead."

Ursula ran outside. "Oh Namkia . . ."

She heaved a sigh of relief seeing him unharmed then glanced at the leopard. "I'll fetch the lamp. Let's have a good look at it."

They examined the leopard closely. Hazekiemba, Haichangnang, and Ali, who was holding Monsieur Coty and frantically stroking the cat in his agitation, hovered in the background, wanting to be sure it was definitely dead before moving closer. Khamba, a low growl in his throat, sniffed at the dead animal. The men eventually came and prodded the cat with their toes, slapped Namkia on the back in admiration, and insisted on celebrating.

"You've saved us a lot of worry by killing the leopard, thank you," said Ursula. She turned to her staff. "From now on we should be able to go about our business without worrying about leopards. Have a good night's sleep boys after your celebration. And now, Namkia, I really must go to the latrine."

Three nights later, Namkia and Ursula were sitting by the fire gossiping. A noise outside cut off their words. It sounded like a leopard cantering the length of the veranda. "Could there have been two leopards?" Ursula whispered. Namkia leapt for the spear, Ursula for the torch. The animal stopped outside the bedroom door. Namkia threw off his cloth, his muscles tense, spear at the ready. Slowly, he opened the door a fraction. Standing close behind him, Ursula shone the torch through the opening. The sight that greeted them stunned Namkia and Ursula into silence. Seconds later, they were laughing heartily, tears running down their cheeks.

Caught in the beam of light was a large rat running for his life from a predatory Monsieur Coty.

Haichangnang returned from Haflong with the mail, which included the usual batch of two-month old newspapers from England. While Namkia spent the evening drinking in the village, Ursula caught up on the news, devouring stories of Britain's struggles—the Blitz, the Battle of Britain, and Winston Churchill's speeches. Although her mother's letters told her everyone was fine, and Grandmama was staying with her in Weybridge safe from the London air raids, Ursula was left feeling unsettled and perturbed.

That night, she tossed sleeplessly, while Namkia gently snored in the corner. She felt no better when morning arrived. After breakfast, Ursula stepped outside the bungalow and took a deep breath of the cool November air. She looked round, drinking in the familiar landscape she loved so much. Normally, she felt soothed and peaceful in this place. Today, she was restless. Lassu, on the mend, licked Ursula's fingers and stood close to her leg, wagging her tail in greeting. Khamba tried to engage Ursula in a game of fetch. She scratched Lassu's head absentmindedly, all the while trying to figure out why she felt so unsettled.

What was wrong? Did she feel guilty being here now that England was in great peril? Understanding dawned. No, not guilt, but a need to be among her own kind, to dance and dine, converse in English . . .

"Namkia," she called.

He came from the cookhouse. "What is it, my sister?"

"I've been up country for almost a year now, and I'm ready for a change of scenery. I've decided to go to Calcutta for a holiday. It's time for a break, and I'm taking you with me."

Namkia's smile slipped.

"My sister . . .," Namkia began fearfully.

"Namkia, you're not afraid of taking this trip with me, are you? Who will be my bodyguard, if you prefer to hide in Laisong?" she challenged, a good strategic move giving her the response she wanted.

"When do we go, my sister?" he asked, his expression was one of pure consternation.

"In two, maybe three, weeks. I'll write to my friends in Imphal to meet me in Calcutta."

Ursula turned away. Her face softened in sympathy at Namkia's plight. He had never been further south than Silchar or north of Kohima, both towns only sixty miles from his village. She knew that the idea of going so far away to a strange city filled him with terror.

It took four weeks to make all the arrangements for the trip. During that time, neither her cajoling nor voluminous amounts of rice beer could lessen the fears she knew were troubling Namkia.

Finally, the day of their departure arrived. Even the staff's admiration for Namkia's going out into the big wide world did nothing to allay his fears. Ursula's conscience pricked her; she felt like she was taking a lamb to the slaughter. She told him what a wonderful time he would have in Calcutta, and what wonderful tales he could tell when he returned. Namkia stayed unusually quiet and resigned. Eventually, Ursula gave up trying to cheer him, and they walked to Haflong halt in silence.

$$* \qquad * \qquad *$$

While the train was halted at Maibong, Ursula passed Namkia's compartment. He was sitting stiff as a starched collar, staring directly ahead, back ramrod straight, stoically preparing for the worst. Naga fruit vendors on the platform persisted in waving and calling to catch his attention to say farewell. When Namkia eventually plucked up the courage to say goodbye, he was almost in tears. Ursula saw that he avoided looking at his beloved hills. She realized he feared he might weaken and embarrass himself by breaking down completely.

At Lumding, they changed trains for the Down Mail. Ursula was relieved to see Namkia cheer up on discovering a stall selling tasty curry. She entered the Lumding refreshment room where she found other Europeans dining, the first white people she had seen in four months. She could not stop staring. The women seemed pale and anaemic; the men craggy and rugged with prominent, almost ugly, features so unlike the smooth Mongol faces Ursula had become accustomed to.

How extraordinary, she thought, that they seemed so strange to her. Stop staring at them, she told herself. She noticed they kept glancing at her as if she was quite mad, but she couldn't tear her eyes away. These people, once so normal to her, now seemed . . . alien.

At Gawahati, the passengers were ferried across the one and a half mile-wide Brahmaputra River to arrive at Amingaon station where Namkia made a friend and the greatest discovery of his life: his own exoticism. He saw himself for the first time out of the context of his place and his own people, and what he saw amazed and delighted him. Because the same cultural transformation had happened to Ursula, she was amused and thrilled to see it happen to Namkia. She had been taken for strange and exotic by many of the Nagas, even to the point of idolatry. Now this was happening to Namkia, and he was quick to use its advantages.

Ursula saw him standing in the doorway of the servants' compartment, as they waited for the train to start, bathed in attention, in all the glory of Naga traditional dress: scarlet blanket, golden yellow necklaces, black kilt and well-oiled, cane knee-rings. Before him a crowd was gathering. At the front were assorted vendors; behind them gaping spectators. An Indian soldier—the man who would be Namkia's friend for a minute— from a military police detachment posted at the station, paraded in the space which remained in front of the carriage. The crowd was asking the soldier questions.

The tilt of his hat, his strutting, and his beaming face revealed his pride, in himself and, by extension, in Namkia. Curiosity got the better of Ursula, who casually strolled past to have a better view. She could not hear what the onlookers were asking, but in his excitement, the Indian soldier raised his voice so she could hear his replies.

"Yes, he is an important person. He is of my own caste. He, too, is a Naga. We may eat from the same dish. Seller! Bring some soda water for my Naga brother! You, there! Bring some cigarettes!"

Both vendors jumped to it, passing their wares up to Namkia with a flourish and ingratiating flattery.

"Nothing is too good. I will pay all." The wiry little man swung round on Namkia. "Oh my brother, take, please, some cigarettes as a present from me. It is so very long since I saw another Naga, and it has made me so very happy."

You old sinner, thought Ursula, watching Namkia, handsome and impressive, posing in the narrow doorway inordinately conscious of himself. What a marvellous figure he must have cut as a young buck. He was impressive enough now! Under the bare lights and the black, barren, girder roof, he presented a magnificently barbaric figure. At the back of the crowd, Europeans were stopping to look. And how Namkia enjoyed it. Without catching Ursula's eye, he was aware that she knew he was enjoying himself. This delighted him and doubled his relish of his own devilment.

With polite reluctance, he took a packet of cigarettes from the vendor, chose and lit one, and said, the crowd hanging on his words, "Yes, my brother, we are both Nagas. I thank you for your presents. Though you are an Ao, and I am a Zemi, yet we are both of the same caste."

The train gave a shrill shriek and jerked forward. Ursula hurried to her carriage. The boost to Namkia's morale would make the trip infinitely better.

At Parbatipur, they changed trains to one without a servants' compartment. Namkia found himself squashed with sixty others in a crowded third-class carriage. The sight of such an exceptional figure aroused the curiosity of his travelling companions. Courteous like all Zemi, Namkia, at first, answered every question fully and politely. But for some of the travellers, thirst for information overrode good manners. Newcomers bombarded him with the same old questions. Earlier inquirers, emboldened by his mild manner, pushed matters to prodding point, to fingering, even to demands for scraps of his dress as souvenirs. His patience began to crumble. Then, in a hushed voice, someone asked, "The plainsmen believe Nagas to be cannibals. Is it true?"

Namkia took a deep breath. "Oh, yes," he said, resettling himself in the small space which appeared as if by magic on the crowded bench. "I couldn't tell you the number of times I've tasted human flesh."

There was a sharp backward movement from his vicinity.

He shifted a little to give himself elbow-room and went on with an air of guileless candour. "In the last famine, my wife and I decided we'd have to eat one of the children.

"We couldn't make up our minds, we had four, you know, whether to eat the eldest, who was ten, because there would be more meat on him, and we could smoke it down, or whether to eat the youngest. He was quite a baby, and we thought maybe we wouldn't miss him so much, and we could easily have another. We argued for hours.

"I decided at last against killing the eldest. He'd been such a trouble to rear. Unfortunately, my wife was fond of the baby. You never heard such a scene. Eventually though, I insisted on killing him, and it really was extremely good, most tender boiled with chillies. But my wife, poor woman, was most upset. She cried the whole time and couldn't touch a mouthful."

By the time Namkia had finished his story, the bench he was sitting on was empty, most of the passengers having retreated, with eyes standing out like organ-stops, to the far side and opposite ends of the carriage. With a final look around him and a benign smile, Namkia spread out his bedding and slept, stretched out in comfort, all the way to Calcutta. Every time a new passenger approached him to suggest he move over, the rest of the carriage cautioned as one, "Look out! Man-eater!" and Namkia would turn slowly over murmuring, "Now the last time I tasted human flesh . . ."

After a thirty-hour journey, they arrived in Calcutta. Namkia found Ursula on the platform and with immense delight, told Ursula the story. She howled with laughter at his mischief.

Outside the station, Namkia froze in fear at Calcutta's swarming crowds and endless streets. "Stay with me, my sister."

Ursula saw the terror return to Namkia's face. "I'll stay with you, my brother."

Poor Namkia, he can find his way about the jungle like a wild animal, but only one minute on the pavement, and he's lost his nerve.

They climbed into a taxi. The porter loaded the luggage in the back. As they travelled to the Great Eastern Hotel, Namkia, sitting up front with the driver, peered in awe at the double-decker buses and the hustle and bustle of the city, while the equally awed driver kept peering to his left, fascinated by the native in full regalia travelling beside him.

The taxi came to a stop in front of the hotel. Namkia climbed out, and completely bewildered, stood looking up at the tall building. He had never seen or heard of a three-story building before. Ursula moved ahead of the porters to the hotel reception with Namkia close behind. She signed in and asked if Lexie and Richard had arrived.

"Yes, miss-sahib, they have already been here for one week."

"Good. Would you see they get this note?"

Ursula scribbled a message arranging to meet Lexie and Richard in the hotel lounge that evening.

"For how long will you be in Calcutta, miss-sahib?"

"Ten days, and I need accommodation for my servant."

She searched for Namkia who had wandered to the dining room. He was looking around him with amazement. Ursula joined him.

"My sister, this place is big enough to put six Zemi villages and still have room for a *morung* in here," he said, nodding towards the large room.

"It certainly is." Ursula waited a moment for Namkia to absorb the wonder of large hotels before saying, "Come, Namkia, we'll go to my room, while I change and refresh myself."

Thirty minutes later, Ursula emerged to find Namkia had managed to survive the wait in the hotel corridor without incident.

"Let's go, Namkia."

"Where to?"

"Shopping, but first we'll dine here. I'll find a member of the hotel staff to show you the servants' facilities, and then we'll go shopping."

Namkia stuck like glue as Ursula made her way through the Army and Navy Stores. Her first purchase was a shotgun. While Namkia and Ursula discussed the various merits and handling of each gun, the bespectacled shop assistant gaped at the exchange in Zemi between the miss-sahib and the hillman. Every once in a while, realizing he was staring, he would shut his mouth and shrug himself into an appropriate demeanour.

Ursula, held the gun to her shoulder. "This one I think, don't you, Namkia?"

Namkia took the gun, tested its weight and feel. The assistant winced. "Yes, it is very good. It will deal well with unwelcome leopards and tigers, my sister."

"And for bagging game for us to eat."

"Nagas cannot eat game killed by a woman."

"So I heard."

Ursula handed the shotgun to the now shaky assistant to be wrapped then moved on to the Ladies Department. With Namkia on her heels, she perused the merchandise: blouses, shorts, underwear, dresses. Fascinated, Namkia examined the headless mannequins dotted about the department, dressed in smart suits and flowered frocks. Then he investigated bodiless heads on pole-stands of varying heights, displaying milliner's creations. Matronly shop assistants' horrified eyes followed Namkia, almost naked beneath his red blanket, as he hunted round the displays with Ursula, who was enjoying the reaction they provoked.

"I think I'll take you to London with me, Namkia," she said, "and we'll visit Harrods."

"I will go with you, my sister, and I will tell Harrods I am a cannibal," Namkia said, and they laughed.

She selected some dresses to try on. A young assistant, pushed forward by the more senior shop assistants, led Ursula to the changing rooms. Namkia was close behind.

The assistant bravely tried to block Namkia's entry into the changing area, but fearful of being separated from Ursula, he dodged past and hurried after her.

"Madam, madam!" the assistant blurted. "This is . . . You are . . . he *really* can't come in here!" She was gasping; her hand clutched her chest. Finally, she took a deep breath to compose herself. "Whatever would the other ladies think?"

Ursula looked back, surprised by the fuss. "Oh, of course, of course." She told a protesting Namkia to stay with the young lady then turned to the assistant. "I'll place Namkia in your safekeeping, while I try these on. Take good care of him. He's nervous in strange places, and he bites when flustered."

Namkia bared his teeth. The assistant paled, staggered, and looked as if she might faint.

Ursula fled to the changing-room, pressing her lips hard together to stop herself from laughing out loud. This is one to write home about, she thought gleefully, holding a chartreuse chiffon gown against herself, studying the colour in the mirror.

*　　*　　*

That evening, Ursula put on her new chiffon gown, dabbed powder on her nose, rouge on her lips, and did what she could to tame her curls with a dampened comb. Leaving Namkia to sleep as a guard in the corridor outside her room, she went to meet Lexie in the lounge.

Richard saw her first. He stood up and waved. "Ursula!" He gave her a warm hug. "You look superb."

"And you, sir, look most handsome yourself. Where's Lexie?" she asked, sinking into the comfort of a deep, padded armchair.

"She'll be here any minute. Would you like a gimlet before we leave for Firpo's?"

"Oh, yes, that would be lovely." She saw Lexie approaching, her freckled face unabashedly welcoming.

Ursula jumped up and hugged her friend.

"Ursula, you look marvellous. You'd never think you'd been out in the wilds for almost a year."

"It's amazing how an afternoon in the Army and Navy brings one back to civilization," Ursula said. After the waiter deposited the drinks on the table, she proceeded to tell them about Namkia and his impact on the shop assistants. "I doubt they'll ever recover."

Lexie laughed gleefully. "You must get him this minute. I've got to meet Namkia."

"You will meet him, but wait till tomorrow. I'll introduce you to my adopted brother then."

"Your adopted brother? Who? Namkia?"

"Yes, I went through a ceremony and was adopted into the tribe, and Namkia took me as his sister to protect my honour, and his, from gossip."

"You're a lady full of the most amazing surprises," Richard said.

"You're unbelievable," Lexie said. "Well, to get you back in the mood for civilization, we thought we'd dine at Firpo's. It's enormously popular, has a jazz band, a cabaret, and good food to boot."

"And a certain young army captain is going to join us there," added Richard.

Ursula looked from Richard to Lexie. "You've found yourself a young man?"

"It's early days yet," Lexie said, "but I do like him. He's witty, charming, a captain in a Gurkha regiment."

"That's wonderful, Lexie. How did you meet him? What's his name?"

"His name is Charles Brown, and I met him when he came to visit friends in Imphal for some duck shooting."

"He and Lexie hit it off at once," Richard said. "I'd like him for a brother-in-law."

"Richard! Let me get to know him first!"

"And me!" Ursula said.

Richard grinned. "I already know he's a good chap. Likes to speak his mind, and he has a keen sense of observation of people and a wicked sense of humour. We spent some hilarious evenings on the veranda with Charles mimicking the club members."

"I'm deliriously happy, Ursula. I think I'm truly in love. What about you? I often think of you living in the hills. Don't you miss civilization? Don't you get lonely?"

"I love my life in the hills. I'm very happy in Laisong. And yes, sometimes I miss being able to go to the dentist and hairdresser, although Namkia's doing a reasonable job of cutting my hair, don't you think?" she said, flicking her curls. "It will be nice to see some shows and go to the cinema and to speak English. I speak Zemi most of the time now, although Namkia would argue with that. He tells me I have a lot to learn before I'm fluent enough to stop making embarrassing gaffs. The same word can mean different things just by the tone of voice you use, and I haven't completely mastered that yet."

"Do you hear yourself? I ask if you're lonely, and you mention this Namkia fellow twice."

"Namkia is a good friend and a kind of mentor. I'm not lonely at all. My life is full. Too full now and then. And not just interesting but fascinating. I'm still making notes and films for the Pitt Rivers Museum and other organizations . . ."

"What about gentlemen friends?" Lexie interrupted. "Do you have one hidden away? Some handsome SDO? I can't see you living with the tribesmen and staying single all your life."

"Where would I find a man who would want to live as I do? Such an entity doesn't exist. So I just don't think about it, because I'll never give up my life for anyone. I've decided that I'll never marry and that's that."

"I'll remind you of that when you meet the handsome stranger who turns your world upside down. I'm going to keep an eye out for him. Just you wait and see. I'll tell him all about my friend living in the hills, and he'll be so intrigued, he'll come knocking on your door," Lexie said.

Ursula laughed. "He'll have to get past Namkia first."

"What are your plans, while you're in Calcutta?" Richard asked.

"Apart from finding a dentist and having a perm, I need to buy more clothes, some books, I've already bought a shotgun, but I'm here for pleasure too."

"Good, we can spend lots of time together," Lexie said.

"That would be super," Ursula said.

"Maybe Charles and I can take you to the zoo and some shows."

"The zoo? You mean with leopards and pythons?"

"Coals to Newcastle," Richard said.

"No, seriously," Ursula said, "I'd like that."

They stepped outside the hotel where the doorman beckoned a waiting gharry. During the ride to Firpo's Richard asked, "You've bought a shotgun? Is there good hunting in . . . where is it? Laisong?"

"Well, there are tigers and leopards that keep scaring my staff half to death by prowling round the camp, and hopefully, I'll be able to stretch my budget by bagging some deer, boar, and doves to supplement our rations."

Richard chuckled. "You're a gutsy girl, Ursula."

"Not really. It's a case of needs must," she answered.

It was only a short distance to Firpo's. Once inside, Ursula surveyed the Louis XV style décor with satisfaction. When they ordered gin and tonics the waiter simply placed a full bottle of each on the table. Ursula looked questioningly at Richard who told her, "At the end of the evening, the waiter estimates how much we've poured from the bottle before he makes out our bill."

"Oh, I see. I've not seen it done like this before."

"Oh, there's Charles." Lexie waved to someone across the room. Captain Charles Brown, looking most handsome in his army uniform, made his way to their table, his eyes glued to Lexie.

Lexie stood up and touched his arm. "Charles, I'm so pleased you could come."

"Pleased to meet you, Charles," Ursula said, studying his candid face and brown eyes surrounded by thick dark lashes any woman would envy. From what Richard had said earlier, Captain

Charles Brown seemed to be lively enough to be a good match for Lexie.

"Ursula," he said. "I've heard so much about you. Lexie's told me everything. Your trips with the State Engineer. Living with the natives and doing anthropological work in the Naga Hills. That's most unusual. I'm full of admiration for women who do the unexpected." He leaned closer to whisper in Ursula's ear loud enough for Lexie to hear, "That's one of the things I like about Lexie."

Lexie glowed with pride and relief that Charles and Ursula were so instantly chummy.

The waiter brought menus. Ursula's mouth watered at the list of entrees. "The menu looks marvellous. I've spent months living on limited supplies and the cooking of a less than gifted cook called Ali."

"Then you must choose your most favourite dishes," Lexie said.

Ursula cleared her plate at each course, savouring every mouthful of the mulligatawny soup, the salmon, roast lamb with vegetables, rich, creamy cheeses and the full-bodied Madeira.

"Just a little better than I'm used to," she said, laughing at herself.

The band started to play, and people moved onto the dance floor. It was impossible to sit still while the popular American swing music of Duke Ellington, Artie Shaw, Benny Goodman, and Count Basie filled the room. Lexie looked radiant as she danced with Charles. Ursula comfortably twirled and jitterbugged with Richard. They made plans to go to the Royal Turf Club for some horse racing, to a cricket match and a picnic, and to visit Eden Gardens. Charles was in Calcutta for one more week, and he and Lexie wanted to spend time together every day.

At evening's end, they returned to the Great Eastern for final drinks in the lounge. Shortly after midnight, Ursula left them to return to her room. She found Namkia stricken with anxiety and dread. He scrambled to his knees and wrapped his arms around Ursula's legs. "Don't leave me again, my sister. Don't leave me again."

"Namkia, whatever is the matter? She lifted him to his feet. Tell me what's wrong."

Namkia told Ursula how he had gone down to the servants' courtyard. "I found my way there all right, but when I came back, I got lost. I made a mistake. I only went up one floor instead of two. I wandered round looking for my bedding. It was dark in the corridor. The other servants did not help me. I leaned over them and shook them awake to ask for help, but they threw their blankets over their heads, some of them gave a cry, and some of them fell on their faces and started praying for the Gods to deliver them."

Ursula chuckled. "Oh, Namkia, with your reputation as a cannibal, they must have thought you were going to eat them."

Namkia was so overwrought he did not smile. "I was feeling most lost and helpless, my sister, wandering in the corridor. I was worried I'd be arrested as a suspected thief and put in jail and never seen again."

"Oh, poor Namkia." Understanding his fright, Ursula patted his shoulder. "How did you find your way back?"

"Someone stuck his head out from under his blanket and told me to go up the iron stairs to the next floor. When I got to this floor everyone hid from me again, and I wandered about till I came round the corner and found my bedding. I was never so happy to see my bed. I fell onto it with a big groan. I am not going to sleep outside any more. I will sleep in your room, on the mat under the punkah. It will be cooler and you, my sister, can keep an eye on me."

"All right, Namkia, you can sleep there. You'll be cooler and more comfortable sleeping under the fan." Ursula went behind the screen to undress. "I'm sure the other servants will feel safer with you out of sight."

Namkia smiled then. "Do you really think they thought I was going to eat them?"

*   *   *

Next day, Ursula took Namkia to the General Post Office, a large domed building with an impressive portico. She left

176

Namkia outside, while she took her parcels to the counter to be weighed and sent off to England. One contained film and the notes she had made about the Nagas; another held tea for her mother. Stepping outside, she found Namkia posing in his tribal finery for a couple taking photographs of him. Hillmen dressed in full tribal dress were a rarity in Calcutta. He caught Ursula's eye, and asked, "So, what do you think of your brother?"

The rest of the morning was spent at Hogg Market where they came across Richard.

"Ursula! Busy shopping? And you must be Namkia," Richard said. He shook Namkia's hand. "I've heard a lot of good things about you. I'm pleased to meet you at last."

"Yes, sahib."

"What do you think of Calcutta?"

"It is very big and very busy and very interesting, sahib."

"What brings you here?" Ursula asked Richard.

"There's a Chinese chap here who turns out marvellous imitations of British shoes. I'm trying to find his shop."

"Oh, we passed it, on this street, only a little way back. We'll let you get on. See you this evening."

Ursula moved on to Bow Bazaar. She had been told the Parsees sold an extraordinary assortment of goods from dried fish to bibles. She was looking for books. Tucked away in a corner she found a second-hand bookshop. Ursula would have liked to browse for hours, but she was concerned Namkia's curiosity would cause him to wander off. She made a quick selection: Tolstoy, Honore de Balzac, Chekov, Dumas, Zola, Charles Dickens, more Waugh, more Dumas and Thackeray, enough books to see her through the next twelve months. Namkia bought three blankets, some tinsel ribbons and a conch shell to make necklaces.

The rest of Ursula's visit passed in a haze of dinners, dances, sporting events, shopping and sightseeing. Part of the time Ursula was able to bribe a hotel employee to keep an eye on Namkia, while she went out with her friends; for the rest, she took him with her, which led to some curious situations with shop assistants staring and people wanting to touch him. Namkia would tolerate it for a while then ask Ursula, "Am I allowed to kill and eat this one, miss-sahib?" a comment which tended to sour people on Namkia-as-attraction.

Richard had taken a shine to Namkia and took him for a ride on a double-decker bus. Another day, Namkia attended a cricket match with the group where his impressive appearance caused quite a stir. Some people admired the hillman's unspoilt-by-civilization naturalness. Some pompous men loudly complained that such people shouldn't be allowed in, and prim matrons spoke haughtily about Ursula's poor judgment in wandering round Calcutta with a naked hillman, never mind bringing him here to spoil their cricket match.

Although she and Lexie had a strong fondness for each other and shared a rollicking sense of humour, Ursula realised they had less in common now that she was living a different life among the Nagas. She was saddened. Her old life had dissolved away, and she was alone in the new. Namkia told her he was having an interesting time in Calcutta, but life there was crazy compared to life in the hills, and he was looking forward to going home.

Ursula, without thinking, said, "So am I, Namkia."

They approached the camp mid-afternoon.

"My sister, I've much to tell the others about Calcutta."

Hazekiemba had seen them coming and alerted Ali to make some tea. Ramgakpa brought a tea tray with a plate of coconut cake to Ursula sitting on the veranda, while Namkia supervised the porters putting the baggage inside.

"I'd like to try out the shotgun tomorrow," she told Namkia when he joined her on the veranda.

"It's against Naga law for us to eat game killed by a woman."

"Perhaps we should have a word with the priest to see what he has to say about it. If he agrees with you, well, Ali and I will just have to eat whatever I shoot."

"I'll talk to the priests tonight."

"Good. I have to figure out some way to celebrate Christmas. It's only ten days away," Ursula said.

"Soon after Christmas," Namkia said, "it's Hgangi, the Zemi New Year Feast to mark the ending of one year and the beginning of another. It starts with Hkakngi, the parting of the dead from the living."

Ursula moved to the edge of her seat. "What happens at Hkakngi?"

"Come with me tonight to talk to the priest. He will tell you. You must ask his permission to watch the ceremonies."

"Of course, I'll come with you, but tell me more now."

She listened with mounting excitement as Namkia explained that Hgangi was the main day of the festivities when enormous wooden effigies are put up at the gate and ceremonially speared by the men and boys, a custom developed from the times of human sacrifice. Learning that the various religious ceremonies, omen takings, and holidays would go on for two weeks, Ursula was delighted. "It looks as if we're in for a riotous time, Namkia."

"It's a lot of fun, my sister."

Before dinner, while Namkia went to tell the others about his trip to Calcutta, Ursula took a bath. She was standing in the tin bath, baling water over herself, when she heard raised voices in the servants' quarters. She hastily dried and dressed and hurried to the cookhouse where she found Ali waving a large knife at Namkia.

"Can't I have a bath in peace? What is going on here?" she demanded.

"I am tired of Namkia bossing me about. It was quiet, while he was away. Now he is back. He's not the only one who has been to Calcutta. I have . . ."

"Enough! Both of you, enough! I'll not have my return disturbed like this. Ali, is my food ready? I want to eat. Namkia, you eat too. We'll go to the village afterwards."

Namkia and Ali glared at each other before turning away. Ursula stomped back to her basha.

After dinner, Ursula and Namkia went to the elderly priest's house.

"The miss-sahib has bought a shotgun to protect us from big cats and to go hunting. I have explained that Nagas cannot eat meat killed by women."

The old man's white hair stood out in the dim interior. "She wishes to go hunting game to eat?"

"Yes, for herself, her staff and even the village, if it is permitted."

The priest addressed Ursula. "My daughter, it is taboo for a Zemi to eat game killed by a woman. It cannot be allowed."

"I understand, my father."

"The miss-sahib wants to know if she can watch the ceremony of Hkakngi."

"My daughter, I will talk to the other headmen, so you can watch the village ceremonies and the stone-dragging.

Ursula, in her faltering Zemi, aided by Namkia, pressed the old man to tell her about the rituals and the underlying beliefs.

"We believe in an after-life, but the dead are reluctant to leave their old homes. They stay there until forced to leave. When someone dies, food and drink are set out for the spirit at every meal, until the priest performs a ceremony of separation. Sometimes, on feast days, large bowls of soapsuds, made from pounded soap creeper, are put out so the spirit can bathe and join in the celebrations with the living. The final parting comes at Hkakngi. Everything the dead will need in the next world—gourds, clothes, tools, seeds, anything not provided at the time of burial—must be provided now." The old man took a sip of rice-beer and continued. "The priest goes to the top of the village and completes his ritual. Afterwards, he walks down the street, calling to the spirits to take their belongings and go. When all the spirits have left the village through the lower gateway and taken the road to the land of the dead, the priest shuts the gate, leaving the village empty of all but the living."

"And I will be allowed to see this?" asked Ursula.

"Yes, I have said that this is so."

Ursula and Namkia left the priest's home. He walked back to the camp with her, and then went to his quarters where he joined some friends from Impoi who had brought two gallons of rice-beer. When he did not turn up for bodyguard duty at the usual hour, Ursula didn't call for him or her hot-water bottle; she was certain he would be too drunk to fill it without scalding himself.

She crawled between the chilly sheets at 9 p.m. However, every time she was about to fall asleep, her toes felt too cold, or she thought she heard Namkia enter the basha, or she heard raucous laughter from the men's quarters. She lay for a long time, wondering whether it was better to go out in a howling gale and tell them to shut up or to stay where she was and try to sleep regardless. At 10:30, deciding they were going to make a night of it, she tumbled out of bed, barred all the doors and windows then leapt beneath the still-warm covers. She was just falling asleep when someone tried the front door.

"Who's that?" she yelled.

A meek voice replied, "It's me."

"What do you want?"

"I've come to sleep." The plaintive voice was slurred.

Ursula gave a huge sigh and climbed out of bed.

"I could ring your ruddy neck for getting me out of my warm bed. You're so bloody inconsiderate. Why don't you get your bloody self here sober and on bloody time!"

She hurried back under the covers. For a long time Namkia stayed outside on the veranda, long enough for Ursula to begin to calm down, relax and slide back to sleep. Only then did he fetch his bedding, come in and lie down in his usual corner. Several lamentable sniffs later, he launched into a well-oiled monologue addressed to Ursula's back.

"I was only late, and I wasn't the only one drunk, and we didn't talk any bad talk."

Ursula immediately wondered what "bad talk" he could have meant.

Namkia continued. "So why is the Presence, not to say my elder sister, so displeased with me?"

The Presence, with her knees curled round her ears trying to keep warm and go to sleep, swore into the pillow.

"All the others were much drunker than me, and they'd all gone home, and no one minded that they were drunk."

Ursula, roused from lovely unconsciousness, said, "Oh, I'm the Presence, am I? Thank you very much! Namkia, shut up! You're still drunk."

Namkia's voice filled with pride. "Presence, I *am* drunk, and I think the Presence had better get a good man to sleep here. I am a very loopy person."

By then it was one o'clock in the morning. Ursula had had enough. She sat up in a fury, bringing loud squeaks to the camp bed.

"Namkia, bloody well shut up! If you don't, I'll use my new shotgun on you!"

Her outburst was met with silence. She settled down again, tugging the blankets over her ears to warm up.

Ten minutes later, Namkia responded, "There's no need to shout. Why do I have to have such a bad tempered sister? I'm only a little drunk."

There was a protracted silence in the basha, broken ultimately by Namkia's contented snores.

*   *   *

The next afternoon and evening, Ursula and Namkia went hunting. They strolled around the jungle where Ursula bagged six doves. She had been hoping for bigger things, but she and Ali would enjoy the tasty treats, and the extra meat would supplement the rations.

As they walked, Namkia pointed out the large stone, three quarters of a mile above Laisong. "We'll move it to the village at the beginning of the festivities to finish the graves of this year's dead. We do this every year."

"It's huge. How do you manage to move stones that size?" Here, she thought, would follow a valuable lesson in the ingenuity of native construction with the bonus of some clues as to how the stones for Stonehenge had been moved. Her reputation would be made at once.

"We carry them uphill and drag them down."

Oh, she thought, nothing magical about that; all done by hard work and muscle power.

"Yes, but how?"

"To move a stone up a slope, we lash strong poles together to make a framework round the stone. Then all the men surround it. They lift the stone and carry it on their shoulders like a litter. To bring a stone down a slope, or along level ground, we lever it onto a sledge made from a forked tree-trunk, and then gangs of men drag it along."

"It sounds dangerous."

"It is. See where the track bends? In the high grass? That ground is 'bad'. Two men have died there during the stone dragging. The first was a young lad out hunting with his friends. It was very hot, and he was bored with the hunt, so he lay down to sleep in the shade of a large flat table-rock, a little way up the hill. In the forest above the rock, the hunt startled a sambhur. It bolted down the hill chased by the men and dogs, jumped clear over the flat rock and landed on the boy. He was killed."

183

"Oh, how sad! What happened to the second man?"

"All the men from the village, with reinforcements from the other villages, were dragging in a large stone. The last man on the rope slipped and fell in front of the sledge. They tried to stop the team of men but they couldn't be heard because of the chanting. The sledge went down over the man, and he died. So they destroyed the stone."

"How on earth did they do that?"

"They cut the lashings and pushed the rock down the slope. Then they piled brushwood over it and logs and dry wood, in a big pile and set fire to it. They kept stoking it till the stone was red-hot and let it burn for a day. Then they carried water from the stream and poured it on the hot stone. The cold water made the stone crack and split into small pieces. Look," he pointed down the slope, "you can see them in the grass."

Ursula peered down the slope and made out the fragments almost hidden by the grass, all that remained of a great stone destroyed as punishment for taking a man's life.

"You will take care tomorrow, won't you, Namkia?"

"I've dragged stones many times, my sister."

At twilight, they returned to the village. The street bustled with activity as field-parties returned with vegetable-filled baskets, and spear-carrying youths, back from their travels, congregated in the *morungs*. Blue smoke drifted upwards from each thatched roof, forming a haze over the village in the still air. A sense of comforting permanence surged through Ursula as she walked down the street into the scene.

*   *   *

After much scrimping and penny pinching, Ursula had managed to save enough to buy a small mithan for Christmas. Haichangnang brought it from Tolpin. Ali killed the beast at the water point and left it for the village blacksmith to cut up. Ursula was about to go and supervise the butchering when Degalang ran to Ursula's bungalow.

"Come, Mother. Come see Lassu. She is pupping."

"Oh, how wonderful," Ursula said and rushed to see. Within ten minutes, Lassu was nuzzling and licking clean three black and white puppies and being very maternal for a first-time mother.

"Take good care of them, Degalang. I'll be back soon."

She and Ali hurried to the water point, her footsteps faltering when she saw the state of the carcass hacked to pieces by machete and axe. Butchered in true Naga fashion, she thought with dismay. So much for the hide I'd planned as a bedside rug and all the steaks, sirloins, and joints I was expecting.

Ali and Ursula charily picked through the mound of bleeding chunks of meat each weighing about one pound. Ali held up a piece.

"Oh, Ali, it takes some imagination to see that as a roast."

"It is the best piece here, miss-sahib."

"It looks like it, more's the pity. So be it. Christmas dinner is salvaged."

On Christmas morning, Ali went to Ursula's bungalow. He was sweating, and his face was flushed. Apologetically, he told Ursula, "I am sick, miss-sahib. I have a fever. I cannot cook today. But do not worry. You need not spoil your holiday by cooking. Ramgakpa knows what to do."

Ursula gave Ali some quinine and sent him to his quarters to recover. She spent the day playing with the puppies, throwing sticks with Khamba and reading Tolstoy. In the evening, Namkia swept into Ursula's living room. With a flourish, he presented the tray holding her Christmas dinner. Ursula stared in disbelief. Something resembling wet, brown string clung, in two or three places, to the soggy bone: her poor joint, boiled to death. Namkia saw her disappointment.

"Last time Ramgakpa cooks for you, my sister?"

"Some Christmas dinner this is. I think I'll open a tin of tongue."

*   *   *

The day arrived for moving the big stone down to Laisong. Ursula stood with Namkia and the priest, looking at the difficult terrain over which the men must bring the stone. Her staff, followed by Namkia and the priest, walked along the path which had been cut out to it. Ursula brought up the rear. She struggled to reach the stone, clambering over logs and rocks on the forty-five degree incline, slipping backwards on loose rock, rubble, and mud. She carried only her camera and was having real trouble. How would the men manage to bring in the mammoth stone? Eighty or so men were taking part. Ursula feared for all of them.

Late in the morning, she raised her camera as the men took hold of the scaffold and drag ropes, two in front and two behind. The cheerleader stood to one side and started marking time with the heaving chant, a slow "Ho ho hoi!" Men and stone began to move, lurching and straining down the steep slope. The drag-teams leaned back, nearly flat to the ground, digging in their heels like anchormen in a tug-of-war. Ursula held her breath and peeped from behind her cine camera when, with a hair-raising rush, the stone and its carriers engaged in a mad scramble to the bottom, and there, checked by the drag ropes, the stone stopped, swaying to and fro at the entrance to the cleared belt.

The slope was so steep only about twenty men were taking the weight at any one time; the rest could barely stay on their feet. With muscles and sinews straining, the men made precarious progress towards the village, swaying and tottering with the stone, occasionally slipping hell for leather down the slope accompanied by frantic ho—ho—ing.

Three times the hulking stone was too much for the men's efforts. It hung impassively above the mass of men teetering downhill into the jungle in a confusion of frenzied effort.

Three times the men managed to halt the slide. But the last time, there was no checking the stone. The men were swung round and down, while the drag teams scrambled helplessly along the ground. Feet ploughed furrows in the loose, leaf mould unable to find a hold. Men were falling everywhere. A frantic note permeated the ho—ho—ing as they fought to halt the stone. Every man and boy among the spectators ran to the ropes. The old headman threw off his red cloth, tugged Ursula's arm and signalled her to join in. She dropped her camera and hurled herself at the nearest empty place on the right-side rope. The men already there were heaving with all their might, heels in, backs to the ground, but the stone was merciless, pulling them down the slope, scraping and tearing skin from their hands, heels, stomachs. They belayed on a tree and were dragged over it. They belayed again on a stouter tree, hung on, and held. At the same time, the rear team took hold. The stone, bobbing slowly down the hill like a juggernaut, checked and finally halted. The ho—ho—ing increased. The stone lurched up a foot. They took in a fraction on the ropes. The stone moved up inch by inch.

Step by step, they worked the stone upwards on a long slant till it reached the path again only twenty yards from the village. Sweating, straining and panting, the teams swept in with the stone, running under the water pipes in a rush of victory before leaving it at the head of the street. The stone, lashed round with ropes of twisted cane, its scaffolding spread halfway across the street, lay still and gray. Women and girls brought out rice-beer for the jubilant and thirsty men.

"Hard to imagine it was crushing men against trees and dragging them down slopes just a few minutes ago," Ursula said to Namkia.

"It was a good morning's work, my sister."

The elderly priest approached Ursula. "We want you to bring your gramophone to the village to entertain the men after all their hard work."

Ursula was delighted to share her H.M.V. hand-crank gramophone, an extravagant purchase from the Army and Navy Stores in Calcutta. Namkia and Ramgakpa brought the gramophone and her collection of fragile, shellac records from camp and set up shop outside the headman's house. Ursula sat on a small stool surrounded by Nagas, and after setting the speed lever, and cranking the handle, she lowered the heavy arm with its needle. The sound of Scottish bagpipes reverberated round the village. Ursula grabbed Namkia and demonstrated a Scottish reel and a Highland fling accompanied by a few Scottish

yells and "och ayes". This cultural diversification was a huge
success, and the young men leapt into action to reel and fling the
night away. The effects of the rice-beer were apparent
particularly in one old headman sitting directly behind her who
was chuckling heartily and appeared to be senile. The priest
squeezed next to Ursula.

"Namkia tells me you killed a deer two nights ago, my
daughter."

"Yes, I did."

"The headmen have decided that you will be an exception
to the law. It will no longer be taboo for the Zemi to eat the
meat that you provide."

Ursula saw Namkia's eyebrows rise.

"I am honoured, my father."

"You seem surprised, Namkia," Ursula said after the priest
walked away.

"Meat is scarce, my sister, but I cannot believe they changed
the law for you."

"It seems the Zemi are a practical people," she said
playfully.

Two days later, when the graves were completed, it was
Hkakngi, the parting of the dead from the living. At midday,
Ursula went to the village with Namkia. They found the street
deserted; not a child, not a chicken, not a dog was out. They
walked through the village; doors were half-closed; here and
there, Ursula saw a woman's face peering; a few men stood well
back on the house porches hidden behind the wood stacks; the
sun glared down on the scene.

When Namkia and Ursula were halfway along the street,
they heard a long cry from behind the upper *morung*. Namkia
pulled Ursula behind a fence and a large boulder.

"The priests have finished their ceremony at the upper
morung," Namkia said. He lowered his voice. "They are going to
come down the street, calling to the ghosts to go. The living
must withdraw in case their souls are drawn away into the
passing crowd of spirits. When the soul goes, the body dies."

The air was still. The old priest came into sight at the head
of the street. He carried a smouldering brand. His white hair

glistened in the sunshine; his voice rang strong and clear in the silence.

"Oh all you dead! Go to your own place and leave the living here. Oh all you dead! It is time to part. Let the living remain, and let the dead go!"

Ursula shivered as a chill passed over, and her hair stood on end. She would have sworn she felt the souls, summoned by the priest's forlorn cries, go by. Across the street, she could see the earth red and raw over the new gravestone. As the old man passed by, the cold intensified, and Ursula hugged herself, despite the bright sun.

The priest turned the corner by the lower *morung*. From behind it, his voice carried back: "Oh all you dead! Go to your own place . . ."

Then silence. Nobody moved until the priest returned five minutes later, proclaiming, "The dead have gone to their own place! The dead have separated from the living!"

His words released the tense spell, which had been cast over the village. Doors opened, householders kicked out squealing pigs, men laughed and talked, and all through the village, life and movement came flowing back.

That evening, Namkia sat with Ursula by her fire. He explained what would happen during the next morning's pig chase. "The staff will go to the village early in the morning ready for when the pigs are shooed out of doors to the catchers waiting near the house." He chuckled. "Some of the bigger boars will be filled with rice-beer first to liven up the chase. The man who catches the biggest pig wins the contest, and the priest takes his kilt."

"Why would he do that?"

"The belief is that anyone so gifted by nature can spare his ornaments for those less fortunate."

"Hmm, doesn't seem like much of a prize, rather the opposite."

"You do not understand prizes, my sister."

The staff left camp before sun-up. By eight o'clock, Ursula was wondering if any of the men would return anytime soon, and when, if ever, she would get some breakfast. A small boy appeared with a message. "Ramgakpa caught the big pig. The priest took his kilt, and now Ramgakpa is the lower *morung*. He cannot report for duty until you send him something to come home in. He says a cleaning cloth will do."

Ursula called Ali, who found a spare kilt, and ten minutes later, Ramgakpa was running past Ursula's basha, flashing an embarrassed smile her way.

Ramgakpa's long absence and the return of the others drunk upset the unstable cook. All morning his shrill shouting at Ramgakpa carried across the compound to Ursula's bungalow. She sympathized with Ali, for Namkia drunk was a force to be reckoned with. The cook, whose religion forbade him alcohol, was the usual recipient of Namkia's drunken rage, which built up to such a crescendo of abuse and insults that Ursula was sure murder would someday be the outcome. Either the cook would take a knife to Namkia or Namkia a machete to the cook. Even so, it was all right as long as the cook remained quiet; for Namkia would eventually rant himself to a standstill, or drop off to sleep, and in the morning indignantly deny his obnoxious behaviour of the night before.

At ten o'clock, a sudden commotion on the slope brought Ursula and her staff running. The men of both *morungs* were embroiled in a fight, which, Ursula learned later, started over a squabble during the pig chase. The two original combatants were in the middle of the free-for-all, each pulling at the other's hair until they were almost on the ground. Friends of the fighters were kicking, struggling, and punching, and every boy in the village joined in this war of fists, bites, nails and kicks. Around the edge of this mêlée, the village elders were hopping and jumping, screeching at the tops of their voices and waving their scrawny arms, not in any attempt to stop the riot but to shriek abuse at the enemy and encourage their respective sons and grandsons.

Ursula looked on shocked and helpless.

A body of women, armed with clubs, came running down the street. Ali, who had tiptoed out barefoot, took one look, screamed in fright, and ran, stumbling in his skirt-like *lungyi*, back to the cookhouse where he collapsed sobbing in Ramgakpa's arms. Wielding their clubs, the women charged into the brawl, grabbed sons and husbands and drove them out with cuffs and clouts to cool off at home.

The old men turned away, grumbling that the women had cut short their sport. Finally, the last of the commotion died down, and Ursula, impressed by the robust way the women dealt with the fracas, returned to her veranda to read her book. She turned three pages before realizing she was unable to follow the tale, her mind still marvelling at the Nagas' hot-headed, volatile nature.

By late afternoon, Namkia was in the village and fighting drunk. Ursula prayed he would stay there. The cook's nerves were in tatters. He screamed at Ramgakpa and slapped him for some trivial annoyance. Ramgakpa had had enough. He slapped Ali back, and leaving him weeping in the cookhouse, dismissed himself from Ursula's service before running off to the village to get drunk with Namkia. The camp was deserted except for Ursula and the cook, who, sniffing miserably, served Ursula's dinner. As night fell, Ursula left Ali to have any hysterics he cared to have. She brought Khamba, Lassu, and the basket holding the pups into her basha for company and barred the door. Kneeling beside Lassu and stroking the puppies, Ursula put her arm round Khamba sitting beside her and declared, "Well, Khamba, I know what my New Year's resolution's going to be. From now on I'm going to celebrate all future Hgangis in civilization."

Ursula was lying in bed, her arms behind her head, watching the approach of dawn bringing light to her bedroom. Loose straws hanging down from the veranda thatch stirred in the gentle breeze. Soon she would hear Namkia open the door followed by his careful footsteps on the bamboo matting as he brought her customary cup of tea. She stretched lazily like a cat, her back arched when she heard cries erupting from the village, blood-chilling in their savagery. Khamba and Lassu snapped up, growling warily. Ursula hurtled to the window, wrenched open the shutters and looked out. Everything was still and quiet. The village was in shadow, and seemed to be waiting in the morning chill for the arrival of warming sunlight, which shone in a yellow wave sliding slowly down the hill behind. Ursula saw Hazekiemba trudging along the narrow path from the water point accompanied by her new gardener Paodekumba, a fuzzy-haired, tough-as-nails, little man with rock-hard muscles. Ursula called to them through the window.

"What's all the shouting about?"

"Boy and girl talk!" Hazekiemba said without slowing. "Boy and girl talk!"

He and Paodekumba marched round the back of the house.

"What in blazes does that mean? And what's it got to do with those terrible cries?"

Ursula threw on her clothes and went looking for Namkia. As she walked to the cookhouse, more cries rent the morning air; their echoes like shock waves lingered.

Ursula found Namkia talking with Hazekiemba.

"Namkia, what is going on in the village?"

Namkia looked sombre.

"My sister, it is not good. Samrangba got drunk, went to the girls' dormitory and tried to rape a girl."

"Samrangba did that! I can't believe it!"

"She's a pretty girl from a good family. He tried to court her, and everyone knows he would rather have had her than the girl he married. But she didn't like him, refused all his advances, and besides, her family thought he wasn't good enough for her. And now he's tried to rape her. I never did like him. Rape is one of the most serious crimes."

Ursula was shocked and frightened. She had never experienced Nagas roused for blood. The sound had terrified her, and she was greatly relieved that, having sacked him a week earlier, Samrangba was no longer a member of her compound.

*   *   *

Too afraid to go near the village, Ursula and her staff kept going to the camp entrance to check what was happening. A mob of riled up men, relatives of the attacked girl, poured from her house and spent the morning roaming through Laisong, screaming for blood, stabbing the ground and shaking their spears. Unable to find the perpetrator, and filled with bloodlust, they raced shrieking and howling to Samrangba's mother's house and tried to break in. They would have killed Samrangba's younger brother but for the arrival of the village headmen, who ordered them to the hurriedly called council meeting, which drew away all but the most blood-crazed madmen.

The council had to act fast to prevent the destruction of the community. Samrangba's crime had caused a huge rift in the village. Bloodshed and the resulting blood feud must be prevented at all costs. The decision was made. Samrangba was the wrongdoer. He must leave the village. Since his own family dare not appear, his wife's family pleaded for stay of sentence, at least until after his wife gave birth to the baby she carried. But the headmen were resolute. Samrangba's offence was heinous. He must go into exile.

*   *   *

Despite Namkia's reassurances that all would be well, Ursula was upset, worrying that something terrible would happen to Samrangba. She and her staff watched the village from the camp. Just before noon, they saw a long line of non-partisans, recruited as village police to give escort, descending the steep street with Samrangba's mother, brother, and wife in their midst. As they stopped outside the bottom house, the last screams of the thwarted killers came from the area of the upper *morung*. When Samrangba appeared, Ursula could tell from his hunched shoulders and hanging head that he was abject, tortured by shame, and in despair. He moved into line. The escort closed up and set off.

"Taking him to Kepelo," Namkia informed Ursula. "They take exiles that no respectable village will accept."

Samrangba's wife and mother were weighed down with pots and clothing, while his young brother, who had come close to being killed, Ursula was told, stared with wide eyes, still apparently, in shock.

Samrangba's uncle stood beside Ursula, who, with her staff, had assembled near the path to see them go. Tears streamed down the old man's crinkled face. Guards and family filed past, descending to the lower gate. Seeing Ursula, Samrangba slowed as if to speak, but when an escort pushed his shoulder to move him on, he did not resist. They disappeared from view down the steep path. The women's cries faded in the distance.

The village court met the following day. Its verdict, banishing Samrangba from living in the village for two years, calmed the hotheads. Later that day, Samrangba astonished Ursula by strolling into camp to see Namkia. As he left, Samrangba smiled and waved. As soon as he had gone, Ursula called Namkia.

"Isn't it risky, Samrangba's being here? Will he be safe? What did he want?"

"Oh, he is safe now the council has made their ruling. He came back for his belongings. He knows he can't be touched."

Namkia looked at Ursula sitting open-mouthed at the sudden turnaround of events.

As if she were a naïve child and he the parent, he said, "It's the Naga way, my sister."

Many times during the spring, Ursula dragged a grumbling Namkia on tours of exploration to ruined villages of the Siemi, a tribe wiped out by the Kachari long before the Nagas settled in the region. Throughout the Barail, the ruins lay out of sight behind ridges and in concealed ravines.

These villages had been built with many defences: multiple ditches, banks, and dry-stone walls. There was one in the Jiri valley, two miles south of Nenglo. But the largest and most notable sites were around Asalu.

Ursula learned of the ruins one evening while talking to Namkia about the beads that he and every Zemi of standing wore. These were strings of old, amber-coloured "spirit beads".

"You're telling me these beads are highly prized?" queried Ursula, rolling his beads between her fingers and thumb. She noted their high gloss, polished from rubbing against his skin and its oils. She brought out her magnifying glass for a closer look. "They look like stone, but . . . my goodness! They're made of glass!"

"No one knows for sure where they came from, but the Zemi believe the Siemi made the beads by a secret magical way using fire and gareo bamboo."

"A secret process? And no one knows how to make more?"

"No one. They're handed down from father to son. They are . . .," Namkia struggled to find the correct word.

"Heirlooms?" Ursula offered.

"Yes, heirlooms. The Siemi put the beads in their graves as part of the grave-furniture. Legend has it that the Nagas found the beads in a hole in the ground made when tree roots pushed up a gravestone."

"Do you know where we can find some Siemi ruined villages to explore?"

"It's foolish to go among the ruins. They're in dangerous places and overgrown by the jungle."

"Namkia, I'm here to do such work. I have to study these places, take photographs, and write about them for the professors in England. We'll start on Monday. We'll need to do it before the rains come in May."

Namkia rose to leave Ursula's bungalow. His face said it all, exasperation and resignation at doing his stubborn-as-a-mule, not-in-her-right-mind employer's wishes. He muttered such thoughts as he left. Ursula, amused she was able to infuriate him so easily, smothered her laughter until he was outside.

Several days later, Namkia led Ursula up a steep, thickly wooded slope south of Asalu. At the top, they stumbled upon mounds, ditches and stone walls, a stronghold bound up in jungle creepers and crumbling under the onslaught of cane thickets.

Excited, Ursula urged Namkia to join her in scaling the outer walls. Once inside, she began to crawl through thorns and bushes. Namkia held back.

"Come on, Namkia! Let's see what's hidden here."

He followed, sighing and muttering, "You've got a screw loose putting us through this to look at these useless ruins."

"Oh Namkia, don't be an old woman. This is exciting!" Ursula said, scrambling over fallen masonry.

"Just what I need, crawling through the jungle with a pig-headed, loony woman."

They slipped and crabbed and slithered across a steep, grassy slope. Ursula lost her footing and would have slid away but for Namkia's quick reaction. He grabbed her blouse and held tight until she found her footing. Such mishaps didn't worry her; she was in her element. This was the biggest Siemi settlement around; at least two hundred houses had existed here, although all that remained were some stone facings to the house platforms. Ursula was thrilled to think she was probably the first European to visit the site.

It did not take her long to realize that wherever they saw massive clumps of gareo bamboo, a Siemi site would probably be nearby. She and Namkia travelled the district for weeks, looking for such sites. One village was divided by a man-made, twenty-foot gully. None of the Nagas living in the area could explain why it was there. In another settlement a long, stone-lined passage cut through the village. Again no one knew why.

Over rice-beer in Asalu, Ursula heard the story of how the Kachari tortured the Siemi to obtain the secret of making the beads. The storyteller was old, crumpled and scarred by deep wrinkles. He had goat-like shaggy eyebrows and patchy white hair.

"The Kachari living in Maibong saw the smoky haze from the Siemi fires as they made their beads," he told her. "The Kachari king sent men into the unknown hills to see what was burning. They returned with a group of captured Siemi. He demanded to know who they were. They told him they were jungle people, that they did not earn a living by digging or cultivation but from making and trading the yellow beads. The king insisted they tell him how they made the beads. The Siemi refused.

"In a fury, the king ordered a metal pot to be made red-hot. He had it put on the head of one of the captives and kept it there until the man's skull burst. Then he turned to the others and warned them that if they did not tell, a similar fate awaited them. The Siemi were not afraid. Each man shouted that he wanted to be next to be tortured. And so, one after the other, they died a horrible death without revealing the secret. He sent men to hunt down the jungle folk and tortured all he could find, but the Siemi preferred to die rather than reveal the process. The remaining Siemi moved deeper into the jungle to hiding places safe from the Kachari, taking their secret with them, and then they were no more."

At Padhekot, site of a Siemi settlement, Namkia bought some beads from a Kuki who said he found them one by one, as he cultivated the soil covering parts of the ancient settlement. Namkia offered to sell them to Ursula. She made some quick mental calculations trying to work a fiscal miracle in order to buy the beads for a museum collection, but had to tell Namkia, "I haven't got forty rupees to spare right now. I'd like to buy them, Namkia, but I'm broke."

Two weeks later, Ursula was dismayed to see Namkia sell the beads to a Hangrum man.

Perched on the open spur, with grassy cliffs below and an open valley in front, the camp appeared to be perfectly situated—or so Ursula thought.

She was working alongside Paodekumba and Namkia in the garden, picking six-inch-long, green caterpillars off the spinach, when they heard Laisong's drums beating the emergency signal to call the men back from the fields.

"Namkia, what's going on?"

Namkia trotted to the path leading to the village, then went and looked at the fields. When he returned, he told her it was a fire alarm. "A grass fire. The brush is dry and the winds strong. They happen every spring. It can be very dangerous."

Ursula looked down the valley. The Laisong men were cutting firebreaks in the ravine; women and girls were hurrying there with water; old men scurried about removing valuables and livestock from the village. The villagers spent the whole afternoon in frantic activity, but by evening, village life had returned to normal.

Ursula and Namkia sought out the headman. "You have a swift response to the fire alarm," Ursula said.

The headman agreed and pointed out that it was not uncommon to see the villagers' possessions packed in *jappas* in a safe place, while the risk of fire was high.

"Is my camp on the spur safe from fires?"

"Oh, no," the headman said, cheerfully. "Flames go sweeping right over it every year."

Ursula looked at Namkia in consternation. "We'll start making preparations first thing in the morning, Namkia."

*   *   *

They stood at the cliff edge after walking the camp perimeter. "We'll cut a firebreak, my sister," Namkia said, "but we can only cut the upper thirty yards of grass and scrub, the rest is too steep for a man to stand and work."

"Let's cut as far as we can, then we'll see what to do next."

After lunch, Ursula consulted with Namkia and her staff who had spent the morning clearing the slope at the cliff top. They decided the only thing to do was burn off the cliff. They would start at sunset when the wind died down, and the men from the village could help.

Late afternoon, Ursula and her staff carried water into camp and soaked piles of sacks. They were prepared as darkness approached. Twenty men from the village came to help. Two men climbed onto the bungalow roof ready to beat out sparks with wet sacks. Three straddled the roofs of the men's quarters. Most of the men were assembled along the cliff top with fire-brooms. Hazekiemba, the caretaker, and his two sons took charge of the water supply, filling buckets, bamboo tubes and Ursula's tin bath at the water point.

The wind dropped. All was still. Haichangnang ran down to the foot of the hill and set fire to the scrub.

Ursula and the men in camp waited. At first, nothing, then minutes later, the air in front of them began to quiver. Tendrils of smoke spiralled. Specks of ash and leaves whorled into view, eddying and dancing upwards. A thin veil of smoke blotted out the hills beyond. There was a sound like the earth itself making a deep sigh. The smoke increased.

"It's coming," Namkia said calmly, sure that all their preparations were adequate.

With a startling boom, a breathtaking shock wave blasted upwards, created by the draught of the one hundred-foot cliff. A wall of flames zoomed up, filled the sky. Ursula gasped for breath as if the air had been sucked from her. She saw the men in the firebreak run to safety, black specks against the vermilion blaze. Namkia grabbed Ursula's arm and spun her round to face the bungalow. Bathed by the flames, it glowed hellishly. Incandescent sparks fell like raindrops onto the dry thatch. The men on the roof swatted and smacked at the thatch with wet sacks. Five seconds later, Ursula and Namkia saw a towering flame arc twenty feet over their heads, reaching for the bungalow. Khamba, Lassu and their pups were yowling in a chorus of panic.

"The house!" Namkia shouted.

Ursula could barely hear him over the roar of the flames. "There isn't a chance. We've got to get the dogs and the kit out!" she cried.

They raced inside. The scene—lamps lit, table laid for dinner as usual—was completely at odds with the frantic activity outside. They tossed books, clothes, cameras, papers and bedding into baskets and boxes. Ramzimba, the caretaker's eldest son, dashed in after them. Grabbing each box and bale thrown to him, he rushed them to the dump in the wet scrub behind the house. Chairs, beds and tables were pitched outside through doors and windows. Ursula and Namkia went onto the veranda. Ramzimba darted out past them, carrying Namkia's spears then returned for the dogs.

Despite the danger and being on the verge of losing the camp, Ursula marvelled at the raging fire. It was a phenomenal sight. She was used to looking out from the veranda to the starry night sky and the dark void of the valley in the evenings. All she could see now between the rail and the eaves was a searing, dazzling mass of flames, roaring upwards for forty feet. Sparks and burning leaves showered the veranda matting. Ursula, and Namkia in his bare feet, stamped and stamped. A man appeared with wet sacks, and handing one to Namkia, began beating the floor. Seeing that the men had the situation on the veranda under control, Ursula ran out the back door to see what was happening in the men's quarters.

On the roofs, silhouetted figures, their chests heaving, were beating out flames. On the ground, dark figures scurried about carrying belongings to safety, lugging water, or slinging wet sacks to the men above. The wind caught the tongues of flames rolling above their heads and fanned it onto the men's quarters. Men leapt from the roof. In seconds, flames transformed the basha into a swirling red shower of fiery debris.

The men on the roofs, pouring water onto the thatch to keep it wet, started yelling, "The water's run out. The roofs are dry. We need water!" Ursula heard them. Seeing flames flaring above their heads, she rushed to the nearest men on the ground, grabbed them, pointed to the flames then pushed them towards the water point shouting, "Water! Water!" Namkia did the same. Men rushed to the roofs with water.

Ursula looked back to check her bungalow was safe and saw a spark fall onto the thatch above the back porch. A flame shot up.

"Not my house!" cried Ursula.

Ali was the only man near enough and, more crucially, tall enough to reach the flame. He gripped the edge of the thatch and jumped up, extinguishing the flame with a few smacks with the flat of his hand. Ursula ran over as he tumbled to the ground and helped the lanky cook to his feet.

"Thank you, Ali. You saved my house!" But he was overwrought and, as usual, close to tears. "For pity's sake, don't cry! Go and sit on the baggage and watch."

The sheet of flames suddenly fell fifteen feet lower. The few remaining sparks blew outwards, away from the camp onto uncut jungle. The men on the roofs flopped, exhausted. The men on the ground sank to their knees among the sacks and buckets and stared at the receding fire.

Then the flames found a patch of dry elephant grass. It crackled. Flames shot up in a churning column. A breath of wind blew flames towards the hen-house. Above the roar of the fire, Ursula heard the geese honking frantically. She ran down the narrow passage at the foot of the garden, calling over her shoulder, "Help me! The hen-house!" Flames flared overhead. Sparks landed in her hair. She beat at them with her hands and dived into the old shed that acted as the hen-house. Two geese flapped there in terror. They scurried under a bench, and as Ursula reached in to grab the gander, she was aware someone had followed her. The goose flew out from under the bench and was snatched up by her unknown helper, who ran outside in the midst of scattering chickens. Ursula tucked the more docile gander under her arm and took off, beating with her free hand at the sparks landing on her hair and shirt.

In the passage ahead of her, Ursula saw Ali running as fast as his tight *lungyi* would allow. He clutched the goose to his chest; her large wings were loose and flapped with fright.

They threw the geese into the cookhouse then, realizing there was nothing else they could do, sat to watch the hen-house catch fire. Flames swooped onto the hen-house, and the instant it should have caught, the flames twisted away, fell and died down, leaving only a dull glow at the bottom of the slope where the last of the fire was burning out in the jungle.

The barking dogs fell silent.

The Laisong men returned to their homes. With their quarters gone up in smoke, the staff went to the lower *morung* to sleep. Ali would sleep in the cookhouse.

"We will have to build new bashas," Namkia said.

Ursula nodded. "Yes, we will,"

They stood in silence surveying the ruins.

"It could have been much worse, Namkia. It's a miracle no one was hurt. Thank goodness most of the camp is still standing."

"Were you frightened, my sister?"

"Yes, I was," she said quietly. "Our scheme to protect us from fire almost burned us alive. What if someone had died?"

It was a thought she couldn't support.

While the men's quarters were being rebuilt, Ursula made as many tours of the neighbouring villages as she could before the rains began. They swept in the first week of May, bringing a heavy mist that hid Nenglo on the hill opposite for months. For long weeks, the monsoon battered Ursula's bungalow on its exposed site, making it impossible to open the front doors. Dampness invaded the house, coating everything—books, clothes, furniture—with green mold. She spent her days sitting under the windows, which provided enough light to read and write despite the dismal grayness of the rainy days.

Ursula decided she now had time to record Naga folklore. She had already heard Namkia's stockpile of stories and three interesting animal-tales from one of Laisong's junior headmen. On a visit to Hangrum, she collected a tale of traditional Zemi life, and that had exhausted all sources of folklore in the Laisong locality.

"I know a storyteller in Impoi. I'll bring him here," Namkia said.

The storyteller duly arrived. Like most of his ilk, he was old and, Namkia said, lazy and poor, but one of the best storytellers he knew.

Ursula wanted to write down the Asa-Munsarung cycle, a collection of connected stories about two characters frequently found in Naga tales, the cunning trickster and his simple friend.

"Do you know these stories?" asked Ursula.

"I know all of them," the storyteller replied.

Ursula looked at Namkia with gratitude. "Then let's begin," she said.

The old man sat down by the hearth. Every afternoon and evening, for twenty-one days, he recounted the tales. His storytelling skills were outstanding: the voice inflections, the use of rhythm and repetition and acting skills to recreate his narratives. He spoke so clearly, Ursula understood his words and was able to type as he talked. Gratified with her growing collection of Naga folklore, she paid the storyteller handsomely with an extra bonus of tea when his work ended.

*   *   *

Life in a semi-tropical climate usually leads to encounters with snakes. Ursula was no exception. The most spectacular examples were almost neighbours. A few yards from the path to Laisong, two highly poisonous hamadryads nested in the bamboo at the foot of the hill. When it was nesting season, the villagers erected a rail and put up a knot of grass to warn passers-by not to wander from the path. There seemed to be a mutual agreement; they would not bother the snakes, and the snakes would not bother the humans.

However, there were the snakes that periodically fell from the bungalow's rafters to jolt her with revulsion, or hid in holes and corners during the hot season to startle her. Fortunately, for the most part, the snakes were not poisonous and easily swept outside.

Ursula discovered the Nagas had a fear and respect for pythons. Namkia told her how, as a young man along with others from the *morung*, he had helped carry one into the village. It was a special honour to do this. The young men slung the python over their shoulders and took it to the *morung*, chanting a special song to alert the villagers. On the way, they drew the snake across a patch of soft earth, which they examined the next day to know their fortune. Once in the *morung*, they allowed the snake to slide freely around while the elders read the markings on its skin and foretold the future. The men then beheaded the snake, cut off its tail, and stripped off its skin—an unsheathing that was difficult, Namkia said, and ugly. They hung up its skin in the *morung* as a trophy. But they did not eat its meat for only the elders are permitted to do this.

206

When there were breaks in the weather, Ursula worked in her garden. The men loved flowers for their ears, so she grew scarlet and yellow cannas for her staff, and pink, white and flame-colours for her own pleasure, with a front row of zinnias and white verbena.

Each afternoon, the men finished work at four o'clock. They bathed, dressed in their finery then strolled along the bed picking flowers, matching and mixing scarlet and yellow with a touch of white to set the whole bouquet off. Once satisfied with the final selection, the men inserted the posy, with much squeezing, stretching and face pulling, into their distended earlobes.

One day, Ursula was pulling dead blooms off the zinnias, a job Paodekumba never bothered to do. A leaf twitched. There was a ripple near her hand. She leapt away and shouted for Namkia. Armed with a hoe, he ran over. Ursula backed up to the bungalow wall while Namkia tiptoed towards the spot where she had been working. They both saw the snake, a large pit viper, curled in a circle on itself, head raised, in a clump of zinnias. Namkia raised the hoe. Ursula held her breath. Down came the hoe with a thwack. Leaves and petals exploded. Namkia swung for a second strike, and Ursula saw the wounded, writhing snake, stuck to the hoe's blade, lifted high in the air.

She winced, and as if that were a cue, the snake flew free and hurtled through the air straight for her face. Jerked into action, she squealed, ducked, dodged right, and the viper smacked into the wall by her shoulder, ten inches from her face. With her eyes squeezed shut, she heard it fall to the ground by her heels with a thump. She leapt away. The snake was alive, cleaved almost in two but moving in muscular spasms while blood spurted from its wounds. Fighting to find her breath again, Ursula gingerly moved away to the step and sat down. Namkia strolled over with his hoe and finished the snake then sat beside her.

"That could have been very interesting," he said.

"Interesting?"

"Yes. If it had hit you and bitten you, it would have been a very unusual accident," he said, with self-satisfaction.

"No need to sound so pleased that you almost caused it!"

"But it would have been unusual, wouldn't it?"

Ursula relaxed. "Yes it would."

What was interesting, of course, was Namkia's set of priorities. Immured as he was to the wild and its predictable threats, the peculiarity of this event struck him more deeply than Ursula's fate. But then, Ursula was well and fine.

They sat on the step while she regained her composure. Looking up, she saw Haichangnang among the garden peas. He loved them and was forever begging a few as a treat. Watching him move along the pea-sticks, Ursula became puzzled by his behaviour and went to see what he was up to. She found him systematically killing the bees crawling on the flowers.

"Oh no, Haichangnang. Stop that!" she cried.

Wounded by her sharp words, Haichangnang told her in a hurt tone, "I am killing the flies that are spoiling the peas, because I like peas, you see."

Ursula, still shaken from the flying viper, took a deep breath to steady herself. She reminded herself to be patient with Haichangnang; he was, after all, simple-minded.

She beckoned Namkia to come over. "Namkia, Haichangnang is killing the bees. Will you explain things to him?"

Namkia drew Haichangnang away to the end of the garden. Ursula stood with her arms wrapped round herself, watching as Namkia slowly spelled out in simple words why there would be no peas for Haichangnang to eat if it were not for the bees. There was a long silence. Haichangnang's eyes blinked repeatedly, he frowned and bit his lip as his mind struggled to grasp Namkia's explanation. Then his mouth fell open; his brow smoothed; he gave a radiant smile, and looked first at Namkia and then the peas. "Oh!" he said, his eyes sparkling with wonder.

*   *   *

During her early travels among the Nagas, Ursula learned that the best way of winning their confidence was to hold dispensaries, and so she had started a dispensary at the camp upon arriving in Laisong. At first, the Nagas only came after a cut had become infected, days, even weeks, after the injury. Eventually, they realized the wisest course of action was first aid at the time of an accident, and it became a normal part of Ursula's day to attend to men who arrived, out of breath and dripping blood on the veranda. With wounds dressed, they left happily, running back to the fields which could be as far as a mile away. She also dispensed copious amounts of quinine for malaria, which was rampant. For all other illnesses, however, they preferred their own magical healing ceremonies.

Ursula never dreamed that one day she might have need of these services, but after an afternoon spent weeding the spinach patch with Paodekumba, Ursula straightened to stretch her back. Something clicked; she buckled; and suddenly, Ursula was in agony with a slipped kneecap.

"Namkia, help me to the veranda," she called.

"Your knee is swelling," he said. "Yes, blowing up like a balloon."

Ursula sat in her chair. "Damn! It hurts like the devil. Bring me an elastic plaster, will you?"

Namkia brought one, and Ursula wrapped it round her knee to hold the bone in place. Upset that there was not a doctor for miles, and there was nothing else she could do, Ursula retreated to her bed, moaning in pain.

Her staff gathered round her. "There's a man in Asalu who can fix out-of-place bones", Namkia told her. "I'll go for him."

"No, it's too far away. Maybe it will click back into place."

Hazekiemba whispered to Namkia then left the room. He returned two minutes later with a machete and a piece of ginger.

"There's only one thing left to do," he said, "a suitable sacrifice."

Hazekiemba sat on the floor ready to divine the trouble. Despite her pain, Ursula's curiosity got the better of her. She propped herself up on her elbows. "Namkia, what's he going to do?"

"He's going to divine with the ginger. It's the one instrument of divination the great healer Herakandingpeo had time to reveal before the spirits killed him; for spirits live by eating the souls of men, and as they eat, the body wastes with sickness. Herakandingpeo's skill as a healer was robbing them of every soul they caught. So the spirits tricked and killed him and made sure he didn't pass his knowledge on. He was only able to whisper this small piece of information about the ginger to his son who arrived seconds before Herakandingpeo died."

Hazekiemba cut the ginger in half. He carefully placed the two halves on the flat of the blade and then spoke to them. "Oh ginger! Tell us the truth, and do not lie. We turn to you for truth. Is it black magic that has attacked our mother? If so, then come down odd; if not, then even."

He tossed the ginger up from the machete. Ursula sat up straighter in order to see. Both halves fell the same way, with the cut side down. "They are even," pronounced Hazekiemba. "It is not black magic." He took the pieces and started again. For fifteen minutes, Hazekiemba tossed and re-tossed the ginger until the pieces revealed that, while in the garden, Ursula had been seized by an evil spirit, which would release its hold on her in exchange for a cockerel.

Namkia left immediately to fetch a cockerel and the village priest. He found the bird, but with the priest unavailable, he returned with the old ex-headman, Samrangba's uncle, who, like most elders, earned extra money by performing minor ceremonies for the sick.

"Everyone must leave," he said.

The staff trooped out. The old man entered the house with his helper who carried rice and beer. They squatted by the hearth in the living room. With outstretched arms, the old man offered the cock to the spirit. "I humbly ask the spirit to hear my petition. I implore you to release our mother. Here is a fine cockerel. Release our mother," he intoned for several minutes, falling into a chanting rhythm.

He then killed and cooked the bird. Small pieces of the liver and some rice were placed on a leaf plate and set out for the spirit. A similar meal was given to Ursula. He poured beer for the spirit and gave beer in a leaf cup to Ursula. Finally, the old man rose, and after proclaiming a prayer for success, told Ursula, "The ceremony has been done correctly. You will most definitely be cured." Then he left, followed by his companion carrying the rest of the food and beer.

I don't feel any better, thought Ursula, but I'm not any worse either.

During the night, she turned over. A stab of excruciating pain woke her. She sat up, swore and . . . the knee clicked back into place. The relief was instant.

"So much for you, demon," she said, "and thanks very much cockerel!"

She fell into a deep sleep. With the arrival of daylight, Namkia brought her morning cup of tea. "How's your knee?"

"It seems to be back in place. I'll see if I can walk when I get out of bed."

Namkia was smug. "Zemi healing works well, doesn't it, my sister?"

"I'm much improved," she said, but thinking, you'll never accept that the elastic plaster may have had anything to do with it.

Later, she limped outdoors. Her staff ran to look at the headman's handiwork. They fussed excitedly, pleased that Naga medicine had cured her knee. Their reaction gave Ursula an insight into how her dispensaries could be more effective by being in tune with the Naga way. When fully recovered, she went to the village to talk to the priests.

"You see, I am walking well again. I am very pleased that the sacrifice was productive. I think it would help my medicine if a priest would work with me in the dispensary. What do you think, my father?" Ursula asked, directing her question to the elderly priest who had adopted her.

The old man, as wise and kind as he looked, conferred with the other priests before answering. "I am sure that with your medicine, aided by our divination and sacrifices, we will be most successful."

From that time on, whenever she held a dispensary, Ursula and a headman could be seen putting their heads together like a couple of hospital consultants. Then Ursula would dish out the quinine, and the priest would sacrifice a chicken. If the treatment worked, they happily shared the credit.

Although Ursula lived at Laisong, most of her staff and friends came from the Asalu area, a region whose economy was steadily deteriorating. Shortly before harvesting, Ursula went on a ten-day tour, her last stop being Asalu. One evening, she and Namkia were hunting pigeon in the parkland. They stepped out of the high grass into a field of rice. Ursula bent down and touched the plants. The crop was ripe but sparse and stunted with only a few thin ears.

"Is this a typical Asalu harvest?" she asked, remembering a few days before, when in a field far to the east, the rice had been brushing her shoulders.

"The soil's exhausted because there's not enough land to rest the fields, so the crops are poor. Each year there is less and less grain in the granaries, and the men must go and work in Kuki and Kachari fields to earn money.

They looked at the field, "If I could find a demonstrator who knew how," Namkia said. "I'd terrace that bit of land of mine at Impoi. It's a good piece, and the Kukis are asking me for it. I've enough savings to get it started. I wouldn't need government money. But who is there who really knows the job? Masang is useless; he doesn't know a thing."

"What about the Kuki demonstrators?"

"What sort of a job would they do for me, a Naga? These streams are steep. We need a man who knows. Why can't we have someone good, a proper Angami?"

They both knew the answer. The Subdivisional Officer had been searching everywhere for a skilled man, but no Angami wanted to come and work for thirty rupees a month. Asalu must continue to subsist on its tragic crops. The hardship this inflicted on the population saddened Ursula and made her feel helpless.

Namkia and Ursula went to Impoi, his home village.

Impoi was located high on a ridge with a backdrop of wild peaks opposite green foothills and hazy plains. "Sometimes," Namkia said, "far to the north, we can see the snow-covered Himalayas above the dust cloud covering the Assam valley."

The thatch on Namkia's *morung* rustled in the constant wind, which blew down the hill, keeping Impoi's climate cool and healthy. Namkia's *morung* was not a large building, for Impoi did not have the manpower for major projects, but it was a house built at a feast of social merit, which bestowed a distinct status on Namkia. He could have gone on to build a higher grade *morung*, but the building ceremonies cost a thousand rupees, and nobody was rich enough to perform them now. The last high-grade house had fallen down some years before, and now there was not one left anywhere in the whole of North Cachar; even the ceremonies were being forgotten.

A mile and a half away, several hundred feet lower than Impoi, on a spur in open parkland, stood Asalu, run down and plagued by malaria. In the grassland around the village, Namkia had shown Ursula rows of stone and monoliths, weathered ruins of ancient settlements and a hundred years of British rule. Where the spur levelled beyond the village, the John Company outpost had been the headquarters of North Cachar for forty years. Almost nothing was left of it now, save the old stone guardhouse, cracked by earthquakes and thrusting trees, and a broad stretch of gravel, which had once been the parade ground. The foundations of a bungalow were hidden by tangled grass.

Out hunting in the area, Ursula and Namkia would go to the site at dusk when the hills were blue-grey and the sunset an orange band along the western plateau.

On their first visit to the site, Namkia pointed out, "There, by the bush, that was the clerks' quarters. Over there were the *sepoys'* lines, and there the rifle range" They had walked to a long-dead tree. "This was the sahib's mango tree. It lasted for a long time after they all left, but it's dead now."

Ursula mused: the sahibs, the clerks, the station, all turned to dust. Her British Empire fading here and under attack at home from barbarians and savages of a different kind. She felt as if these were Roman ruins and she were one of the last consuls in an outpost. Nearby, the village was failing too. Dying like the twilight. A sense of foreboding overtook her, and she loosed a long and mournful sigh.

Ursula and Namkia were fishing at the big pool in the valley, one of only a few that Namkia claimed was safe. There were other pools in the area, inviting bowls of refreshing water in glades and bowers of shade. One was overhung by a gray rock. Ursula thought its golden-green water would make a perfect diving pool, but Namkia would have none of it. It was a python's lair he told her. The snake draws men into the water by magic and drowns them. The pool must be avoided. Ursula smiled inwardly each time Namkia reminded her of this Naga belief and insisted on protecting her from the danger. Respecting his wishes, she resisted the cool, tempting waters where the python lurked.

Khamba's growling alerted Ursula to the approach of a man from Kepelo to disturb their enjoyment at soaking up the sunshine after an extremely wet rainy season.

"Oh, my mother, I am Masang's brother. He is very ill. He asks that you come to see him."

Before Ursula could answer, Namkia spoke, his voice dripping with scorn. "Do you think the miss-sahib can travel to Kepelo and back in one day? Does Masang think the miss-sahib is a village woman to come running like a dog at heel? Let Kepelo take the trouble to build a camp, then the miss-sahib will come."

Masang's brother flushed with embarrassment, mumbled an apology, and slunk away.

"Kepelo is only four miles away. I can easily go and see him," Ursula told Namkia.

"He is not a good man. It is best to stay away."

"I haven't seen Masang for a long time. You drove him away with your hostility."

"I do not like him."

Annoyed, Ursula raised her voice. "And you made it obvious, didn't you? Once we settled in Laisong, you drove him away by your rudeness. Whenever Masang came into the house, you walked out instead of interpreting, and so he visited less and less. He hasn't been round for months, and now he's sick. I'm going to Kepelo to visit him."

"I am not going with you."

"Fine! I'll take Haichangnang."

There was a long, bristling silence. Then Ursula asked, "Why don't you like Masang?"

Namkia paused to consider the wisdom of telling her what he knew. "He used you. He claimed you were the goddess Gaidiliu."

Ursula's jaw dropped. The answer was completely unexpected. "Why on earth would he do that?"

"Because Masang was a prophet of Gaidiliu's. When she was arrested and sent away, he was sent to prison. He lost his standing without her power. But Gaidiliu promised to return in another form, one that her enemies would not recognize. When you turned up, he decided that Gaidiliu had chosen to return as a miss-sahib. What better disguise and what better way to become important again?"

Ursula mulled over Namkia's words. Despite Masang using her this way, she was still fond of him; after all, he had been her friend before Namkia.

"I will still go to Kepelo to see him."

"Then you must go with Haichangnang. I want nothing to do with Masang."

Early in the morning, Ursula set out for Kepelo with Haichangnang who carried a pouch full of drugs. They travelled eastwards. Kepelo lay in a pass near the village of Haijaichak where they left the road and climbed steeply through graves, stones, and woods. They walked between the granaries resting on bamboo stilts and stepped into Kepelo's wide village street.

Seeing Ursula, the villagers flocked to her, touched her clothes, clamoured for her blessing, and forced gifts upon her.

Just like it was at Guilong.

Only now, Ursula understood.

Masang's brother appeared and brought her through the crowd. He led her to Masang's house. Ursula felt like a biblical prophet with the horde on her heels. She stepped through the doorway into the murky darkness. Behind her, Masang's brother closed the door on the throng.

It took a moment for her eyes to adjust. A fire burned on the hearth between three stones. The family sat behind it. To the side of the fire, lying on a mat on the floor, was Masang. Any doubts she may have had about coming vanished in an instant. It was clear Masang was dying.

Gone was the rough, tough, rascal she knew. He was a skeleton, covered by a cloth, on a floor mat. Of his powerful, muscular body there was no trace, only toothpick limbs and a skull-like head with deep shadows for eyes and teeth which seemed too large for his shrunken face. When she kneeled beside him, she looked into sunken eye-sockets, and Masang's yellowed eyes stared up at her. His bony black hand groped for hers.

"My mother Goddess, save me," croaked Masang. "I am afraid to die."

Ursula looked across the fire to Haichangnang. She saw the look on his face and understood. To Masang, Ursula was, and always had been, reincarnated Gaidiliu.

She sat with him most of the day, Masang drawing succour from her presence when awake, although he was mostly semi-conscious. He occasionally asked his goddess to save him. His hand lay in Ursula's like a child's. Whenever Ursula moved away, he moaned, and the skeletal hand rose to pull her back.

She was glad it was Haichangnang with her and not Namkia. Namkia would rebuke Masang and be delighted he was dying. Haichangnang sat quietly, watching from across the fire, his face filled with pity. Her heart filled with love for the small, gentle man offering occasional words of sympathy and comfort.

In the quietness, Ursula thought over all that Haichangnang had told her on the way to Kepelo.

Contrary to Namkia's opinion, Masang had believed that Ursula was Gaidiliu right from the start. At the welcoming celebration for Ursula in Laisong, he had declared her godliness.

217

The more stable Nagas, including Namkia, refused to believe him. The majority positioned themselves on the sidelines to see what would happen next. The faithful took his pronouncement as gospel, which explained why, in the beginning, some villages were not comfortable with her visits, and in others, she was mobbed.

She recalled Philip Mills' story of Gaidiliu complaining how it was hard work being a goddess. Indeed, from her own short experience, Ursula could not agree more.

Haichangnang had said that the outlawed Dikheo, Gaidiliu's main henchman, had paid a visit to Ursula's camp with a group of villagers bringing her presents. Ursula vaguely remembered a tall, strong-looking ruffian who had stared and stared at her. That had been Dikheo, the henchman, risking his life to investigate Masang's re-incarnated Gaidiliu.

Ursula failed the test.

As word spread, the number of visitors to Ursula's compound dwindled away. Only Masang, and the few he led, believed. Everyone knew of it but Ursula, and Namkia, presuming Masang was using Ursula to regain his lost status as Gaidiliu's right-hand man, kept him away from Laisong.

Then Masang lost his government job. Dikheo, the henchman, met his fate. His life as a fugitive came to an end when he was surprised at his home by a unit of the Assam Rifles and shot dead. And now Masang was dying, asking to be saved by the goddess for whose sake he had been beaten and jailed. He clung to Ursula's hand.

She stayed with Masang until evening when, with a final gasp and a beseeching look at his goddess, he died. As she left, the villagers again swarmed her. They viewed her as a deity, and she was patient and indulgent with the throng, knowing that this would be her last appearance as the goddess Gaidiliu. With Masang dead, it all would end.

Gaidiliu could not have wished for a more devoted servant than Masang.

In December, Ursula went to Calcutta on her annual holiday. This time she took not only Namkia but Haichangnang as well. Namkia insisted.

"Haichangnang must come with me," he told her. "Last year when I came back and told the villagers all I had seen in Calcutta, they did not believe me."

"Really?"

"They called me a liar!" he said indignantly. "Haichangnang hasn't the brains to tell a lie. He will be a safe witness."

Ursula had her own reasons for taking them to Calcutta. Japanese activities in the Far East were bringing the war closer, and she was well-aware of the dissident rumblings among the disaffected Zemi looking to flout the ruling British should they become embroiled in warfare. Ursula wanted to show Namkia and Haichangnang the War Weapons Exhibition in Calcutta, hoping it would be something they could use to dissuade the more mutinous groups from rising in revolt.

Once in Calcutta, they wasted no time in going to the exhibition. Namkia and Haichangnang were resplendent in full tribal dress. They were a third of the way round before attracting the attention of the other visitors who whipped out their cameras and formed a solid wall in front of the two Nagas. Cameras clicked and flashed, cine cameras whirred. The hillmen grinned, posing with proud dignity and patience. The scene reminded Ursula of newsreels she had seen as a girl, where Hollywood royalty disembarked from trains at Victoria station or from liners at Southampton to face flashguns popping and cameras grinding and reporters yelling, "Look this way, please!" Ursula smiled at her friends, surely the most photographed men in Calcutta.

Officials hurried over. "In return for publicity pictures," one official told Ursula, "you can have the run of the exhibition." A friendly sergeant-major took charge of Namkia and Haichangnang and led them round the exhibition, explaining the intricacies of the different weapons. An hour later, he came looking for Ursula. "The lads've had their fill for now, and it's getting hot. I'll take 'em off to the canteen for some ice cream, if that's all right with you, miss."

"I'm sure they'd like that." She took the opportunity to sit down and drink a large glass of lemonade. At lunchtime, the sergeant-major returned with Namkia and Haichangnang. "Whenever you want to park 'em, miss, you bring 'em along to me. I'll keep 'em happy."

Ursula still had to trail Namkia and Haichangnang round with her while she shopped, but most days she gratefully left them with the sergeant-major, who plied them with ice cream— they adored the stuff—and cool drinks and kept the overly curious onlookers at bay. The hillmen thought the world of him.

Lexie and Richard timed a return visit to Calcutta to coincide with Ursula's. Lexie's fiancé, Charles Brown, was absent, having been posted to Europe. Ursula danced, went to the cinema and dined out with some of the many soldiers on leave. On the few occasions they discussed Japan's intentions in the Far East, they agreed that life in India would continue as usual; both the war in Europe and the war in China were a long way away. They really had nothing to worry about, except loved ones who were being sent to the war zones.

Returning to North Cachar, Ursula felt a twinge of regret to find Jack Dawson gone, replaced by a new SDO Edwin Perry. She braced herself to go along to the bungalow at Mahur to introduce herself. She had already discovered that many district officers were disapproving of a woman alone.

As Ursula walked up the garden path, a tall, slim man came out of the bungalow. He strode down the steps, arm outstretched, with a guileless and boyish smile.

"Hallo, I'm Edwin Perry, and you," he said, after looking at Namkia and Haichangnang, "must be Miss Bower. May I call you, Ursula?" He took her hand and shook it vigorously. "Jack has told me all about you. Come and have a cup of tea." All trepidation left Ursula. She had found an ally.

*   *   *

Back in Laisong, Ursula sat at her camp table, writing letters home. Namkia expressed an interest in writing to Ursula's mother too.

"After all, you are my sister, so under Naga law, she is my mother."

In Zemi, he dictated a letter to Ursula, which loosely translated, said:

My mother,

I don't know how to read and write. It is very bad, and I am much ashamed. If I knew how to write letters, I would write one and send it to you. That would be very good. I am like a stone and don't know anything, only how to eat rice and drink beer.

Beneath the words he printed his name, NAMKIABUING ZEMI.

Satisfied with his efforts, Namkia went to tell the others of his achievement. Ursula was left wondering what to write to newly engaged Lexie, who feared Ursula was missing the experience of marriage, motherhood, domestic life. "It's just that I'm so happy," Lexie had said, "I want to be sure you're as happy too."

How to put into mere words her contentment, the hold this place, these people, had on her? Here, she had been mother to many, sister to Namkia, goddess to some, doctor, helper, gardener, provider of food, ethnographer, linguist, anthropologist and archaeologist. Ursula patted Khamba's flat head and tapped the paper with the end of her pen then filled her fountain pen from the bottle of black ink and began:

It's hard to explain the ache I feel for this place after being away in Calcutta or on a tour. There's my little bungalow, not very pretty with its gray and brown bamboo matting walls and woodwork. But my heart leaps with joy when I step into camp and catch sight of its sagging thatch and latticed railings. I love being awakened by streams of sunlight forcing their way through cracks in the shutters and watching the sun climb across the Jenam valley with the colours of the grass, wood, and forest brightening as if touched by a magic wand. There's the jungle trying to unroll its green carpet into camp, kept at bay by the men working in a line across the slope, rhythmically slashing and cutting to drive it back. I can sit on my veranda and look at the garden with its kaleidoscope of flowers, blossom-covered bean stacks and bee-covered peas. The men gather there just before dusk, assessing Paodekumba's care of the plants, offering advice as they walk up and down the rows. I watch the swallows swooping and diving, the camp belonging to them as much as to us. There's such an air of permanency. Below the bungalow are some outcrops of rock. I go there and sit, sometimes for hours, and look over the Jenam River, studying the convolutions of the river gorge and watching the sparkling ribbon of water, Rangalang working in his field, or the shimmering pool where Namkia and I fish.

But mainly, it's the atmosphere I love, its essence. The Barail is a barrier between the outside world and us. We pass to the far side by walking over the hill to Asalu. Below is the railway where the clang and clatter and piercing train whistles combine with soot-filled steam to sully the peace. Then we return behind the Barail, where there is an everlasting tranquillity.

I've painted an idyllic picture, and so it is, but life is also hard and uncertain. We soon patch up a quarrel; anything can quickly bring life to an end, a fever, a falling tree, and, apart from my dispensaries, medical care is days away. We live in the present with a simple honesty, which brings an easy contentment. Without the distractions of material wealth, spiritual values are experienced more clearly.

Life may be short here, but it is rich and human. Friendships, loyalties, and kindnesses are felt more and have greater meaning. Every simple pleasure is enjoyed as if for the last time, making life rich and sensual. I think the Zemi are much happier than any European could ever be.

I saw how flushed with happiness you are now that you have found Charles to love. I am truly happy for you, Lexie. Be happy for me too. My happiness has a softer glow, a warmth, which sustains me in everything I do and everything I am. We are both extremely lucky, only in different ways

Ursula sent Haichangnang to Haflong with her letters. He returned with newspapers carrying headlines of Japan's attack on Pearl Harbour. Later bundles brought news of the fall of Singapore and the invasion of Burma. Ursula noted these events with dismay, but they seemed so far away, in a different reality that surely could not touch them. The daily routine behind the Barail claimed her attention, the need to re-thatch the house, the blacksmith's illness, life in Laisong going on as before. Then a letter from Lexie arrived, urging Ursula to leave North Cachar and go to India. At first, Ursula dismissed Lexie's fears, but the warning nagged at her until, at the end of March, she decided to find out what was going on. She wrote to Lexie saying she would soon be arriving in Imphal.

*   *   *

The truck stopped outside Richard and Lexie's bungalow. Ursula, Haichangnang, and Namkia climbed down as Lexie rushed outside, elated to see Ursula on her doorstep.

They hugged and bussed each other on the cheek. "I only received your letter two days ago," Lexie said. "I've already replied telling you not to travel here. We're all prepared for evacuation at twenty-four hours notice."

Ursula was stunned. "I didn't realize the situation was so serious."

"Oh, but it is. Come in. We'll have some tea, while I bring you up to date." Lexie turned to her servant. "Ranjan, take the miss-sahib's men to the servants' quarters for refreshments, and bring us some tea, please."

Once settled, Lexie looked as if she might break into tears. No doubt her fears for her brother and, Ursula knew, for Captain Charles Brown had been weighing on her.

"Ursula, the war is upon us. The men are ready for call up. You must leave Assam and move to India. It's not safe here. The Japanese are pushing through Burma to India."

"You really think they'll invade India?"

"Why not? From what we've heard, they seem unstoppable."

Ursula pursed her lips. Her jaw hardened. "I'm not letting any Japanese army drive me from my home. I'm staying in Assam."

"Ursula, be sensible! The Japanese do horrible things to the women they capture. You must leave."

"No, I absolutely will not!"

For the rest of the afternoon, the arguments flew back and forth, continuing when Richard returned that evening. Even facing twice the force, Ursula would not be moved. Richard sighed surrendering to Ursula's stubbornness. "There may be something you can do to help," he said.

Ursula, immediately excited, said, "What's that?"

"Thousands of refugees are fleeing over the Burmese border. They're travelling along the jungle trails and getting lost in the mountains. The few who survive the journey are in a dreadful state. There's an SOS out for women to volunteer to help the refugees."

"That's a wonderful idea." Ursula paused to think. "I can organize a team of Zemi to search the trails for refugees. We can bring them to safety." Carried away with enthusiasm she continued, "I'll go to the authorities. I'll go as soon as possible. You come up with the most marvellous suggestions. Thank you, Richard."

Lexie protested, "Ursula, I'm sure the kind of volunteer work Richard had in mind was something less dangerous, such as feeding and caring for the refugees when they arrive. Please listen. Don't be reckless."

"It's not a question of being reckless. It's a question of using our knowledge of the jungle to find and guide the refugees to safety. We can be much more help that way than putting food in their bellies if they manage to make it."

*   *   *

Ursula returned to Laisong intent on recruiting a team of Zemi volunteers. It was a more difficult undertaking than she expected. The Zemi were aware that refugees were flowing into India from Burma. With rumours flying that the Japanese were closing in on the border, they were tense and afraid. Ursula overcame their reluctance with Namkia's help. Together they reassured the Nagas that the British would not abandon Assam and that anything they did to help the British would be recognized as the actions of friends. Ursula then travelled with Namkia to Shillong where she stayed with Philip Mills and his wife, while she spent two fruitless days trying to convince the army to use her and the Nagas on any of the refugee routes where they could be of use.

Ursula spoke first with Colonel Ashcroft, who adamantly refused to allow Ursula and her team to search the hills. The very thought caused him to flush red, and his features knotted in absolute refusal.

"Miss Bower, conditions on the trails are appalling. They're littered with the decomposing bodies of those who didn't make it. You would literally be walking over the diseased corpses of people who've collapsed and died on the road."

"But you're already using hillmen to help you. My Zemi and I are strong. We know our way in the jungle. We're not just up to the job, we're perfect for it!"

Colonel Ashcroft spoke in a clipped and precise manner. "Yes. Right. As you say, we are sending tribesmen to catch the refugees as they come over the frontier. But . . ." Ursula saw how much effort it was costing the colonel not to show his irritation with this woman who simply would not be put off. ". . . we are not sending women into the area because conditions are so dreadful. If you are really keen to help, I suggest you contact Mrs. Reid, the Governor's wife. She's organizing a volunteer force and would welcome your help."

Angry and frustrated, Ursula left his office.

"What is it, my sister?" asked Namkia.

"They won't let us go into the jungle to find the refugees. Or rather, they won't let me because I'm a woman. Still, I'm not dead yet. Come on, we're going to see the Governor's wife. She's looking for volunteers."

Ursula cursed rarely, but she could be poisonous with her tongue when angered, and she was angry now. The oaths came softly, under her breath, but they were venomous. She trudged to the headquarters of the volunteer services.

"Wish me luck," she said to Namkia before going inside.

She was directed to Mrs. Reid's office where she tapped on the open. An older woman, with jet-black hair smoothed back into a bun and spectacles perched on the end of her nose, was searching through a filing cabinet drawer.

"Mrs. Reid?" asked Ursula. "I'm Ursula Bower. I want to offer my services to help the refugees."

"Good afternoon, Miss Bower. Come in."

Mrs. Reid gave Ursula a crisp handshake. She gestured Ursula towards a battered chair before shutting the drawer and seating herself behind her desk.

"I've lived with the Zemi Nagas for several years doing anthropological work, and I want to offer our services to search the jungle for refugees."

Mrs. Reid studied the young woman before her. "I see." Mrs. Reid's elbows rested on her desk, fingertips steepled

"Then too," Ursula continued, "I've run dispensaries and treated every kind of wound and sickness, on a daily basis, for all my years here. With my staff, I can deal with . . ."

"By 'your staff' do you mean the hillmen? Natives?"

"Yes. They're quite good. We treat malaria, jungle sores, snake-bite and . . ."

"I see. An interesting proposition, but the army seems to have that end of things covered. What we desperately need are volunteers to provide refreshments at the stations where the trains, bringing back our wounded soldiers, will stop. I'm sure you would want to help where you would be most useful, wouldn't you, my dear?"

"Refreshments?" Ursula repeated, stunned.

Here was a dodgy situation. She was obviously not going to be allowed to help in the way she wanted, and she could hardly refuse to help wounded men, but being a kind of field waitress seemed a total waste of resources.

Mrs. Reid's waiting smile was bogus. She wanted to keep Ursula where women belong—and she had used maimed and injured Englishmen for leverage.

Well, thought Ursula, if I want to help, and I can't help any other way, it looks like it will have to be this. "All right, we'll do it. When and where do I report?"

*   *   *

"Lumding! That's where we're being sent! Lumding junction!" Ursula blurted out on returning to the Mills' home. "She said that's where most help is needed! Damn and blast the woman . . . and the army! What a ruddy waste of our talents! Sorry for the language, Philip." Ursula's cheeks were flushed, her eyes blazed. Philip Mills chuckled. The corner of his wife's mouth twitched as she tried to suppress a smile, amused by Ursula's youthful frustration.

"Come now, calm down," Mrs. Mills said. "We know you'd much rather be trekking through the hills. But to Mrs. Reid you're an unknown quantity. She might even be wondering if you're quite insane."

Ursula opened then closed her mouth twice as if to speak before bursting into laughter. "I'm sure you're right. I suppose people do think I'm a bit strange, don't they? Well, I've committed us to Lumding, so we'll do it."

"The war has arrived, Ursula," Mr. Mills said. "Who's to say for how long? You may yet get your chance to show your mettle, especially if you impress the authorities with your hard work at Lumding."

"Are you sure you don't want to leave?" Mrs. Mills asked.

"Assam, you mean? Oh, no. I couldn't possibly leave my home or the Zemi. No, we're all in this together. I'm here for the duration."

*   *   *

At Laisong, while she waited for her orders to arrive, Ursula pondered how this disruption to routine would put a strain on her relations with the Zemi. Leaning on the veranda railing, she watched Paodekumba hoeing the garden, Ramgakpa bringing a chicken from the hen-house, and Khamba tumbling with Lassu as they chased one another round the men's quarters. This was her family. Would their ties be strong enough to stand the test of this separation, this war? Maybe she shouldn't expect too much.

On the last day of March, Ursula received orders to proceed to Lumding. The gardener, caretaker and Ali were to remain behind to take care of the camp and the dogs. Namkia, Haichangnang, Ramgakpa and Degalang were going with Ursula to Lumding station, which they feared much more than the Manipur refugee routes.

Word of their impending departure spread round the village. A deputation of headmen swept into Ursula's compound.

"We object to the Governor's orders sending you away. The country is in a disturbed state and could be invaded at any time," they complained. "It's no time for a young woman to be out and about alone. We suppose that the British, like the Zemi, take care of their own people. If whatever Europeans responsible for your safety are not prepared to look after you, then we, the Zemi, will. We, as a tribe, will take full responsibility. So, we forbid you to leave the shelter of the hills."

Ursula, touched by their concern, pointed out that orders were orders. She had no choice but to go. The headmen were not convinced. They sent Ursula's porters, who had gathered in the compound, back to the village.

"You must stay put," they told Ursula. "You are not to leave. We're going to see the SDO at Haflong."

They turned on their heels and marched from her camp. An hour later they were leaving the village for Haflong. Perry later told Ursula that on arriving at his office the next day, they made their demands. They were taking responsibility for her safety.

"I argued, reasoned and pleaded with them to no avail. The headmen of Laisong refused to budge. Finally, I promised, 'Gentlemen, come hell or high water, I will take personal responsibility for the miss-sahib's safe return to Laisong.' That must have satisfied them for they returned to Laisong."

When Ursula congratulated Perry for his knack in dealing with the Zemi, he returned the compliment, saying, "All congratulations to you. You've inspired loyalty such as I've never seen—loyalty and, I dare say, love!"

On his return to Laisong, the elderly priest informed Ursula, "The SDO is going to take responsibility for you, my daughter. Therefore we will allow you to go to Lumding."

When Ursula and her group left Laisong, Namkia was strangely silent on the way down. On their last night in the hills, at Asalu camp, Namkia spent the evening hanging round Ursula's hut. He would walk towards the hut then veer away at the last minute, stand for a moment as if undecided as to what to do next then wander off only to return and repeat his actions a few minutes later. Ursula kept glancing his way. Something was up, but she wasn't sure what. Namkia would, she knew, get round to telling her when he got up the nerve.

Ursula had lit the hurricane lamp and was sitting at her table, writing, when Namkia barged in. Before Ursula could move, he dropped to his knees in front of her and wrapped his arms around her. His head went down on her lap. He burst into a flood of tears. Shocked, Ursula looked down on his heaving back too stunned to do or say anything. It took some seconds before she found her voice.

"Namkia, Namkia! Whatever's the matter?"

He wept loudly. She shook him, tried to lift him off her lap. He buried himself closer and continued sobbing. Ursula pulled herself free and stood up. Namkia's head and arms fell onto the empty chair where he continued crying. Ursula looked about her wondering what to do. She remembered, in the bedroom, some rum, in the *jappa*. She rummaged round until she found it. Returning to the living room, she found Namkia still crying as if his heart would break. She threw the tea in her bamboo cup out of the window and poured a stiff tot of rum.

"Namkia, come on, drink this!"

She pulled at his shoulders, shoved the cup to his mouth. "Come on, now! Drink up. It will calm you down."

Namkia swallowed. Gradually his sobbing lessened. He sat up, sniffing and gulping for air while he regained his composure.

When he finally calmed down, Ursula said, "Well, what's the trouble?"

Namkia stood up and seated himself on the edge of the bamboo table. "It was all right before I left Laisong. I didn't mind a bit, and I wasn't afraid to go. But now my wife and mother have been at me, and I don't know what to do. Suppose Assam is invaded and abandoned without a fight, as they say it's going to be?" He cast an anguished look at Ursula. "Suppose we can't come back? Suppose raiding breaks out again in the hills when the British go? Who'll look after my wife and children? I was in the village today and heard what they're saying."

"What are they saying?"

"They say this isn't our war, and we ought to leave it alone. We aren't Japs; we aren't British; we're Zemi. What's it to do with us? We've been together now, all of us, for two years; we're like family. How can I leave you? What about my children? Oh, my sister, I feel like I'm being torn in two. Which way shall I go?"

Ursula went and sat at the table. "Well, I don't know what's going to happen either. But my home's at Laisong, and I'm coming back to it whatever happens. After all, Lumding isn't far; we can walk home in four days. As for the rest, I don't think you Zemi will be able to stay as neutral as you suppose, certainly not if the Angamis and Kukis take sides. And I doubt if you'll find the Japs a fair exchange for the British. From what I hear, they're rather more like the old Kachari kings you talk about, who made men lick knives, and flayed the soles off their feet, and made them walk thorny logs."

"From the talk I've heard, I think so too," Namkia said.

"In the meantime, thousands of people are coming through from Burma in a devil of a state. I've been told to go down and help, and I'm going, with anyone I can find to go along with me.

If you people won't come, it's my bad luck. I've had the orders, not you."

Namkia slipped off the table and wiped his eyes.

"Dear elder sister, don't be afraid. We're all in this together."

He held out his hand and they shook on it, and Namkia went off to his quarters. Three days later, on a hot, dark night, after an uncomfortable and chaotic trip, the group, with Namkia, arrived at Lumding.

NAGA QUEEN

Lumding was a fine example of planning gone awry. The railway junction—its platform, signals, sheds and yards—was built in a clearing hacked from the Nambhor Forest. The junction was meant to connect the Hill Section Line with the railway running through the Assam Valley, only the junction ended up a mile and a half from where the town had been constructed. Town and junction survived in seclusion, in separate clearings nudged by eclipsing greenery, connected by tracks which tunnelled through the jungle on a narrow strip of bare land liberated from the forest's clutches.

"Oh, I'm so glad to see you. Do come in," said Mrs. Rankin upon Ursula's arrival in the town. Mrs. Rankin had a teapot's shape and a wren's quick, darting movements. She quickly made arrangements for the Nagas to stay in the servants' quarters and turned back to Ursula. "You have no idea how delighted I am to receive help at last. There's a lot of work to be done to get the canteen started, but I won't burden you with that tonight. We'll talk in the morning. You must be tired and hungry. Let's deal with first things first."

By virtue of her husband's position on the railway, Mrs. Rankin had taken it upon herself to see that the retreating soldiers and refugees would at least receive some refreshment on their long journey to the hospitals of India. Over breakfast, Mrs. Rankin told Ursula of her difficulties.

"As yet, we have nothing really at the junction. No cookhouse, store, hut, food, fuel, not even a place for you and your staff to sleep." She puffed up her ample bosom. "But we'll soon have you fixed up with everything you need. Just leave it to me."

As soon as breakfast was over, and while it was still relatively cool, she took Ursula and her men to Lumding junction.

"You can see the place is totally disorganized. Many workers have disappeared fearful of a Japanese invasion."

Ursula and her staff looked around, took in the confusion and exchanged concerned glances. The yards were choked with wagons loaded with bamboo and other building materials, which, in the panic, no one had claimed. Unforwarded consignments left lying around overflowed from the siding onto the main line.

The morning silence was torn by the distant shriek of a steam whistle.

"The mail train," Mrs. Rankin said.

Lumding junction burst into life with a sudden frenzy of trucks being shunted from the main line to be squeezed into crammed spots, while the mail train huffed and puffed impatiently at the signal. Once the train had passed, the trucks were released from their tight corner to again block the main line.

"Who are those people at the far end of the platform?" asked Ursula, seeing Indians bustling about.

"They belong to a Nationalist organization. They've just started their own canteen for the Indians coming through. You know, of course, that Indians, for religious reasons, can't eat food prepared by Europeans. Most of the refugees and soldiers are Indian, so they'll be kept busy. Not that you and your men won't be busy too. The work is going to be hard. So, what will we need here?"

"Some type of counter to put the food out, a place to heat water for tea?" suggested Ursula.

"You'll also need a place to stay, but until one is built you will, of course, live at my house."

Mrs. Rankin swabbed the sweat beading on her brow and looked about her. She patted her neck with her handkerchief. Then she pulled a pencil and notebook from her handbag and started jotting items down.

"Well, this is a long list. Can't stand here wasting time; there are things to be done. Let's scout around. Maybe we'll find something here."

The group searched the rail yard for materials to construct a canteen.

Mrs. Rankin pointed to a corner. "Those steel girders there, we'll have those. No one else seems to have claimed them. We can prop them on timbers, and I'll see if I can find some tabletops to rest on them. That will make a fine counter."

Pointing to the refreshment room, Ursula asked, "Is that still going to be out of bounds for the refugees, even in this emergency?"

"I'm afraid so. It wouldn't be acceptable. But the British officers will be able to go there, while you're attending to the men."

Ursula held her tongue, her practical mind dismayed that convention should rule at a time like this.

*   *   *

Ursula and her men depended on Mrs. Rankin's hospitality during the two weeks it took for the canteen to be up and running. Meanwhile, Mrs. Rankin was a one-woman tempest of energy and activity. She commandeered the girders she had discovered and conjured up tabletops. Using her husband's authority, she took charcoal stoves from the engine sheds and badgered someone to build a small, whitewashed rest-house at the edge of town for Ursula and the volunteers. It was completed the day Mrs. Rankin's husband heard he was being transferred.

"I hope you hold up, Ursula. The Governor's wife Mrs. Reid is doing her best to persuade the ladies to come and help here, but she's finding it difficult. I'm so glad you came to do your share. Mrs. Rankin patted Ursula's arm in encouragement. "Goodbye, Ursula."

The rest-house provided little privacy as there were no separate quarters for the men. There was only one big room where Ursula slept on her camp bed, and Namkia and the other three Zemi slept on the floor under a convoluted tangle of mosquito nets attached to her bed, the table, chair, a nail-head and anything else that jutted out. When Ursula saw the completed rest-house, she knew it was going to be tough on the men; awake or sleeping they were all going to be herded together with her.

It was the start of a gruelling daily routine. At 2:30 a.m., a messenger knocked on the window of the rest-house to deliver a telegram to Ursula, giving the number of refugees scheduled to come through on the trains that day. She retired to the bathroom to bathe and dress.

At 3:00 a.m., she woke the men. In the only cool hour out of the whole day, they made their way, one and a half miles in the dark, to the station. They were weighed down with wood for the fires, which they had cut the night before, and bread for sandwiches to feed some of the one to two thousand people being brought through on the trains. Between six and sixty of the travellers would be Europeans; the National Congress canteen would feed the remainder. Both canteens supplied tea to any and all of the men.

Ursula and her helpers plodded over the tracks shining in the starlight. They soon became familiar with the dark shadowy buildings and green and red glowing lights of Lumding junction. Arriving at the thatched shed with the cookhouse behind it, the group made for the railway coal bunkers and staggered back covered in soot and coal dust with loads of coal to light the fires. Then they carried sixty gallons of water using four-gallon kerosene cans with a wooden bar across, one in each hand, which they stacked near the fires. While the water boiled, Ursula and the Nagas cut sandwiches and set out the mugs.

As dawn was breaking to the accompaniment of birdsong, the Hogermeer family arrived with their servants to help with the early shift. Mr. Hogermeer, a Dutchman, worked for an export company. He arrived in Assam as a young man and had married a beautiful Anglo/Indian lady. They and their two daughters, aged twenty and twenty-one, worked faithfully every day during Ursula's stay.

At five, heat descended on the junction as the first train of the day chugged in. Billowing steam, the train emerged from the green foliage with its brakes screeching, metal on metal, and its buffers clanging against each other. The sun-bleached brown, old-fashioned, high carriages, blistered by peeling paint, clanked over the points.

The trains arrived jam-packed with hot, thirsty, weary people, many of them ill with dysentery and cholera, all of whom had been trapped on the trains for at least twenty hours without food or water.

Owing to the breakdown in communications, officials in Shillong believed the refugee trains passed through during the night, reaching Pandu in time for the morning meal. The reality was they spent the night in sidings, while troop trains poured up the line. So it was that each morning at Lumding, a howling mob of hungry, dehydrated refugees of all colours and creeds spilled from the train. Ursula was in equal measure filled with compassion for the sorry travellers and livid at the administrators.

The Indian coolies, with no regard for sanitation, rushed from the train to relieve themselves around the station and canteen areas. Those ill with cholera, dysentery, and all sorts of other diseases freely used the latrines on the trains when they were standing at the station. The sewage of eight hundred or so people was concentrated in two hundred yards of track. As the day grew hotter, the stench increased, flies swarmed in, and over time, conditions became unbearable. On her first day, anger at the squalid conditions overcame the urge to retch. She was shocked to see Namkia and the boys also reeling from the foulness.

The work challenged even the most hardened.

The hours between five and seven were a blur. Tired, demoralized passengers on this first train of the day gratefully gulped down thirty gallons of tea. The volunteers served and poured, fetched and carried, washed mugs and dishes and dealt with crises and scalds. Then the train pulled out, leaving Ursula and her helpers leaning exhausted on the counter stained from spilt tea and tea leaves and littered with crumbs and dirty dishes.

By the time the train had been swallowed by the greenery, they were already washing dishes, wiping the countertop, sweeping and cleaning before returning home in the increasing heat for a brief rest, housework and breakfast.

At ten o'clock, they were again lighting the fires, making sandwiches and tea for the 11:00 a.m. mail-train, carrying wounded soldiers from the Burma front and more refugees. Temperatures were rising to 90°F, 100°F. Ursula and her helpers buttered three hundred buns in a small hut. A huge furnace in the adjoining kitchen added to the sweltering conditions. Sweat trickled down noses, stung eyes, soaked shirts and drained them all. Flies buzzed everywhere, round ears and eyes as a blur of hands flipped knives back and forth, spreading the runny liquid over crumbly bread.

Most of the wounded could not leave the train to go to the canteen. There were also numerous dysentery cases. Ursula and the Nagas boarded the train carrying four gallon buckets of tea in each hand and were followed by young Anglo/Indian women helpers from Lumding carrying sandwiches. In the carriages, it was stifling and even hotter than the 100°F temperatures outside. Ursula and her helpers, with sweat dripping from their faces, tea sloshing, muscles straining, rushed along the twelve carriages trying to reach each of the some two hundred men too sick to leave the train. With the train scheduled to stand for only twenty minutes, it meant they could only attend to people in the first few carriages, who were already clamouring for a second cup before Ursula reached half way down the train.

Ursula noticed with displeasure that as soon as the trains stopped, officers removed themselves to the refreshment room, giving little thought to the men under their command. Then one day, one outstanding brigadier arrived on the train. Eschewing the refreshment room, he stood with his foot on the step of the carriage, defying the stationmaster, the engine driver, and everybody else who wanted him to move, until each and every one of his men had tea and a sandwich. It warmed Ursula's heart to see him with a mug of tea in one hand directing the canteen staff. "Those chaps down there haven't had anything yet."

"Those men can have their second helping." He picked a bun from a passing Naga's tray. "See those men are taken care of."

From inside the train, the wounded could see Ursula, her clothes soaked with sweat, running at the double with her heavy cans of tea. They leaned out of the windows, grinning and shouting, "It's all right, miss. Take it easy, miss. Now don't worry, miss."

When she boarded the train, Ursula often found seriously injured men, whose wounds were putrid, whose uniforms were tattered and bloody. She ached for her medical kit, for the Naga healers, for time to minister to these valiant, suffering men. Gallant men as well: when they saw the genteel Indian/Anglo ladies pouring tea in the canteen, they stayed on the train so as not to upset the ladies with their bloodstained bandages and uniforms. Ursula patrolled the train, checking every carriage to see that no one missed receiving refreshments. She found a soldier whose leg was in plaster up to his thigh struggling to get out of the carriage with the help of his friends.

"Here, here," called Ursula. "Don't you bother going to the canteen. Stay where you are. We'll get you something."

"Oh no, miss," he smiled brightly. "It's all right. I like walking in India." He was lifted off the train, and with his arms round his friends' shoulders, he hopped to the canteen.

In the next carriage, Ursula found one man whose uniform was covered with blood.

"Are you wounded?" she asked.

"No, miss. Well, at least not much."

He must have been beside a man who had been hit. "Look here, go and get some tea. Can you walk?"

"Oh yes, miss, but there's ladies there, and I didn't like to go. Might upset them the state I'm in."

"You must be dying of thirst, though. All right, here you are," Ursula said, passing the man his tea and bun.

"Thank you, miss. Thanks for the tea. I was gasping for a drink."

On one train, Ursula found a soldier who had collapsed. On examining him, she found a septic shrapnel wound in his neck. She stuck her head out of the train and shouted for Namkia.

"Find someone to help you get this man off the train. He needs a doctor, now. Can't wait till he arrives at the hospital." The man was carried from the train and taken into Lumding when the train departed.

As the trains pulled out, men hung from the windows, waving and shouting. "See you on the way back, miss." "See you on the road to Mandalay."

At first, the Indians manning the National Congress canteen were standoffish, but as it became apparent that Ursula's group desperately needed help if they were to attend to all the wounded soldiers, they abandoned their spare time and joined Ursula's helpers. In time, the canteens were unofficially integrated with supplies drawn impartially from both.

By twelve thirty, the rush was over. The wounded departed. The station baked in the hot sun. One or two scavenging pi-dogs sniffed around. Ursula and her Nagas cleared up then walked to the rest-house in the stifling heat to bolt down some food before returning to light the fires at 2:00 p.m. An hour later, the up mail-train arrived filled with troops heading for Burma. This was the last train of the day except for the occasional one that passed through carrying trucks, ambulances, and mules to the front. After cleaning up, Ursula and the Zemi collected drinking water to bottle ready for the next day. At six o'clock, they returned to the rest-house to cut wood to take to Lumding the following morning. Then they bathed and ate. If Ursula were lucky, she would be asleep by eight o'clock once the accounts and correspondence were completed, but usually it was after nine before she switched off the light and collapsed onto the camp bed.

And at half past two in the morning, it all began again.

Ursula was to be relieved after two weeks at the canteen. A letter arrived from Mrs. Perry saying that Mrs. Reid had left on April 17th. The women who were supposed to relieve Ursula immediately began sending their excuses and refused to do a damn thing that was remotely uncomfortable. The next day, a letter arrived from a Mrs. Freeman informing Ursula that she could not possibly allow her daughter to work at the canteen. She was much too young and genteel to do such things.

239

"Damn and blast!" Ursula exploded. "Another relief isn't coming. This woman says her daughter is too young to do such work. Hah! She's older than I am for goodness' sake! Didn't take long for the ladies to kick over the traces once Mrs. Reid left, did it, Namkia?"

"The British ladies don't seem to like hard work."

Waving the letter about, Ursula continued her tirade.

"The other canteens on the line have four or five lady helpers and large canteen and domestic staffs. I'll write again and tell them we desperately need someone to relieve us. Maybe someone will show up before we collapse."

There was no lessening in the number of refugees and wounded arriving at Lumding. There were no nurses, orderlies, and most of the time, no Medical Officers available to travel on the trains with the wounded. People died on the trains from disease and lethal wounds, but they died too from neglect, and the lack of the most elementary treatments and lack of fluids. As Ursula carried tea along the trains, she looked out for corpses, particularly on the refugee trains where family members tried to hide the bodies from the authorities. After a few weeks, patrols were organized to search the trains and remove the bodies for burial.

And the gruelling work continued.

By early May, after four exhausting weeks, Ursula and her men were buckling from the long hours and hard work. Letters continued to arrive full of reasons why no one could come to relieve them.

Over breakfast, Ursula told Namkia, "I can't do anymore. I'm exhausted and so are all of you. I'm writing to tell them we're quitting at the end of this week."

"My sister, the wounded soldiers keep on coming. We have seen their suffering and their courage. We can't quit. They're putting their bodies as a shield between the Japanese and us. We must be here to help them when they come."

Ursula studied Namkia. The Zemi were an emotional people. She had noticed her staff working furiously at the canteen without any urging from her. She realized that helping the wounded soldiers had become a personal matter, a debt to be repaid.

"You're right. I'll try one more time to find a relief, but I can't keep working sixteen hours a day on so little sleep."

Ursula's relief arrived in the person of Mrs. Peak, a gray-haired grandmother. Sixty-five if she's a day, thought Ursula. Mrs. Peak was a cheerful, sunny, yet down-to-earth personality, who felt she could take on the world.

"These young women just won't have hard work, will they, Ursula?"

Ursula felt sorry for her. She had no idea what she'd let herself in for. Well, thought Ursula, I hope she can last the course. But that wasn't Ursula's worry now. She'd been set free, released from a huge burden, one that had proved almost too big for her to carry. Now she was going home to recuperate.

As zombies, Ursula and her staff stumbled aboard the Haflong train and immediately fell asleep on the benches.

The group staggered over the Tolpui pass and along the path to Laisong. Hazekiemba saw them coming and hurried to meet them with a jug of rice-beer.

Ursula and the men sank to the ground to rest. The look of concern on Hazekiemba's face made her think they must be a sorry sight, not the same strong folk who strode out of there six weeks before. They had worked themselves to a standstill.

At the camp, they fell into their beds for a week. In the world outside, the Burma army was beating a fighting retreat to the Manipur border. Imphal was bombed. The Japanese invasion was imminent; women and children were leaving, all while Ursula and her volunteers lay oblivious in an exhausted sleep.

The arrival of the monsoon at the end of May halted the invasion. The rains fell thick and fast, a grey wall behind which Laisong huddled. Wild gale-force winds lashed the bushes. Downpours mashed the flowers and swept the garden soil away. Rain clattered against the outer walls of the bungalow like handfuls of pebbles flung against the matting. Lines of wet clothes hung throughout the inside of the house unable to dry in the steamy, smoky rooms.

Letters arrived. One from Lexie told Ursula she was leaving Assam to work for the British Legation in Tehran. Lexie urged Ursula to leave too, "but knowing how stubborn you are, you probably won't, so at least promise me you'll stay safe." Another letter, from Mrs. Perry, told Ursula that her relief at Lumding had collapsed after one week and returned home on a stretcher.

"Poor dear," Ursula said to Namkia, "how she lasted that long I don't know. It laid me out, not to mention four very strong Nagas I know. It was really tough going, wasn't it?"

"It was hard work but good work, my sister." Namkia chuckled. "I'm glad it's over. Don't involve me in any more of your bright ideas."

On the first clear day after three weeks of winds and torrential rain, Ursula was hanging damp clothes on the line outside when she caught sight of three visitors to her compound: skeletons, three walking skeletons. She dropped her pegs in horror on recognizing them as men she knew from Asalu.

'Come. Come sit down."

She led them to the veranda then ran for Namkia.

"Namkia! Headmen from Asalu are here. They're starving. Why? Is there a famine?"

"Yes, there is a famine in Asalu."

"Why didn't you report it? Why didn't you tell me?"

"They were keeping it quiet. They didn't want the government to know."

"Good heavens! Tell Ali to prepare some food, and then come to the house."

Ursula hurried back to her bungalow. A lump formed in her throat at the pitiful sight of her friends, mere shadows of the men they once were. Lank hair covered skull-like heads. Their skin was dry and tight over jutting bones of ribs and cheeks.

"Namkia tells me you have a famine in Asalu. You must tell the SDO so he can help you."

"No, we do not want the government to know about the famine. Would you lend us some money to buy rice to see us through until the next harvest?"

"There is no need to borrow. If you tell the government, they will help you out with relief."

"Oh no, we cannot do that. Last time we had a famine, the government said they would provide us with free relief, and then they made us pay for it all."

Ursula looked to Namkia for an explanation. He told her the story of a previous famine.

"A generation ago, a government clerk from Haflong brought bags of grain to the village of Asalu. He opened them up and told the starving villagers to help themselves. Many did. Years later, they learned that the grain was not a gift but a long-term loan to be repaid with interest—something the clerk forgot to tell them. Brothers, descendants, heirs of dead-and-gone men, youths who had not even tasted the borrowed rice, found themselves liable for its repayment. It was a terrible blow to the village. As no one had expected this, no one had budgeted for it. In the end, the headmen solved the problem by a house-to-house levy throughout the village. That is why Asalu will not go to the government even though the silos are empty after losing their rice crops last August to a plague of grasshoppers."

"This is all because of one stupid clerk," Ursula argued with the headmen. "He was irresponsible for not explaining the relief was a loan, but that was one man, not the government."

"No, my daughter, it was a crafty deception by the government, and we, in Asalu, swore that we would never again accept help so mean and allow our suffering to be exploited."

"But you are entitled to free relief," Ursula persisted.

The headmen refused to consider it and again asked for a loan.

"How bad is it, Namkia?"

"There are no grain reserves. Been none for years."

The headmen continued, "We depended on the earnings of the able-bodied men, but a measles epidemic has laid them all out. There's nothing left. The people are starving. Everyone who can stand, even grandmothers, search the woods for frogs, beetles, roots and edible leaves."

"Listen to me," said Ursula. "You are entitled to free relief. If there is any charge for it, any interest to pay back, I will pay it." Ursula was serious in her offer, although she had no idea how she would manage to pay back anyone with her precariously low funds.

Still the headmen refused. "If we take the government's grain, they will be down on us to squeeze every penny they can from us. We will not take the government relief."

Ursula's heart was breaking at the stubbornness of her starving friends. She gave in and paid out the loan. That evening, she wrote to Perry and made arrangements to travel to Asalu.

Perry wrote back at once, saying her report had shocked him. His predecessor had given no hint of problems, and there were no indications from the records. He immediately sent a man to Asalu to investigate. The shell of Zemi secrecy was cracked. Perry, still new to the district, faced a full-blown famine.

He and Ursula worked together. As soon as he could, he found porters to take twenty loads of government free-relief rice to the village. He followed two days later with more supplies. Like the clerk a generation before, Perry and Ursula opened the bulging sacks and urged the villagers to take it. Silently, the people looked long and hard at Ursula, Perry, and the rice, and turned away.

Arguing and cajoling, Ursula and Perry persuaded those in most need to take a little. Ursula's Asalu friend Miroteung, whom she had seen a few months previously, lying laughing on his porch bench, tossing his chubby baby in the air, returned to the village fresh from the baby's burial almost too weak to stand. He sat against the doorpost.

"Please, Miroteung, you must take some rice," Ursula pleaded. "You've been ill, so has your wife."

Miroteung shook his head, too exhausted to speak. He would not touch the rice.

"If there's any catch in it, any interest to pay, I'll make up every last anna myself, I swear I will." Ursula's voice was breaking with emotion.

Reluctantly, Miroteung nodded, but he wouldn't take more than ten pounds. He was so weak Ursula called Ramgakpa to carry it down for him.

When she felt she had done all she could, Ursula returned to Laisong. Perry arrived to see her a week later.

"How are things in Asalu?" Ursula asked as they sat down to tea.

"The worst sufferers have been fed. We seem to have prevented immediate tragedy, but only just. Thank goodness you found out. It was a near thing. The Asalu headmen said deaths from starvation would have started that week."

Comparing notes, Perry and Ursula agreed heart and soul that something should be done about the Zemi. "We can't let this horrible misunderstanding with the government continue,"

Perry said, "but for the life of me, I can't think of a way to end it."

Ursula considered. Perry was a fair and just officer, well-liked and freely accepted by the Zemi, indeed as no officer has been for a dozen years, or so Namkia had told her. But the trouble was far too deep-rooted for his personal influence to cure. Something much bigger was required.

She said all this to Perry and he nodded, not immodestly, simply as one who values the truth. "If we're lucky," he said, "we'll get that chance, the opening we could use. We'll just have to watch for it."

Next day, Perry returned to Haflong. The unrelenting rains unfurled in curtains. Ursula and her staff snapped and squabbled like bad-tempered children, their nerves still in tatters after Lumding.

Then malaria attacked Ursula again and took her down. She lay helpless. For a day and a night, Namkia never left her room; every time she stirred, he was sitting by her side; at night, he slept beside her bed and woke at her slightest movement. As she improved, an awareness of his gentle care and devotion pierced Ursula's mind; this was a new Namkia.

July was marked by a dysentery outbreak at Nraitsak, a new and virulent strain brought in by refugee trains infecting the line as they travelled through. From the line, it spread outwards into the hills alongside. Nraitsak's elders decided that as medical treatment must be carried on over long periods, and as a doctor would need feeding and housing all that time, they would economize by keeping the outbreak secret and end it by the time-honoured sacrifice of a large pig.

It was a tragic decision. A month later, the situation came to light when a man Ursula had treated once before for dysentery developed symptoms and sent a messenger to Ursula for help. By this time, twenty people out of a population of sixty were dead.

Since Ursula's return from Lumding, the atmosphere in North Cachar had been tense. The Japanese lay just beyond the Burma border; all manner of rumours were flying. The Zemi were afraid. Mangled reports, misinformation and gossip overstated the British defeat in Burma and exaggerated Japanese prowess. Once the rains ended in the autumn, an invasion seemed certain. Ursula and the Zemi pondered what to do when that happened. In Manipur, the Kabui, Zemi, and Lyeng Nagas met to decide on joint action in the event of a withdrawal by the British administration. They wrote to Ursula to ask if she would stay behind to be their leader. Amazed, Ursula showed Namkia the letter.

"Well, of course you must, my sister. The Zemi know you, trust you, and look up to you because you get things done. You are a leader."

"I doubt I could be a Naga leader, Namkia. But I'll tell you this, if an invasion comes, I mean to stay."

"Colonel Rawdon Wright is on his way to see you," said Perry's letter contained in August's bundle of mail Haichangnang brought from Haflong.

The next day, around midday, Ursula spotted a European man accompanied by Nagas on the path beyond the village. She sent Degalang and Khamba with a note, inviting the colonel for lunch. An hour later, they returned alone.

"Didn't you find the colonel?"

"Oh yes, my mother, he sends you a message." Degalang handed Ursula her slip of paper.

She opened the note to find the colonel's reply scribbled in the margin.

"So sorry, but I've got a gammy leg. I'd better go straight to the rest-house."

"Can't the colonel walk properly?" Ursula asked Degalang.

"No, he's very lame and travels slowly."

Ursula called Namkia, and they went down the east path, expecting to meet the colonel's party at the bottom, but they were nowhere in sight. Ursula and Namkia searched the road for tracks. Finding none, they followed the road back towards Asalu, finally coming across the party just before the western pass.

It was obvious why the colonel's progress was so slow. A broad stretch of bandage showed between his stocking and his shorts. Unable to bend his knee, he was struggling to walk. Additionally, the colonel was not a young man; grey flecked his dark moustache, deep seams bracketed his mouth and furrowed his forehead. Ursula judged him to be in his mid-fifties.

She approached and held out her hand. "I'm Ursula Graham Bower. I hear you've come to see me."

The colonel shook her hand. "I certainly have, Miss Bower. There's a lot I want to talk to you about. Sorry I couldn't accept your luncheon invitation. Maybe you'll have lunch with me at the rest-house."

"Certainly," Ursula said. "Let us show you the way."

At the rest-house, Ursula and Rawdon Wright tucked into bread and sardines on the cool veranda.

"I've heard a lot about you," she said. "You know Mr. Jeffery, don't you?"

They discovered they had many mutual friends, including Philip Mills.

"I met your parents once, during a weekend on a country estate in England," he told her. "Assam used to be my old stomping-ground. Used to be an officer in the Assam Rifles between the wars. Had a hell of a job joining up again when war broke out. I'd retired, and I had this gammy leg, collected in the Kaiser's war. There's still an open wound in it. Managed to get in the RAF in the end. A ground job." He looked at Ursula and smiled, a shy, boyish smile. "Then the war came near Assam, and I began to raise heaven and earth to get out again. Finally, I was allowed to come, but only for desk work when what I really wanted was to get back into the hills with my Gurkhas.

"So what are you doing here?" Ursula asked. "This isn't desk work."

Rawdon Wright got straight down to business. He leaned forward in his chair opposite Ursula.

"I belong to a guerrilla organization, a unit known as "V" Force. Our job is to recruit the hill-tribes for service as scouts. The Japs are standing along the length of the Burma border. Behind us, in India, the Congress Party has stirred up widespread trouble, apparently to coincide with a Japanese invasion force in the near future. With the end of the rains in sight, we expect the Japs to press forward as soon as they can."

"Once the rains are over?" Ursula was shocked.

"Most likely. Possibly. The fact that they haven't moved yet might be because they're watching the Congress Party's rising. If it scores more success than it has at present, or even if it doesn't, the Japs are likely to attack India the first chance they feel strong enough. 'V' Force is therefore actively interested in the border areas, and among them North Cachar and that part of Manipur which lies in front of it. Several tracks cross this stretch, converging at Haijaichak and from there running to the railway. The district will be of importance if an invasion comes, and meantime it would be as well to stop spies and enemy agents from infiltrating the area, which they could easily do from the wayside stations."

The colonel leaned back in his chair, looked at Ursula and asked, "What do you think about recruiting a Watch and Ward?"

She felt a flicker of excitement. "What do you want me to do?"

"We've got to set up a network, anything from five-to-ten men in selected villages covering key points—the passes, fords, main tracks and trails—so that Watch and Ward can spot and report any unauthorized movement in the hills and give news of aircraft movements."

He brought out a map and spread it on the table.

"There are the tracks, the road from Kohima, the Naga paths from Maovom and Impuiloa meeting at Haijaichak in the eastern end of the pass. The only other route, from Hangrum, comes out at the west end of the pass by Laisong rest-house, and Laisong covers that."

Ursula traced a route on the map. "There's a possible route from Hangrum up the stream-beds and by Tolpui, which cuts out these; but it's difficult and would need local guides. Hangrum covers that."

"One thing's clear, Ursula, nothing can be done without the Zemi. Not only are they in the majority, but their villages lie at every strategic point. The Kuki villages are small and scattered and tucked away in corners in the hills. Only one Kuki village, Khuangmuel, near the Naga Hills border, occupies an important position. The Zemi have everything else that's going to matter. As a former commandant in the Assam Rifles, I know from first hand experience all about the Gaidiliu goddess fiasco and the political situation with the Zemi. What do you think they'll do?"

Ursula frowned. "I don't know. There's a sound element. That interpreter of mine, Namkia, is one of them, and he carries quite a bit of weight. Asalu and the Impoi group can be relied on. That's where he, Namkia, lives. Then there's a big group, the biggest I'd say, which doesn't want to get mixed up in anything, just wants to be left alone. Then there's the old crowd, Gaidiliu's lot. There aren't many of them now, not that one knows of anyway, and it's hard to say what influence they've got. But all the Zemi are really pretty sticky."

Ursula told him about the famine and other things she knew that would make recruiting the Zemi into Watch and Ward difficult.

"I'd like to go out to the Plains by way of Hangrum to see the country for myself," Rawdon Wright said.

"I'll go along with you as far as Hangrum. I know them a bit by now, and they know me. They won't hold back from me as they would a stranger."

"Eight o'clock start all right?"

"Fine, I'll raise some porters at Laisong and see you in the morning."

Next morning, they left the rest-house promptly at eight. As they walked along the bridle path, Ursula discovered how much the colonel's leg hindered him. They were barely making one and a half miles an hour. It was a steep climb out of the Jenam valley to the Nenglo ridge. Narrow Naga paths provided short cuts, which left out several hundred yards of road. To get down a steep slope, Rawdon Wright had to lean on a man's shoulder. On the narrow short cuts, where no one could walk beside him, he crawled up on his hands and knees. Despite his intense pain, he uttered not one word of complaint.

"Why are you making this trek with such a bad leg?" asked Ursula, after he apologized for the fifth time for delaying her and urged her to go on ahead.

"I spent many years in Assam," he told her, "and more than anything, I loved my Assam Rifles. And of course, there're the hills, the rivers, life in the open. I came back full of hope and joined 'V' Force, but it's manned by young men. I felt they were laughing at me, a desk-bound crock. So I begged to do this reconnaissance, and I'm going to do it if it kills me. As long as my leg will carry me, I can convince myself I'm not a has-been."

Progress to Hangrum was slow in August's steamy heat. During the halts, they stopped talking about the road and spoke instead of fishing and the people they'd known in Manipur. Rawdon Wright told Ursula about his most memorable salmon fishing trip to Scotland when the fish had practically jumped into his keep-net. Ursula told him of one fishing expedition she made with the Nagas.

"Shortly before you arrived, we all went fishing. The men diverted a stream and picked the minnows, shrimp and whelks and so on out of the dry bed. I wasn't much good with the shrimp and minnows, but I was hot stuff with the whelks; they were just about my speed. Anyway, after six hours work, we came away with, I would say, two pounds of assorted produce and that included crabs. But all the men seemed quite pleased."

Ursula enjoyed the halts, where the colonel, a superb conversationalist, entertained her. She felt they could have been sitting on a Club veranda.

After several more hours trekking, Ursula told him, "We've just reached the last summit, the one that overlooks Hangrum. I can see the headmen waiting on the outskirts of the village by the upper *morung*. They'll be in a panic at the arrival of a Colonel Sahib; anything scares Hangrum. So I'll go on ahead with Namkia. The others will bring you into the village."

As Ursula and Namkia approached the village, the headmen came to meet them. Before Ursula could say anything, Namkia spoke up. Ursula had never seen him so excited.

"That Colonel Sahib, he's not a man. He's a tiger! He's got a wounded leg. He got it in the German war. His bearer told me. He climbs up the hills on all fours, like a bear. He comes down the hills like this, on a man's arm. And not one word, not one! The courage! Anyone else would be weeping aloud by now. I tell you he's not a man, he's a tiger!"

Ursula, Namkia and the headmen watched the small group descend the dozen zigzags of the opposite slope. When Rawdon Wright reached Ursula and the headmen, they were unable to speak, so awed were they by his courage.

The next day, Ursula and Rawdon Wright went round Hangrum. As was the norm with strangers present, a silence hung over the village, only this time the hush was not hostile. The villagers all looked at the colonel as Namkia did, Ursula as well for that matter. Such was the man's courage it could not be commented on, only watched in reverence.

Sitting over drinks in the rest-house veranda at sunset, Ursula and Rawdon Wright looked out over the green hills of Manipur.

"I'm always amazed by the beauty of the ridges when they're tinged red by the setting sun," Ursula said.

Rawdon Wright looked at Ursula.

"I believe you're like me, you poor thing. In love with the hills."

"I believe I am."

"Fair warning, nothing else in this life and nowhere else on god's planet will quite do after living here." He shook his head then sipped his drink.

That evening a deputation of headmen from Hangrum arrived.

"We want the Colonel Sahib to have a litter. We will have one made. We will arrange the porters. We will provide men free of cost, as a gift from the village," Namkia translated.

Rawdon Wright shook his head. "Tell them I'm a soldier. I'm not going to be carried about the country like a woman."

Namkia translated back to the Hangrum elders then said to Ursula in Zemi, "The Sahib got his wound in the war. It's nothing to be ashamed of. Nobody questions his courage. He ought to be carried; he shouldn't go on as he is."

Ursula told Rawdon Wright of their concerns, but he would have none of it. The next morning, Ursula, Namkia and the headmen stood outside the bungalow, watching the colonel's white shirt as he climbed slowly and painfully, with the aid of the interpreter's shoulder, over boulders, gullies, and slippery red soil. At the last turn of the road he stopped and waved. Ursula and the elders waved back. Then the white shirt was lost from sight. Nobody said anything. There was too much to say.

Ursula received a couple of letters from him later. Then he fell ill. That last gesture, the reconnaissance, had been too much. His leg amputated, he died three weeks later. Perry informed

253

Ursula of Rawdon Wright's death just as the scheme he had started, North Cachar Watch and Ward, was coming into being. The news brought her to tears.

"Perry, he told me he was unhappy anywhere but here, and I think he died well and no doubt happy that he had proved he was no old crock."

"That's something."

"And then there's Watch and Ward. I want his scheme to be a success. In his honour, as it were."

She and Perry resolved to build the finest network they could.

Colonel Critchley, a tall, young "V" Force officer, arrived at Laisong in October and interviewed Ursula in her bungalow. Satisfied with "V" Force's newest recruit, the colonel presented Ursula with a sheaf of papers, a bag containing one thousand silver rupees fresh from the Haflong Treasury and said, "There you are, Miss Bower. You can go ahead now and recruit the Zemi and Kukis. You'll be working closely with SDO Edwin Perry, so when Watch and Ward is up and running, you can contact us through Perry." And then he left.

A few days later, Ursula met Perry in Asalu. Sitting on the veranda of the rest-house, they discussed the possibility of reconciling the Zemi with the government.

"This is the chance we've been waiting for," Ursula said.

"Yes," Perry said, "but we must keep every promise we make, especially about providing them with guns."

"Just one slip up will make things worse than ever; we'll never get them back. This is a wonderful opportunity that's fallen into our laps. Now it's up to us."

"Where are you going to start recruiting?" Perry asked.

"I thought Hangrum."

Perry's eyebrows lifted in surprise. Ursula saw his expression and laughed.

"Yes, I know. It must be my contrary nature. Why else would I start but with the toughest challenge?"

As Ursula returned to Laisong, she stumbled and twisted her knee so she and Namkia did not arrive in Hangrum until a week later. As she sat and rested her leg with Lassu's latest batch of month-old puppies tottering and tumbling around the living room, Paodekumba, her tough, wiry gardener came to see her.

255

"I've heard that you want scouts. I will be a scout, starting today," he told her.

He was their one and only scout for the first two weeks of Watch and Ward.

In Hangrum, Ursula and Namkia put the Watch and Ward scheme to the headmen. The headmen responded with alarm and disapproval but not outright rejection.

"We must put the matter to the village," they said.

Namkia and Ursula impatiently cooled their heels in the rest-house for a week before Hangrum held the public meeting. The headmen invited Ursula and Namkia to go along and thrash it out. About fifty villagers turned out for the meeting. Many carried babies on their backs. They sat, stood or squatted around the open space in front of the headman's house. Namkia and Ursula sat on a bench facing the crowd. The headman sat beside them to act as chairman of the debate.

He stood up and explained why Ursula and Namkia were there. Then Namkia took his turn to state their case. He did so, powerfully. He had barely sat down before people were leaping up, hurling accusations and denials at each other, and just as abruptly sat down.

A Hangrum man jumped up. "You'll take us away! It's a trap!"

Namkia stood up. "No! It's an honest offer!"

"Why should we fight for the sahibs? We didn't fight for the Kacharis. We didn't fight for the Manipuris. Why should we fight for the British?"

Namkia stood again. "Why shouldn't we? Did the Kacharis or the Manipuris stop the Angami raids? Haven't the sahibs done that? Haven't they given us roads and salt markets? Haven't they given us protection and peace? Don't we owe them something for that?"

"I say it's a trap! They want to take us away! What about the Lushai War? We sent porters for that. How many returned?"

He was right there. Ursula recalled that most of the Zemi porters had died of cholera.

Namkia rose. "That was fifty years ago! They've got new medicines now. You can get injections against these things.

Don't quote the past at me! You won't be taken away. It's all for service here. Here, in your own village."

Ursula got to her feet. "You'll be paid. You'll get guns."

"This is our country, isn't it? Why shouldn't we look after it?" Namkia challenged.

The debate grew more heated. Opponents jumped up one after the other like pistons in an engine; Namkia and Ursula leapt to their feet in turn to reply.

"Lies! Lies! Lies!" shouted a man almost in their faces.

Ursula sprang up. "It's not lies, but the truth! If you Zemi won't do it, then the Kukis will. Or else troops will come here to do the job for you, and will you like that? I'm offering you guns! Guns! Where are your guns? When did you last have some?"

"Bring your troops in! Let them do it!"

"All right!" Ursula shouted. "You didn't like it before, did you, when the troops got off with your girls? Don't scream at me later if things go wrong! Fools! We've got guns for you! You've been disarmed for ten years. If you do the job well, you'll have a chance to keep them. Fools!"

"Lies! Lies!"

"Truth!"

"You'll take us away!"

"You'll serve here!"

"Lies!"

"Truth!"

"You'll take us away!"

"We won't!"

The debate had developed into a childish shouting match, and the meeting ended, as Zemi meetings did, by everyone, as if by silent signal, abruptly getting up and going home.

As the last stragglers drifted away, Ursula felt frustrated and depressed. "We didn't convince them, Namkia."

"A few people have been coming to me to ask about Watch and Ward," he said, "but you can see most of the village is against it. They won't play unless they're forced to."

Travelling to Asalu and Impoi, Ursula and Namkia found so many eager candidates they were able to be selective in choosing men to be scouts. The pay Ursula offered was not high, only ten

257

to fifteen rupees a month, but the two villages were still impoverished owing to the famine. Working as scouts enabled the men to escape the financial trap, which forced them to work in the Kachari fields. Also, as Ursula and the government had helped them in the famine and kept their word to them about free relief, the villagers trusted them. The government had helped them when they were hungry, now they felt they should help the government.

By the time Ursula had reported back to Perry, all the smaller Zemi villages and Kuki settlements she and Namkia had approached were cooperating. Only Hangrum and two nearby villages, Shongkai and Baladhan, were resisting.

"I'll talk to them," Perry said.

Ursula and Namkia returned to Hangrum accompanied by Perry and some Watch and Ward recruits. The discovery that the smaller villages were supporting the scheme shocked and disturbed Hangrum's residents. Hangrum, because of its great size, had dominated the area for years; now for the first time ever, little settlements, under Namkia's leadership, were flouting Hangrum's authority. Not knowing what to do next, Hangrum berated the Watch and Ward recruits who had come with Ursula and the SDO.

"We have always decided what is right for the tribe, and you're going against us!"

"To the devil with Hangrum's dictatorship," the recruits retaliated. "We've made our own decision."

At the council meeting, Perry rebuked the villagers for their fearfulness and lack of cooperation. Headmen from Shongkai and Baladhan were also present at the meeting. Volunteers for Watch and Ward from their villages waited in the wings ready to be produced, or not, depending on how events played out. Seeing the swing towards Watch and Ward, the headmen suddenly jumped up, dashed from the meeting and returned with their candidates. They praised the Watch and Ward scheme loudly as they propelled their recruits towards an astonished Perry still in the middle of the council meeting.

Stunned, Ursula whispered to Namkia, "Did you know about this?"

As shocked as Ursula, he shook his head.

"I'd say it's all over bar the shouting," she said.

But Ursula was wrong. As the council continued, it became obvious that the large village was so at odds with itself it was incapable of deciding anything.

"I'll give you one week to make arrangements to join us," Perry told them. Then he and Ursula's party moved down the ridge to Baladhan.

Next day, as Ursula's group returned to Laisong via Hangrum, the headmen met them on the way to the rest-house. They gushed such profuse greetings Ursula immediately realized something was amiss.

"Has Hangrum found its recruits?" she asked.

"Oh yes, we have."

The two elderly headmen scrambled to offer them beer. Ursula caught Namkia's eye across the lip of her cup. His suspicious expression said it all. Something was not right.

The headmen arranged to bring the recruits along that evening. With some nail biting and nervousness and avoiding Ursula's eyes, the headmen marshalled the recruits in the rest-house at four o'clock.

No wonder they're so nervous thought Ursula, eyeing the recruits. Of the ten candidates, only three had two good eyes. None was under forty; most had no teeth; and one was crippled. She didn't blame the elderly headman. He was a decent old chap in his way, but at his age, the village was just too much for him with its political factions and infighting.

Ursula took a deep breath then spoke her mind. "Hangrum is a large village, is it not? With a hundred and twenty houses, correct? I know you have many strong, young, healthy men, men who could be the type of scout and runner we want. I can see you have tried to fulfil your quota, but only of men whose loss could not possibly be felt by the village." She stopped pacing, stood in front of the headmen and waved her arm towards the volunteers. "You seem to have swept the village for the lame and the blind. I expected better." Ursula paused, stood to her full height, then dismissed them with, "Take these men away, and find us men who are at least in one piece."

The headmen looked down at the floor and glanced sideways at one another. Ursula could see they had expected her response. Relieved of the onerous task for which they had been press-ganged, the candidates shook off their cloud of resignation and, in a cheerful mood, hurried back to the village.

Next day, the headmen arrived with a fresh selection. Ursula recognized a couple of the original crew, but the rest of the men seemed reasonably fit and they lacked the air of acquiescence of the original bunch. Smiling, she looked across at Namkia.

Blast! She saw something was up by the way he wrapped himself in his red blanket and stood aloof from the proceedings, Ursula could tell Namkia was expressing disapproval about something. The agitated old headman was stuttering so much, Ursula could not understand what he wanted.

"Namkia, what's he trying to tell me?"

Namkia reluctantly approached, his mouth turned down in repulsion.

He eyed the men with distain. His voice dripped with disgust. "These recruits are so lily-livered, they want you to swear an oath on your life that in no circumstances will they be sent away."

He turned on the headmen. "Sahibs don't take oaths. A sahib's word is enough. If a man is a liar, then he isn't a sahib. An oath! Tch! The idea!"

Ursula stepped forward to Namkia. "I don't mind," she whispered, "What I've to say is true."

Namkia relayed this to the headmen and the recruits. Then, dissociating himself from the proceedings, he leaned against a veranda-post and looked on.

The instant the recruits heard that Ursula agreed to take an oath, Tseva, one of the volunteers, pulled out an egg from under his cloth and handed it to Ursula. Namkia came out of his detachment to tell Ursula what to do, but Ursula stopped him. "I know what to do, Namkia. Don't coach me."

She silently thanked Professor Hutton, of Cambridge, for the wonderful advice he had given her so long ago. Would it work?

She went outdoors and dramatically lifting her arms to the sky, she repeated the words of the oath, calling on earth and sky to witness that what she said was true, and then offered her life as forfeit if she lied.

She then began reciting a long passage from Alexander Dumas in her best French. As she chanted and sang the lines, Namkia looked shocked. The whole village was agog, and some young men stepped away from Ursula, impressed and afraid.

Then she flung down the egg.

Ursula knew that among the Nagas an oath is a matter of such magnitude it is avoided as much as possible in village court cases. Death is considered so inevitable should the person swearing the oath break it that there is no further dispute—he wins his case outright. If Ursula took the oath, it would be conclusive proof of her honesty.

The egg hit a small rock; shell and yolk splattered far and wide. The headmen and recruits hurried down the veranda steps and anxiously looked for traces of the egg. They found tiny particles as far as twenty yards away splashed on gravestones, specks of shell outside the kitchen, yellow splotches on the gravel path.

Awed, they came back to Ursula and said, "The egg is completely dispersed. What you say is true."

Satisfied, they went off to the village.

By early December, Watch and Ward was operating in a triangular area. The Jiri River from Khuangmuel south to the confluence with the Jenam formed the base, and the apex touched the railway at Mahur. The plan was to extend operations along the Barak River from Henima village down. Three main cross-country tracks converged in this key area.

In every village covering an entrance or exit to that triangle, Watch and Ward had a small group of scouts, usually five, and where necessary, a pair of runners. Runners were stationed by arrangement with the *morungs* at every stage along the main routes so that in an emergency, news and orders could travel immediately. The scouts' job was to find and bring to HQ possible spies: all strangers passing through who were not hillmen or government servants or otherwise accounted for with special passes issued by either Perry or Ursula. A rubber-stamped symbol of a crown that the illiterate scouts would recognize adorned each pass. The scouts were also to report crashed aircraft and generally to keep Ursula and Perry informed.

The main difficulty in the beginning was to put some mettle in the Zemi who had felt downtrodden for so long. After the first week, distressed scouts began complaining, "Without red cloths, nobody recognizes our official authority. We must have red cloths."

"Yes, you must," Ursula agreed, wondering where she was going to find a batch of red blankets when civil supplies had dried up because of the war.

She sent Haichangnang with a letter to Perry stressing the urgent need for red blankets. Perry sent an SOS to "V" Force HQ at Barrackpore where, by fair means or foul, the quartermaster managed to procure nineteen scarlet British

Military Hospital blankets and promptly dispatched them to Mahur for Ursula's scouts.

In the early days, "V" Force HQ did not always mesh with Ursula's needs. Drafts and the Haflong Treasury's opening day failed to coincide with Ursula's payments to the scouts, all one hundred and fifty of them. At the beginning of November, after meeting all Watch and Ward's financial commitments out of Critchley's initial one thousand rupees, Ursula sat at her dining table counting and recounting her last few coins. How on earth would she manage for the next six weeks with only thirty rupees to keep her staff, two dogs, their pups and herself?

Ursula toured over two hundred miles in the mountains in those six weeks. She felt the gods were looking after her by the abundance of squirrels and pigeons that presented themselves to her shotgun to supply her cooking pot.

Straight from this tour, Ursula went to Shillong for Christmas where she stayed with Mr. and Mrs. Mills. Her scrawny appearance shocked them.

"Ursula, you look quite gaunt!" Mrs. Mills blurted out. "Doesn't she, Philip?"

"Have you been ill?" he asked.

"No, not ill. 'V' Force seems to be having some hiccups in making its payments to me," Ursula told them. "I'm finding it a struggle to keep going, but I daren't complain."

"It's ridiculous to be in this situation. Why can't you complain?"

"Philip, I'm a woman, a freak in the job. They told me they'd send a British officer to take over sooner or later. I don't want to give them an excuse to fire me."

Once Ursula and his wife retired to bed, Mills, in his official capacity as the Governor's Secretary, wrote a scathing letter to "V" Force's commanding officer. It had the desired effect. In the New Year, to Ursula's delight, she was put on a captain's pay, and "V" Force allowed her rations, which helped greatly with prices soaring and supplies scarce.

Colonel Scott, the quartermaster general "V" Force, came to see Ursula to discuss her needs. She found him to be particularly sympathetic.

"Tough for a woman," he told her. "Always wrong twice, once for being wrong and once for being a woman. Don't worry, Miss Bower, I'll sort things out."

And he did. Her teething troubles were over. From that day on she lacked for nothing.

*   *   *

Ursula's immediate commanding officer Colonel Binny, who commanded "V" Force Assam Zone, arrived in January to inspect Watch and Ward. More importantly, he brought the promised guns, which Ursula had insisted on for her scouts. The Zemi had never had many firearms, though most Kuki villages had at least two; whatever guns the Zemi had owned were confiscated in the "troubles."

With guns in their hands, a wave of confidence passed through Watch and Ward scouts, confidence in Ursula and confidence in "V" Force because they had fulfilled the most important and apparently the most impossible of their promises. And, most importantly, they had confidence in themselves because they were now armed. It didn't matter that the guns were ancient muzzle-loaders, which took two minutes to reload. Supplied with powder and shot, the scouts instantly became at privileged elite, encouraged to spend their leaves in any village where game was damaging the crops. It was good target practice and a great boost to morale.

A few weeks later a couple of woebegone scouts arrived at Laisong each carrying a weapon which looked like a stock with a spring attached. The guns they had received had barrels made of coiled sheet metal and were not very solid. When used, the barrels had burst and unwound themselves. As nasty as the repercussions were, Ursula could barely keep a straight face. She hastily appeased them with the promise of the best of the next lot of guns to arrive.

*   *   *

In the spring, while Ursula was away in an inaccessible part of the south Barail, telling off idle scouts, promoting keen ones, and inspecting their weapon training, Binny sent a British signaller from Imphal with a convoy of stores and rations. Having travelled directly to Mahur without passing through Haflong, he had no pass and didn't know he needed one.

The signaller managed to find some porters and march his loads through Watch and Ward's lines to Laisong, much to the consternation of the scouts from Impoi and Asalu. Wrapped in their red blankets, they doggedly brought up the rear of the procession.

Paodekumba was in charge at Ursula's camp. The scouts hurried to him.

"The soldier has no pass."

"Why have you let him through?" said Paodekumba. "You know your orders."

"Yes, but he's a sahib. How can we arrest a sahib?"

Tough-as-nails Paodekumba would have arrested anyone or anything, but he didn't like to make a mistake.

"Ramgakpa," he called, "take the sahib some tea."

While the signaller drank his refreshments, Paodekumba conferred with the scouts in the men's quarters.

"He must be a Jap spy."

"How do you know? We've never seen a Jap before," said one of the scouts.

"He has black hair, doesn't he?" said the head scout from Asalu. "Whoever's seen a sahib with black hair? Europeans are either fair or brown."

"That settles it. He's a Jap spy," said Paodekumba. He sent Degalang to the village for reinforcements. Ramgakpa served the oblivious soldier's supper. Paodekumba found a piece of rope and briefed his raiding-party. As he led the men across the compound towards Ursula's bungalow, a runner arrived with a message. Ursula had reached Mahur and would be back in two days.

Paodekumba regretfully called off operations.

When Ursula arrived at Laisong, the signaller came from exploring the vegetable garden to meet her.

"Hello, Miss Bower, Corporal Richards. Am I pleased to see you!"

"Haven't my men been looking after you?"

"Oh yes," he said, as they settled on the veranda, "only . . . the Nagas gave me porters to come up all right, but they don't seem to understand that I want to leave again. I've been here two days."

It must have been a nerve-wracking two days thought Ursula as she quieted Khamba who was prowling around with a sullen growl in his throat. Khamba obviously didn't like the poor man.

"Excuse me a minute, Richards. I'll have Khamba taken away so you can relax."

Ursula moved to the end of the veranda and called Degalang to take Khamba. Instead, Paodekumba arrived in a rush.

"Who is he? Why's he here? He doesn't have a pass. Is he a Jap spy? D'you want him captured? I've got the men here."

"What men?"

Paodekumba turned towards the men's quarters where the men from the village sprang from their hiding places, full of hope, bringing the rope with them.

"I would have captured him before," said Paodekumba. "But I thought I'd better wait till you came back. Can we do it now?"

With mounting disappointment, Paodekumba listened to Ursula's explanation of the signaller presence in Laisong.

"I really hoped he was a Jap," he said.

Hidden deep in the woods, on top of one of the steepest, highest spurs on the south Barail stood Khangnam, a Zemi village of fifty houses. It could be reached only by climbing precipitous Naga paths like ladders, so remote that touring district officers rarely went there.

When "V" Force affairs took Ursula to the village, she delighted in discovering it still had its stone defences. All other Zemi villages had allowed theirs to fall into moss-covered heaps of rubble.

"Once the Japanese have been dealt with," she told Namkia, "we'll return to study these defences more closely."

"Another one of your crazy ideas," he said, less than thrilled.

The building of a new airfield at Kumbhirgram brought a new excitement to the Naga Hills: flying aircraft. They flew daily through the Barail passes, sometimes ruffling the thatch on Namkia's *morung* at Impoi and sometimes rattling the garden fence at Laisong. Sometimes, planes crashed in the jungle. Then Haflong police forwarded messages to Watch and Ward to search for aircraft, but the sparse information and confused directions supplied were, more often than not, inadequate; they needed a special set-up.

The only village in Watch and Ward that neither commanded a route nor covered a ford was Khangnam. What made the village so special was the hill just above it. From the top, one could see a red oblong carved out of the Silchar plain, the new airfield at Kumbhirgram, and almost the entire face of the south Barail. By virtue of the village's position, Khangnam became an observation post and search party base. The lookouts' camp stood on a ridge beyond the village, giving a clear view south to the plains, shimmering in the heat, or north to a sweeping green valley with a backdrop of Barail ridges.

One morning about nine o' clock, Ursula and Namkia were walking to the village. The path travelled along the ridge between large rocks and then down over an outcrop to the broad street. They had just reached the outcrop when they heard the drone of aircraft high above.

"Planes," Ursula said, looking up and around without seeing them.

"A lot," Namkia agreed.

"Are they ours?" She stood still and listened. "They don't sound like ours."

People crammed doorways, listening, anxiously looking around. The planes came into view, two large formations of bombers accompanied by fighters, invisible except when seen as a speck glinting in the sun. The air throbbed as the aircraft passed over, heading for the plain.

"They must be ours," Ursula said, sounding puzzled, "but I don't recognize . . ." Stunned, she stopped in mid-sentence as a puff of smoke erupted from the plain; then another and another and another; then the boom of gunfire reached her ears. Suddenly, from Kumbhirgram, there came the whoomp, whoomp, whoomp of bombs.

The airfield could not be seen from the village, only from the top of the hill. Everyone began to run. In seconds, all the males from the village were strung out along the path to the summit: small boys racing in front with dogs at their heels, being overtaken by youths from the *morungs*, elders throwing off their cloaks to run faster, while girls and women shrieked and dashed for home. Namkia was gone from her side in a flash. Last in line, Ursula panted along some distance behind everyone, alone except for one of the headmen who tactfully slowed down to trot along beside her.

When Ursula reached the viewpoint, a haze of red dust hid the airfield. The hum of departing bombers faded into the distance. All eyes were pinned on the dust-cloud from where came the sound of explosions. Was it gunfire or exploding ammunition? She waited in suspense for the dust-cloud to disperse, watching as it swirled away over the plain to reveal smoke rising from buildings on fire.

Namkia pushed through the crowd to Ursula.

"The guns hit one! We saw something falling. We couldn't see where it went because of the sun."

"Was it in our area?"

"More over Manipur way, I think."

Excitement over, the men returned to the village, babbling about all they had seen. Over the campfire that night, Ursula and Namkia discussed the day's events to reiterate to the "V" Force lookouts the importance of their work. Then next day, Ursula returned to Laisong.

Some days later, the Kuki wet-demonstrator hurried into camp, accompanied by a porter carrying a large, lumpy sack.

"We've found something in the jungle, miss-sahib."

He waved his hand to the porter to reveal his load. The porter tipped the sack, tumbling splintered, gray-painted plywood over Ursula's feet.

Aircraft wreckage! Ursula squatted down. Ferreting through it, she found a varnished piece of wood covered with Japanese characters.

"Where'd you get this?"

"In the jungle near where the Jiri and Jenam Rivers meet. There's a lot of it. It came down burning. The villagers were frightened by the gunfire and ran to hide under their houses. They believed the bombs could blow whole mountains away."

Ursula scribbled a note to Perry to tell him it seemed a Japanese plane was down. Having sent Haichangnang off with the letter, she called Paodekumba.

"I want you to take a patrol at once to find the plane's wreckage and look for survivors," she told him.

"At once, Mother," he said and was off like a shot.

After Paodekumba left, Ursula couldn't settle. Next day she told Namkia, "Get ready. We can't miss out on the excitement. We'll go to Baladhan to meet the patrol."

Perry landed at Baladhan an hour after Ursula, and an hour after that Paodekumba's patrol arrived.

"We found the wreckage," Paodekumba told them, "but it was only a shot-off wing, not the whole plane. We scouted round a bit, but the jungle was thick, and we didn't find the rest of the plane."

"Good work," Perry said. "Pity there were no Japs about, eh?"

"Big pity, sahib," Paodekumba replied with feeling, running a finger across his throat, leaving no doubt as to the fate of any Japanese survivor who might fall into his hands.

Paodekumba left to go into the village. Ursula and Perry ate curried bully-beef and rice by the campfire.

"Bother! I thought we had something there," Ursula said.

"We were out of luck today, but it's not likely anyone survived the crash. Anyway, it looks like we'll soon have enough to keep us occupied. The possibility of a Jap invasion is growing by the minute."

As Perry talked, Namkia loomed from the darkness beyond the fire. "There's a party in from Hangrum to report."

It was Tseva and his co-leader, a wild hunter from the lower *morung*.

"Ten men in uniforms and armed with rifles and a man who seems to be their officer arrived at Hangrum this afternoon," he told them. "They didn't have a pass or a guide. We don't know who they are or where they came from. They're camped at the rest-house."

Ursula and Perry looked at one another.

"It wasn't a whole machine." Perry said.

Ursula was galvanized. "Perhaps the rest of it came down somewhere."

They sent Namkia and Tseva into Baladhan to find Paodekumba and all the men they could raise. Shortly after, Paodekumba trotted into camp.

"Here." Perry handed him a note. "This note has orders for the strangers. If they try to leave after reading this, you must stop them . . . somehow."

Paodekumba grinned in delight at the prospect of some action then left with his torchlight patrol, while Ursula and Perry packed ready to leave at sun up. Next morning, as they marched along the ridge behind Hemeolowa, they were met by two Nagas with a note. Perry opened it.

"That ends the Jap theory. It's from the lieutenant of a Railway Operating Unit sent to look at the wreckage."

Half an hour later, outside the rest-house, they met the lieutenant, a small Anglo-Indian with a pencil thin moustache.

"Good morning," Perry greeted him, snapping off a salute. Looking past the lieutenant, Perry appeared startled. "What on earth's all that?"

In the hollow where Ursula had flung the egg and sworn the oath, ten uniformed men with rifles were standing beside six loads of baggage. Surrounding them were nearly fifty Hangrum men, including the headmen, Paodekumba and the scouts. There were also a goat, and two chickens in a basket, and surprisingly, right in the middle of it all, a long-poled bamboo carrying-chair.

"Why the litter?" asked Perry. "Is one of your men sick?"

The lieutenant looked at the carrying-chair as if he wished it would disappear and hesitated before replying. Ursula and Perry, sensing his evasion of the question, glanced at one another before looking back to the small man.

"My corporal's got fever," he said, the words tumbling out in a rush. "It was a pleasure to meet you both, but we need to be off."

His haste seemed suspicious.

"It's too late for the porters to march and return," Perry said. "You may as well stay the night and set off in the morning."

The lieutenant wrung his hands. "No, no, I really must go."

"And I really must insist," Perry said. "There are tigers in the area. Wouldn't want anything to happen to you, would we?"

Despite the lieutenant's reluctance, the SDO's words compelled him to stay.

Over dinner, the lieutenant told them he had been sent to report on the aircraft wreckage. "But the information I was given was completely wrong as to the route I should go and the travelling conditions." He showed them his written orders.

"Surely his C.O. was joking," Perry said, handing the orders to Ursula to read.

271

"This is so off-beam, it has to be a joke."

"No, no," the lieutenant said. "From the start, I was disinclined to fulfil my mission. I didn't realize you were ahead of me, or I would have turned back at Hangrum, leaving the Japs to take care of themselves. But the Nagas delayed me."

"You would have disobeyed orders?" Perry asked.

"Yes, I would."

"What do you think would have happened to you if you had?"

"Oh, I would probably have been transferred to another unit. I've been transferred many times since I entered the service."

Ursula looked at Perry. She could see he felt the same as she did, ashamed and sickened at the poor example this pathetic man was setting the Nagas. She saw Paodekumba waiting outside.

"Excuse me, gentleman," she said, getting up and leaving the rest-house. She moved away with Paodekumba to hear his report.

"We got here in the early hours and delivered the note to the officer as I was told. But next day, he pestered the headmen for porters. They put him off as long as they could. And then they became afraid he would use force, so they told him they would bring some porters to the bungalow. But we weren't really going to let them leave. I had a plan. As soon as the officer laid his hands on the farewell gifts—the goat and the chickens—the porters were going to jump the men and grab their rifles. I'd picked some men to help me jump on the officer, while the porters were going to get the men. Then you turned up and spoiled the fun."

"So that's what was going on when we arrived. Good work. But weren't you scared to tackle the sahib and his men?"

"Sahib!" scoffed Paodekumba. "Call that a sahib! He's the laughing-stock of Hangrum! Didn't you know? He was carried up in a litter! He told the headman he was over forty and too old to walk."

"How shameful! The headman himself is well over sixty. Mind you, he can outwalk me," Ursula said.

"The officer's too scared to sleep in the bungalow because of the ghost."

"What ghost?"

"The one the headmen told him about. Every time the bungalow cracks and creaks, it's a sign the ghost is around they told him. He spent last night in the kitchen with his men!"

Ursula and Paodekumba shared a short chuckle at this fatuity.

Then Paodekumba turned angry and said, "What do you suppose those who are not loyal to the government are saying? They've been asking how the sahibs will beat the Japs if their officers are like that. What am I to answer? Tell me that!"

"This is not a good officer, Paodekumba." Ursula looked at him expectantly. Emphasizing her words, she continued, "*Especially* as he is frightened of ghosts."

Paodekumba brightened, catching Ursula's drift.

"Goodnight," she said, with a mischievous smile.

Ursula returned to the bungalow, took Perry aside and passed on what Paodekumba had told her. "That bloody man's a total disaster as far as propaganda goes," Perry said through clenched teeth.

Ursula was bitter. "He's destroyed all the good that Rawdon Wright's courage created."

Perry slammed his fist down on the veranda rail. "Damn it! I'm livid! I haven't been this angry in years."

They stood in silence, looking at the stars, while Perry lit and smoked his pipe and calmed himself. As they turned for the rest-house, Ursula said, "Oh, don't be surprised if we have a visit from the resident ghost tonight."

Perry raised questioning eyebrows.

Ursula grinned. "We'll teach the lieutenant to come here spoiling all our hard work."

The first raps had the lieutenant leaping from his bed and running into the living room. He was still fully clothed. His face was gray. He held a revolver in one hand and a shining electric torch in the other.

"Did you hear that, the ghost?"

"Don't worry," Perry said, from his chair where he was reading by the lamp. "It usually quiets down before midnight."

"The ghost is pretty well harmless," Ursula added, "except to strangers."

The lieutenant shrieked and ran back to his room.

Perry smiled with grim satisfaction. Ursula covered her mouth to muffle a fit of giggles.

First thing in the morning the lieutenant hastened away on foot. Not long afterwards, Paodekumba reported that the officer had the two litters waiting out of sight. He'd stepped into one and his corporal into the other to be carried away.

"God help us!" said Perry.

Attendance at Laisong's daily drill sessions had drastically fallen off. Delighted that Ursula had provided them with guns they could use for hunting, the Naga scouts at first religiously attended her drill sessions, but then started skipping them in order to go hunting. Namkia was becoming increasingly angry and frustrated with the villagers.

"Don't worry," Ursula said. "I know how to deal with them. I'll do it the Naga way. Make sure everyone comes to camp in the morning."

Next morning, the scouts gathered in front of Ursula's bungalow. She walked out and sat on the veranda steps.

"Sit, sit," she told them, waving her hand for them to draw closer.

The men gathered round and squatted down.

Smiling, Ursula looked around, making sure she caught each man's eyes. They wriggled, uncomfortable with the knowledge they had let her down.

"I want you to listen to my song," she told them.

The men looked at each other in surprise. They had been expecting harsh words.

Ursula began singing, a Naga Romeo and Juliet story, about a boy and a girl whose families would not allow them to marry. Her song described how the young couple made a suicide pact, tying their hair together and vowing to jump from a cliff holding hands. The scouts listened enthralled as Ursula continued. The girl jumped, but the boy brought out a knife and cut the knot in the hair. The girl fell to her death. Full of shame at his cowardice, he returned to the village. On the path, he saw a bird of ill omen. He never married, and years later he was buried in a grave next to his childhood sweetheart. Two bamboos grew, one from each grave. The one from the girl's grave grew tall and strong; the bamboo from the boy's grave was deformed and bent over at the top.

The song ended. Ursula's voice fell silent. She was no longer smiling. Her face serious, she again looked at each man. The scouts were chastened, looking down at the ground and shifting about. Namkia watched Ursula with admiration. She never needed to mention poor attendance at the drills again.

The song-as-lesson stratagem had occurred to her instantly and naturally, and Ursula realized how fully she had changed. She was not thinking "like a Naga," rather she now was a Naga. She was Namkia's sister and, well, she smiled to herself, *everyone's* mother. She was made from two cultures and loyal to both. Both were in peril and needed the best from her.

Except for the pleasant surprise of Lexie's letter informing Ursula of her marriage to Captain Brown, the remainder of 1943 passed without incident as Ursula toured hundreds of miles round the villages, promoting hard workers and boosting morale.

March 28th, 1944 found Ursula glued to the midday news coming over the amenities radio. It was not good. The news bulletins didn't say much, but it seemed the Japanese attack along the Manipur front was making progress.

Ursula chewed her lip with concern. Perry's brief note in the last mail had warned her to keep her eyes open. She wished he had said more. He had access to better information than she. Ursula knew he was not always able to pass it on for security reasons, but . . .

She stood up and moved to the veranda that overlooked her compound. Watch and Ward has been up and running for eighteen months. On the whole, this past year had been a good one. There was that bad outbreak of smallpox in two of the villages. She frowned. Too many died because of that negligent vaccinator. Then there was the famine straight afterwards. Thank goodness for "V" Force relief.

Ursula folded her arms across her chest and smiled with satisfaction as she remembered the rice, salt, and medical help they'd received. Never before had the Barail known such assistance: a full-time medical officer and all the drugs—quinine, mepacrine and sulphur—they needed, plus guns, red blankets, powder and shot, everything that was promised. The authorities certainly pulled out all stops to win over the Nagas. Ursula then thought of her discussions with Perry, and how they had gained experience in handling guerrillas. After several discussions on the subject, they agreed to agree with Dundee, who said that no one could lead a Highland army who had not shaken every man in it by the hand. They followed Dundee's example, knowing that for the Assam hillmen any leader was the first among equals and nothing more. The hillman's allegiance and loyalty were not to the unit but to the leader, who could count only on the men with whom that personal attachment existed.

Ursula returned to the living room and began a letter to her mother. A few minutes later, Namkia came in.

"Strangers coming, my sister."

"Who is it?"

"Two *Sepoy*-Sahibs."

Hearing the clomp of heavy boots on the veranda, Ursula went to the door and found two British sergeants. "Hello. Come in. What's up?"

"Well . . .," said the first sergeant and tailed off. He looked to his companion for help, which was not forthcoming, then took a deep breath and turned to Ursula. "It's like this, Miss. Fifty Japs crossed the Imphal road at Kangpokpi about a week ago, and they ought to be 'ere by now. We wondered if you'd 'eard anything of 'em. We've been sent from Silchar to see."

Suddenly feeling weak, Ursula grasped the doorjamb as the familiar hills, visible above the veranda rail, seemed, momentarily, to leap closer, rotate left then right, then settle back to their usual positions. Ursula steadied herself.

"Well," she heard herself saying in a bright voice. "You might as well have some tea, while we talk it over."

She sent Namkia to arrange the refreshments.

North Cachar Watch and Ward was the farthest of all back areas. For eighteen months they had lived behind a belt of defences a hundred and fifty miles deep. Now, suddenly, the sergeants were telling her there was nothing. "Apart from the defended boxes at Imphal and Kohima, the rest of the area is filled with advancing Japs. Looks like they're trying to cut the road at Kohima and capture our supply dump at Dimapur."

"Where's the front line now?"

The sergeant hesitated before telling her, "Twenty miles be'ind you on the railway. You're the only thing between it and the Japanese."

"What force have you got to meet them?" asked the second sergeant.

"A hundred and fifty native scouts, one Service rifle, one single-barrelled shotgun, and seventy muzzle-loaders."

"Where do you think's the best place to put your men to give warning of enemy approach?"

Ursula moved the cups to one side and laid a map on the table.

"Along the line of the Jiri River," Ursula said, tapping the blue line on the map. "That would give us one day's warning before the Japs arrive."

"Looks good," the sergeant said. "We'd better set off and report back. We'll do our best to send you some 'elp from Silchar. Good luck, Miss Bower."

Ursula watched them leave from the veranda. Before they were out of sight, she was already pondering how to send the scouts forward without creating a panic.

She called Namkia.

"Some Japs have been seen advancing in our area, and we need to find out where they are. The sergeants are going to see that troops are sent from Silchar to help us."

"But we need to know where the Japs are now," Namkia said. "I'll fetch Paodekumba and the scouts from the village."

"Send runners back to call up the best men from Impoi, Asalu, Pangmual, Hange and the villages to the rear," Ursula said.

The scouts began arriving in Laisong that evening. Next morning, Ursula told them the Japanese were moving into the hills, and Watch and Ward must form a screen along the Jiri to warn of their arrival. The scouts looked anxiously at one another and muttered they were being sent into danger. Seeing the effect of her words, Ursula was thankful they didn't know all that she did.

Unconcerned by her orders, Paodekumba told the men, "Stop squawking like old women, and go and do what we're paid to do." He picked up his rifle, scowled contemptuously at the scouts and moved out. The scouts, some grumbling, some silenced into shame, followed his lead.

When the compound emptied, Ursula looked around and realized that her camp, with its steep-sided hill and one narrow approach road, was a perfect trap. It would be safer to sleep in the jungle, but if she did that, it would panic the men. She needed to act unperturbed, make it business as usual and sleep in her own bed.

She slept fitfully, alert at every sound. The nights seemed endless. Then Perry sent a note summoning her to a conference to be held at Mahur, April 1st. When she arrived, groups of soldiers, standing around waiting to be organized or marched off some place to defend Assam, crowded the station. Ursula found Perry at the rest-house. "I've never seen the station so crowded," she said.

"We're pressing any troops we can get our hands on, sections of this, platoons of that, Railway Maintenance Units, Railway Defence Troops, anything that can march and hold a rifle."

After perfunctory introductions in the rest-house's tiny lamp-lit room, Ursula and thirteen army officers, all strangers to her, conferred. They concluded that the Japanese were probably coming, but they had no idea from which direction.

"We have to find out. There aren't enough troops to protect the length of the line," one colonel said.

"There's no wireless communication. We need to improve communications," said another.

"We use the railway telephone," Perry suggested, "with code-words since the clerks all down the line listen." He was in the middle of explaining that "one elephant" meant "ten Japs" when there was a tap on the door. A colonel opened it to find a soldier standing there.

"Mr. Perry, sir, I've a message," he said, handing him a note.

Perry read the note, thanked the soldier and returned to address the meeting.

"I've just received a message that somebody's turned up on the Silchar border with forty elephants."

A murmur rippled round the room.

A colonel pushed back his chair. "I'll go and see what's what," he said and hurried outside.

While he was away, the conference decided to send out a patrol at company strength to see if they could find the fifty Japanese that had turned up ten days before."

"Those Japs should be as close as fifteen miles to your HQ, Miss Bower," one officer said.

"You must come out if things look bad," Perry told Ursula.

Believing the Nagas would fold if she left, Ursula refused to consider leaving an option. Ignoring Perry's concerns she said, "This is a 'V' Force job. If they're out there, we'll find them. I'll signal HQ."

Ursula's immediate commanding officer, Binny, was out of touch in Imphal, but she could still communicate with main HQ in Comilla, where it had been relocated along with army headquarters. She wondered if Colonel Scott would back her or order her out of the area; she thought the latter.

As the conference broke up, the colonel returned. "Managed to sort it out—eventually. The message wasn't code. There's some blighter on the Silchar border with forty real elephants." He laughed. As his words registered, they all laughed and for the moment, tension in the room melted.

Thinking that if she was out on patrol, she could not be ordered out, Ursula signalled headquarters. "Going forward with the patrol to find out what's happening. We need guns. Send thirty rifles so we can arm the best of the scouts."

Namkia and Ursula set out for Laisong the next day accompanied by Captain Willy in command of a company of the Chamar regiment, which was to patrol her area. Willy was thirty or so and an old hand to the area. They had planned to arrive at Laisong that evening, but the sixty troops were new arrivals from the plains and out of training, so the first night was spent at Asalu. The following day the men were struggling. Four collapsed before reaching the pass. Willy and Ramgakpa were each carrying one man's equipment. Namkia stopped to help the third man. Donning the stricken soldier's netted tin hat, he flashed a look of misgiving to Ursula as he hoisted the Bren gun onto his shoulder then with his other hand lifted the fallen soldier to his feet. When the fourth man went down, there was no one to spare but Ursula. Willy charged up and down the line, coaxing, scolding, joking, keeping the men moving. He bent over the fourth man and shook him.

"Come on! It's not far."

The man responded with a groan followed by, "Can't. Can't go . . . on."

Willy took hold of the fallen equipment. "All right, don't worry. The Miss Sahib'll carry your kit for you. Up you get. Come along."

The Indian soldier grabbed his equipment, leapt to his feet and red-faced was marching off before Willy finished speaking.

Everything was normal and quiet at Laisong. There was no news from the scouts on the Jiri and no sign of Japanese. Willy spent the day in the rest-house with Ursula discussing plans for the patrol, then at sunset, he and his men moved off to sleep in the forest. Ursula gave him a Laisong scout as guide and runner.

Ursula spent the best part of the next morning soothing Willy.

"I don't mind telling you," Willy said, "your scout scared the living daylights out of me. I thought he'd seen a sniper, and it turned out all the excitement was over his bloody supper."

He proceeded to tell her that as they walked along the old road up the valley the previous evening, the scout suddenly stopped, tugged Willy's sleeve and pointed up at a tree.

"Jap sniper, I thought. Damned if I could see him. I ducked and peered. The scout was pointing and gesticulating, whispering excitedly. The whole column had now come to a halt. It was dark and shadowy in the dense woods at dusk. All our senses strained for any sign, sight or sound that meant danger. With a cluck of impatience, the scout raised his gun and fired.

"The men flung themselves down and sideways into the bushes and ditches with a frenzied clicking of rifle bolts. Wide eyes searched frantically for the enemy. Then with a loud thump, a dead squirrel fell in front of my nose, and the scout, looking very pleased with himself, picked it up and moved on."

"He did well to shoot it with the muzzle-loader," said Ursula laughing.

"He gave my men the jitters."

"Take heart, Willy. If he can spot a squirrel hiding in a tree at dusk, he'll surely find any Japs about."

Ursula and her scouts left with the patrol next day to go to Thingje. The heat was intense, like walking in an oven, and the road was baked to concrete. After Thingje, they marched to Hangrum then returned to Laisong on the sixth day, having obtained no information about the fifty Japanese in their area. Ursula left the Chamars preparing camp by the river and wearily climbed the eight hundred feet to Laisong.

Degalang came to meet her.

"There's a "V" Force Sahib here," he told her.

Hot and sticky, Ursula trudged along the veranda and looked through the door. A fair-haired captain was sitting by her table. Seeing her, he stood up. Fearing she was to be pulled out of the area, a shooting pain jabbed the pit of her stomach.

"I'm Albright. Scotty sent me along."

"Hello, I'm Ursula Bower."

"I've brought something for you." The captain nodded towards a pile of boxes on the floor in the corner.

The surprise of recognizing the stack as long cases of rifles and tommy-guns, rations, boxes of ammunition, and grenades, took Ursula's breath away. "V" Force was backing them up!

Albright brought her up to date with the news, telling Ursula that 2 and 3 V Ops, Imphal and Kohima areas, had been dispersed.

"The Jap advance has scattered our men all over the map. Those blasted Kuki scouts! Most of them were playing a double game. Apparently, they still hold a grudge from some rebellion years ago, so they joined up with the Japs and led them to every camp and cache set up by their 'V' Force officers."

"Did the officers manage to get out?"

"Most of them are missing, but they're coming in by ones and twos. Hopefully, most of them are safe. Murray of 3 V Ops, a damned good man, made a fighting retreat from Shangshak and beyond, ambushing the enemy thirty-five times in as many miles. Ruther has reached Kohima. Betts is still missing. HQ staff has been sent out right and left to fill the gaps, and down at HQ, Scotty's struggling on almost by himself with the clerks."

"We'll send out word to the scouts to watch for 'V' Force officers coming out. With a bit of luck, they'll soon turn up."

Japanese forces swept into Assam.

Ursula read then pocketed the orders Haichangnang had just brought from Perry. She was to hang on as long as possible and watch the road for the enemy advance. As soon as she made contact, she was to warn Haflong then get out—fast. Ursula wondered if Watch and Ward could meet the demands placed upon it.

With shocking speed, the Japanese overran the area before Ursula could organize a screen between the Barak and the Jiri Rivers. Without the screen, she was in the dark about enemy activity. Watch and Ward's front line was in the Haijaichak pass. The most she could expect was one hour's warning. Without a field telephone or wireless, the likelihood was no warning at all.

They had set up a chain of beacons, supplemented by relays of runners from the front line to Laisong and on to Haflong. If the beacons were set alight, it meant contact with the enemy. In a letter, Perry told her he'd had some anxious moments seeing smoke from spring grassfires flaring up, thinking they might be warnings.

Ursula's idyllic life in Laisong was no more. She and her scouts trekked the area, hunting for Japanese troops and finding none. She was afflicted with worry. She had no idea where the Japanese were or what they were doing. Ursula, her staff and her scouts lived in a state of readiness for a speedy departure. If they picked tomatoes, they took their tommy-guns, all the while checking the beacons and the camp's exit as they worked.

At night, they travelled a mile from camp to sleep hidden in an area of thick scrub honeycombed with hideouts hollowed out below foliage level. One man stayed in camp as sentry, while Ursula and her men slept in their jungle warren. If the Japanese appeared, the sentry was to fire a shot and flee to safety. Every night, they changed sleeping places so no outsider ever knew where they hid in the wide stretch of scrub. Cattle trails, pig paths, game runs, and "V" Force tunnels criss-crossed the area. If their hiding place were discovered, they would not be all trapped together. They had caches of food buried along the most likely escape route and another one in a ravine behind Impoi, where they could lie up for a while if they had to. Each morning, they crept back to camp, scouting to see if the enemy had been there. The loss of her secure, happy place gnawed at Ursula. The paths she had safely walked with her dogs were now places she must watch for danger and be alert for ambushes.

Despite pressure from government officials, Ursula had no intention of getting out. If she ran, the Nagas would collapse. Even with her presence, she didn't expect Watch and Ward to hold. The men hadn't been trained for active service. They had been chucked in at the deep end without preparation, weapons or support. She would not blame them if they cracked and returned home. It was never intended they should face this.

Ursula also worried about the problems her staying could cause. Word had come that the village of Jampi, three days away, was in friendly contact with the enemy, who had offered the village a reward of one hundred rupees for her head.

One night, hiding in the scrub, she told Namkia of her intention to stay no matter what.

"It is good that you stay, my sister."

"That may be so, but I see it causing some problems. I'm much too tall to conceal myself in a Naga village, and then there's the problem of my light skin and hair. It stands out a mile. The Japs may come and torture the villagers to reveal my whereabouts. You know I can never give myself up. If I am taken alive by the Japs, I will be slowly tortured to death. You've heard the stories as well as I, and it's not something I want to happen to me. If things really get desperate, I'll shoot myself."

Namkia flinched at her words. "No, no, my sister, you must not think such things."

"Yes I must. And when I shoot myself, you must cut off my head and take it into the village to show the Japs. They'll

285

recognise the light hair and complexion and know it's me. With a bit of luck it won't come to that. But if it does, you must promise me you'll do it."

Namkia was solemn-faced. "I'll do it, if I have to."

A week later, at the height of the crisis, all of Ursula's personal staff came to her bungalow. Namkia spoke for the men.

"My sister, we want to go on leave to see our families."

Ursula's heart sank.

So this was the finish.

"Yes, of course you may go, Namkia," she said. "Take care."

Ursula was alone in her compound except for Ali and the cat. Lassu and Khamba had been sent to friends in Shillong. She spent a miserable day and night wondering what to do, stay or leave for a safer place. Twenty-four hours after their departure, Ursula was overjoyed to see the men climbing the path to her camp.

"Namkia, you've returned! That was a short leave."

"Long enough for our needs, my sister."

It was not until the next day that Ursula realized Namkia was without his deo-moni beads.

"Namkia, why aren't you wearing your beads?"

"I've left them with my sons. All the men left their heirloom necklaces with their sons when we went home."

"Why did you do that?"

"We are going to die, so we went home to make our wills and arrange for our families' keep. Now we wear only our burial beads."

"You came back to meet the end with us?" Ursula stared at him open-mouthed.

Seeing Ursula's amazement, Namkia explained, "After all, which was the better thing? To desert and live, and hear our children curse us for the shame we put on them; or to die with you and leave them proud of us forever?"

Ursula continued to stare, speechless at the bravery and loyalty of her staff.

Namkia grinned and shrugged. "It's the Naga way, my sister."

Albright came to Laisong and brought with him updated news of the war. He told Ursula that a series of bloody battles had brought the Japanese advance ever nearer to Imphal. Rather than have his troops retreat in a haphazard manner, General Slim, the commander of 14th Army had another strategy. His troops were to pull back from the Burmese border, drawing the Japanese into the Imphal Plain towards "Administration Boxes." These were maintenance areas for the soldiers, laid out with supply depots, ammunition dumps, vehicle parks and dressing stations. Albright said that Slim, having studied how the Japanese fought and reacted in battle, knew they would repeatedly throw themselves upon the "Admin Boxes'" defences, making it easy for Allied troops to annihilate them. If cut off by the enemy, the men in the boxes were going be supplied by air. Thus all non-combatants were being evacuated.

The evacuation began early with nurses, followed by units of Bengali and Madrassi Pioneers, marched out under their officers across the Tamenglong subdivision, where they were gathered up by Ursula's Watch and Ward network. The Pioneer companies had little food, and Ursula had none to spare. Her units could only send the soldiers on to the railway as fast as possible. Although the evacuation of thousands of personnel had been planned, no one thought to send food to Mahur for them. The soldiers camped in the market sheds beside the railway, hungry and disgruntled.

Forty men deserted from the first Pioneer Company to come through Ursula's area. "V" Force scouts spent two weeks rounding them up and bringing them out. One group brought to Ursula's camp included an RAF gunner with a ginger handlebar moustache. He exchanged salutes with Albright.

"Good afternoon, what are you doing here?" Ursula asked.

"Asking myself the same question. George Winters, Royal Air Force," he introduced himself, offering his hand.

Ursula, then Albright, shook his hand.

"Did your plane come down?" Albright asked.

"I thought it did, but then it didn't."

Ursula's eyebrows lifted in query.

The gunner hurried to explain. "Well, the plane, a Vultee Vengeance, crew of two, got into difficulties, went into a spin. I thought it was about to crash, so I baled out. The plane was still spinning when it disappeared behind a hill. I landed unhurt, ran to the top of the ridge and saw a fire at the bottom of the valley. Tore down the hillside and through the jungle to help the pilot, but when I got there, it was only a small grass fire. No sign of the plane at all."

"So what did you do?" Albright asked.

"Well, I didn't know what to do. Didn't know if Imphal was east or west. I was standing there scratching my head, when these Naga chaps came along. I must admit I was very nervous. Didn't know which side they were on. Managed to ask them by signs if they'd seen the plane. 'Oh yes', they said."

Twirling his hand at the wrist, the gunner mimicked how the Nagas indicated what had happened.

"The Vultee had come spinning down like this, then straightened out and went off," he made a roaring sound and spread his arms as if flying, "like that!"

He laughed heartily at his predicament. "Anyway, they took charge of me and led me to a bridle-road."

"To where the Pioneers were coming through," Ursula added, feeling proud of the Nagas' contribution to his rescue.

"Yes, and here I am, missing my wings and walking out."

They sent George Winters on to the railway.

Some weeks later, Perry took great delight in regaling Ursula and Albright with the sequel. "The Vultee returned safely to Imphal, and the pilot jumped out shouting, 'Hey, George, that was a near thing, wasn't it?' And discovered there was no George. It was ten days before they heard of his whereabouts."

Ursula and Albright had their hands full. When the Japanese overran the camps at Kanglatombi and other points along the Imphal road, there was little organized evacuation of personnel. Large numbers of men scattered, fleeing to safety with their arms and ammunition. The hungry men surged westward through the hills. Most of these men were new recruits and ill-disciplined. They were not regular troops, but men drawn from every creed and part of India to provide every kind of auxiliary service—drivers, mechanics, water carriers. Along with the hordes came pastors and teachers from the mission stations, a few Naga refugees and half-naked soldiers, prisoners who had escaped from the enemy, mostly men of the Gurkha Parachute Battalion, some of whom had bayonet wounds courtesy of their Japanese torturers. All had to be collected, questioned, helped, fed, clothed, doctored, disarmed if necessary, and sent to the rear.

Within days, the armed stragglers were creating serious problems. The situation was already out of control in Manipur between the Barak and Jiri Rivers. The Nagas gave the soldiers all the help they could and were rewarded with beatings and lootings. The villagers took to the forest; normal life came to a standstill. The disruption permeated westwards to Ursula's area, affecting morale and threatening the whole intelligence network.

Ursula and Albright put their heads together to discuss the best way to tackle the disruption to Watch and Ward. Both agreed that, with only twenty armed scouts and an under-strength platoon of Mohendra Dals, Nepalese State Troops, they did not have the manpower to deal with the situation. Disheartened, Ursula slumped in her chair, then, as if summoned by a genie, a British captain, his face red and sweaty from the climb up Laisong hill, appeared in the doorway.

"Good afternoon, are you Miss Bower?"

"Yes, I am."

"I've got a platoon of Gurkhas for you."

"What? You have what? How wonderful!"

"Excuse us," Albright said, leading Ursula onto the veranda. "Ursula, you can't possibly take charge of them. You're a civilian. There'll be repercussions."

289

"We can't look a gift-platoon in the mouth, especially now."

"No, I insist. You, a civilian, cannot take charge of this platoon!"

Overhearing their discussion, the captain interrupted. "Excuse me, Miss Bower, Captain. I don't care if you have a problem accepting the platoon. You'll have to take it up with my superiors. My orders are to leave the platoon under Miss Bower's command, and that's what I'm doing."

Ursula and Albright looked at each other. Ursula smiled triumphantly. Albright tightened his lips.

"Would you care for a cup of tea before you leave?" she asked the officer.

"That I would, Miss Bower. Then I'll check on the men before I go. They're making camp down the hill, beside the river."

Several days later, Albright was still disconcerted about Ursula's command of the Gurkha platoon.

"The men are not likely to take orders from you, Ursula. How are you going to pull rank when you don't have rank-badges?"

Ursula thought for a moment then brightened. "I know," she said then hesitated.

"Yes, go on," Albright encouraged.

"We could split your pips. You could wear your captain's pips on the left shoulder, and I could wear mine on the right."

There was a complicated silence. Albright narrowed his gaze at Ursula. Then he slapped his knee and burst out laughing. "Excellent solution," he said. He released the pips from his epaulette. "There's the difficulty of how the men are to address you. They can't call you lieutenant because you're a civilian."

"Have them call me GB," Ursula said. "There'll be no confusion with that."

*   *   *

A thunderstorm blew in while Watch and Ward practised ambushes along the old road in the Jenam Valley. Ursula, Albright, six Gurkhas, Namkia and a couple of Naga scouts raced for shelter at the rest-house. With rainwater cascading from the eaves, Ursula and Albright leaned against the veranda posts, gossiping with Khuala, a Lushai doctor who was treating the people coming through the area.

"Here comes someone," Albright said, suddenly. "My, they're wet!"

Two running Zemi, one wearing a red cloth, splashed through the puddles and jumped onto the veranda out of the rain. The men were not familiar to Ursula, but their haircuts indicated they were from the Thingje group. The taller man stripped to his soaked kilt and stood there, wringing water out of his cloth when he was not waving his arms and ranting to Namkia.

Namkia translated. "These are headmen from Impuiloa, a village just across the Jiri Valley. Five walking-out soldiers have just come through the village. They looted the headman's house as well as some others. These two ran ahead of the looters by a shortcut. They say the gang ought to be at Haijaichak by now."

Albright called the six Mohendra Dals and headed up the road. The Laisong scouts and Gurkhas carried rifles. Ursula had a Sten gun, pistol and kukri; Albright had his pistol and a tommy-gun. Thankfully, the rain stopped as quickly as it started. It was four miles to Haijaichak along a scenic, winding road beside a stream. The group was tramping through the small wood on the outskirts of the village, when two Nagas raced round the next bend. They slowed to a trot on seeing Ursula. One was the village head scout, the other his lieutenant.

The head scout Hailamsuong had the worst job in Watch and Ward. Whichever way the Japanese came over the hills, his group would be the first to make contact. All roads converged on Haijaichak. The whole warning system of North Cachar depended on him. Everything had been working well until the stragglers arrived. Now looters were assaulting his men almost every day. When driven from the observation post, the loyal scouts moved to the hillside scrub and resumed their watch for Japanese, while a runner went to Laisong for help.

"That band of looters must have arrived in the village," Albright said.

"Just what I was thinking," Ursula agreed.

The two men trotted up to Ursula.

"It's those stragglers!" Hailamsuong said. "They drove us out of the lookout and went into the village. Then they started to loot the place, and the people ran to the woods. The soldiers are still in the village. There must be thirty of them. Come and get them out!"

Thirty of them! Not good odds, thought Ursula. Leaving the cover of the woods behind, they crept along the path below the village. There was no one about. An old Zemi came out of the woods above them and shouted something, but they could not catch his words. Everything was quiet. They halted at the bottom of the path leading up to the village. Two scouts stepped from their hiding places in nearby bushes and joined the group. At that moment, an armed man wearing a tin hat strolled out of the village and looked down at them. No one moved. The man walked away into the village.

Ursula gasped in disbelief. "He must have taken us for another band of stragglers."

Albright pushed her behind a big standing stone. "You, the corporal and all the Nagas stay here. If we get in a jam, well, use your head and join in."

Ursula hated to be left out, but before she could argue, Albright and the five Gurkhas were walking up to the village. Ursula and the Nagas waited under cover by the lookout hut. They could see the Gurkhas searching among the empty houses with fixed bayonets. Ursula was admiring how the Gurkhas were not in the least bit concerned about the odds of five to one when she heard Hailamsuong's anxious voice behind her.

"Will there be shooting, my mother? My wife and child are hidden in my house."

"The Captain Sahib is very clever," Ursula said with conviction. "He will take the men without shooting, if he can."

They stood by the lookout hut, waiting for the shooting to start.

Albright and the Gurkhas moved cautiously between the houses. A Watch and Ward scout appeared from behind a house where he had been keeping watch and pointed to the large house at the end of the street. "All the looters are in the *morung*, cooking a meal."

Ursula could remain hidden no longer. She moved quickly, with practised, noiseless agility, to join Albright as he crept up to the *morung*. They looked through the window and saw the whole band there. The pillagers had cooked a meal and were sitting in the middle of the room eating. Not expecting any opposition, the looters had stacked their weapons along the walls. Albright tiptoed back to his men and gave his orders. While Ursula kept breathless watch, the Gurkhas stepped up to the windows and doorways and aimed their rifles at the men inside.

"Hands up!" Albright shouted.

The stunned men surrendered without a fight.

When Ursula entered the *morung*, she found thirty glum prisoners sitting quietly with their hands on their heads. The Zemi, watching events from the hills, poured back through the streets. Most of the plunder was recovered and piled on the veranda by the front door. Villagers hurried to claim their possessions, all the while hurling insults at the perpetrators through the open doorway.

Albright spoke to Ursula. "There's not much else we can do here, GB. We've impounded their weapons and ammunition, bagged twenty-one rifles, nine Stens and three thousand rounds."

"We'll escort the prisoners to Mahur and hand them over to the field security section." Ursula said.

"We'll need porters to carry the weapons," Albright said. He disappeared with Namkia to find the headman in order to commandeer firewood baskets from each household. Weapons and ammunition were stacked in the baskets.

"My goodness, Albright, we could certainly do with keeping it here," Ursula said, distressed at letting the rounds of ammunition go.

The dejected prisoners filed out of the village. Two elated Gurkhas marched in front with four behind, followed by Ursula, Albright, Namkia and the Laisong scouts with the Zemi porters bringing up the rear, carrying the weapons. One of the looters, a

Bengali from an auxiliary unit evacuated from Imphal and leader of the gang, made a run for it.

"Stop or I'll shoot!" Albright shouted.

The soldier ran on, ignoring the warning. Albright brought him down with his machine-gun. The fusillade of bullets gouged off a deep line of flesh and bone across the man's back, and as he lay dead, face in the dirt, flames flared briefly, scorching his cloth jacket.

Albright was shaken to the core. He was a staff captain, not a combat soldier. "I had no choice . . . ," he said, looking anguished.

"Namkia, find the *jappa* with the rum and give him a drink." Ursula turned to Albright. "Shall I organize a burial party?"

"Would you?"

"I'll see to it. Truth be told, Albright, I'm so mad about them looting Naga villages, I don't care about the gory mess."

The whole event turned out to be a fortuitous experience. The Gurkhas, who had not known what to make of a lady officer, and the Nagas, who wanted to know if the army was really going to protect them or not, decided they meant business. It was a boost for morale and confidence.

A week later, the army supplied a Bren gun post for Hailamsuong. There were no more incidents at Haijaichak after that.

Fresh from the siege at Kohima with its pitched battles and bloody hand-to-hand fighting, Lieutenant Tibbetts, a "V" Force officer, arrived at Ursula's camp, bringing a half-section of the 3rd Assam Rifles. The lieutenant stayed only long enough to introduce himself, explain the men were exhausted from the fight at Kohima, then left. The soldiers retired to beds squeezed into the servants' quarters and slept. Forty-eight hours later, they emerged refreshed, cleaned the camp until it gleamed, then looked around for the enemy.

Lance-Naik Supbahadur Rana, left in charge of the Assam Rifles, was a Gurkha. A thin man in large boots, he had a small turned up nose, large ears and black hair with a strong widow's peak. He arrived at Ursula's door, stood smartly to attention and saluted.

"Come in," Ursula said, thinking he had a strong resemblance to Mickey Mouse.

"Where are the Japs, GB? Now that we are rested, we want to go out and kill some more as soon as possible," the Indian lance-corporal said.

Ursula liked his spirit. "We've had rather the same idea ourselves. Unfortunately, there are none around. We've managed to get in touch with a few Naga villages beyond the Jiri, and now that we have a wireless transmitter, we're in communication with Tamenglong."

She pulled out a map. "We're here." She tapped the dot marking Laisong. "The Japs are well back of the Barak and in the area behind and around Kangpokpi."

For a moment the Indian corporal was crest-fallen. Then he grinned. "We will train ready for the day we run them down."

A week later, there were further changes of personnel at Laisong. The Mohendra Dals, who had been increased to a full company under their own officers, were withdrawn and sent to Nungba. They were replaced by a company of Mahrattas under Captain Archer, a dark-haired, dark-eyed man with a strong roman nose and a suntanned face.

Archer built a miniature range between the bungalow and the garden, and he and his men began training as many scouts as possible to use rifles. As for Namkia, he was training as well, learning to use a tommy-gun. One day, in the middle of rifle-practice, a low-flying Japanese Zero swooped over the camp. Everyone rushed for cover. Ursula dived into the only refuge left available, the large cookhouse drainpipe.

When the flap was over, she crawled from the drain, her uniform covered in grease and grime.

"What a mess I'm in. That wasn't very gentlemanly, leaving me the drain," she laughingly chided the men.

Not two minutes later, a Kuki woman entered the camp with her young baby and family members.

Ursula went to meet them. "Hello, do you want me?"

"Yes, Mother. We want you to name my baby daughter."

"Of course," Ursula said, "but I must change my clothes first. Sit on the veranda for a moment."

A cleaned up Ursula returned and took hold of the infant. She smiled, stroked the baby's cheek and thought of what to call her.

"I name this child Victoria Elizabeth," she said.

The family signalled their approval and brought out the rice-beer to celebrate.

Archer was awed. "GB, you're the only 'V' Force officer I know who calmly squeezes in the naming of a baby between arms training and air raids."

*   *   *

As a result of the fighter plane's visit, Archer decided he must have a new campsite, one well-concealed from the air. He and Ursula studied the east face of the hill. It appeared to be one of the few places that met this requirement.

"We could cut platforms to hold the buildings, and the bamboos and jungle provide fair cover," Archer said.

He and Ursula went to reconnoitre by crawling up a well-trodden game trail, which came in from the main path.

"This'll do," Archer said, surveying the place as best he could from the all fours position. "We'll have the platforms along either side, and the path will do nicely through the middle."

Ursula, also on her hands and knees, looked down at the path and saw a large, feline pug mark baked into the hard mud.

"You may have trouble with game," she said. "This is a main run."

"Oh they won't come when they smell humans about. After all, it won't be a small camp."

And so they called in the villagers to cut platforms and build huts, and Archer and the Mahrattas moved in.

Next morning, Archer came to Ursula's compound eager to recount his experiences of his first night in the new camp. "I was in bed, smoking a last cigarette before turning over. The mosquito net was down. Some big beast pushed the door curtain aside, came padding in, and lay down on the floor beside the bed.

"One of GB's dogs I thought, sitting up. It wasn't completely dark in the hut, but I couldn't see the thing; it was too close under the side of the bed. Then I remembered; your dogs had been sent away to Shillong.

"A village dog then, I thought. I looked over the edge of the bed, but the mosquito net obscured my view. It was very dim like I said, but whatever it was didn't look like a village dog. It seemed bigger, the shape not quite right. It was then I broke out in a cold sweat. It was a very large animal, and I knew for sure it wasn't a dog.

"I was afraid to move. The bed seemed to creak even as I held my breath. My cigarette was burning away, almost to my fingers, and I daren't move. Then my throat began to tickle. Did my best to control it, but it was no good. I put my hand over my mouth and gave a muffled cough.

"The beast rose up by the side of the bed and sat there like a dog," Archer said, his voice incredulous. "It was a leopard. I was terrified. It looked right at me, gave me the dirtiest look it could muster then stalked out. A minute later, my men, who'd seen it leave the hut, came charging in. They barged into me in the doorway where I'd staggered to catch my breath."

By the time Archer had finished his tale, Ursula was sitting on the edge of her seat, her hand over her heart. "Good grief!" she said. "What a lucky man you are!"

"Luck had nothing to do with it," Albright said, laughing. "The leopard didn't fancy him. Didn't smell like an old goat."

A secret meeting of British Army officers took place at Ursula's camp at the end of April. The officers, colonels and majors, elected to meet at Laisong because of its convenience and seclusion. They were to discuss, along with other matters, the role of the Nagas now that the Allies were starting to turn the tide against the Japanese.

Ursula told her staff that some sahibs were coming, which was nothing out of the ordinary as officers frequently came in for various reasons. The afternoon before the conference, half a dozen arrived at Ursula's bungalow. During the evening, they had serious discussions about the Japanese invasion and the siege of Kohima and Imphal, but some light-hearted moments too. One colonel raised hearty laughter with his tale:

"I was sitting in my field tent when a Naga arrived appearing most concerned. 'Sahib, Colonel Sahib,' he said, 'a Japanese officer has sent word to my village. He is asking if he can bathe in the bathtub he knows we have there. What shall we tell him?' I must say I was surprised. The Naga waited expectantly for my wise reply. 'Tell the Japanese officer he can't use it,' I told him. 'Tell him there's a British officer sitting in it.' A huge grin appeared on his worried face. Then he began to laugh until tears streamed down his cheeks. It was so infectious, I was laughing hard with him. 'That's a good joke, Sahib' he said, then ran off."

The officers squeezed into Ursula's basha, sleeping on camp beds in the sitting room and veranda. Shortly after dawn, they heard an aircraft some way off, very high. It was circling over to the southwest near Hangrum. Ursula and the officers were just beginning to stir with first light when the woomph of a bomb landing a long way off reached their ears. Seconds later, they felt

299

shock waves through the floor. Everyone leapt out of bed and ran onto the veranda in their pyjamas. They searched the sky, but the plane was so far away and so high, they couldn't see it. It dropped two more bombs then flew away. The excitement ended. Nothing further happened. Still, the event reminded everyone how unstable was their position and how swiftly and unexpectedly their lives could end.

About four o' clock in the afternoon, conference attendees saw a body of men running down the far slope across the valley on the track from Hangrum. The villagers arrived at Ursula's camp carrying baskets of bomb fragments.

"A plane flew over early this morning and dropped three bombs on the village," they told Ursula. While the officers examined the bomb fragments, Ursula explained, "Hangrum's built on a knife-edged ridge, so it would be hard to hit the village."

"That *would* make it hard to hit," one officer said. "It's hell trying to do a supply drop without someone on the ground marking the area. The villages just don't show up well in mountain country."

"Anyway," Ursula continued, "they missed Hangrum, but left three craters in the fields outside the village. Do you think word got out about our conference, and the Japs were really trying to bomb Laisong?"

"Undoubtedly," answered a major.

"But where did the leak come from?" Ursula asked. "My people didn't know anything except that some sahibs were coming. The leak must have been somewhere further back in India."

"Undoubtedly," the major said again. "But it's probably not treason you know, only indiscretion. Chaps who blather on about everything they hear or see put the rest of us in danger."

"It's a good job the villages are indistinguishable from the air," another officer said. "At least nobody's been hurt, and no damage done except to the nerves of Hangrum."

Ursula explained to the villagers that the sahibs were pleased no one in Hangrum had been hurt. As they left, Ursula noted the villagers were actually preening themselves because they had been regarded as important enough to be a military target.

The conference ended. The Nagas were to continue playing an important role, informing Fourteenth Army of Japanese movements. Bower Force was to be supplied with four wireless transmitters for a wireless network. Four posts, one at Laisong, one at Silchar and two more in the hills to the south in Manipur, would each have a signaller and a soldier to protect him. Albright and Ursula, who had been manoeuvring for weeks for permission to move forward to report on the enemy, had strongly argued their case to the officers, but they would have to wait until further discussion at HQ for an answer.

The officers departed, leaving Ursula gloomy with the frustration of a further delay to their plans. Albright consoled her, "GB, you must understand, the authorities have the wind up about your safety. Don't worry; we'll keep pushing for it."

In the middle of May, Bower Force received permission to move forward. Albright, the instigator of the scheme, had been recalled to HQ and would not be around to see his efforts come to fruition. Instead, he was relieved by Captain Bill Tibbetts, a displaced "V" Force officer. Ursula watched his party's approach and smiled. Tall, fair-haired Tibbetts was ascending the hill, hanging on to the tail of a ration-convoy mule.

He strolled into Ursula's compound and, with a friendly grin, introduced himself. Ursula shook his hand. "Pleased to meet you, Captain Tibbetts."

"We met before in fact, momentarily. I don't blame you for not remembering, but I say, I do remember you, Miss Bower. You prefer GB, don't you?"

The words were barely out of his mouth when joyful howls of greeting erupted from Tibbetts' old comrades, the Assam Rifles. Surprised to find them still at Laisong, Tibbetts grinned with delight. "I hope you'll excuse me, GB. I'd better say hello."

"Off you go. I'll rustle up some tea."

Shortly after his arrival, Ursula and Tibbetts were in the bungalow when they heard an aircraft approaching from the south. The Mahrattas leapt to their machine-gun and drew a bead on the plane diving down on them. Ursula and Tibbetts rushed out of the bungalow. The plane was coming out of the sun, and they couldn't see it properly. Tibbetts, who had been in anti-aircraft before joining "V" Force, at last made out the silhouette against the sun. It was the British communications plane, known as the Imphal taxi, used for transporting senior officers from Imphal to Silchar and Calcutta. It was heading straight for the machine-gun trained on it and about to bring it down.

"Oh my God!" he cried, "It's one of ours!" He raced down the spur like a gazelle with a lion on its tail, yelling to the machine-gunners, "It's one of ours! Don't shoot! Don't shoot!"

Responding to Tibbets' shouting, the machine-gunners lowered the gun. The plane flew on unharmed.

Ursula caught up with him. "Bill, my heart was in my mouth. Thank goodness you stopped them in time or heaven knows how many senior officers would have ended up as mess in the vegetable garden."

Tibbetts was livid. "The stupidity of it, flying low over the site of a machine-gun post! Probably doing a bit of sightseeing, trying to see you. With brains like that they're as much use as a concrete parachute!"

The signal they had been waiting for arrived. Bower Force was on the move. With six Assam Rifles, fifteen scouts, Ison the signaller, the young British private who was to protect him, and one hundred Zemi porters, they moved up. They were preceded by a Mahratta patrol bound for Kangpokpi area, and followed, Ursula hoped, by Archer and his company, who were to sit at Tamenglong with Bower Force and harry any Japanese that Watch and Ward found.

"We're marching none too soon," Ursula told Tibbetts. "The rains are almost upon us, and we have the Barak to cross."

They arrived at the cloud enveloped Hepoloa rest-house in driving rain. Below, in the valley, they saw the Barak River running fast and red with silt.

There had been two disasters at the three great falls when people on rafts had been swept to their deaths. The North Cachar porters were terrified of the big river and panicked. Putting down their loads in the rest-house compound, they refused to go one step further. For thirty minutes in the stinging rain, Ursula and Namkia argued with them under the dripping pines. Finally, they induced the porters to move. The men picked up their loads and galloped the two miles down the steep, slippery hill to reach the river, while it was still fordable, all except the two men on either end of the pole carrying the cumbersome wireless transmitter.

These two, at Ison's urging, kept to a more careful, sedate pace to take care of the set. Ursula, Namkia and Bill Tibbetts followed, scrambling hand and foot down a newly cut track through the sodden bamboo-jungle. To their relief, they found the river surprisingly shallow. With Bill and the Assam Rifles leading, they waded across the river, the porters rushing across to be out of its clutches.

A flood had wrecked the old suspension bridge. At Bower Force's request, the Subdivisional officer at Tamenglong had arranged for it to be reconstructed for their line of communication. On the far bank were an overseer and a gang of workmen. But, for some inexplicable reason, they had moved it fifty yards upstream, from hard, high ground to a sandbank.

"I don't like the look of that," Ursula said. "It seems far too low. The Barak's a dangerous river. It takes the heavy rain off the hills and can rise thirty feet in six hours."

"Well, it's across. There's nothing to be done now," Bill said. He turned to go then noticed Ursula looking around. "What is it?"

"Just looking. I camped here five years ago while on tour with Mr. Jeffery, the State Engineer. The camp's disappeared under the grass and creepers. It looks much wilder without the bridge." Ursula was thinking, too, of how quickly the jungle consumes all traces of human occupation.

The party left the stream and began the long climb up the cliff heading for Tamenglong. One of Watch and Ward's Kuki scouts met Ursula at the Kabui village with a note from the SDO which said: "Tamenglong has just been strafed in error by the RAF. Duck if you see fighters, in case the misunderstanding has not been resolved."

"We'd better send a signal off as soon as we arrive," Tibbetts said.

Tramping on, they covered the last few miles of the twenty-five mile journey and arrived at the outpost of Tamenglong. It hadn't changed since Ursula's last visit some years before. The fort was still there along with the pines, the streams, and the bungalows perched hither and thither. But the red, tin roofs were peppered with holes, courtesy of the RAF and, consequently, leaked like sieves in the pouring rain.

Ursula's party settled into the rest-house to wait for Archer. Ison, the signaller, tutted over the defects in the wireless transmitter caused by the march over the hills and strived to repair it in order to signal HQ.

After some hours of work, he informed Tibbetts, "All set, sir."

"Good. Send this: Inform the RAF that Tamenglong is now in Allied hands. Would they please not strafe it?"

Heavy, gray clouds concentrated in a rolling boil over Tamenglong, driving in low and steady from the southwest. And of Archer and his company of Mahrattas there was still no sign.

Ursula invited the SDO to dinner. They discovered he had been left alone in Tamenglong since the invasion started and was feeling the strain.

"I've had no orders or support, and I don't have much in the way of resources," he told them, smacking his lips in appreciation of the tot of rum he was drinking. "But I've developed an intelligence screen a full three days march away."

"How long does it take for the information to reach you?" asked Tibbetts.

"Oh, less than twenty-four hours by relay runner." The SDO paused, his face pinched. "In the middle of April, when the Japs were nearest, we found the Kuki *subedar* in charge of the Assam Rifles in the fort had been in communication with the enemy. He claimed he was trying to tempt them into an ambush, but his message was ambiguous to say the least, and with the Kuki record of betrayal, it was no time for chances. Even Jampi village, west of the Barak, was helping the Japs."

"Yes, I know," Ursula said. "They were prepared to sell my head to the enemy for a hundred rupees."

"So I heard," the SDO said.

Tibbetts laughed. "Really? How insulting! We pay two thousand rupees to the natives for every serviceman they rescue from the jungle."

"Anyway," the SDO continued, "I arrested him and sent him down for court-martial. And then there was Sharp."

"Sharp?" Ursula said.

"A young Indian Civil Service officer, who'd served in Imphal and knew the district well. He was hastily taken into the army and sent out to organize an intelligence screen in the gap between Watch and Ward and the Imphal-Kohima road. But he never reached Tamenglong. There were fifty Japs reported in the area. It's almost certain they captured and killed him. It's very sad." The SDO took another mouthful of rum, moving the warming liquid slowly round his mouth before swallowing. "We haven't found his body yet."

Everyday, reports came in of enemy foraging parties. The Japanese, obviously unaware of Bower Force's presence in Tamenglong, were leaving supply dumps unguarded and only using two or three men to escort mule convoys. Ursula and Tibbetts traced their routes on the map. Enemy troops were only three or four days distance from them, travelling through the villages, levying food. The two sat in the rest-house, champing at the bit, wondering when Archer would arrive so they could go after them. Rain dripped through the holes in the roof, pine branches scraped against the tin, and between the trees they could see the hills where the enemy lurked.

"I don't intend to sit twiddling my thumbs any longer," Tibbetts said, after intelligence reported a virtually unguarded forage dump in the Imphal Plain. "What say you we plan a raid, GB?"

"By Gads, sir! An excellent idea!" Ursula said, playfully. Then, becoming serious, she added, "What do you have in mind?"

"I'm thinking we should raid the forage dump on the plain. We could reach it with a night march from Tamenglong and attack it at dawn with machine-guns and grenades. It's chock full of rice. We'll burn it. That should deprive the Japs of a month's supply of food."

"We've only the Assam Rifles and a Mahratta patrol," Ursula said.

"I'll signal HQ again and try to find out where Archer is with his company."

The reply when it came informed them Archer was in hospital with dysentery, but a platoon of Mahrattas would be sent for the raid.

Tibbetts made the arrangements. Ursula found the guides. Captain Archer's substitute, a nervous Punjabi subaltern, arrived after an interminable wait of five days, but the Mahrattas were itching for a fight. The party set out with Bower Force scouts and guides.

Two days later, the platoon returned. Archer's *subedar*, Saronki Sayib, went to see Ursula and Tibbetts. While at Ursula's compound, the *subedar* had taken Ursula on as a daughter. To Ursula, there was no better soldier or nicer person than dear old Saronki Sayib. So she was shocked when Saronki entered the office where she and Bill Tibbetts were sitting, tore off his tin hat, threw it on the ground and burst into tears.

Ursula leapt from her chair. "Saronki, what is it?"

"The regiment's been shamed by that windy boy turning back when we were almost in sight of the dump. If only the Captain Sahib or you, Captain Tibbetts, had been with us, we'd have made it."

"What happened, Subedar?" asked Tibbetts, his voice low and tight.

"We got to within six miles of the dump when the lieutenant lost his nerve and ordered everybody back again. We're veterans! Veterans of the Western Desert! Good soldiers brought to this, this . . . disgrace!" Tears of shame streamed down his face.

"Oh, Saronki," Ursula said, "yours is a fine regiment. We know what you could have done if you'd been allowed to. We'll talk with the lieutenant."

Saronki picked up his tin hat and wiped his eyes. "Give him a good talking to. Tell him how to be a soldier." He turned to leave, his shoulders slumped with dishonour.

The minute Saronki stepped out the door, Tibbetts exploded. "Damn it! This was not a difficult raid! What was the man thinking?"

They sent for the young subaltern who, when questioned, explained they were running late, and it was getting light. He thought it too dangerous to continue with the mission.

That wouldn't have stopped the Mahrattas, Ursula knew. They'd have gone in. It was still early enough to have caught the Japs on the hop. She was filled with disgust and frustration.

The platoon rested a day, then left. Mild dysentery broke out, attacking all in camp except Ison. Tibbetts had it so badly he was almost incapacitated. Then in June, they received a signal that two hundred Japanese and a field gun were approaching Tamenglong. They were ordered to withdraw immediately but to leave Ison behind with the wireless transmitter.

Usually amiable and unflappable, Tibbetts broke. He angrily waved the paper Ison had handed him. "This is a false report!"

"More than that," Ursula said, "it's absolute nonsense. If there were two hundred enemy soldiers in the area advancing on Tamenglong, the screen would have picked it up. What do they think we're doing here? Picking daisies?"

"I'm not happy at having to leave Ison behind either," Tibbetts said.

"Neither is Ison, judging by his expression when he brought you the signal."

They fell silent, deep in thought, the wind taken out of their sails by this blow to their efforts. Ursula broke the silence. "If Ison has to withdraw, the Nagas will see him out. They'll get him through to the rear all right."

"All this bungling. What are they thinking? I'm sick and tired of it!" Tibbetts shouted.

"Albright went to enormous trouble to make it all happen, and someone else at a stroke has wrecked the lot. It's so disappointing." Ursula started pacing up and down. "You know what it is, don't you? Some fool's got the wind up about me being here and won't be happy till I'm further in the rear out of the danger zone."

Tibbetts stood up. "I'll tell everyone we're leaving tomorrow."

Foul weather matched their mood as they packed up. The day they left, in drenching, pounding rain, Tibbett's dysentery flared up again. He looked ghastly, and Ursula worried he would not be able to make the journey. At the river, they found the new bridge had been washed away the previous day.

"If we go to Joute, we can cross on the ferry. It's only about eight miles south," Ursula said. "Can you make it?"

"Don't worry about me," Tibbetts said.

The party took the road south to cross the river further down at Joute.

Tibbetts, sick and limping with fever, kept going, dosing himself at intervals, never letting up or complaining. In the bottom of the valley, the path suddenly plunged into almost virgin jungle. Ursula lost sight of him. Ahead of her was a small ravine. There were the leading scouts on the far side. Bill should be fifty yards behind them, but she couldn't see him. She felt sick with worry. If he'd fallen out and collapsed in the jungle, it could take days to find him—*if* they found him. Then she heard the crash of bamboos in the ravine and loud swearing. Ursula peered over the edge.

"Thank God," she said, seeing Tibbetts stumbling around in a mud-hole among the splintered ruins of the bridge he had been crossing.

They spent the night enjoying the hospitality of a Joute Kuki. Tibbetts felt better the next day, and the party pushed on. At Hepoloa they came on ninety men of the Observer Corps heading for Tamenglong with quarters and mule transport for Bower Force.

"The whole show's gone ruddy haywire," Tibbetts said.

"I don't care," Ursula said. "I just want to get back where things are sane as they were in the old days under HQ."

The party travelled east in a haze of soaking wet exhaustion, through mists and torrential storms, down the narrow cleft of the Jiri gorge, up the far side, over the hill, and into the

Haijaichak pass by the stragglers' road, to the little look-out and the Mahrattas' trenches, and all the friendly sights of home.

Ursula was due for leave and took it, leaving Tibbetts in charge.

*   *   *

She found adjusting to the more civilized life of Calcutta almost impossible. Not only was she estranged from Calcutta's social milieu by her life in the jungle, but the hard times of war as well. It was an effort to undress for bed after sleeping so long in her clothes. She had worn trousers for so long that dresses and skirts felt strange, and she felt undefended, somehow, in them.

Nights were the worst times. Lying in the dark, in bed, in her pyjamas, Ursula tossed and turned, feeling anxious and unprepared in case of a night alarm. It was difficult getting used to the idea of security. The second and third nights, she awoke to find herself groping on the floor for her Sten gun.

The transition came gradually, with a permanent wave, shopping, dancing, dinner with friends, dates with servicemen with time to kill, and many afternoons in the hotel's tearoom.

Then it was time to return home to Laisong.

Ursula stepped down from the train at Mahur dressed her Calcutta clothes, a short-sleeved yellow dress with tailored pleats that hugged her hips. She wore a white, brimmed hat set at a jaunty angle and smart two-inch wedge-heeled shoes. With no sign of Namkia, Haichangnang and the Laisong porters, who were to escort her back to camp, Ursula entered the waiting room. Inside were two American GIs. The soldiers eyed the glamorous woman coming through the door then rushed to pull out her chair and offer her a cigarette.

"Mind if we join you, ma'am?"

"Not at all."

The men settled themselves at the table. At first they made small talk. Then they began telling her stories they had heard of an extraordinary British woman.

"She lives in the hills with the tribesmen in crummy, primitive conditions," one said.

"Yeah," the other added, "we read all about her in the newspapers. They call her the Naga Queen. Have you heard of her?"

"I can't say that I have," Ursula said.

The soldiers continued with more stories of the Naga Queen.

"Really!" she responded. "Frankly, I find it hard to believe."

"Oh, it's for real, ma'am. This broad can kill leopards and heal the sick."

Keeping a straight face, Ursula leaned forward, her chin resting on her hand. She made her eyes grow wider as the embellished stories strayed further and further from the truth. Then, with a flurry of feathers and beads, Namkia and the others arrived. She jumped up, collected her bags and headed for the door. On the threshold, she turned to say goodbye to the servicemen. Their mouths hung open, jaws almost touching the floor.

"Bye, boys," she said with a cheery wave and a sweet grin then turned on her heel and vanished into the night.

Shortly after Ursula returned to Laisong, Bill Tibbetts was recalled to active service. The war was pushing into Burma, and he was needed there. Watch and Ward was now a back area.

She shook his hand. They had been through a season in hell together.

"I'm always saying goodbye to my friends. Be careful, Bill, and give the Japs what for."

Bill held on to Ursula's hand. "Don't worry about 'Bones' Tibbetts. Just you mind your own head. It's worth one hundred rupees I hear."

Ursula continued to tour the area to pay the scouts and ensure they were still at their posts. Touring in the monsoon was taxing. Matches wouldn't strike. Cigarettes grew mould whiskers overnight. Clothes were never dry. The paths were ankle deep in mud. In one area, they needed to be extra vigilant because elephants had been along the track, leaving footprints twelve inches deep in the mud, and nettles hemmed in this part of the trail, so if someone slipped and tumbled, they'd receive a painful sting.

At one village, two of the locals and one of Ursula's Assam Rifles went out to shoot pigeon. An hour later, the *sepoy* ran breathlessly into camp.

"One of the men has been attacked by a bear, miss-sahib. He's bleeding."

"I don't have any instruments," Ursula said. "We'll have to see what we can do without them. Get some water boiled, Namkia."

She brought out the bandages. Streaming with blood, the victim staggered into camp. "Come, sit here." She examined his wounds. "Luckily, they're bites and not claw wounds. That would have been really nasty," she said briskly.

The *sepoy*, who'd had the gun, paced up and down in a flap, doing his best to avoid watching Ursula treat the attack victim's wounds, reproaching himself that he should have taken action, but hadn't been able to.

"What happened?" asked Namkia.

"As we passed along the base of a steep slope, a bear charged down the hill and attacked the last man in line. He slashed at the bear with his machete and managed to drive off the beast. The mauling was over so quickly, the man ahead of him with the spear had no time to get back, and I was in front with the gun and never saw the bear at all."

"It was just bad luck," Namkia said, "and not your fault."

*   *   *

During a break in the weather, Ursula sat on the veranda, enjoying the sight of her staff wearing sweet-scented, buttercup yellow flower sprays cascading from their ears. She found the colourful contrast of the yellow against their black hair, coppery skin, and red blankets fetching. Her people were, she decided, the most beautiful on God's earth.

She opened the letters that Haichangnang finally managed to bring her on his second attempt to collect the mail from Haflong. (The first time, he'd found the post office closed for a public holiday, and instead of searching for the head clerk at his home, the poor fool had returned the thirty miles home empty-handed.) Ursula had to send him back again.

A letter from Captain Tibbetts described conditions now that the Japanese were in full retreat to Burma. He had found roads littered with unbelievable numbers of enemy dead and abandoned equipment. He'd come across a Japanese staff car with four dead Japanese sitting inside and Japanese field hospitals abandoned, wounded and all. Hundreds of dead, dying and starving enemy soldiers were being found in every village and position along the routes. He ended, "I've been having a high old time blowing up a Jap ammo dump and, incidentally, a lot of Japs. We slipped away leaving hell and high water going on in Jap circles. I bet you wish you were here."

But Ursula didn't.

She was engrossed in her life at Laisong and her Watch and Ward responsibilities. Then in November, with the Imphal Plain clear and the war now on Burmese soil, North Cachar Watch and Ward was disbanded.

Perry, Captain Albright and Colonel Scott came to Laisong for the final meeting along with the Deputy Commissioner. All of Watch and Ward's men came in. The village and Ursula's camp were crammed. Magulong village, which had the best dancers of the Zemi, sent a specially picked party for the entertainment. Because of the war, mithan were priced beyond Ursula's means, but Namkia scoured the country and found a massive pig.

It was a cool, bright day when the men were paid off. A small camp table stood in front of Ursula's bungalow. The wind snatched at the piles of papers and certificates, and the "V" Force officers had to continually catch them before they fluttered away. Ursula solved the problem with tins of sardines as paperweights. Three sides of the table were packed solid with the gathered scouts, a mass of red blankets and jet-black heads, relieved here and there by the Kukis' white turbans and edged by the dull jungle-green of the Assam Rifles.

Deputy Commissioner Pawsey made a short speech, praising the efforts of the Naga scouts and stressing the importance of their help in turning the tide of the war. "The Japanese are on the run, and the British government is very grateful to you."

One by one the scouts approached the table to receive their presentations. They were given ivory armlets, knives, certificates or cash bonuses, and some received guns thanks to Perry having persuaded the civil authorities to allow men who had done an especially good job to keep their weapons. They each took their discharge papers and retired.

When it was Namkia's turn to be called to the table, the Deputy Commissioner told him, "You have worked very hard for North Cachar Watch and Ward. Without your help, it very well may not have got off the ground. I am proud to present you with the British Empire Medal for Meritorious Service. It's well deserved."

He placed the silver medallion around Namkia's neck. Namkia was beaming and proudly posed for Ursula, who had left the table to take photographs of the presentations. Then it was her turn. Pawsey called her to the table.

"Miss Bower, formerly known as GB of Bower Force, General Slim wants you to know your services were invaluable to Fourteenth Army, and he greatly appreciates your help and your network of scouts. It is with great pleasure and gratitude that I present you with the Member of the Most Excellent Order of the British Empire Medal for Meritorious Service." Pawsey placed the silver cross round Ursula's neck. A surge of pride ran through her.

"Thank you, Deputy Commissioner. Pleased to have been of service."

She posed for army photographers. The disbandment ceremony was over. Men who had been given their guns ran to the end of the spur where Albright was supervising a shooting competition with flasks of powder for prizes. Other people participated in jumping competitions and sports. Late in the afternoon, food was served and rice-beer flowed. The camp was awash with bordered Kuki cloths, scarlet waistcoats, and the Magulong dance-troupe in dance-dress with huge Tam o' Shanters of wound cotton thread and hornbills' feathers quivering in the stiff breeze. As if on cue, the spectators formed a circle; Magulong began to dance; they danced all night.

Watching the celebrations, Ursula was sure her war was over, but she was wrong.

At breakfast the next morning, Scott told Ursula, "We've been thinking of using your services in jungle training camp. Would you and some of your men be interested in a job at Badapur as instructors?"

Ursula was thrilled to be of further use in the war. "Absolutely! And I'm sure the men would be interested."

Battered boxes, rifles, and Ursula's Sten gun were loaded onto the mules. Porters picked up the rest of "V" Force's paraphernalia. The Assam Rifle escort marched off along with Perry, Albright, and Colonel Scott. The long line of porters wound away up the village street and was glimpsed one final time where the road climbed the spur. *That was where we first saw Rawdon Wright,* Ursula thought with a sigh. *It seemed an age ago.*

"The camp feels empty now, Namkia," Ursula said.

Grumpy from the large amount of rice-beer consumed the previous night, his only response was an abrupt, "Uh."

That afternoon, Ursula sat on the veranda, sipping tea as she watched the gardener tend her vegetables. She absently stroked Khamba's head, recently returned from his stay with her friends in Silchar, and mulled over the past few years. *We're all civilian again, but it's not the same. Too much has happened. The scouts returning to their villages with well-earned, treasured guns, they're not the same. They put their trust in us and we in them—and we didn't fail each other. The Zemi suspicion of the authorities has gone. Only two years ago, I wouldn't have believed it possible.*

She roughed Khamba's ears. Then, raising her glass of lemonade, she toasted their success. *"Cheers in absentia, Perry. We managed it. No more glass wall."*

315

Shortly before Christmas, Ursula, Namkia and twenty of her best scouts arrived in Badapur to teach jungle survival techniques to Royal Air Force pilots.

Tucked away in the jungle, travel along a streambed provided the only means of access to the camp. As it was the cold, dry season, the stream was low. To reach camp, they travelled by jeep on a dirt road by one of the tea gardens before plunging into water. The jeep had a snorkel on it, and stakes marked the channel to avoid driving into deep holes during the three-mile drive upstream. In between courses, Ursula and the camp officers often went out for the evening in nearby Silchar, and as they drove back to camp, they frequently saw tigers and elephants.

The Nagas' main job was to teach stalking and hunting techniques and how to make things from bamboo, such as shelter, tools and weapons. "You can make just about anything from bamboo," one amazed airman said, "from a house to a cigarette holder."

On the other side of India, at Babhaleshwar near Bombay, was another jungle training camp with instructors from Kingdom Watch and Ward. A friendly rivalry developed between the two camps as they competed with one another to see what they could make out of bamboo. Kingdom's staff made an exquisite cigarette case and challenged Ursula's staff to do better. Ursula's camp, rising to the challenge, responded with a Christmas card made of scraped and flattened bamboo and won the contest.

Ursula may have been teaching jungle survival techniques, but she was only a short distance from civilization. At Christmas, she attended the British Other Ranks dance, deeming it the best of the three dances she attended. One party included a tame bear and a phenomenal milk punch nicknamed "dynamite." An RAF band provided the music. The dance was held outdoors, and a full-size banana tree towered over Ursula's table.

"If the food's a let down, I can always munch on bananas," she said to a young private who laughed at her quip a bit too long and a bit too loud. She would have liked to have looked more glamorous, but in the chilly night air, she frequently had to put on her sweater and even her camel hair coat to keep warm.

Some of the local planters came to lunch at another party held at the mess. The cooks provided food that would have been the envy of chefs at the Savoy, and the Nagas, having been hunting, brought in venison. The planters went away well-dined and well-wined on rum punch. Even the jolt of an earthquake didn't dampen the festive spirit.

The jungle training camp had inadvertently been built across an elephant trail, and one bull elephant often appeared at the camp in the middle of the night. The first intimation of an elephant problem happened in the early hours one morning. Ursula woke aware of a torch beam outside her tent and someone at the tent fastenings. She looked at her clock: 2:15 a.m.

"GB!"

"What is it?"

"There's an elephant outside."

Ursula threw on her coat over her pyjamas and emerged from her tent into the cold night to find the young adjutant with an electric torch, peering into the darkness, which crackled with elephantine noises close at hand.

"Right," Ursula said. Knowing the commandant was grumpy when his sleep was disturbed, she played the devil, saying, "Wake the major. The ejection of unauthorized elephants from military premises should be performed by the O.C. of the unit or by an officer designated by him for that purpose."

The surprised adjutant stared at her open-mouthed then hurried to the major's tent. Ursula grinned at his retreating back.

The major appeared in his pyjamas. He was rubbing his eyes and scowling.

"I don't hear any ruddy elephant," he said after listening for a minute. "I'm going back to bed."

A smile tweaked at Ursula's mouth as she and the adjutant duly returned to their respective tents. Ursula could hear the elephant resume its meanderings among the bamboo. At that point, she heard the servants exiting their tents, chattering like monkeys, afraid the elephant would come into camp and trample them. The servants began banging bamboos around the fire. The elephant competed by crashing and clambering about in the trees, on the other side of the river. Ursula finally had enough. She threw on her coat, flung the tent flaps aside and rushed out of her tent.

"Will you all shut up and scram!" she yelled.

The servants beat a hasty retreat to their quarters. The elephantine noises stopped.

"And peace reigns," Ursula said, satisfied.

She turned back to her tent. The distant browsings of the elephant started again.

"See what you started," she called to it then fell into bed.

Next morning, on the far bank of the stream, they found the tracks of a solitary elephant. He appeared again one day when Ursula and her Nagas were teaching the pilots stalking and hunting techniques. The large bull elephant walked into the middle of her class. Thinking discretion was the better part of valour, Ursula used hand signals to indicate they should withdraw silently into the jungle. It was as good a time as any to see if her students remembered the hand signal lessons she had been teaching.

They had.

Instructors and trainees tiptoed safely away.

One of the drills the Nagas taught the pilots was how to approach a village they were not sure was friendly. "First, you are to approach a villager and try to make friends with him," the major told the airmen. "If he doesn't run away in fright, he'll go into the village to convey your request for help to the headmen. While he's away, you are to find a place to hide. It has to be a place from where you can watch to see whether the villagers come back in a friendly fashion, or if they come rushing back armed to the teeth. It also has to be a place from where you can easily retreat without getting trapped."

Then came the part the Nagas really enjoyed, throwing themselves wholeheartedly into the spirit of things. The Nagas, to a man, could run faster than the trainees, especially uphill. On one particular occasion, when the Nagas, role-playing a hostile gang, arrived at a pilot's hiding place, his exit route was up a steep hill. The pilot, a fit, athletic man, was making good going, or so he thought. A Naga, overtaking him at twice his speed, tapped the airman on the shoulder. The pilot's shocked expression had the whole group howling with laughter for days. Lesson learned?

Make sure your escape route is downhill.

The final test for graduation from the three-week course arrived. The airmen were taken twenty miles away by jeep, left in dense jungle with only a compass and emergency rations, and told to find their way back to camp. The commandant, an ex-Burma forestry officer, had taught them that if they came across a tiger, it would probably not be hostile.

"The one thing he wants," the major reminded them, "is to be left alone. You'll hear a deep growl in the thicket. When you do, turn round, and quietly creep away. He'll go back to sleep and won't interfere with you. Right, GB?"

"Well . . ." Ursula began.

Two of the men returned to camp full of praise for the course and the advice given to them. They had stumbled on a snoozing tiger. The tiger growled. Desperately hoping their instructors knew what they were talking about, the two crept safely away.

"We didn't really believe you till then, but what you told us worked like a charm," they said.

"Hrrmph!" the major said, winking at Ursula. "You're the first ones to return in one piece to tell us it works."

At the end of March, Ursula's tour ended. The Nagas wanted to return to their villages to burn and prepare the land for cultivation. Ursula was offered the opportunity to return as instructor, but even though teaching in jungle camp had been fun, she decided against a second detail. "It's time to go home, boys," she told her men. "I'm ready for more domestic pursuits."

Back in Laisong, and finally feeling relaxed, Ursula received a letter from Colonel Betts, a "V" Force officer with ten days leave to spare. He had heard there were rare species in that area and asked if he might visit her compound to go butterfly hunting. She dashed off a brief affirmative reply explaining the procedure for obtaining passes and porters, then eagerly opened a package from her mother, containing the long-awaited Penguin paperbacks she had requested.

*　　　*　　　*

When Betts set out for Laisong with his Gurkha orderly, it was not an auspicious beginning. He missed a train connection then missed Perry who was to organize passes, help him find porters, and inform him how to reach Laisong. Betts had to sit about waiting for both. Then the monsoon broke as he and his orderly entered North Cachar. Soaking wet and weary, they reached the Tolpui pass and sat down to rest.

"What the hell am I playing at?" he rhetorically asked of his orderly, Lohengrin. "I'm on a wild goose chase encouraged by my romantic sister, Patience. I should know better."

He had poured his heart out to her about how lonely he was, and how he wanted to settle down with the right woman as soon as the war was over. She had told him to find the "Naga Queen" he had written about in his letters. It was obvious he was fascinated with her. "Faint heart never won fair lady," she'd said, wagging her finger at him.

She was right.

And so he had devised a plan to visit the "Naga Queen" in her camp. Sitting at the top of the pass in the pouring rain he felt a damned fool. *She could be as ugly as sin, a hard-faced, horse-toothed Amazon. She might throw me out on my ear.* He was in turmoil. Should he turn back or go on? He decided to draw lots and cast around for stems of grass.

"What are you doing, Colonel Sahib?" Lohengrin asked.

"Deciding what to do," Betts said.

Lohengrin giggled. "You're afraid of the Naga Queen."

"Certainly not! Just deciding what to do."

"There's no Naga king to worry about, Colonel Sahib," Lohengrin said, chuckling, "at least, not yet."

Betts ignored his orderly's amusement and concentrated on the task in hand. *Long straw, she's a horse-faced harpy. Middle one, she's a peach—but she won't have me. Short one, she's a peach and says yes.* He closed his eyes and extracted a straw. Betts stood up and pulled his beret firmly on his head. "Let's go."

"You picked the right straw, Colonel Sahib?"

"I picked the right straw," he answered with a smile and set off marching through the downpour to Laisong.

*   *   *

Namkia rushed out of the rain into Ursula's bungalow.

"The butterfly sahib is arriving, my sister."

"With it raining so hard? I didn't think he would come."

She went out by the back door to take a look. At her heels, Khamba was barking. She saw silhouetted against the grey sky a tall, lean, dripping colonel in jungle greens, a short, sodden Gurkha orderly and three soaking Asalu porters. The colonel hailed Ursula with relief.

"Do come in, Colonel, and dry out. We'll have some tea. Namkia, take his orderly and the porters to the kitchen for tea and to dry out, and ask Ramgakpa to lay on a bath for the Colonel Sahib and make up a bed in the guest bedroom."

The colonel scraped off his soggy beret, revealing his fairish, but greying, thinning hair. He was a handsome man, looking older than his years, worn out by fighting and deprivation but still full of spirit and a hungry sort of energy. Betts was ecstatic.

322

The "Naga Queen" was a peach. His enraptured glance raked over her quickly.

"I'm Tim Betts. Pleased to meet you at last, Miss Bower, or do you prefer GB?" he asked, shaking her hand, taking note of her sun-bleached hair and frank grey eyes and wondering how such a shapely woman had managed to remain single with Assam full of lonely soldiers and so few suitable women available for marriage.

Ursula was aware of his interest in her but chose to ignore it. It was commonplace among officers deprived of female companionship. "Please, call me Ursula. I was GB when I was a 'V' Force officer, and those days are over now."

"Then I'm Tim. I hoped on many occasions to bump into you at one of the 'V' Force meetings, but I always seemed to miss you."

Ramgakpa appeared with hot tea. "The Colonel Sahib's bath will soon be ready, mother."

"Thank you, Ramgakpa."

Ursula turned to Tim, taking in his tanned face and bright blue eyes. "Why did you hope to meet me?"

"Well, to be honest, I was curious about what a female 'V' Force officer would be like."

The picture of a hefty opera singer wearing a horned helmet singing in some Wagnerian opera immediately sprang into Ursula's mind. "And now that you've met me?"

"I'm pleased to see you seem quite normal. No horns on your head, no big muscles like an Amazon. Just a normal looking woman who's been doing an incredible job."

Hearing his comments about the horns, Ursula almost burst out laughing. We must be on the same wave length, she thought, but said instead, with a grin, "I'm relieved you find me normal."

While the colonel bathed, Ursula returned to her correspondence, shaking her head and smiling at his ingenuous compliment. She had written to Philip Mills, looking for fresh ethnographical work. He had suggested the Daflas in the northern hills west of the Brahmaputra River. She thought she would go once the monsoon ended.

*　　*　　*

After his bath and a change of clothes, Tim returned to the living room. From behind his back, he produced a bottle of sherry and some chocolate.

"I brought you a small gift. I hope these are to your liking."

Ursula was surprised and delighted. "Oh, how thoughtful! This is a wonderful treat! Let's have some now. I'll fetch the glasses. We'll sit by the hearth so you can warm yourself by the fire." She picked up a chair. Betts hurried to help her. She had lifted five times the weight of the chair many times but allowed Tim Betts his gallantry and stepped aside.

She felt snug, sitting in the light of the flickering flames, talking to this man. He shared with her some of his activities as a "V" Force officer and told her that he had been hearing stories of her deeds for the past eighteen months and was pleased at last to be able to meet her. Every once in a while he threw a log on the fire. They discovered they had a number of mutual acquaintances.

"I was a coffee planter in southern India, the Nilgiri's, before joining up."

"Will you go back to that when you're demobbed?"

"No, I don't think so. Being a planter doesn't bring great prospects. And I don't think I'll be staying in the army. I'm too much of a maverick. Being in 'V' Force was just up my street with few restrictions and more autonomy than most army officers manage to have. I was bored to tears with the job I had before 'V' Force, which was ferrying coolies by train from southern India to Assam. When it's all over, I'd like a much more interesting job, possibly as a political officer."

"Where's your family?" asked Ursula.

"They live in Winchester. My father was in jute, but he's retired now."

"Oh, do they know the Carpenter-Garniers? I went to school with their daughters."

"I believe they're some sort of distant cousins through marriage," Tim said. "Do you know Hal Carpenter?"

"Yes, I do."

Tim told her a story. "I remember going on a hike with Hal; we'd be about sixteen at the time. It was just before I left England to come to India. Anyway, we were having a peaceful walk through a meadow, along the riverbank, minding our own business, putting the world to rights, when we heard a loud bellow followed by the thudding of hooves. The ground was shaking. We looked round to see a Hereford bull bearing down on us. Hal ran up a tree, a large oak, thank goodness. I jumped in the river. Had to swim downstream to the next field then find the farmer to come to Hal's rescue. The family laughs about it every time we get together."

Ursula put her head back and laughed. "Believe it or not, I heard about your escapade with the bull. Hal's sister Christine told me about it."

There was a comfortable silence. Captivated, Tim found it hard to take his eyes off her.

"How about you? How did you end up living here with the Nagas?" he asked.

"Well, I've always had a yearning for adventure. Must be in the blood. I belong to a service family. Daddy's a navy commander. I grew up hearing my uncles' and great uncles' tales of their marvellous adventures. Only problem was, I was female, and it was men who had the adventures, not women. I was most disheartened about it all. Then a friend invited me to visit her in Imphal. We toured the Naga Hills with the Civil Surgeon and the State Engineer, and you might say I lost my heart to the Nagas. I found great satisfaction in doing something useful by bringing them medical help while at the same time making films about their culture for anthropological societies at home. I came and never left."

"You must have some amusing stories to tell."

"Thousands!" Ursula said. She thought for a moment. "There was the time I took my staff into Haflong to the cinema. We had a three-day orgy of watching films. They saw the War Bonds show, *Sixty Glorious Years,* which they enjoyed so much they saw it twice. There were some Indian films, but they didn't understand the talk very well. The boys preferred the English films so they could watch the vagaries of the sahibs. They saw

Johnny Weissmuller in action in *Tarzan Escapes*. I thought they'd love it, but no; they said coldly, 'it had too many monkeys in it.' Namkia said seeing the black cannibals in Tarzan made him feel positively white. Surprisingly, they much preferred the travelogue on Czechoslovakia. However, when we returned to camp, all I heard for days were poundings on chests, Tarzan yells, and the soprano squeals of Maureen O'Sullivan."

Betts' hearty laugh joined Ursula's throaty chuckle at the picture her tale conjured up.

"What are your plans while you're here, Tim?"

"I'd like to stay for a few days. Laisong seems to be magnificent butterfly ground. Perry told me he caught two rare *Calinaga* on the spur here only a few weeks ago."

"Well, there's plenty of space in camp now the army's gone. You can use it as a base. Let me know when you want picnic lunches, and I'll arrange it. In the morning, I'll show you the best places to go."

That night, after retiring to bed, Ursula stretched and smiled to herself. *I enjoyed this evening. He can certainly tell a funny story. He'll be fun to have around, and as a guest, he shouldn't interfere with my work too much.*

* * *

After breakfast, Ursula and Tim huddled over a map while she showed him the areas she thought would be the most fertile hunting grounds. As she pointed out the tracks, his hand strayed towards hers. Ursula moved her hand away. He's been on the frontline too long, she thought. His hand wandered towards hers again. She moved it a second time and this time, Tim took the hint.

They dined together each morning and evening. She found him to be very likeable and easy to get on with. She liked his craggy face, crooked smile and the straightforward honesty in his eyes. With his store of amusing stories, he was entertaining company. Even Khamba liked him. However, Ursula was puzzled. For a man who was an ardent collector, who had only ten days leave, she would have expected him to hurry off with his net as soon as the chill was gone and his prey on the move. But at ten o' clock and even eleven, the colonel would still be hanging about the compound as if reluctant to go chasing butterflies.

On the fourth day of his stay, he returned to camp early in the afternoon. Ursula was in the kitchen making a cake when Namkia entered.

"The Colonel Sahib wants to see you, my sister."

Khamba, lying by the door, lifted his head.

"What? He's back already? It's only one o'clock! I'd better see what he wants."

She wiped her hands on a cloth and brushed the flour off her trousers before going outside. Khamba rose from his bed and gave a lazy stretch, first one rear leg then the other then followed Ursula out the door.

Tim was pacing up and down beside the garden, head down, hands linked behind his back with the air of a man with something very much on his mind.

Ursula fell into step beside him. Tim seemed agitated. She wondered if he'd been recalled and had to leave at once. A lively Khamba trotted at her heels. Up and down they paced. When Tim came to the end of the garden, he wheeled and strode back to the other end followed by Ursula and Khamba. The first two turns he stayed silent, and Ursula wondered if he had received bad news. Then he began mumbling about how he had first heard of her on his arrival at "V" Force HQ where she was being called the Naga Queen.

Ursula was puzzled by this utterance and supposed he would soon get to the point.

Tim droned on. She kept turning her head towards him, trying to catch his words. Khamba, enjoying the impromptu romp, kept looking up at Ursula.

Tim cleared his throat. "After hearing about you, I knew you were the woman I wanted for my wife. I even tried to scrub Bill Tibbetts' name off the orders to substitute my own to come to support your unit, but he walked in at that point, so I was stymied." He chuckled. "You should have seen the Colonel's face when I asked for leave to come here. He wanted to know why I needed to go on leave. Told him it was for the purpose of matrimony. I was going to propose to the Naga Queen."

Tim stopped abruptly by the cannas and, filled with trepidation, took a deep breath. "So, Miss Bower, this is it. Will you marry me?"

Khamba sat down and, looking from one to the other, watched the proceedings with interest.

As if struggling to move through waist high molasses, she brought her mind to Tim's words. "What did you say?"

Now that the words had been said, his agitation disappeared, replaced in a heartbeat with an earnest confidence.

"I said, will you marry me?"

Ursula was dumbfounded. *I didn't see this coming. How could I have been so blind?* She stared at his attractive face, his straight nose, the tenderness in his eyes. She opened her mouth as if to say something then closed it several times before managing to say, "I'll never leave the kind of life I'm living now. I can't be the usual sort of wife. I . . ."

Tim took her hand, his voice gentle. "Ursula, if I'd wanted the normal and ordinary in a wife, I would not be asking for *your* hand in marriage. I've been thinking about this for months. My visit to your compound has shown me you're the special someone I want to share the rest of my days with."

"Oh, well, that's all right then."

From Tim there was a sharp intake of breath. "Is that a yes?"

Tim was so surprised his dream of the past eighteen months seemed to be coming true that he looked like a man who'd been hit on the head.

"Yes? I . . . Well, I . . . Hang on! You're a very nice man, and we have a lot in common. When we know each other better, it's possible, maybe probable, that we could find grounds for matrimony." Ursula was spluttering and flailing. "I have to think about this. This is my first marriage proposal . . ."

"That's splendid! Absolutely bloody marvellous! You've made me a very happy man, Ursula."

"I really can't rush this. I need time…"

But Tim wasn't listening. He was already leading a dazed Ursula into her bungalow. "This calls for a drink to celebrate. It's been a shock for both of us."

"Yes, it has," Ursula said, her voice sounding to her ears as if it came from a distance.

Tim took hold of her arm and turned her round to face him. She felt the strength in his arms. After towering over the Naga men for so long, Ursula was aware of his tallness, and she looked up at him. He tilted her head back and brought his lips to hers, covering her with passionate kisses. Ursula stiffened. She'd always thought kissing a nauseating and overrated pastime. To her surprise, she found herself enjoying the experience. She melted into his embrace then panicked and wriggled free.

"We must be careful. My staff frowns on such behaviour in public. If Namkia came in, he might misunderstand and attack you."

Tim laughed softly, kissed Ursula's forehead then grabbed his signet ring and shoved it on her finger.

"There, that makes it official. Let's have a tot of rum to celebrate."

A wave of panic hit Ursula. In shock, she moved to the rations cupboard, took down a bottle of rum and two glasses and held them to her body. She stood for a moment, composing herself before returning to the living room, her eyes wide in an apprehensive face. Tim, in seventh heaven, didn't notice her pallor.

Full of joy, he poured two glasses of rum and held up his glass. "To us."

"To us," Ursula responded numbly, clinking his glass. "Tim, about *us* . . ."

"Oh, Ursula, we can do so many exciting things together. I've always wanted to go to Tibet and China, explore the Himalayan foothills. How would you like to honeymoon there?"

At the mention of a honeymoon, she was filled with an impending sense of doom. Stalling, Ursula steered the conversation to safer ground while she struggled to subdue her emotional seesaw. "One of my great uncles walked across Tibet into China. I'd sit and listen to his adventures for hours when I was a child."

"I'm so glad you like adventure too. For years I've been looking for a woman who shares the same passions, and now she's sitting right here with me. I can hardly believe my luck." Tim squeezed Ursula's hand. "Once the war's over, I'll try for a political officer's job. We'd still be somewhere in India or Burma, watching out for the tribes. Could you bear to leave Laisong to do that with me?"

"Yes, I'm ready to leave Laisong. In fact, I've been corresponding with Mr. Mills to find another area to go to for my ethnographical work."

All evening, Tim talked animatedly about their future. They would do this together; they would do that. He was so engrossed in the picture his mind conjured up, he failed to realize that Ursula, now filled with dread, was not sharing his joy.

She spent a sleepless night, her mind in turmoil. One minute she was thinking she should marry him and what was she fussing for? He was as pleasant a chap as she'd ever come across. The proposal had just been a shock. Then the next minute she was fearful about losing her independence. She was used to making her own decisions. She'd been in command of soldiers. Could she give that up? Would he want her to? Would married life agree with her? Probably not. She had too much to lose. Ursula felt as if she was sliding into the abyss, and wanted to stop the fall.

*   *   *

The next morning at breakfast, Tim's heart was in his mouth thinking Ursula had changed her mind when he saw she was not wearing his ring. He said nothing about it and neither did Ursula. They decided to go for a walk, but before leaving, Ursula returned to her room. She took the ring from her dresser and rolled it in her fingers as she stood in front of the mirror, looking at her reflection. She decided it would be a mean trick to return the ring before she'd really considered his proposal, especially as he seemed overjoyed at the prospect of marrying her. She slipped the ring on her finger and returned to the living room. Seeing it, Tim's smile was radiant.

"Let's find Khamba," Ursula said, "and make the most of this good weather."

They hiked the path towards the Nenglo track.

"I'll try in these next few days to show you as I really am. I know I have little to offer a woman. I'm thirty-eight. I've lived on my own for too long, so I'm selfish and self-centred, and lacking in enterprise."

The unflattering picture Tim painted of himself made Ursula hopeful he was having second thoughts too. Her panic subsided. "You sound as if you're trying to put me off the idea of being engaged to you."

"On the contrary, with a woman like you as a partner, I'd have something to live for. I think there's every chance I'd make you a good husband. To my astonishment, I fell head over heels in love with you the moment we met."

Unnerved again, Ursula said, "I can't say I feel the same way, Tim. It's almost as if I'm the rare butterfly you came for. And netted. I feel captured almost . . ."

Tim gently put his finger to her lips to silence her.

"There'll be no killing jar nor will I pin you down. Warm friendship and companionship would be all I'd ask of you at first. Then, as we get to know one another better, hopefully your feelings for me will grow."

They had only two more days to spend together before he had to leave. Tim tried to pin Ursula down to a date for a wedding within the next couple of weeks.

"This is only an unofficial engagement, Tim, until I have a chance to talk to Mr. and Mrs. Mills. They're my closest friends, and I trust their advice. And I certainly don't want to rush into anything. If I do make it official, I'd want at least a six months' engagement."

"I'm afraid I'm rushing you," he said, "but under the circumstances, I don't feel I have much choice. I had to propose now, or our ways may have parted never to meet again, and all my life I would have regretted losing this opportunity."

"I just need time to consider what being married to you will mean for me. I like the way I live. I don't want to change it."

"This is exactly how I would like to live too. If I get a political officer's job, we can stay away from civilization and help the natives."

On hearing his words, Ursula relaxed enough to enjoy finding out more about this man who cared for her and accepted her as she was.

*　　*　　*

The day of Tim's departure arrived.

"Ursula, I know it's a hell of a gamble on your part. Please don't change your mind after I leave or think this is an affair that can't last."

"I'll meet you in Shillong in three weeks, when I visit Mr. and Mrs. Mills, and in the meantime, I'll consider everything you've said."

"Is their advice so important to you?"

"Yes, they've taken the place of my parents while I'm away from home. I respect their opinions."

"Give me the chance, and I'll do my best to see you never regret it. I also won't say anything about our engagement in Shillong or make a public announcement until you give me the word. I love you more and more every minute, my darling. Take great care of yourself till I see you in Shillong."

He kissed her, looked deep into her eyes and then left the bungalow.

Ursula was relieved, the pressure to marry gone along with Tim's departure. Nevertheless, she would still think seriously about marriage to Tim Betts. He loved her as he found her, had no desire to change her. He was well-educated, seemed like he would be a good match and acceptable to the family. He had shown her how sweet a kiss could be, and he was attractive. All she had to do was quieten her doubts. She touched his ring on her finger.

The well-worn train clanked down off the Hill Section and into Badarpur junction on a July afternoon. From inside her carriage, Ursula saw Tim waiting on the platform, his face knotted by a worried frown. He looked panicked, until she saw him spot Namkia's red waistcoat weaving through the crowd towards him.

"Hello, Namkia. Where's the miss-sahib?"

Namkia led Tim along the congested platform to Ursula stepping from the carriage. Tim looked as if he wanted to sweep her into his arms and kiss her passionately, but, restraining himself, he said simply, "I'm glad you came." He took her arm to help her down, the only physical touch he could have in front of her servants.

Shading her eyes from the sun, she looked up at him and smiled. "So am I."

Namkia and Haichangnang picked up her luggage, and Tim roused himself enough to lead the way through the press of bodies to his jeep.

With Namkia and Haichangnang perched in the back, they bowled along the flat road, stretching westwards along the foot of the hills as far as the eye could see, heading for Shillong.

Tim leaned close to Ursula so her staff would not overhear. "I've been posted to Burma in the Military Administration. I want to get married straight away."

"No, it's too soon! I want a six-month's engagement!"

"Once I'm sent into Burma, I don't know when I'll be able to see you again. It certainly won't be often. I want us to be married. I don't want to risk losing you while I'm away."

"No, I won't be rushed. It's six months at least."

They would not reach Shillong that night and would have to stop at Dawki. Tim's conversation for the rest of the drive stayed on neutral ground as he digested Ursula's words.

Over dinner, Tim was so captivated by Ursula he could hardly keep his hands off her. He brushed her hair back from the nape of her neck and pleaded his case for an immediate marriage. Ursula insisted on six-months.

It was stalemate.

And yet, the enormous effort he was making to restrain himself, and his despondency at her refusal to marry at once, touched Ursula's heart. Tim stopped pushing, and Ursula regarded him with a new approval. The evening relaxed into a companionable tête-à-tête. She felt she could enjoy life with this man, but marriage was a big step, and she wanted to confer with the Mills first.

Next morning, they set off on the last leg of the journey. On the outskirts of Shillong, they encountered a long convoy of trucks bearing down on them on the wrong side of the road. MPs in a jeep, in front of the convoy, waved them to the side of the road. Tim pulled in behind a blue Austin Healey. The two vehicles sat there while the convoy roared past almost close enough to scrape their paint. When the car ahead didn't move during a lull in the traffic, Tim pulled round it.

"Stop!" cried Ursula. "It's the Mills!"

She jumped out of the jeep and ran back to the car. Mr. Mills, laughing with surprise at the coincidence, got out to meet her, then talked to Tim, while Ursula sat with Mrs. Mills in the front seat. Mrs. Mills welcomed her with a peck on the cheek. "It's so good to see you. How long will you be in Shillong?"

"Well, I'm not really sure. It depends on your advice. I wrote you about Colonel Betts' proposal."

"Of course you did. A very nice man he is too."

"You've met him?"

"Yes, indeed, He called on us soon after he left you at Laisong and announced he intended to persuade you to be his wife. We're both quite taken with him, my dear. In fact, we think he's delightful, a perfect match."

"Tim called and introduced himself? That's showing initiative!" Ursula said. "I was going to ask your advice about marrying him six months from now, but he's going into Burma and wants to marry immediately. I'm not sure that's a good idea."

"My dear girl, have the wedding at once. Philip and I had only known each other eight days when I accepted his proposal, and we've had a very happy marriage."

"I don't know if I can do that. I'm afraid. It will be such a drastic change."

Mrs. Mills patted Ursula's hand. "I had cold feet right up to the wedding, but everything turned out well. Once we were married, I realized I was very fond of Philip, and I've continued being very fond of him ever since. Besides, marriage is such a gamble anyway. Go ahead. Marry your handsome colonel. Mr. Mills and I think he's a decent chap. Tell him yes."

Ursula returned to Tim's jeep stunned by the Mills' advice not to wait. It was the last thing she had expected. She spent the remainder of the journey deep in thought, revising her ideas on marriage.

Tim dropped Ursula and the Nagas at the hotel, while he went to the officers' mess. For two days, they explored Shillong, the hill station becoming the backdrop for their battle of wills. On top of Shillong Peak, Tim pressed Ursula to marry him. She said, "No." She also said, "No" at the racecourse, Police Bazaar, and the spectacular Elephant Falls. With the shadows lengthening on the second afternoon, they were sitting in the jeep, overlooking the American Remount Depot on the Gawahati road, watching several hundred mules in the depot.

"Ursula, please reconsider. I don't want to go into Burma a single man. I want to know I'll have you waiting for me each time I come home on leave. Now that I know you just a little, my life will seem so empty without the permanency of marriage."

Taking her silence for another refusal, Tim's heart sank.

But Ursula had made her decision.

"Yes."

"Yes? Yes? Oh, Darling!" Tim kissed her hard then held her at arms length to look at her amused face. "You've made me the happiest man in the world. I don't know what it is about looking at mules that made you change your mind, but I'm so pleased they're here." He pulled her to him, kissed her again.

Ursula laughed, having made the decision, she was elated. "We'll need a special licence."

"Yes, we will," Tim said. "It's getting late. Let's go."

With squealing tires they tore round Shillong in search of the padre and licence, and when those details were settled, Tim dropped Ursula outside the hotel. The first person she saw was Namkia.

"Hello, my sister."

"Hello, Namkia." She took a deep breath. "I have something to tell you."

Her tone of voice attracted his full attention.

"In two days I'm going to marry the Colonel Sahib."

Namkia was stricken speechless.

Ursula laughed with delight at taking him so completely by surprise. "Namkia, it's the first time I've ever seen you at a loss for words."

*   *   *

Next morning, Ursula wrote a letter to her mother and then called Mrs. Mills with the news.

"I need your help. I've a wedding to organize. I'm in desperate need of a trousseau. I've been economizing on clothing while prices have been so high, and now all my underwear and nightwear is so shabby, it's totally unsuitable for a bride."

"You must come round at once. We'll sort something out."

Ursula arrived at the Mills home within the hour.

"Come into the bedroom. I've already pulled some clothing from the dresser for you. How are you doing?"

"My feet have suddenly turned very cold."

"Pre-wedding jitters. Nothing to worry about," Mrs. Mills said, briskly. She held up a cream satin nightgown with thin straps. "If you like this, I'll lend it to you for your wedding night."

"Oh, it's beautiful," Ursula said, thinking of her usual worn flannel pyjamas with patched seats and elbows. She couldn't remember the last time she had worn such luxurious nightwear.

Mrs. Mills asked her servant to bring some tea, and while they drank it, pulled out pencil and paper and started jotting down everything they needed for Ursula and Tim to put on a good show: cake, dress, invitations, flowers, pretty underwear, nightwear, photographer, newspaper announcement. She listed things for Tim to do and made another list for Ursula before whisking her off to the stores to search for items on the list. At one shop they found some bright red, silky Chinese pyjamas. Mrs. Mills bought a pair for Ursula, and Ursula bought another. At the next store, they found some cotton frocks, a dinner dress, and a long, pink brocade dress ideal for the bridal gown. They stopped to order flowers then a cake and arranged the reception at the Orchid Hotel before breathing a sigh of relief.

"We've made a good afternoon of it, Ursula," said Mrs. Mills. "Why don't you bring Tim to dinner tonight so we can get to know him better?"

*   *   *

For Ursula, the following forty-eight hours passed in a blur punctuated with glimpses of a harassed Tim. Ursula spent her wedding day morning bathing, packing and having an early lunch. Then she started to dress for her wedding. Mrs. Mills arrived to help.

"Your hands are shaking," she remarked.

"I hadn't noticed, but I'm not surprised. I'm feeling slightly sick."

"I've arranged for the best photographer in town to take the photographs so your family will at least see how especially beautiful you look today," Mrs. Mills said. She opened her handbag and took out a jewellery case. "I've also brought you something borrowed, the pearls I wore on my wedding day." She stood behind Ursula and fastened the clasp. "They'll bring you luck and, I hope, a marriage as happy as ours."

Mr. Mills called for her with the bridal car. Ursula felt like she was leaping from a plane without a parachute.

"Wait," Mrs. Mills fussed. "You're far too pale. Where's the rouge?"

She rubbed some on Ursula's cheeks till she had a healthy glow. "That's more like it. Off you go."

Ursula left with Mr. Mills, who was to walk her down the aisle. She was shivering as if it were cold. Mr. Mills patted her hand and made soothing noises. The car drew up at the church. Ursula looked out the car window and took a deep breath.

"Ready?" asked Mr. Mills.

She looked at him with saucer eyes, nodded and stepped from the car.

At the church door, seeing the church packed with "V" Force officers and Shillong's leading citizens, she checked, overcome with panic, feeling she was making a ghastly mistake now that the moment had come.

Mr. Mills firmly took her arm and whispered, "It's all right. We all feel afraid at this point."

She looked down the church and saw Tim, his shoulders hunched and tense, like a groom expecting to be ditched at the altar. At that moment, he turned to see if she had arrived. She glimpsed Tim's relief at seeing her before the best man nudged at him to turn his eyes front.

The organist played *Here comes the Bride*. Mr. Mills tugged her into motion. She felt hot then faint in turns, and then she was beside Tim. Catching a whiff of the brandy he'd needed to steady his nerves, she immediately felt calm. A sense of normality returned. Things were running true to form for a Bower wedding. She relaxed even more when Tim, with his hands shaking and Ursula's hand sweating, had difficulty putting the ring on her finger. By the time they signed the register in the vestry, Ursula was reconciled to being married.

The couple left the church to find a guard of honour of Assam Rifles, who formed an arch of kukris over the couple.

Looking at the short Gurkhas, Tim said, "Duck well down or we'll be scalped."

"And that's no way to start a honeymoon," Ursula said.

The bride and groom had a fit of the giggles.

Haichangnang and Namkia, wearing his British Empire Medal, stood guard on either side of the church door. The couple posed for photographs before jumping in the car, which carried them to the reception. On the steps leading to the hotel's hall, a bearer met them with two glasses of hock.

"I need this, don't you?" asked Tim.

"Yes, I do."

With a clink of glasses, they gulped down the wine and grinned at each other.

"You've done it now, girl. Are you all right?"

"I'm as right as rain," she told him.

They were sent off from the reception amid showers of rice. Tim's brother officers had seen fit to tie a tin can and an old boot to the back of the car taking them to the small cubicle-sized room at the officers' hostel with its strawboard partition walls where they were to spend their wedding night.

Inside the small room, Ursula felt embarrassed and awkward at undressing in front of him. Sensing her shyness, Tim said, "The walls are very thin, aren't they? Enough to put you off."

"Well, there is that. Our neighbours could be in for an interesting night," she said, laughing and then became serious. "It's just so strange to have you in the room with me." Covering her confusion, she light-heartedly spoke in a Scottish brogue. "Good grief, mon, I hardly know yeh. We've nay been properly introduced."

Tim laughed and wrapped his arms round her. Copying her Scottish accent, he said, "We can soon rectify that, m'lady. We could start with a Scottish reel, a Highland fling, or would m'lady prefer to toss the caber."

Ursula dissolved into laughter—and at that moment, she fell in love.

*   *   *

339

Tim had managed to obtain more leave before joining his new post. They left by train to spend their honeymoon trekking round Darjeeling and Sikkim. With them went Namkia, Haichangnang and Tim's orderly, Lohengrin.

For sixteen days, they hiked through Sikkim and Tibet, discovering they shared the same goofy sense of humour and a sense of what was wonderful and amazing. Ursula was happy. She had made a good match.

Tim went off to Burma as soon as they returned to India; Ursula and her men returned to Laisong. The day following their return, Ursula looked up from her correspondence to see a formal procession of all her staff advancing towards the house with Namkia at its head. Looks like the boys are going to ask for a pay raise in view of my status as a married woman, she thought. The men lined up before the table with solemn faces. Ursula felt a twinge of alarm. Was this something more serious?

Namkia stepped forward and looked Ursula in the eye.

"The Sahib," he said, "is all right."

The tribe, having delivered judgment, trooped out.

She wondered what they'd have done if he was not?

The Japanese surrender on September 2nd 1945, took everyone by surprise. Tim, in his capacity as a British Army officer, was working for the Burmese government in Burma's Shan State. A serious famine was raging, and he could not be released from his post. For months all he could manage were flying visits to his new wife until his return to India in the spring of 1946.

Warned by Ramgakpa that Tim was coming, Ursula hurried down the hill to meet him, her eyes shining with love. The only acceptable public display of affection was a tight squeeze of the hand, but Tim's smile clearly revealed his joy in being with Ursula again.

"I've missed you so much," Tim said.

"I've missed you too."

"I've been demobilised," he said as they climbed the slope to Laisong. "I'm trying for a job on the North-East Frontier. Is that something you would want to do with me?"

"Of course I would. Any idea when you'll know?"

"It could be weeks, even months, but I do so want this job."

That evening, nestled by the hearth of the roaring fire, Ursula told him she was in the middle of preparations to bring in Magulong's dance troupe to perform in Haflong at the VJ Day celebrations.

"I'll be leaving for Magulong in a week. Are you up for it?"

"Wouldn't miss the chance to go on a trek with you for anything."

"Magulong is really my favourite Naga village."

"Then why do you live in Laisong?"

"Perry wanted me to be reasonably close to him in case I got into trouble." Ursula threw a log onto the fire. "I first came across the Magulong men in 1940 in Asalu camp when a party of them came in looking for shelter during a storm. That was on my first trip in North Cachar. Apart from that, I had no real contact with them except occasionally coming across them as salt traders heading for Mahur market. They live in Manipur State, thirty miles away across the hills, outside of British India. Then in June 1944, Bill Tibbetts and I recruited scouts from the village to watch the Barak crossings. That summer, their headman, Khutuing, came to Tamenglong to see us. The village had a dysentery outbreak. Many died. We quickly sent the 'V' Force doctor there and provided the village with free relief later on."

"Why do you like Magulong so much?" asked Tim.

"It was when they first appeared for the 'V' Force show. I saw them as they really were, splendidly barbarous as Nagas used to be. Colourful and untamed. They had taken heads but danced like Nureyev. For drive, discipline, skill, and for sheer zest, they make our North Cachar Zemi look like a flock of sheep."

*   *   *

Ursula and Tim did not start for Magulong until May. They travelled east, down into the narrow Jiri Valley. As they reached the top of the far hill, it started to pour. They climbed into Maovom in sheets of rain, with ankle-deep water running down the path. From Maovom, valleys and hills stretched one after the other. The party marched and climbed, up and down, through grass, scrub, bamboo and forest. Monsoon clouds shrouded the crests ahead. From Saipimual, they climbed through dark woods, picking their way through elephant-trails among splintered and scarred trees laid waste by the gargantuan beasts that left water-filled footprints like hip-baths in the soft soil.

They arrived at the little camp at Bungsang. Magulongs's headman, Khutuing, met them there. He was short and muscular, dwarfed by the taller men with him. Ursula remembered thinking him unimpressive when she had first met him and was surprised he could be the headman of such a vibrant village.

But on talking to him, she and Tim discovered that at eighteen years of age, he had taken a head during the Kuki rebellion. Among his heirlooms he had two long tails of black hair cut from his victim's head. He took them out on great occasions, wearing them as ear ornaments so the wavy tresses fell far down on his bare shoulders and chest.

"Because I have taken a head," he told them, "I'm entitled to the great human-hair shield, the *ge-ʒe*. You don't see them in Magulong now."

He described how the young men used to carry them in sham fights, leaping, bounding, scissoring their legs, and making war-play until the long black tassels whisked and flew. Khutuing's eyes shone at the memories. Ursula asked more questions about his headhunting activities.

"I'll show you how we let the village know we've taken heads," he said and proceeded to demonstrate a head-hunter's war cry. It was a deep, humming chant, and as he sang, Ursula's skin crawled.

The next morning, the party set off for Magulong. Moving down the ridge, they sighted the village across a grassy valley. It stood on a spur jutting out from a high, wooded range behind. Ursula and Tim could see cliffs in the woods on the high, steep hill. The ground fell away sheer and smooth from the village, the path zigzagging downwards in twists and elbows, past waterfalls, past huge grey rocks, under crags, and into the valley bottom.

They halted. From their feet, a narrow, stepped track, hemmed in by tall reed-grass, ran down to meet the descending path. As they stood, they heard the faint, sweet sound of distant singing.

Ursula and Tim stared and listened. The songs were distant, haunting. They took out their field glasses and searched the hills. Then they saw, on a ledge of rock a little below the village, young men and girls singing.

All through the long, hot trek through the grassy valley, the distant singing called a welcome to them. As they moved nearer, crawling up the rugged opposite slope, the singing came down full and clear, the girls' high voices blending with the boys'. At the back of Ursula's file, the Nagas answered them verse for verse, while they climbed the last half-mile to the village gate.

The sound of Ursula's party's singing had brought out the villagers. Singing elders, children, and housewives crowded the gate. Escorted by the young men and girls still singing, the party turned towards the gate.

"This is wonderful," Tim said. "I feel like we're in an operatic extravaganza."

"The name Magulong means the people who chant as they work, welcome visitors and see them off."

The entrance rose steeply in a narrow flight of steps. They stepped through a gap in the cactus hedge into an airy village street. Dark, weathered houses dotted the spur. They walked along the street followed by singing villagers.

The village council, set in a row, were in a nearby wide street. Ursula and her group approached. In front of the council stood a line of bottles of rice-beer, at least forty of them Ursula reckoned. There was a small bull-mithan tied to a post. One of the elders stood up and began to speak.

Namkia and Khutuing explained. The village knew that Tim and Ursula had been married by the sahibs' laws and rites, but on behalf of the tribe, there ought to be more. It was only right that the miss-sahib, who was a Zemi, should also be married by tribal rites as well—the only rites the Zemi recognize. Magulong, therefore, proposed to see it done. "Do you agree?" asked Khutuing.

Surprised and delighted, Ursula and Tim gladly gave their consent.

There were three days to wait before everything would be ready for the ceremony, days which Ursula and Tim filled by exploring the area. Ursula also observed Khutuing in his work as headman and marvelled at his strength of character and leadership. Although young for the job, Ursula never heard him raise his voice. He hardly ever gave an order. One word and the warriors did as he said. Magulong functioned like a well-oiled machine, while North Cachar headmen shouted and cuffed, raged and ranted and produced no results at all.

She was relieved that Magulong rather than a North Cachar village had taken the initiative to provide her with a Zemi wedding.

*   *   *

Haichangnang arrived at Magulong with the mail. A letter for Tim informed him he had his appointment in the North-East Frontier service—the Subansiri Area, which was the last unexplored tract. The news meant they could only spend two more days in Magulong before leaving.

The wedding ceremonies were set in motion. First, Khutuing adopted Ursula by the name of Katazile, meaning "Giver of All," because of the "V" Force relief, which had saved Magulong from famine. Tim next presented Khutuing with a spear, the gift of respect, and one hundred rupees as Ursula's nominal marriage-price. Khutuing replied with the cloth of betrothal, a crimson-bordered full-dress cloth of Magulong and its groups.

Then came the ceremony proper. The village priest strangled a cockerel and took omens from the way it crossed its feet. The bird was cooked and placed in a special dish. Khutuing gave Ursula a cane-rice basket, the symbol of wifely duties, as well as an axe, a hoe, and a spindle.

Ursula and Tim walked from Khutuing's house and back to the camp, man and wife by Zemi law.

And Ursula suddenly felt utterly and deeply married, sworn to Tim by laws and in a manner that felt more profound than the church ceremony in Shillong. She was a Zemi wife, who loved her man as he loved her.

Khutuing's lieutenant carried the dish of cooked fowl and set it down in the hut for the couple to eat.

The first formal meal of married life concluded the Zemi ceremony but not the celebrations. The party began at four that afternoon in the dark, smoky hall of Khutuing's *morung*. Vats of rice-beer filled the back room. The young men and warriors of both *morungs* were in attendance, as were the elders.

In the huge hall with its two pillars and fires burning on the floor, everyone danced and sang in the smoky darkness till the sun went down. They were still singing and dancing when the moon went down and long after the cockcrows at sunrise. Even when the housewives woke to the day's chores, they were still dancing. At ten o'clock, Ursula and Tim urged Khutuing to bring the party to an end. Chanting, singing, and dancing, the partygoers saw the bride and bridegroom to their hut. Gathered about the doorway, they sang goodbye, ending with a wild, ringing, barbaric chorus. They threw the notes out, chord on chord, in a magnificent crescendo, a mass aria. Up went Khutuing's arm. The whole band checked on one sustained note. There was a second's pause; then "Hoi!" it was over.

Ursula and Tim left next morning. Half the young men in the village wanted to go with Ursula to work because the village suffered from the Barail disease—shortage of land and chronic poverty. Ursula took their names and said she'd send for them later. Elders, women, and warriors said goodbye. Priests blessed the couple. Khutuing would accompany Tim and Ursula to Laisong. They finally left the village after collecting gifts, advice, blessings, and farewells. As they dropped down the long, winding track to the stream, the boys' and girls' voices followed, singing the song of farewell to a girl who marries outside the village.

At the bottom of the track, between the high walls of reeds, Namkia discovered a small boy carrying Tim's shotgun. He was eight years old and the leader of a pack of boys who had been catching butterflies and locating birds for Tim in the scrub surrounding the camp. His presence in the party was unauthorised. In an ominous silence, elders and headmen surrounded him.

"What," asked Khutuing, "are you doing here?"

The boy's tears overflowed. His nose ran. He gave a loud sniff. "I want to go away and work for the Sahib." His voice was small and sad. "He gives me plenty to eat."

"Have you your father's leave?"

"No."

"Go home," Khutuing said.

Mutely, the small figure handed over the gun. Heartbroken, and with his head bent, he turned round and trudged home. The column resumed the climb to Bungsang.

As the group reached Saipimual, the weather broke. Torrents poured from gunmetal skies. Paths gushed like gutters. The bridgeless Jiri River lay between the column and Laisong. Ursula, worried about how they would cross, relaxed when the rains thinned to a drizzle as they neared Maovom. But it was a premature hope. During the night, heavy rain thundered on the palm-leaf thatch, and they woke to steady rain and low cloud. Khutuing reported the Jiri could not be crossed at the ford.

"I've sent men to start a bridge. Go down later in the morning, and it should be over."

When the rain let up, Ursula, Tim and the rest of the party struggled along difficult paths towards the narrowest part of the Jiri. A man came and told them the bridge wasn't ready. With the rain increasing, they stacked their baggage underneath a stilted field house then climbed up to the platform to eat their lunch. Khutuing left with Namkia to help the bridge-builders.

An hour later, with a lull in the rain, Ursula and Tim went to find out what was happening. The only people to be seen were five shivering, wet Kukis sitting on the riverbank. Ursula had never seen the Jiri in such a spate. The red, silt-tinged water roiled and lunged, lashed and heaved, roaring by with flotsam that disappeared downstream in the blink of an eye.

"Where is everyone?" Ursula asked the Kukis.

"We started to cut down a big tree to use as a bridge," said one of the Kukis. "But the river kept rising, and when the tree fell, the water flowed over it. Two men managed to get across, and they've gone to Thingje to fetch help."

Everyone was drenched and cold.

"Let's collect some brushwood from under the bushes where it's dry," Tim said. "We'll light a fire."

The Kukis dragged up a couple of logs, and Tim lit a big fire. The Kukis squatted round it, shivering. Then Khutuing appeared from out of the woods with the Maovom men and a load of bamboo.

Tim said, "Our married life so far has been full of challenges to be home, together."

Ursula squeezed Tim's hand. "It's fitting that Khutuing will build a bridge to allow us to reach home."

It began to rain again as Ursula and Tim stood by the fire, watching Khutuing, almost single-handed, bridge the seventy-five foot wide river. He knew how to make a cantilever span in the Zemi manner, which the Kukis did not. The men pushed, hauled, laid stones, and cut lashings under his direction. First, the upper bamboos went in, well-weighted down by stone revetments rammed against the bank, followed by the footway, four long, sturdy bamboos thrust home into the soil and lashed to the upper pieces. They managed to fix one supporting trestle close in to the bank, but after that, the deep, fast flowing water made underpinning impossible.

The rain fell more heavily, pelting down with a dull roar. All were soaked. The Kukis' wet, coarse cloths clung to their skin. Khutuing had shed his cloth and wore only his kilt. He took a long, thin bamboo rod, cut to form a hook, and slowly walked out onto the shaking footway with it.

The wet, slippery bamboos forming the footway were not yet tied down and bounced under his footsteps. Carefully, he reached up with the hooked bamboo, caught the overhead span then pulled it down until the upper span began to spring. Keeping the tension on the bamboo rod, Khutuing sat down and straddled the footway. He locked his legs below it, passed the straining bamboo rod under, bent it round, held it, and made it fast, to complete the first support. The Kukis passed him another hooked rod. Still sitting, he fished for the span on the other side and repeated the process. Staying straddled over the footway, he moved up three feet and began again.

Rain thundered on their backs. Tim and Ursula saw the river rise. It began pounding at the bank. The water's roar deepened. Ursula bit her lip with anxiety as the water climbed over the stone revetments, the butt-ends of the bridge bamboos, and over the end of the footway. Still Khutuing worked. The rainfall was a solid curtain between them and the far bank.

Tim tensed, ready for action should Khutuing fall. "If he slips, he hasn't a hope in hell."

"If he falls, we'll both jump in after him, and I doubt any of us will come out alive," Ursula said.

The footway was so slippery, so shaky and unstable that the Kukis would not venture along it. They passed the needed bamboos out to Khutuing, who could not turn round in case the footway tilted. With every movement, he bounced and swayed up a foot or two or a foot sideways as the bucking bamboos slipped and swung about. The water lapped up another couple of inches, covering the first lashing at the bank end of the footway.

Suddenly, they heard a new note in the river. The Kukis at the near end of the bridge ran and fell as they scrambled toward the banks. Branches and limbs of a giant tree, rolling down on the flood, loomed over the group, heading straight for the bridge and Khutuing.

He didn't run, but walked calmly back towards a trestle to watch the tree strike. It hit the bridge squarely. The bamboos creaked and snapped; the structure tilted. The tree turned, twisted, veered away then was gone, swirling clear of the bridge into the rapids below. Khutuing returned to work, testing the footway, mending broken ties, and sat down to his job as though nothing had happened.

Then on the far bank, men of Thingje village appeared. They called to Khutuing. He shouted a reply. The villagers disappeared into the trees. The rain had eased, and Ursula could see them scrambling and bobbing about in the woods before they returned to the bank, dragging bamboos.

His work done, Khutuing joined Ursula and Tim at the fire. They made tea and drank it, while Thingje men worked feverishly on the far side. Out and out, their side of the bridge grew. Its footway met Khutuing's. The upper spans tapped each other. The men on the far side ran out other bamboos and covered the gap. Up went the side-hooks; under went the lashings. They finished the bridge at four o'clock.

Before moving from the fire, Tim told Khutuing, "Watching you build the bridge was the most amazing feat of engineering I've ever seen."

Khutuing grinned. "Now we must see if it works."

He crossed the bridge first, testing it as he went. As he jumped off into the scrub at the other end, Ursula, Tim and the porters followed. An hour later they arrived at Thingje camp. It was still raining.

From Thingje it was a wet but uneventful journey to Laisong where they had a camp to pack. Khutuing discovered Ursula and Tim did not have a picnic basket. While they and their staff packed and hammered cases shut, he sat in a corner and made them one, calmly working the cane with the same detachment from the confusion around him as he had at the bridge.

At last everything was packed and Ursula ready to leave. She was taking along two boys picked from a dozen applicants from Magulong. It was time to say goodbye to Khutuing. He held out his hand.

Ursula and Tim soberly shook hands with him.

This gesture had special significance. They were not just two white people who called him "Father" for fun, but were linked to him in a relationship of great emotional depth. The handshake was a public expression of this.

"Go well, son-in-law. Go well, my daughter. Bring my grandchild to show me if you can."

"Remain well, my father," each replied.

Khutuing turned and left. Ursula watched him leave. His head was bent. She knew he was crying.

Dogs, boys, baggage, Namkia, Ursula and Tim took the path in the opposite direction, the path leading to Mahur station. On the way, Ursula bade farewell to her friends at Asalu and Impoi, where Namkia's oldest son joined the group. At Mahur, the worn, grubby train came clanging in. Boys and servants loaded the luggage and scrambled for seats. Stepping from the train, Ursula stood in front of Namkia, who had walked the last mile in increasing misery. Her heart ached for his sadness. She couldn't imagine life without him.

"It is time for me to go, my brother. I have had no better friend, protector and teacher than you. We've been through a lot together. You shall always have a special place in my heart," Ursula managed to say before her voice broke.

"And you in mine, my sister." His voice wavered. A sob escaped his lips.

"I go with a good man, Namkia. He will look after me, be my friend and protector."

"My heart is heavy, but you must go with your husband. It's the Naga way."

Ursula squeezed his hands then jumped onto the train. It jolted, pulled slowly away. She leaned from the window, Tim behind her, and waved farewell. Namkia was standing in his red cloth on the platform, watching the departing train. Tears streamed down his grief-stricken face.

Glossary

Anna	A coin of Indian currency (1/16th of a rupee)
Basha	Hut made of bamboo with walls of bamboo matting
Chaung	Burmese for small river
Gharry	A horse-drawn wheeled vehicle
Havildar	A sergeant in the Indian Army
Jappa	Tall, covered carrying baskets of plaited cane and bamboo
Kukri	A sharp, curved Gurkha knife
Lance-naik	A lance-corporal in the Indian Army
Morung	"Batchelor halls", large houses serving as clubs and dormitories for village men and youths
NCO	A non-commissioned army officer
Punkah	A mechanical palm leaf fan for cooling a room
Rupee	Indian currency
SDO	Sub-divisional Officer
Sambhur	A large deer
Sepoy	An Indian Army soldier in European service
Subedar	A captain in the Indian Army

About the author

Pauline Hayton hails from the northeast of England. She left her probation officer job in her hometown of Middlesbrough to emigrate to the United States in 1991 with her husband Peter. They live in Naples, Florida, willing slaves to four abandoned cats that adopted the couple.

After listening to her father's war stories and reading his tattered wartime diaries, she felt compelled to write her first book about his WWII adventures as a Royal Engineer in the British Army. The result was *A Corporal's War* first published in 2003.

While researching *A Corporal's War,* she stumbled upon Ursula Graham Bower's story and knew instantly that she would write a book about this extraordinary woman. *Naga Queen* was the result, a novel based on eight years in Ursula Graham Bower's life

During her research for *Naga Queen,* the author became friends with Ursula Graham Bower's daughter, Trina. This led the author and her husband into sponsoring Mount Kisha English School in the remote Naga village of Magulong. *Chasing Brenda,* a comedy/adventure novel is based on a 2011 visit the author made to Magulong. Royalties from Hayton's books go towards educating the more than one hundred children in the village.